Death
Sits Down
to Dinner

ALSO BY TESSA ARLEN

Death of a Dishonorable Gentleman

TESSA ARLEN

Death Sits Down to Dinner

MINOTAUR BOOKS
A THOMAS DUNNE BOOK
NEW YORK

A THOMAS DUNNE BOOK FOR MINOTAUR BOOKS.
An imprint of St. Martin's Publishing Group.

DEATH SITS DOWN TO DINNER. Copyright © 2016 by Tessa Arlen. All rights reserved. Printed in the United States of America. For information, address St. Martin's Press, 175 Fifth Avenue, New York, N.Y. 10010.

www.thomasdunnebooks.com
www.minotaurbooks.com

Library of Congress Cataloging-in-Publication Data

Names: Arlen, Tessa, author.
Title: Death sits down to dinner : a mystery / Tessa Arlen.
Description: First edition. | New York : Minotaur Books, 2016. | A Thomas Dunne book.
Identifiers: LCCN 2015043804| ISBN 9781250052506 (hardcover) | ISBN 9781466854284 (e-book)
Subjects: LCSH: Countesses—Fiction. | Upper class—England—London—Fiction. | Murder—Investigation—Fiction. | Great Britain—History—Edward VII, 1901–1910—Fiction. | BISAC: FICTION / Mystery & Detective / Historical. | FICTION / Mystery & Detective / Traditional British. | FICTION / Mystery & Detective / Women Sleuths. | GSAFD: Mystery fiction. | Historical fiction.
Classification: LCC PS3601.R5445 D44 2016 | DDC 813/.6—dc23
LC record available at http://lccn.loc.gov/2015043804

Our books may be purchased in bulk for promotional, educational, or business use. Please contact your local bookseller or the Macmillan Corporate and Premium Sales Department at 1-800-221-7945, extension 5442, or by e-mail at MacmillanSpecialMarkets@macmillan.com.

First Edition: March 2016

10 9 8 7 6 5 4 3 2 1

To Chloe, Toby, and Georgia

Acknowledgments

It has been a perfectly thrilling experience to write the second volume in the Lady Montfort series and I have much to be grateful for. My greatest thanks as always go to my husband. His steadfast belief that I will be successful in everything I do—if I just knuckle down and do it—and his wonderful sense of humor only added to the fun of this past year. And here I am again thanking those who have been so generous with their support and time in that interesting period known as the "writing process."

Thank you to my daughters, family, and friends for graciously putting up with all the vagaries of a late-blooming novelist with kind patience. Your generosity is always much appreciated—as is your telling me where to get off when my insecurity looms too large.

Kevan Lyon, my agent and advocate in this still very-new-to-me world of publishing, never ceases to impress me with her patience, her commitment, and her wisdom.

To the team at Thomas Dunne and Minotaur: Thank you all for whipping me into shape! We none of us complete our books successfully without the help of our publishers and their talented staff. My thanks especially to my editor, Anne Brewer, for her keen observations and thoughtful guidance; to assistant editors, Emma Stein and Jennifer Letwack, for their huge, hard work to keep me on track; to David Rotstein, who gave me yet another stunning cover; and to Shailyn Tavella, my publicist, for her creative ideas and her delightful enthusiasm. Also: to Toni Kirkpatrick, who gave me my start at Thomas Dunne Books, and for her kindness and generosity.

And last of all to all my readers who told me on Facebook and Goodreads how much they enjoyed my debut: thank you. I hope you enjoy Clementine and Edith Jackson's new adventure as much as I have enjoyed writing it!

Characters

Montfort House in Belgravia, London

Clementine Elizabeth Talbot, the Countess of Montfort: our amateur sleuth, welcome everywhere in fashionable London society

*Mrs. Edith Jackson: housekeeper at Iyntwood, Lord Montfort's country estate in Buckinghamshire, and Lady Montfort's fellow sleuth

Ralph Cuthbert Talbot, the Earl of Montfort: Lady Montfort's long-suffering and loving husband

Harry Talbot, Viscount Lord Haversham: the Talbots' only son and heir and enthusiastic aviator

Mr. White: the Montfort House butler

*Mrs. "Ginger" Harding: the Montfort House cook

First footman

Second footman

Edna Pettigrew: the Countess of Montfort's lady's maid

Herne: the chauffeur

Mr. Ernest Stafford: contract landscape architect at Iyntwood

*Cooks and housekeepers were referred to as Mrs. out of respect even if they were unmarried.

The House at Chester Square in Belgravia, London

Hermione Kingsley: elderly patroness of England's largest charity
for orphans, the Chimney Sweep Boys

Adelaide Gaskell: Miss Kingsley's pretty, paid companion
Mr. Jenkins: Miss Kingsley's geriatric butler
Martha: first housemaid
Eliza: second housemaid
First footman: working name John*
Second footman: working name James*, real name Eddy Porter
(also known as the Clumsy Footman)
Macleod: chauffeur
*Often footmen did not work under their own names, but worked
under the house names. James and John were typical working
names for footmen.

Other guests invited to Hermione Kingsley's party to celebrate Winston Churchill's birthday

Winston Churchill: First Lord of the Admiralty
Captain Wildman-Lushington: Royal Marine, aviator, and
Mr. Churchill's flying instructor
Captain Sir Parceval Vetiver: punctilious aide to Winston
Churchill
Marigold Meriwether: Vetiver's superbly dressed young fiancée
Sir Reginald Cholmondeley: old friend of Hermione Kingsley
and chairman of the board of governors for the Chimney
Sweep Boys

Aaron Greenberg: sophisticate and extremely rich banker
Veda, Lady Ryderwood: a beautiful widow with a superb singing
voice

Trevor "Tricky" Tricklebank: Hermione Kingsley's nephew and
only surviving member of her family

Jennifer Wells-Thornton: the young woman Tricky is expected to marry

Maud, Lady Cunard: wife of Sir Bache Cunard of the Cunard Shipping Line, and rich American patroness of the arts and arch gossip

Lord and Lady Wentworth: rich aristocrats

Sir Vivian Hussey: patron of the arts

Friends, well-wishers, and policemen

Chief Inspector Hillary: educated and intelligent member of Scotland Yard's CID

Mavis Biggleswade: matron of Kingsley House, home of the Chimney Sweep Boys

Olive, Lady Shackleton: friend of Lady Montfort

Gertrude, Lady Waterford: friend of Lady Montfort

Sir Thomas Beecham: conductor of his own orchestra, man about town, and lover of Lady Cunard

Gladys Robinson, the Marchioness of Ripon: charismatic patroness of the arts who brought the Ballets Russes to London

Nellie Melba: Australian opera singer and international superstar

Death
Sits Down
to Dinner

Chapter One

A wet and miserable late-autumn day had turned into a bitterly cold winter night as the sun sank unseen below a horizon obscured by a bank of thick gray clouds. The wind veered to the east and the first strong gust gathered force from the estuary and bellowed up the Thames, blowing sprays of puddle water into the air and plastering wet leaves against the legs of those unfortunate enough still to be hurrying homeward.

Tucked away in the quiet comfort of her bedroom at Montfort House, Clementine Talbot, the Countess of Montfort, and her maid, Pettigrew, were absorbed in the leisurely business of dressing her for dinner. As they went diligently about their work, engrossed in the particulars of choosing the right shoes for her evening dress and making difficult decisions on the appropriate jewels for the occasion, they enjoyed an intermittent exchange of information on the new cook who had recently taken up her appointment at Montfort House.

"Her food is quite *nice,* I suppose, considering how young she is and not even French, but from somewhere in the north of England; some *industrial* town like Newcastle or . . . Sheffield." Clementine suppressed a smile at Pettigrew's grudging praise. Her maid viewed all changes in the Talbots' London house servants' hall with skepticism and was not naturally given to enthusiasm.

The search for the new cook had been a long and worrying business. Clementine was well aware there was little enough to entice her husband away from the family estates at Iyntwood to London. But once convinced he should make the effort, it did not do for him to eat his dinner at the Carlton or White's, where he heard horribly exaggerated accounts from his friends of lucrative rents garnered from the lease of their London houses to the nouveaux riches.

"Lord Montfort must not eat all his meals at one of his clubs when he comes up to town, White," Clementine had reminded the Montfort House butler when after weeks of interviews he had found no exceptional candidate. "It prompts him to question the prudence of keeping on the expense of a full establishment in London." She knew the butler would understand the wisdom of *this* thinking. "It is absolutely vital that a first-rate cook be found before his lordship's next visit."

White had certainly more than redoubled his efforts. And when the perfect candidate accepted an offer of employment a collective sigh of relief had resounded throughout the household belowstairs that their future employment was once again secure. And upstairs, Clementine had given thanks that she would continue with a house of her own to stay in whenever she chose to come up to town.

Persuaded by his wife that the domestic crisis was over and breakfast, luncheon, and dinner at Montfort House would no longer regrettably remind him of Eton, Lord Montfort had come up to London for the first time in months. He had enjoyed a delectable dinner of veal consommé, succulent trout in crisp blanched almonds, game quenelles and truffles, followed by a roast goose with a red-currant glaze, and pronounced that London was almost civilized.

"Her food not only tastes sublime, it looks wonderful, too,"

Clementine said, regarding herself critically in the looking glass. She wondered if wearing her hair piled high toward her forehead was flattering now that she had reached her forties.

"She's got her little ways though," said Pettigrew and wrinkled up her nose. Clementine knew, of old, that her maid could never resist taking some of the gilt off the gingerbread; it was almost expected of her.

"I think you should wear the diamond circlet when we do your hair this way, m'lady." She held her choice over Clementine's head, and they both gazed thoughtfully into the glass.

Clementine shook her head. "No, it's a bit too ornate for this evening." Pettigrew produced a more modest affair. "Yes, that will do nicely." She returned to their earlier conversation. "What little ways?"

"Well, nothing at all really, m'lady. She gave us a nice beef stew for dinner the other day for servants' dinner, called it by some French name. It had two bottles of wine in it." And catching Clementine's startled look, Pettigrew used her fading-away voice to say, "Oh no, m'lady, not the good stuff." And feeling that more explanation might be required: "Just some of the ordinary from France she said it was. Does wonders for the cheaper cuts of beef." Clementine's shoulders came down a notch, and Pettigrew continued, "Anyway, she announced at servants' dinner today that she would prefer us to call her by her nickname." She paused and glanced at Clementine in the looking glass.

A little warning bell began to chime in the distance and Clementine struggled for outer calm. It was hard enough to find and keep good servants in London without making things any more complicated than they already were. There was a shortage of talented cooks who were also sober, honest, and didn't cause havoc belowstairs. Now one merely prayed that the new candidate would fit into the claustrophobic and tightly knit group whose members made up her servants' hall. But Pettigrew no doubt expected a reaction to her tidbit and Clementine dutifully obliged.

"Her nickname? Oh really? How awfully nice of her!" Clementine said in a bright sort of voice. While it was important to take an interest in the lives of those who worked for her, she believed it best not to involve herself in the servants' social interaction with one another, it only made muddles.

Pettigrew, concentrating on the finishing touches to Clementine's hair as she fixed the diamond half-circlet firmly into place, took a moment to reply, "Yes, m'lady, she is a nice young woman, very friendly. But as Mr. White says, it's important to observe decorum and the proper respect for each other." Pettigrew was a traditionalist, a member of the old school of personal servants, and would be appalled, thought Clementine, if anyone other than her family called her Edna. She hurried to agree.

"Of course, he's absolutely right; important to observe social convention, saves a lot of misunderstandings in the long run. What *is* her Christian name by the way?"

"I think it might be Ethel, m'lady. But she said, 'Just call me Ginger.'" Pettigrew pulled her mouth into a tight knot as she slid in the last hairpin and lifted her eyes to gaze with reproach at Clementine's face reflected in the looking glass.

"Ginger," Clementine was puzzled until she recalled her only meeting with the new cook. "Ah yes, all that glorious titian hair. So do you? Call her Ginger, I mean." She was careful to maintain only a polite interest.

"No, m'lady, we most certainly do not." The lines around Pettigrew's mouth deepened. "We may not be a sophisticated bunch belowstairs, but we have our standards. We call her Mrs. Harding, as we ought."

"And very right and proper, too," was Clementine's only comment.

They lifted their heads as they heard a powerful gust of wind chasing down the street.

"Hark at that, m'lady, wouldn't be surprised if we lost a few roof tiles tonight." Pettigrew, happily complacent they were not her roof tiles, searched for the left hand to the pair of Clementine's evening gloves. The bedroom windows rattled in their heavy frames as another gust clouted the front of the house.

"Yes, it's definitely taken a turn for the worse," Clementine observed, equally unworried. "Thank you, Pettigrew. No need to wait up, we'll be back late. But perhaps come in before I leave to make sure I have everything." A small puff of smoke blew back down the chimney.

Pettigrew laid the gloves on the dressing table, retrieved Clementine's evening handbag from the bed, made a quick inventory of its contents, and laid it next to the gloves. She reached over to her mistress and carefully smoothed the neckline at the back of her dress, then hurried off to the servants' hall for a nice cup of hot cocoa and, guessed Clementine, for further assessment of Ginger's other interesting eccentricities.

Clementine walked over to her bedroom window and pulled back the heavy velvet curtain. The draft creeping in around the edges of the window frames struck cold against her bare arms, but she leaned forward to look down the street in time to see a quick blue flare at the bottom of the square as the lamplighter lit the last lamp. She watched him climb down his ladder, swing it up onto his shoulder, and stagger into the wind, his cap pulled down on his head and scarf tied tightly up around his neck. In the light from the lamppost outside Montfort House she watched the last of the leaves that had blown off the plane trees in the center of the square fly upward, as if trying to reattach themselves. She let the curtain fall back and with an exaggerated shiver turned back into the welcoming brightness of the room; a log fell in the grate and a pretty gold and ormolu clock chimed a silvery half past the hour. The door opened and Lord Montfort walked into the room

"What a wretched night," Clementine said and recognized, too late, her husband's raised eyebrows and slightly downturned mouth—customary indications of reluctance and resignation in the face of duty—and realized she had said the wrong thing.

"'Wretched' isn't what springs to mind. 'Unbearable' is more like it." Her husband walked over to the fireplace and, flipping the tails of his coat out of the way, sat down in a chair, his legs extended and crossed comfortably at the ankle. He must have heard his tone and decided it sounded ungracious because he looked up at her with an appreciative smile and said, "You look rather nice. Is that new?"

She cast an assessing glance at her dress in the pier glass. She thought the color beautiful, a shade of rich, old gold, the narrow skirt falling in three diagonal layers of lace-edged tulle from a fitted bodice of pomegranate-red silk velvet, with delicate gold tulle split sleeves to just above the elbow.

"Yes, it's from Worth. Like it?"

"Yes, very much, perfect color for you." He always appreciated the trouble she took to dress in elegant clothes with simple lines.

She smoothed down the front of the dress and went to sit at her dressing table, head tilted to one side to put on her earrings.

"How's Olive bearing up?" He was making a supreme effort to shake off low spirits as he politely inquired after her afternoon round of visits.

"She's in a bit of a fluster over poor old Sir Thom." Clementine laughed as she referred to one of her closest friends and patron of the arts, Olive, Lady Shackleton, and her ongoing fascination with Sir Thomas Beecham, conductor and director of his own symphony orchestra; he was also the managing director of the Royal Opera House at Covent Garden and impresario of His Majesty's Theatre, and privately referred to by the three of them as Sir Thom, because of his tendency to stray, like a male cat when the moon was full, from his current mistress, Maud, Lady Cunard.

"Oh, and the Shackletons will not be with us for dinner tonight," Clementine said, delivering what she knew would be bad news.

"Shackleton not coming to Hermione's tonight?" His dismay was palpable. The last lifeboat onboard the sinking ship of his evening had been found to have a hole in its bottom.

Clementine did what she could to reassure: "But Henry and Emily Wentworth and Aaron Greenburg will be there. And do you remember Lady Ryderwood? We met her at the Waterfords'. No? Yes, of course you remember her. She is the widow of Sir Francis Ryderwood; they lived on the Continent."

The company of Lord Montfort's good friends Henry Wentworth and Aaron Greenberg, with the added attraction of one of London's most lovely widows, did little to dispel gloom that had probably been building all afternoon. Clementine knew what was causing her husband's despondency, but she did nothing more to try to convince him that their evening would be enjoyable. It was too late: his morale had already taken a nose-dive, so all efforts would be wasted.

At tonight's dinner there could not be enough old friends to make the evening palatable for her husband. The principal guest, the man whose birthday was being celebrated at the house of their close friend Hermione Kingsley, was the First Lord of the Admiralty; a man whom Lord Montfort had never approved of and whose company he took considerable pains to avoid. There were plenty of men who held positions of power and responsibility in government with whom Lord Montfort got on quite well, in spite of differences in their politics. Winston Churchill was not one of them.

"The one thing I can never forgive Churchill for is his treachery . . ."

"Treachery"? Surely this was a bit steep? All the man had done was leave one political party to join another. He had merely left the Tories to join the Liberals. Clementine prepared herself for a long list of Churchill's many faults.

"Treachery rewarded by a meteor-like career from a lowly undersecretary," her husband reminded her, as if she could possibly ever forget, "to home secretary in just six years . . . not to mention his self-aggrandizing and grandstanding."

Well, of course he has a point. Winston Churchill's habitual indulgence in passionate rhetoric can be rather trying.

"But worst of all is the man's complete nincompoopery and his . . . well . . . his showing off."

Clementine tried to find patience. *Please, not the Siege of Sidney Street again.* She sighed as she recognized the prelude to her husband's favorite diatribe toward a man he despised.

But she was evidently not to be spared. The slums of Whitechapel, made notorious by Jack the Ripper twenty-five years earlier, had provided the backdrop for a calamitous incident in Winston Churchill's early career as home secretary. The police had made a telephone call to Churchill for permission to call in military support in the arrest of a gang of desperate Latvian thieves who had killed three policemen in an armed robbery and were now trapped in a dilapidated, terraced house in Sidney Street.

"What I can't begin to understand is Churchill's determination to thrust himself forward and rush off to join a scene which was already verging on the edge of violent disaster. It was an action most unsuited to his position. Dispatching the Scots Guards from the Tower of London should have been enough. But his appalling display of eagerness to *personally* direct their efforts in storming that shabby little house was undignified." Like most men of his background, Lord Montfort despised public displays of enthusiasm, he thought them vulgar and demeaning. "And he used field artillery, for God's sake!"

He stared ferociously into the flames leaping in the fireplace and Clementine knew he was not quite finished.

"Of course the house caught fire and the fire brigade was called. And what did the ridiculous man do?" He gave his wife a look of outrage, as if she had been responsible for egging on Churchill's childish behavior, and she sighed.

"He refused to allow the firemen to put out the fire! What could he have been thinking? When the house was a smoking wreck, two pathetic bodies were found charred beyond recognition and the rest of the *gang* had miraculously *escaped*. All of this watched by a growing crowd of Londoners *and* the newspapers. I am not surprised public and official outcry was tremendous."

Clementine knew her husband would never forgive or forget the incident, as it served as an indication of Churchill's true character.

"I'll never forget the sheer arrogance of Churchill's self-justification after the Sidney Street debacle or forgive his outrageous encouragement of brute force and violence. What did he say when pressed for a reason for this deplorable display? That he thought it 'better to let the house burn to the ground than risk good British lives in rescuing rascals.' And then a year later the blighter is made First Lord of the Admiralty—unforgivable!"

He shot his wife a look confirming that his usual good humor had left him hours ago.

"However much I am devoted to Hermione Kingsley and her selfless efforts on behalf of her charity, I simply can't imagine why she would have to court a friendship with someone as detestable as Churchill. I find him to be a pugnacious and wholly obnoxious bore, he monopolizes all conversation. The thought of an evening celebrating his birthday makes me want to hop on a train for Iyntwood and give my guns a thoroughly good cleaning." He caught her eye and laughed, and to her relief he shook his head. "Yes, I know, I know . . . the man somehow manages to bring out the worst . . ."

"Yes, it's rather unfortunate. I had hoped that everyone else would provide a buffer. I'm sorry, darling, but you simply must—"

"Get a grip. Yes, I know I must, and I will. Of course I will. But I am not happy about it. Feel I've been put on the spot."

She turned back to her dressing table and picked up her gloves and evening bag, as a signal that it was time for them to go.

"Aaron Greenberg is lovely company, and so is Henry Wentworth in his own way."

"Yes, you are right, Clemmy, but neither of them is as dynamic and witty as Churchill. So they won't get a word in all blasted evening."

Clementine sought a distraction; it wouldn't do for him to keep on in this vein.

"Olive told me this afternoon that Lady Ryderwood is to sing a duet with Nellie Melba at Hermione's charity event next week; such an honor for her. Melba only sings privately for royalty now and is celebrated across the world—her season in America was a colossal success. And Olive says her temper is even more terrifying now that she is famous and she still absolutely refuses to sing at Covent Garden. How long has her feud with Sir Thom been going on for now? Is it two years since he told her she was 'uninterestingly perfect and perfectly uninteresting'?"

Lord Montfort shook his head and chuckled. "You can be quite sure he has said far worse than that to her. Melba may have a silver voice, but she has a tongue of brass and she loves a good scrap with her conductors. Just pray she behaves herself at Hermione's charity event and doesn't feel the need to shriek directions at the pianist."

"Oh, she will be quite the grande dame; the Chimney Sweep Boys charity event is heavily attended by royalty. Lady Ryderwood is going to sing for us tonight, a sort of informal dress rehearsal for the charity event. Olive says she has an exquisite voice, and you have to admit she is very lovely."

"Yes, I remember her husband well. Nice chap, terrible health after the Boer War. Didn't they spend the rest of his life somewhere in the Balearics? Died recently, didn't he? I heard that he was confined to a wheelchair, awfully bad luck for an ex-cavalry officer. Shame really, horses were his passion."

"All I know is that she returned to England this spring, recently widowed. We met her at the Waterfords'. I rather took to her."

More chimes announced the hour. Pettigrew arrived to wrap Clementine up in her sable fur, pulling its deep collar high up around her ears. Even with this layer of insulation around her she could still hear her husband's voice quite clearly as they walked downstairs to the hall.

"Do you know the swine has commissioned two more super dreadnoughts at two million blasted pounds a throw? Heard about it in the club this afternoon, the wretched man is collecting battleships like a damn schoolboy. I have never known anyone as hungry for war as Churchill; Kitchener can't hold a candle to him."

The butler helped him on with his coat and handed him his scarf and hat. He turned at the foot of the stairs, held out his arm, and walked her to the front door. She rather wished that they were not going out after all.

Clementine buried her gloved hands deep inside her fur muff as the butler opened the outer door and let in a draft of air so frigid that husband and wife huddled together as they went out into the night. Clementine raised her muff to shield her face. "Thank you, White; looks like winter is finally here," she said through clenched teeth.

"It's bitterly cold out there, m'lady, but Herne has a foot-warmer and plenty of rugs in the motor. There will be a thermos flask of hot coffee for you on the way home."

On the way home. She sighed as she thought of the evening ahead and was quite envious of White, no doubt anticipating a cozy evening of leisure in the servants' hall eating coq au vin.

"Good heavens, White, we are only driving half a mile; we've hunted in worse weather than this." Lord Montfort took his wife's arm and she marveled at his determination not to be swerved from his dislike for the evening, it seemed that he was determined to wrong-foot everyone tonight.

Chapter Two

Hermione Kingsley's dinner party was a glittering affair of sumptuous food, faultlessly served to an elegant gathering representing those who patronized the arts, who came from some of the oldest families in the country, or who were merely astonishingly rich. Hermione had chosen her guests carefully, Clementine thought, as they were ushered from the bitter night air into a drawing room thronged with beautifully dressed men and women, each one of them a sure touch for Hermione's Chimney Sweep Boys, the largest and most prestigious charity in Britain for the orphaned children of the destitute.

But, as predicted by Lord Montfort, Winston Churchill, at his most expansive, did indeed monopolize the conversation at dinner from his place of honor at the head of the table throughout a procession of eight delicious courses.

Clementine had had the privilege of being taken in to dinner by the First Lord of the Admiralty and seated on his right. Mr. Churchill was in fine form and kept them all entertained with an effortless flow of convivial chatter. He dwelled at considerable length on his tussles with the leaders of the suffragette movement. His determination not to be henpecked by the formidable Mrs. Pankhurst and the most intimidating of her three daughters, Cristobel, was another anecdote deftly recounted from his days as home secretary.

Halfway through dinner, Clementine glanced at her husband to see how he was faring. They had finished some poached turbot and empty plates were removed to make way for tender slices of roast duck in a red-wine sauce with game chips. She was grateful to see he had turned from Lady Cunard, who always seemed to believe it was her duty to fascinate everyone in sight, to Lady Ryderwood on his left. *Oh the relief of it*, thought Clementine. *Lady Ryderwood is a perfect dinner companion for Ralph.* Indeed, the lady in question was lovely to look at, attentive and intelligent, and if she flirted she did so with subtlety and restraint.

There was a bray of laughter from Hermione's nephew, Trevor Tricklebank, who was enjoying the company of Marigold Meriwether at the far end of the table. Trevor was a good-natured but fatuous ass of a young man thoughtlessly dedicated to good living. She wondered what her husband would say if their unmarried daughter, Althea, were to fall in love with a drone like Trevor.

She glanced across the table to the upright figure of Captain Vetiver, Churchill's chief aide at the Admiralty, who was seated next to Mrs. Churchill. Would they prefer perhaps someone as consciously perfect as Captain Vetiver for a son-in-law for their independent daughter? Captain, the Honourable Sir Parceval Vetiver, third son of the Duke of Andover, was impeccable in every aspect, but might be rather unforgiving if his wife was not quite as faultless as her husband. No, he would never do for independent Althea, always happier in the great outdoors than in the drawing room.

Her gaze traveled on down the table to the young man seated at the end. He was awfully young and handsome in the scarlet coat of his dress uniform. *What was his name again? Washington? No. Ah yes, Wildman-Lushington, Captain Gilbert Wildman-*

Lushington, Royal Marines. She nodded to Sir Reginald Cholmon-deley, on her right, as he launched into a prolonged explanation as to how the New Year's Honors List was compiled; no doubt he expected to be elevated to the peerage in the New Year for his considerable efforts on behalf the Chimney Sweep Boys charity.

Sir Reginald is the sort of man to be congratulated rather than enjoyed. Clementine felt her eyes swim a little with the effort of keeping them fixed on his face as he elucidated on his charitable obligations.

Deeply Anglican in his outlook, Sir Reginald was always ready to produce a ponderous moral fable to illustrate any aspect of human frailty, and this evening there were to be no excep-tions. Countless dinner parties seated next to, or within earshot of, Sir Reginald had taught Clementine long ago to remind her-self that the man worked only for the good of the deserving poor, which in this frivolous day and age demanded true beneficence and unrelenting hard work. Sir Reginald's eyes were shining with the energy only the zealous possess, and she forced herself to pay attention.

". . . Always so generous with his donations . . . Mr. Green-berg might not be of our faith . . . but God's way are mysteri-ous . . ." Sir Reginald's pale blue eyes were fixed on her face, and having grasped the gist of his monologue, for the next several minutes Clementine allowed herself to mentally drift away.

Her conversation with Captain Wildman-Lushington had been far more interesting to her than any to be had with Sir Reginald or Churchill. He flew aeroplanes in the new Royal Naval Air Service, he had explained, his young face glowing with pride and enthusiasm. He flew a Farman-type pusher biplane, whatever that was, and he knew her son, Harry Talbot, Viscount Lord Haversham—not personally, he had hastened to assure her, but by reputation as a fellow pilot.

Clementine had never truly come to terms with what she

hoped was her son's passing infatuation with aircraft and flying. In fact, she had kicked up such a fuss about his involvement with Tom Sopwith and his aeroplane manufactory in Kingston last summer that when the dust had settled in the Talbot family and everyone was talking to one another again, Harry had asked her never to bring up the subjects of "safety" and "flying" in the same sentence again, since it caused her so much distress. Denying her the opportunity to learn exactly what happened when one launched oneself into the heavens in what she considered to be a badly wrapped brown paper parcel, tied with string.

The moment Captain Wildman-Lushington had introduced himself, she had deftly cut him away from Hermione's other guests and interrogated him, using the words *safety* and *aeroplanes* as often as she wished. Their conversation had been illuminating once she had translated some of the strange terms the young pilot used, the vernacular of flying she supposed. Clearly delighted that someone in this eminent crowd actually wanted to talk to him at all, Captain Wildman-Lushington had been informative as he accounted for his invitation to dinner.

"I am here this evening as the guest of the First Lord of the Admiralty, Lady Montfort. Today I was appointed his personal flying instructor." He almost blushed with pride.

"Mr. Churchill went aloft?" Clementine realized that this was a term used for what you did in a hot-air balloon or when sailors scrambled up a ship's rigging. She struggled for the right word. "I mean actually went . . . ?" She lifted her hands upward.

"*Up,* Lady Montfort." He was beaming and trying not to swagger at the evident pride he felt at being connected to the First Lord of the Admiralty in such a dashing way. "Up, with me this afternoon, in my plane. He did frightfully well. Of course he's been up before but this time he actually took the controls."

"Great heavens, so it's considered to be quite safe then?"

She had actually seen an aeroplane and couldn't imagine Mr. Churchill's considerable bulk crammed into such a fragile container.

"Well, yes. But flying has its risks, even today." He laughed the deprecating laugh of the truly brave or, perhaps, the completely unimaginative.

The captain was tall, fit, and alert, with clear, steady gray eyes in a firm, round face that shone with health as a result of wholesome food, untroubled sleep, and no doubt masses of exercise. Captain Wildman-Lushington personified anyone's ideal of a young man of derring-do. Now here was someone she would have been delighted for Althea to be interested in. Like her daughter, the young man before her relished the active life of doing. *Yes,* she thought, *he is most certainly a doer before he is a deep thinker.*

Now as she finished her duck and turned a listening face to Sir Reginald Cholmondeley, she cast a quick, assessing glance at Mr. Churchill. *How old is he? Older than I am, surely.* She calculated; yes, he was easily in his late forties. She was later to discover that he was celebrating his thirty-ninth year, making him a surprising three years younger than herself. Mr. Churchill was balding and his heavy-limbed body was going to fat. He had downed at least a bottle and a half of wine during the first part of dinner and was still eating and drinking with enthusiasm.

If a specimen as physically unfit and as unmuscled as Mr. Churchill could fly an aeroplane, then surely they must have ironed out all those wrinkles that made them such death traps only two short years ago? Keeping her expression responsive to alterations in the conversational tone of Sir Reginald's lecture on the importance of charitable giving, she went back in her thoughts to her earlier examination of the young flying officer.

"And how long have you been flying, Captain?"

"Ohhhhh . . ." He squinted one eye and struggled with the arithmetic. "Let's see now. Ah yes, started in May. So that's . . ."

"Six months! You've been doing it for just six months and you were appointed to take up one of England's chief ministers! Why, Captain, that's astounding!"

"Yes," he agreed, struggling to look modest. "It is rather. Your son has been flying at least a year longer than I have, of course, and is far more competent. Mr. Churchill is awfully keen to sign Lord Haversham up to the RNAS soon as possible, so we can get this whole show on the road before we go to war with Germany."

He was completely oblivious of her appalled silence. *I don't know what's going on in the world,* she thought as Captain Wildman-Lushington rhapsodized on about pusher biplanes. *Here I am thinking war with Germany is still a laughable bit of posturing, and people like Churchill, Vetiver, and apparently Harry are planning on taking battles into the air.* "Do you imagine, Captain, that there is a place in war for these machines?" she asked

"There most certainly is," came the blithe unheeding reply. "Mr. Churchill believes all wars of the future will be fought in the air. Sea battles are a thing of the past really. And of course enemy reconnaissance is a piece of cake from an aeroplane."

If there was to be war with Germany, and hopefully if they all kept their heads there wouldn't be, then Harry would be careering around in the sky in something as unpredictable and fragile as a "kite"—Wildman-Lushington's term. Clementine stared in horror at the bright young man in front of her and had nothing whatsoever to say.

Her preoccupation continued through to the end of dinner. Only self-discipline and a strong sense of social obligation helped her to contribute in the evening's lighthearted chatter. But with Mr. Churchill on her left she had merely to incline her head in a parody of fascinated interest, as he talked inexhaustibly on any topic. He was now in the middle of an account of his near brush with what he called his "attempted assassination" by an enraged and militant suffragette at a country railway station in Hertfordshire.

"She was a big woman." Churchill gestured from the center of his chest outward with both hands. "She had an unattractive flat straw hat perched on her huge head." His alert eyes glanced around the table and he lifted his voice so all could enjoy the joke as he paused to finish the last of the wine in his glass which was immediately replenished by the footman. "I was waiting on the platform at Tring station for the half-past-four with my wife." Here he bowed his head to Mrs. Churchill, seated farther down the table, next to Sir Vivian Hussey. "We were anxious to be home: our youngest had chicken pox, we were tired and in need of our dinner. Well, long story short, this buffalo of a woman came up behind me as the train came steaming in at a fast clip. Just as it started to slow down she gave me this terrific buffet from behind. Of course I wasn't expecting to be booted off the platform and I went staggering forward, completely caught off-balance. I remember seeing the pistons of the engine turning in front of my nose and fully expected to go down on the rails and be squashed quite flat." Here he laughed—a big man's laugh; a genial man's laugh. *The laugh,* Clementine thought, *of the truly successful, who always get what they want.*

"My life, as they say, flashed before me. And as my body reached a tipping point," he seesawed his outstretched arms to encourage them to join in the joke against him, "I felt this reassuring grip on my shoulder. A powerful heave and I was righted in an instant and dragged to safety by my vigilant, coolheaded, and remarkable wife. And as of course you know, Mrs. Churchill is in favor of the franchise for women." He smiled down the table at his wife, who had been listening attentively. *How many times has she heard this story?* Clementine wondered in sympathy, as Mr. Churchill's anecdote was greeted by huge laughter, and a little smatter of applause from the sycophants in the group. She glanced across at her husband, whose face was set as he stared down at his plate.

"What happened to your assassin?" Sir Vivian, who knew what it was like to be pursued by angry women, asked to further laughter.

"She was arrested for assault with malice and sent to Holloway Prison, where I believe she set fire to her cell!" Winston sat back in his chair. His eyes glistened as he took generous sips from his glass. "Quite batty of course, these women, and as they age they get battier and take bigger risks, and not just with *my* life," *he has become the politician again,* thought Clementine, "but with the lives of all of us. It's an unnatural lust for power in womankind, and a power that . . . will . . . not . . . *be given*." She noticed that he had a way of intoning his words almost through clenched teeth as he spaced out each one and then grouped the last two together in a rhythmic and emphatic pattern, and if she listened carefully she could still detect his tendency to lisp. She sat back in her chair, fascinated. He wasn't exactly likable, she thought, but he was impressive. He had effortlessly dominated a gathering of at least eighteen people throughout dinner with deft and wicked wit. He had certainly gained her preoccupied attention.

A footman pulled back Hermione Kingsley's chair so she might stand up from the table.

"Dear Winston." Their elderly hostess smiled at the incorrigible charmer seated at the end of her dining-room table. "We will leave you all to enjoy your port and cigars."

Clementine regarded the upright old lady with affection. Hermione had all the fearsome traits of her mother's generation.

Her angular frame looked incongruous and gaunt in a gown of pink satin and deep lace ruffles, and her iron-gray hair was swept up in the pouf that had been fashionable at the end of the last century. Hermione waved an imperious hand, telling, not inviting, the women to join her.

Chapter Three

There are those among us who enjoy that brief interlude after dinner when we women leave the men to their port and cigars and disappear to powder our noses and relax among friends to indulge in topics exclusive to feminine interest. And that all depends on who those women are, thought Clementine, as they left the dining room in chattering groups and crossed the spacious inner hall to the wide marble staircase that climbed to the second floor. She caught the tail end of Lady Cunard's laying down the law to Hermione and Lady Wentworth about the merits of employing Rosa Lewis, London's most celebrated chef and owner of the Cavendish Hotel, to organize one's dinner party, instead of employing a full-time French chef and butler, and felt this part of the evening might wear a little.

But, to her delight, on arriving in the salon, Clementine found herself immediately engaged by the more amiable of her husband's dinner companions. Lady Ryderwood's dark eyes lit up as Clementine approached her and she deftly steered her off so that they might talk alone.

When Clementine had first met Veda Ryderwood she had been instantly drawn to her, finding her to be a woman comfortably at ease with herself no matter what the occasion. She had a low, unhurried and musical quality to her voice, a quick, bright mind and a well-developed sense of humor.

"Tell me, Lady Montfort, do your really enjoy opera? I find so many of my new friends say they do and then discover that it is actually the Royal Opera House they enjoy." There was not a shred of criticism in Lady Ryderwood's tone, just baffled amusement and an invitation to laugh at the philistine attitudes of the day toward important things like serious music.

"I'm afraid it is a bit of both for me. But I definitely have my favorites: I prefer Puccini to Verdi and Mozart to Wagner. But I have to admit I love the dazzle of lavish sets and lush costumes. I must be a bit of a philistine." Clementine often found that her attention wandered between arias.

"Oh no, not at all, I think opera is about the combination of superb music and spectacle. Will you be in London for Tetrazzini and Caruso's performance in *Butterfly*?" And Lady Ryderwood sought her opinion on the season's offerings and listened attentively to Clementine's choices. In exchange she had some amusing observations of some of the more notable Italian opera singers who had become popular in London.

"They are all as sweet-natured and humble as they can be, slumming it at the opera house in Milan, sharing rooms and dressers, makeup and costumes, everything. Then they spend a season in New York, and return to Europe to scowl, tantrum, and cry, 'What's this? I always have a daybed in my dressing room in America! No, my dresser and wardrobe must be in a separate room, I simply have to be alone to prepare!'" Lady Ryderwood nodded her head and laughed. "One season at the Metropolitan Opera and they are transformed into divas, it's quite astonishing!"

Coffee was served and brandy was offered as they chattered on. Mrs. Churchill and Jennifer Wells-Thornton gathered around Marigold Meriwether, offering congratulations on her engagement to Captain Vetiver and to admire her elegant white moiré silk dress. This was the one she had worn to be presented at Court, she proudly informed, and one that obviously came from a top Paris fashion house. Lady Wentworth sat in quiet conversation with Hermione. Adelaide Gaskell, Hermione's companion and general factotum for the Chimney Sweep Boys, searched through a stack of music as she was to play the piano accompaniment for Lady Ryderwood's singing when the men came up from the dining room. Only Lady Cunard remained separate from the group; she roamed the salon sipping brandy as she waited for the men to join them. *Never one for female company,* Clementine remembered, as she noticed the restless figure pacing the room; she had always found Maud Cunard to be competitive with her own sex.

Clementine's attention was momentarily diverted from her conversation with Lady Ryderwood by the arrival of Sir Henry Wentworth and her husband, closely followed by Captain Wildman-Lushington; they were all talking about hunting. As the salon began to fill with male voices and laughter, Clementine became aware of a fluster and a good deal of agitation on the other side of the room. Hermione Kingsley's voice was raised in irritation and Marigold Meriwether's in surprise and anger. The footman had clumsily spilled coffee on Marigold's splendid dress and instantly Hermione was in charge.

"Down to the kitchen and bring up a glass of diluted white vinegar and a towel," she instructed the hapless servant. They all watched the dark stain spread upward from the hem of Marigold's gown, and the footman sped off on his errand, almost colliding with Captain Vetiver, who was standing by the open door.

"Oh dear, he'll take too long and it's moiré; perhaps vinegar will ruin it." Hermione cast about for a better alternative. "Adelaide, Adelaide, where are you? There you are. Run to the drawing room and bring up a little pure spirit . . . and a towel . . .

don't forget the towel!" Adelaide Gaskell left her sheet music and scuttled out of the door, leaving the rest of the women to surge around Marigold. Handkerchiefs were produced and little blots and dabs made on the dark stain. Marigold Meriwether, a statuesque blonde with large, pale blue eyes, stared stonily ahead, her face set, ignoring the activity at her feet.

"Baking soda, a thick solution in a little water," Lady Wentworth advised.

Hermione went to the door, calling back over her shoulder as she went, "Baking soda, that'll do the trick. I'll get it myself. And if it doesn't, Marigold, it's only one panel . . ." And off she went intent on her errand.

Marigold turned to Mrs. Churchill, her eyebrows raised in anguish as she cried out, "Oh, oh, oh. It's quite ruined."

"Nonsense, Marigold, not ruined at all. That panel can be easily replaced. There is no need to fuss." Mrs. Churchill turned to Lady Wentworth. "Nothing will get that stain out, it's coffee. What a pity." Then back to Marigold: "My dear Marigold, you must try not to be so . . ."

Maud Cunard, never one for gathering around women, especially those younger than herself, said to Clementine, "It astonishes me how hard it is to find decent servants in London these days. Most of them lack any useful skills. You take them on and lavish hours in instruction, and then off they go to someone else." Clementine was not particularly surprised that Lady Cunard couldn't hang on to good servants, as her weekly entertainment schedule alone would be grueling for any household.

"Hermione has kept every one of her servants for decades, Lady Cunard. Her butler, Jenkins, has been with her since she was a young woman."

"Such a mistake to keep an elderly butler; his hands were quite unsteady at dinner. I thought I would be deluged with peas, and he offered me the fish twice." Not waiting for Clementine's response, Maud Cunard was off to cut Sir Vivian away from any possible conversation with frivolous and pretty little girls like Marigold Meriwether and Jennifer Wells-Thornton, which left Clementine free to join Sir Henry and her husband's conversation on the merits of a cold compress to prevent lameness after a rigorous day of hunting.

So involved was their discussion that she was only briefly aware that poor Adelaide was back in the room, waving a little glass of clear spirit and timidly approaching a silent Marigold, who was still failing to be a good sport about the coffee stain.

Poor thing, Clementine thought, *now she has to try to deal single-handedly with that very put-out young woman; I wonder if I should go over and help her?* She turned to Lady Ryderwood, whose eyebrows were raised in amusement at the display of temperament from the pretty Marigold. Adelaide was holding out her little offering to a frozen-faced young woman who had all but crossed her arms under her bosom and was refusing to look at her.

They were saved from the unpleasant business of trying to make things right by the arrival of Mr. Greenberg and the return of Hermione, who, having lost interest in saving the dress, announced it was time for them to enjoy some music.

"Lady Ryderwood has agreed to sing for us." Hermione extended her hand to welcome Lady Ryderwood to come forward. "Some lovely songs by Puccini."

There were exclamations of delight, and all the guests moved to the far end of the salon and took their seats. Veda Ryderwood gave Clementine's arm a nervy little pat with such a chilly hand that she shivered, and Lady Ryderwood laughed in apology: "So sorry to startle you, Lady Montfort, performance nerves. *Che gelida manina.* I should be singing *La Bohème* and not *Butterfly.*" She floated gracefully to the piano to help a harassed Adelaide find the music for her accompaniment and, when that was accomplished, to stand quietly in front of the piano, smiling to her audience.

"I hope you all enjoy Puccini as much as I do." She nodded to Adelaide and said simply, *"Un bel dì vedremo."* And a murmur of appreciation welcomed the opening chords of the famous aria "One Fine Day" from *Madama Butterfly*.

Hermione beckoned Clementine over by patting a chair next to her at the back of the room by the door.

Is it possible, thought Clementine as she sat down next to her mother's oldest friend, *that someone as tiny and fragile as Lady Ryderwood might open her mouth and effortlessly pour forth such exquisite and yet powerful sound?* She listened spellbound to the perfect control of Veda Ryderwood's pure soprano in her enchanting rendition of Butterfly's heartbreaking song of faith and hope.

But unfortunately, as Lady Ryderwood reached the penultimate stanza of her aria and everyone leaned forward in anticipation of the song's devastating finale, the door opened behind Hermione and Clementine and Winston Churchill tiptoed conspicuously into the room. He had patently been enjoying a cigar downstairs, as a dense cloud of smoke accompanied him.

Churchill's arrival was made with unerring timing, almost, it would seem, as if to purposefully upstage Veda Ryderwood's performance. *And,* Clementine thought crossly, as she turned her head to see his caricature of apology—a stubby forefinger lifted to his lips as he stood among them—*he is interrupting my favorite part of the song.* Butterfly, abandoned by her American husband and almost destitute with only her loyal maid and her little son for solace, cries out:

> *Tutto questo avverrà, te lo prometto.*
> *Tieni la tua paura, io con sicura*
> *fede l'aspetto.*

I promise you this
Hold back your fears—
I with secure faith wait for him.

As Lady Ryderwood sang the last words, Clementine saw her cast such a look of anguish toward Churchill that Clementine wondered if he would be easily forgiven for his bungled entrance.

As polite applause and little cries of delight died down, with Lady Wentworth and Mrs. Churchill lifting handkerchiefs to the corners of their eyes, Mr. Churchill, with one hand over his brow in a gesture of calamity, somehow found the courage to face Lady Ryderwood. He was embarrassed, or at least making a good show of embarrassment. And Lady Ryderwood forgave him. With a slight shrug of her shoulders and a little laugh, she shook her head. "No, dear Mr. Churchill, it's all right, I was nearly finished, really."

And Churchill, always ready to stage-manage a good moment, and clapping his hands to show both his appreciation and his apology, slowly approached Lady Ryderwood to take her hand and bend over it, an unctuous impresario feting his leading lady.

Mr. Churchill's interruption and subsequent enthusiasm for Lady Ryderwood's performance had everyone on their feet and walking toward the singer standing by the piano.

Clementine was turning to smile her appreciation to Hermione when she noticed the footman, who had been in attendance by the door, start in surprise, lean his head toward the paneling of the door, and then swiftly turn and open it. From downstairs there came up to them a cry of such magnitude that Clementine was afterward surprised that no one else had heard it. But Hermione's guests were clustered, unheeding to the harsh sound of a voice far less musical than that of Lady Ryderwood, around the diminutive soprano standing at the far end of the room. Miss Kingsley, however, leaped to her feet with surprising agility for a woman of her years and pushed the footman away from the door.

"Is that Jenkins?" Hermione cried as she took Clementine by the arm. "What on earth . . . ?" she exclaimed as she pulled her through the open door.

As they started down the stairs to the inner hall, Clementine was immediately aware that Hermione's elderly butler was leaning against the wall outside the dining room, palms braced to stop himself from falling.

"What is it, Jenkins?" cried his mistress, halfway down the stairs. "Jenkins, what has happened, are you all right?"

But all the poor man could do was wave to the dining room and gasp the words, "The cloth . . . all over . . . the bloody . . . cloth."

Chapter Four

Clementine, faster on her feet than was her friend, was several strides ahead of Hermione and reached the dining-room door first. Leaving her hostess to administer to the elderly butler, she pushed open the right-hand panel of the double doors and entered the dining room.

The long table clothed in heavy white damask stood out in the dark of the room, its candelabra burning a bright path down the center. Cigar and cigarette smoke still lay in a heavy pall over the mingled scents of jasmine, roses, and rich food. Clementine paused at the top of the table and spoke to the figure seated at the far end of it.

"Sir Reginald?" She peered down the length of the table. "Don't you want to come upstairs to join us for—?" She stopped, deeply embarrassed. It was clear that the gentleman was quite drunk. Clementine's lips formed a moue of disgust. The man was tedious sober; heaven forbid that he was now incapable. Sir Reginald's heavy shoulders were slumped forward, presenting a balding crown since he was facedown among the walnut shells littering the cloth. Annoyed with herself for barging into a potentially embarrassing situation, Clementine half turned in exasperation. She wished she had left it to Hermione to come into the room first; Sir Reginald was *her* oldest and closest friend

31

after all. She decided it prudent to retreat, took a step back, and noticed that Sir Reginald in falling forward had knocked over two glasses of half-finished port; a dark stain crisscrossed the cloth in front of him.

But something wasn't right here. Her mind was trying to escape from what her eyes were observing. It was trying to wriggle away from the truth, which was slowly assembling itself as a bewildering fact before her. A wave of alarm raised the hairs on her arms. A primitive call to race for safety surged through her, a powerful summons to run for home. The practical voice of instinct commanded, *Get out, now,* and she was conscious of a surge of adrenaline that pricked behind her knees and made her legs ache. But another voice, far cooler in tone and less urgent, suggested she move forward and investigate; there was no danger here. Intellect won out over ragged breath and bounding pulse, and she started to walk toward the slumped figure.

"Oh dear God . . ." Clementine half turned to the door as Hermione Kingsley came into the room. Hermione took in the situation at a glance and lifted a hand to the light switch on the wall. The seated figure at the table jumped fully into focus in the harsh electric light just as Clementine's mind made the connection, causing her to step backward in shock and fear bumping up against Hermione, who was moving forward. The two women collided, stepped apart, and walked rapidly down the dining room on either side of the table.

Sir Reginald did not move. He did not look up at them with eyes glassy from too much port wine to apologize with slurred words. He remained humbly head-down among the debris on the cloth, the bright light glinting on a few strands of hair plastered carefully across the gleaming surface of his balding pate.

As Clementine arrived at the bottom of the table, she emphat-

ically understood that Sir Reginald was sprawled out on its surface not because he was dead drunk; he had toppled forward for
an altogether different reason. Again she disobeyed the shrill
voice within instructing her to leave the dining room and sum-
mon help from upstairs, from the servants, from the men in the
salon, from her husband. She remained where she was and took
in a breath to steady herself. *Slow down, slow down.* She felt her
heart leaping along at an alarming rate, a wild March hare racing for its life. The scent of jasmine was overpowering in the
airless room. An incongruous image flashed in her mind of a
moment in her childhood, of a hare racing across the hot red
earth of the maidan in Madras, her dog, Rosie, in full cry; herself running in her white starched pinafore from under the
claustrophobic shade of a jacaranda tree. The room dipped and
swayed around her; the tropical scent of jasmine was sicken-
ingly sweet, the splash of blood on her pinafore vivid.

Breathe, the cool, rational voice instructed, *slow breaths.* She
obeyed and the stifling heat of the stamped red earth of the
maidan and the incessant, monotonous call of the baza bird receded. But the unpleasant metallic smell of rust and salt remained
and became stronger in the thick, oppressive atmosphere of the
dining room. She held on tightly to the back of the chair she had
been seated in throughout dinner and felt sweat break out on
her palms and in her hair. In another world and time, the dog
caught the hare, and rolled it over and over on the hard-baked
clay of the parade ground.

Hermione, on the other hand, appeared to be made of sterner
stuff, and well she might be, for Clementine realized the poor
woman was mistakenly still under the impression that her old
friend was merely unconscious. She took hold of Sir Reginald's
heavy shoulder and shook it, crying sternly "Reginald? *Reg-
in-ald.* Whatever is the matter?" And turning to her butler, who

had returned to the dining room and was standing motionless in the doorway: "For heaven's sake, Jenkins, what are you thinking? Have you telephoned for the doctor? I think he's had a heart attack."

Jenkins and Clementine looked at each other in complete understanding, and Jenkins said in an elderly quaver, "Ma'am, I am afraid . . . Sir Reginald is dead. I'm afraid he might have . . ." He stopped and looked helplessly at Clementine, beseeching her to say the words for him.

"I'm afraid he is dead, but not from a heart attack, Hermione." The sound of her own voice, clear and steady, brought Clementine fully into herself, and she bent down until she was almost crouched on the floor, and peered up at Sir Reginald. She saw something hard and shiny sticking out from the middle of his chest. The starched front of his white evening shirt and waistcoat, his dark coat, the cloth that hung down from the edge of the table—all were stained in what she now understood to be congealing, dark blood. A wave of nausea burned her throat and she heard herself observe in a neutral and dispassionate voice, "I think that's a knife handle sticking out of his chest."

"Don't be so ridiculous, Clementine, what can you possibly be saying?" The old lady's voice was angry and Clementine looked up and saw that Hermione's face was ashen and uncertain, and that the upright old body had started to sway. Clementine darted around the back of Sir Reginald's chair and helped Hermione away from the table and back up the room toward her butler. Supporting her with one arm, she motioned to Jenkins for his help, as Hermione had become almost a deadweight in her arms.

As Jenkins and Clementine, with Hermione sandwiched between them, came through the dining-room door and into the hall, the first of Miss Kingsley's guests came down the stairs. Their faces bore nothing but polite inquiry, until they took in the indomitable figure of their hostess, always commanding in every situation, a curled-up husk, between her butler and Clementine.

Aaron Greenberg, followed by Captain Vetiver, was the first to reach them. Mr. Greenberg gently took Hermione's hand and then, as she began to fold inward, lifted and half carried her into the drawing room.

Captain Vetiver clattered down the last steps, had a quick exchange with the butler, and started back up the stairs two at a time.

Clementine was aware only of tremendous confusion as guests ran past one another on the stairs, some descending to go into the dining room, others ascending halfway to tell them not to go down. Something terrible had happened and naturally everyone must see for themselves.

She watched Sir Vivian run down the stairs and walk swiftly into the dining room, followed by Lady Cunard, to be abruptly pushed by him back into the hall.

Lady Wentworth had an arm around Marigold Meriwether, who was howling like a shocked baby as they came back through the dining-room doors. Lady Ryderwood was standing at the base of the stairs, her face as white as chalk, and Captain Wildman-Lushington ran across the hall, demanding to know from the butler if there was a telephone in the house. From behind the green baize door to belowstairs a housemaid's head emerged, followed by another.

Clementine found herself encircled by strong and protective arms.

"What is it, Clemmy, what has happened?" She heard her husband's voice and felt a wave of tremendous relief, as if she had been searching in vain for his familiar face in a strange land. Her body was stiff and cold, but her mind was racing.

"Reginald Cholmondeley is dead," she said. "He's in the dining room. He was murdered."

And then she heard the unmistakable voice of Mr. Churchill. He reached the bottom of the stairs, barking questions to Captain Vetiver, who was right at his elbow. He ordered everyone to stop talking, get out of the dining room, and stay in the hall. Shouldering past Henry Wentworth, he walked up to her.

"Lady Montfort, what did you see? Try to tell me exactly how you found him."

"Sir Reginald was sitting at the dining-room table. He was bent over, his head on the table. I thought he . . . Then I saw the knife handle sticking out from his chest. His evening suit and shirt had blood . . ." She felt her husband's arms tighten as Churchill said, "My dear lady, please tell me you did not touch anything?" and heard her husband reply, "That's enough, Churchill; you'd better go and investigate. Take Vetiver with you, and remember not to touch anything, either of you."

For a moment Clementine thought that Churchill was going to respond, but he shot a thoughtful look at Lord Montfort and then abruptly turned on his heel and walked away, his head thrust aggressively forward, lower lip jutting, brows lowered. He briefly gestured Vetiver to follow him and they disappeared through the door. Clementine heard his voice above the exclamations of shock from those around her. "Gentlemen, please wait for me in the hall."

Clementine found herself thinking rather irreverently, *He's taking over, just like at Sidney Street; I wonder if the Scots Greys will be called in.*

The composure Clementine had found so easily to be hers in the dining room left her at this moment. She felt drained and quite exhausted. Her mouth was dry from too much wine. Her feet were ice cold and her mind was off on a track of its own. Her husband, with his arm around her, took her into the drawing room. And there was Hermione, sitting bolt upright in a large wing chair. The old lady's aged face was the color of ancient ivory, but otherwise she seemed quite as usual, Clementine noticed, in a detached kind of way.

Lord Montfort took his wife to a sofa and sat down on it with her. He drew her toward him and told a startled servant to bring brandy.

"Do not go into any of the receptions rooms for it," Lord Montfort instructed. "Go to the cellar and bring up a fresh bottle, and do it without talking to anyone." Then he turned to her. "Oh, my poor darling, you are so frightfully cold. I think you are in shock." He took off his evening coat and pulled it around her shoulders.

The footman must have run, Clementine thought, because he was back with a brandy bottle, a decanter, and a tray of glasses. *Funny,* she thought, *I am noticing everything, but I don't yet quite understand what it is I am seeing.* It was as if her brain were disobediently lagging far behind, refusing to take in another fact that might cause anxiety and distress.

"Good. No need to decant it," said her husband as the footman set down his tray. "Now go and see if you can find Lady Montfort's coat. And please bring Miss Gaskell in here for Miss Kingsley."

"I'm quite all right, thank you, Ralph, no need to worry about me. But I do need to know what is going on in my house." Hermione rose to her feet, accepted a glass of brandy, and drank it in one long swallow—a swallow that caused a shudder to reverberate throughout her thin body—before she walked purposefully toward the door.

Aaron Greenberg beat her to the threshold. "Quite enough for one night, Hermione. Churchill and Vetiver are taking care of everything. Please come and sit down."

Clementine watched the footman stir up the embers of the fire and add more logs. Aaron Greenberg said to Lord Montfort, "I think it would be a good idea if I asked all the women to come in here, until we know exactly what has happened; it's not right for them to be milling around in the hall." His voice expressed disapproval: the fairer sex should not be subjected to even a glimpse of such a sordid sight as a bloody, dead body.

"Of course, good idea, Greenberg." Lord Montfort barely glanced at him; his concern was only for his wife.

And then the room was full of feminine voices exclaiming in shock or inquisitive with questions. Clementine, sipping her brandy and huddled deep into her sable, was remote from all of them. She saw again Sir Reginald's bald shining head with three thick strands of hair slicked across it, the dark stain on his shirt-front when Hermione had shaken him upright. Sometimes the images were clear, sometimes they were blurred, as if the dining room were still full of cigar smoke. Other images came and went: Hermione instructing her butler to call for the doctor, the feeling of the old lady's upright body sagging into her arms. She remained in isolated thought as the room filled with people. The men stood in a solemn group by the doorway in silence, the women together in twos and threes to console or support as they watched the men out of the corners of their eyes. Everyone was waiting for Mr. Churchill to come back from the dining room.

"Adelaide, where on earth have you been, my dear? I was *so* worried." Hermione was again on her feet, and glancing up at the young companion, Clementine thought that Adelaide Gaskell had been crying, not tears from shock and horror but the sort of concentrated crying that causes swollen lips, eyelids, and noses. The sort of crying that leaves you with a headache and the sort that Clementine had not indulged in for years.

"Brandy," ordered Hermione, turning on the footman who had spilled the coffee on Marigold's dress. "Oh for heaven's sake, it's over there. If there's none left then get some more. Now, Adelaide, my poor dear girl, come and sit down here next to the fire."

Hermione Kingsley, who often erred on the brusque and matter-of-fact, insensitive to the needs of others who were not from the destitute class, was speaking to her companion in a gentle and consoling tone. Clementine was reminded of the voice she had used to her little girls when they had fallen off their ponies and were too frightened to get back on.

She always felt rather sorry for any young woman who had to earn her living as a companion to an elderly spinster or widow; it must be the most trying existence, she thought as she watched Adelaide Gaskell sit down next to the fire, with sideways peeks to see if the other women thought it permissible. Miss Kingsley wrapped a shawl around Adelaide's shoulders as tenderly as if she were a baby, taking her young hands in her long, bony, wrinkled ones and trying ineffectually to warm them. The young woman ducked her head and sneezed, and Maud Cunard got to her feet and glared at her with disgust.

"What are we waiting for?" she demanded of Aaron Greenberg, who, having decided that Hermione might now be left, was trying to slip out of the room, muttering something about a telephone call.

"We are waiting for the police, Lady Cunard. They will be here directly and will want to talk to all of us." Mr. Greenberg was instantly attentive.

"All of us?" Maud replied. "Well, all of us aren't even here. Trevor Tricklebank left after dinner and so did Jennifer Wells-Thornton. And I am not going to sit around all night waiting for a policeman to talk to me about something I know absolutely nothing about. Tell him he can call on me on Wednesday afternoon if he honestly thinks I can be of any help. Now," she turned to the butler standing in the doorway, "get my coat and tell my driver to bring around the motor. Hermione, I will call on you as soon as all this fuss has died down." Her meaning was clear, she was not to be considered a part of this catastrophe. Her name must not be mentioned in connection with what was obviously a scandal waiting to break. She gave Adelaide Gaskell another glare as she swept from the room and Adelaide diligently bent over her handkerchief and sneezed even more loudly.

Chapter Five

Detective Inspector Nigel Hillary arrived at Chester Square at half past midnight. The excitement caused by Sir Reginald's murder had long evaporated, leaving Hermione's guests in much the same mind as Maud Cunard. All of them, except Mr. Churchill, who was holed up in the library with Captain Vetiver, were sitting silently in the drawing room, drooping with exhaustion and brooding over their involvement in a soon-to-be public scandal.

We are all speculating like mad as to which one among us had reason to kill a perfectly harmless, stout, middle-aged man, whose only fault was that he was self-satisfied and pretentious. Clementine, still planted on her sofa with a plate of untouched salmon sandwiches on a little table at her elbow, looked around the silent room. The rallying effects of brandy consumed after the shock of finding a dead body in the dining room had worn off the group of society's bright and chatty partygoers, and when Detective Inspector Hillary strolled into the drawing room he was greeted by the collective blank stare of a group with one thought among them: *Talk to me first so I can go home.*

With perfect timing, Mr. Churchill was back in the drawing room before the policeman had a moment to introduce himself. Clementine was once again reminded of Churchill's extraordinarily assertive side when it came to directing the efforts of others as he assumed control of the policeman's arrival. He quickly made introductions, scrupulously correct with the order of precedence, she noticed with some amusement. Standing among them, chin thrust forward, gesticulating with a pink pudgy hand, Mr. Churchill intoned their names, watching the young policeman to make sure he was impressed by the elite throng he found himself among. It was only later that Clementine was to understand the importance of Churchill's involvement and the effect it would have on the nature of the Metropolitan Police inquiry.

"And unfortunately three of us are no longer here for you." Churchill waved a majestic arm around the room as if to conjure those missing to their places. "Miss Kingsley's nephew, Trevor Tricklebank, left immediately after dinner with Miss Wells-Thornton to go . . . ?" He turned to Miss Kingsley, who answered that her nephew had gone on to a ball at the Desmonds' with Miss Wells-Thornton.

"And Lady Cunard left well over an hour ago," put in Marigold Meriwether, coming off as rather pert. "She asked us to tell you that you are welcome to call on her next Wednesday if you think she can be of any help."

Mrs. Churchill expressed her disapproval of Marigold's determination to insert herself by fixing the girl with a long, thoughtful stare calculated to silence her. It had its effect.

Clementine was surprised at how young Detective Inspector Hillary was. He was a pleasant- looking man, about the same age as Captain Vetiver, and tall with broad shoulders, which she noticed he had squared as he walked into the room. *Probably feels a bit overwhelmed by Churchill,* she thought. Hillary was wearing a well-cut suit and looked as freshly turned out as if he were off to dinner at one of the nicer gentlemen's clubs. He had looked them all over thoroughly during Churchill's introduction and now he said, "Thank you, sir," to Mr. Churchill before turning to address them all. "I would like to talk to each of you, separately, before you leave. And please make arrangements to stay in town until this investigation has reached its conclusion, or I have given you permission to leave. There is no doubt I will be following up with each of you within a few days."

He turned to Miss Kingsley and asked which room he could use for his interviews. She was about to reply when Churchill started toward the door, left hand extended, and shepherded Hillary out into the hall and left to the library. *He has magnanimously decided to share his headquarters,* thought Clementine, *and obviously his is the first appointment with Detective Inspector Hillary.* It was a full twenty minutes before Mr. Churchill appeared among them again.

"I must away from you now, my dear Hermione, but I will return in a few days to see how you are doing." Churchill crossed center stage, exhibiting a blend of solicitous concern and reluctance to leave, thereby depriving the old lady of comfort and reassurance. "Come, my dear," to his wife as he extended a husbandly arm.

"Thank you, Winston, but I think I will remain with Hermione tonight, if you would send the motor back for me tomorrow morning."

Clementine was impressed with Mrs. Churchill's independence and her husband was obviously used to it. He paused only long enough to make a little speech to all of them: regrettable and tragic circumstances, absolute faith in the Metropolitan Police force, best in the world—the sort of heartening twaddle that was expected to soothe troubled souls. Clementine recognized the measured tone he had used earlier at dinner. His politician's voice, she remembered. "It would . . . be . . . in *everyone's interests* . . . to those of us here . . . and in the . . . *criminal investigation department* . . . to maintain complete . . . and . . . *absolute silence* about what has happened . . . *here tonight.*"

He strode out of the room, leaving them to their cold coffee and curling sandwiches.

A police sergeant came into the room and stood portentously in the doorway. "Miss Kingsley?" he asked, looking around the room for the butler to help him. "Inspector Hillary will see you now, please."

"I think it would be better if he spoke with Lady Montfort first." Hermione did not get up from her high-backed wing chair. She reminded Clementine of an old tortoise sticking her head out of her shell to see if winter was over.

"Beg pardon, ma'am, but Inspector Hillary asked for you, so would you mind stepping into the library?"

Hermione rose from her chair and crossed the room, and the others sat on and waited.

Clementine was called next.

Clementine felt as if a year had crawled slowly by before she could lay her tired body down in her bed at Montfort House. It had certainly taken an age before Detective Inspector Hillary had allowed them all to go. His thoroughness had known no bounds, and Clementine was still considering her interview as Lord Montfort tucked her up in the back of their motorcar.

Detective Inspector Hillary's manners had been faultless, but she had felt clumsy and unprepared. As he took her through the events of the evening, Clementine noticed that his notes, which lay before him on the surface of the desk, were neatly organized in columns. She could see the information he had written down from his session with Hermione in the second column and couldn't help but wonder if this method was a useful way of tracking where suspects were at the crucial time. She narrowed her eyes but still could not decipher his handwriting.

The questions began. Clementine strove to be as accurate as she could with her answers. Finally, the inspector's quest for detailed minutiae was over. He put his pen down, and his sergeant drew a heavy line in pencil across his shorthand notebook. Lord Montfort's interview, which had followed that of his wife, was far shorter; they were released from Chester Square with further reminders from the sergeant to contact Detective Inspector Hillary if they remembered anything more. Certainly they must expect a follow-up interview within a few days.

They were driven home to Montfort House through silent, empty streets slick with ice. A heavy frost glazed pavements and rooftops, glittering dully under the light of a full moon. The wind having cleared the sky of clouds had died away, leaving a black night bright with stars. The going was treacherous and they heard Herne swearing softly to himself as he carefully negotiated a turn in the road. Swathed in travel-rugs in the back of the motorcar, their steamy breath fogging its chill interior, they sat in silence. They had been under way only five minutes and already Clementine's feet were numb and her face was stiff with cold. As she stared out of the window at the bare boughs and branches of trees crystalline in the streetlamps, she felt she had been transported to another world, a world of black and silver, a metallic world with deep, dark shadows and glittering hard-edged surfaces.

"We are nearly home and then we can warm you up a bit." The grumpy man who had reluctantly spent an evening in the company of someone he didn't approve of had disappeared. She turned away from the window and looked into her husband's tired face and thought what a dear he was underneath his well-bred courtesy and careful reserve. She put her hand in his and leaned back against him. His arm came around her shoulders, pulling her close. She turned her head and buried her cold nose in the astrakhan collar of his coat.

"More than anything, I want to be in bed. I'm not sure I can sleep, but most of all it would be nice to have you close."

"When ugly things happen in life, wretched, wasteful, and senseless things, I always find myself profoundly grateful for what I have," he said, and she realized how comforting the sound of his voice was in the dark. "I'll tell White to make sure we are not disturbed and we can sleep late."

They drew up outside their house, and Clementine felt she was sleepwalking up the steps to the front door. When she finally gained the warm sanctuary of her bedroom, Pettigrew, who had been sitting by the fire, stood up and, tutting with disapproval at the hour and Clementine's ice-cold hands and feet, came forward to help her out of her clothes. With deft, kind hands she put Clementine into her nightgown and dressing gown and sat her down by the fire to warm her feet.

And then with relief and joy, Clementine found herself being helped into her bed. *The bliss of smooth sheets and soft blankets.* She leaned gratefully back against familiar pillows and her feet found, and sandwiched themselves on either side of the hot water bottle. A cup of warmed, malted milk was carefully placed between her hands and as she sipped, she felt the tension begin to ease. Between half-closed lids she watched Pettigrew moving quietly around the room. And then her maid was gone and her husband was climbing in beside her. She put down her cup and switched off the light on the table next to her bed.

Ah, the blessed dark, she thought, as she closed her tired eyes and let her limbs become heavy.

Her husband pulled her close and buried his nose into the nape of her neck. After a while he said, "Will you call on Hermione tomorrow afternoon?"

"Yes, I suppose I'll go round and see how they are faring, poor things."

"I thought Adelaide Gaskell looked quite ill."

"She has not been too well just recently. Mr. Churchill decided to invite the young marine captain, so poor Miss Gaskell had to make up the numbers. Then Hermione decided she was a better accompanist for Lady Ryderwood."

"Well, that was rather one-sided of her. I thought Maud Cunard was going to do the honors." His tone made it clear that he thought Hermione selfish.

"Well, that would explain why Maud was in such a bate. She was a positive viper about Hermione's poorly trained servants." Clementine remembered the complaints about inadequate butlers.

"She's always a positive viper. Probably Sir Thom has been wandering in the moonlight again. I'm surprised he wasn't there, must have been his night off." They giggled and Clementine felt her world right itself.

She was drifting off to sleep when he spoke again.

"How did your interview with Hillary go?" His voice was quite bland. *Just a polite question then,* she thought, as she replied, "I thought he was a bright sort. Not like our brush with the Metropolitan Police at Iyntwood."

She remembered with unwelcome clarity an earlier summer when Lord Montfort's nephew had been murdered at Iyntwood, and their house overrun with policemen, interviews, suspicion, and interminable fuss.

"Yes, I thought he was more than competent. Well educated, too, went to Stowe actually and Cambridge." These were important elements to a gentleman's existence, and they were ones that reassured her husband that they were in the right hands.

"Oh, good for him." She was falling asleep now.

"So I was hoping you could leave it all to him."

"Leave what to him?" She was wide awake.

"The investigation into Sir Reginald's murder, my darling. Will you promise not to interfere and let the nice, bright boy work without benefit of your help?"

The trouble with marriage, thought Clementine, *is that after decades of sharing life's woes and successes, of forgiving each other's frailties and coming to rely on each other's understanding, we end up knowing too easily what the other is thinking.* She experienced a moment of duplicitous guilt.

Her feet had warmed and her nose felt less like a peak of ice on her face. With these minor comforts in place, she had been pondering on the events of the evening. Prompted by Hillary's earlier questions, her stunned mind was now finally obliging by beginning to piece together the evening. There were still some blank bits, but she knew if she allowed herself within the next days she would remember everything she had seen or heard tonight.

She slid her now-hot feet off the hot water bottle and tucked them into the cool sheets at the edge of the bed.

"You see, you are off in your own world." There was a slightly censorious tone to the voice in the dark. "You haven't even heard my question. I hope you are not planning on involving yourself in this investigation, Clemmy, there's no reason to."

"I'm not off in my own world. I was thinking about Hermione and her musical evening for the Chimney Sweep Boys. I expect she'll have to call it off." A little ripple of guilt as a plan started to form itself.

"Oh I don't think so. That would upset Nellie Melba and most of all her greatest friend, Gladys Ripon. Anyone who enjoys going to the opera or the ballet does not upset London's most powerful patroness, the Marchioness of Ripon." He was laughing now. "God forbid, we might be barred from either place. No one would dream of doing that without thinking through the consequences quite carefully. Hermione has an able butler, and Adelaide Gaskell will rally after a few days' rest. Anyway she could always move the whole thing somewhere else. Claridge's does a good job."

"Jenkins is not up to organizing an event of that size and importance." She remembered Maud Cunard's scornful observations of the aging butler's incompetence. "And by the time Adelaide recovers it will be too late. It's less than a week away and it's the greatest event of the year for the charity!"

She could tell he was losing interest; he gently slid her off his lap and rolled over onto his left side.

"I think I'll offer Jackson's help, she could organize the charity evening standing on her head. Anyway, she has nothing else to do at Iyntwood with both of us in town until this is over. She'll have plenty of time to organize things for the hunt ball when we return to the country." She was thinking out loud, a huge mistake. Lord Montfort was instantly alert and turned back to face her.

"Why drag the poor woman up to town in this weather? I think housekeepers prefer to stay on their own patch, and not gallivant around the frozen countryside in November."

"Nonsense, Ralph, she'd love it. We are just around the corner from Harvey Nicks; perfect place for her to potter around and criticize the price of everything and say how much better Selfridges is for a bargain."

"As long as that's all she does." She heard his exasperation, but it was resigned exasperation. "As long as you are both busy with the simple pleasures of the Christmas season and not off together scouting around for clues."

Well for pity's sake, thought Clementine, *how could he make us both sound so vulgar? Like two prying and poking old ladies.* She remembered how restrained, methodical, and sensitive they had both been not to transcend the bounds of propriety when her husband's nephew, Teddy Mallory, had been so horribly murdered. How they had collected every scrap of information, every tiny detail, without asking direct questions while the entire household both above and below stairs had been thrown into confusion and chaos by the most bungling and intrusive of police inquiries. An investigation headed up by a man with an ax to grind against the aristocracy as he trampled hither and yon, without making a speck of progress, always ready to arrest the wrong man especially if he came from the upper class. It had taken skill, intelligence, and intuition to piece together those scrupulously gathered remnants of information. And then Mrs. Jackson, in one brilliant stroke, had found the last piece to their puzzle and created a whole and perfect picture of what had happened on the night Teddy Mallory had been so brutally killed. After which Clementine, observing strict gender protocol, had dutifully taken their information to Lord Montfort, so that through him Chief Constable Colonel Valentine had brought the culprit to bear in all official correctness. And Clementine and Mrs. Jackson had gone quietly about their everyday lives as if nothing had happened at all.

Her mind was superbly alert now. *Funny how that happens; you feel quite sleepy, ready to say good night, and then you get annoyed about something, and there you are as bright as day.*

"I think that's less than fair, Ralph," she said with genuine reproach. "We did nothing that could possibly be construed as unconventional; it was you and Colonel Valentine who made the arrest."

"Yes, it was. And I would be utterly grateful if it was Detective Inspector Hillary who made the next one. This is a different situation entirely and I am entirely relieved that you see it that way too."

Chapter Six

The next afternoon, Clementine returned home rather confused after her visit to Hermione Kingsley. Not surprisingly, the old lady had rallied; Miss Kingsley was of a generation that did not allow disaster to affect the standards of behavior. Personal distress was best kept tightly under wraps, concealed under a mask of locked-down composure.

Correct deportment aside, the elderly woman's face was leached of all color, her skin almost transparent, Clementine observed as they sat in the drawing room to drink tea. There was a feeling of the absent about Hermione, as if she didn't quite register where she was. Clementine glanced over at the butler, Jenkins, who appeared to have suffered the worse from the garish business of Sir Reginald's being stabbed to death in his mistress's house. If Hermione was temporarily absent, her poor old butler had never quite returned from his shock of last night.

Jenkins stood in the doorway to the drawing room, watching over the Clumsy Footman, who had blundered so badly the night before as he served coffee. The older man's large, imposing head was held erect, but Clementine saw that his hands were trembling slightly as they hung by his sides, and she could not decide whether this was due to age or to anxiety. And there appeared to be a strange, rather vacant look in his eye, which struck her as a bit disturbing.

But the reason Clementine came away from Chester Square, puzzled and perplexed, was Hermione's complete refusal to talk about the preceding evening. She did not acknowledge in any way that a murder had been committed in the dining room of her house and, what was even more worrying, did not refer to the evening at all. With increasing concern she realized that Hermione had taken completely to heart Churchill's instructions that Sir Reginald's death not be discussed among her household and guests. She had apparently dismissed the incident completely from her mind. Her party for Winston was something that had never happened. *How extraordinary,* Clementine thought. Sir Reginald had been a friend of Hermione for years, the mainstay of her charity, raising thousands of pounds over the decades and acting on her behalf in the House on every reform that affected the lives of the children and orphans of the impoverished. Their friendship had been so close over the years that if Hermione hadn't been so much older than Sir Reginald, everyone would have fully expected them to marry. Yet, for the duration of their afternoon together, Hermione's lips were compressed in a thin line on the subject of her friend's death. She had kept the conversation exclusively on the topic of her charity evening, even though the man who had worked unstintingly for its cause had been killed in her house.

Clementine had been quite ready to follow the old lady's lead; it was important to bide one's time if you wanted information. And so the two of them had sipped tea, nibbled around the edges of their hot buttered toast, and kept their conversation focused on the evening that would take place next week, with or without the sterling efforts of Hermione's paid companion, Adelaide Gaskell.

"How is Miss Gaskell?" Clementine had been quick to ask this question, since it did not trespass on the forbidden matter.

"Poor young girl, her head cold has settled in her chest. I'm quite sure she has bronchitis. Dr. Brewster came over this morning and has prescribed linctus for her. Now she must stay in bed and rest, he says, otherwise she might well contract congestion in the lungs." The tired old eyes blinked twice but Clementine did not take this as regret for Hermione's selfish behavior of the night before.

"How will you manage next week?" Clementine had finally ventured.

"Adelaide is a thorough young woman; she has kept records of all previous charity evenings. Jenkins will manage under her instruction." She was firm on this point then, thought Clementine as her eyes swiveled over to the old man standing by the door, whose tremor, it seemed to her, was even more pronounced.

Now was the time that Clementine should have recommended moving the charity recital to Claridge's Hotel, calling in the talented skills of Rosa Lewis, or suggested postponing the event, but she did no such thing.

"If I might make a suggestion, Hermione." She cleared her throat. "I would be happy to send for Mrs. Jackson. She is extraordinarily efficient, has arranged both our summer and hunt balls year after year. Each one a resounding success, as I am sure you will remember."

The old lady leaned forward a little in her wing chair. "But can you spare her, Clementine? Won't she be needed to organize Christmas?" Hermione made it sound as though Saint Nicholas relied entirely on Mrs. Jackson to ensure that his yuletide festivities were a single shared experience for every Christian soul worldwide.

"Yes, of course we can spare her. We will be here in town for the next week or so . . ." She didn't say why, because they were not talking about murder investigations just yet.

"My dear Clementine, how generous of you; I would be so

grateful. Mrs. Jackson is so impressively able. Would you telephone to her?" Like Clementine's mother, Hermione still demonstrated the habits of an older generation, born in an age without newfangled contraptions. The telephone, an artifact with a dubious provenance, was a necessary evil Hermione had reluctantly installed last year, along with electric light in the servants' hall. Even so, she never went near the instrument, which was kept in a far corner of the library behind a potted palm, dusty with disuse as there was an extension in the butler's pantry. It was Jenkins who, like a medium in a séance, spoke to the telephone, her intermediary with the outside world.

Quite pleased to have accomplished her mission, and ready to get things moving, Clementine had rapidly finished her tea and taken herself off to Montfort House. She asked White to telephone to Iyntwood and instruct the butler, Hollyoak, so he might inform Mrs. Jackson to ready herself for a trip up to London.

"Mrs. Jackson will stay here at Montfort House and go over to Miss Kingsley in Chester Square every day to help with organizing her charity recital. I know we have a full house in the servants' quarters, so I think it would be best if you put Mrs. Jackson in the old nursery. She will be comfortable there and it won't inconvenience anyone."

If White was surprised that Iyntwood's housekeeper was to be lodged on the third floor of the house, rather than in the attic bedrooms on the fourth floor with the other female servants, he did not betray any curiosity. He merely bowed his handsome head and murmured that all would be taken care of. Then he asked where Mrs. Jackson would take her meals.

"Her meals?" Clementine was momentarily mystified. "She will take her breakfast with you belowstairs or in her room if she chooses to, her luncheon and dinner wherever she happens to be. I am sure Mrs. Jackson will tell you what she wants, White."

"Then she will not take her meals with the family?" He obviously wanted to be clear on this point, she thought.

"Certainly not, White. Whatever gave you that idea?"

An unsuspecting Mrs. Jackson had awakened at the Talbots' country house, Iyntwood, to a snow-filled morning and had decided to go for a nice long walk that afternoon with the dogs. From the moment she had pulled back her curtains and discovered that it had snowed in the night, she had decided to make the best of this glorious winter day. Perhaps she would stop off for a cup of tea with her friend Mr. Stafford, who would be busily at work drafting plans for an extension to Iyntwood's rose garden to be started in the spring.

She always enjoyed a long walk in the first snowfall of the year, and at half past two she pulled on her stoutest boots and changed into a thick wool skirt. She buttoned her coat to her throat and wrapped a bright, cherry-red scarf, knitted for her birthday by the first housemaid Agnes, up around her neck and pulled a felt hat low over her ears, completely covering her glossy, dark auburn hair. She had just picked up her gloves when there was a knock on the door of her parlor.

"Come in," she called, and the hall boy came into the room and stood respectfully in front of her.

"Mr. Hollyoak says good afternoon, Mrs. Jackson, and asks you to join him belowstairs." The boy took in her bulky walking garb. "Soon as you can, he says."

And that was it for her walk and her pleasant cup of tea with Mr. Stafford in his cottage on the edge of the park. She changed back into her pinstripe skirt and white blouse and went downstairs to the butler's pantry. At five o'clock, after yet another change of clothes and dressed in her best dove-gray Sunday suit and hat, and carrying a small suitcase, she boarded the express train at Cryer's Breech station for Marylebone.

There was a sense of adventure in the air as the train began to pick up speed, and Mrs. Jackson in her second-class compartment, prettily flushed from her run along the platform to catch the train, was quite pleased at her summons to London. It would be pleasant to do some shopping with Miss Pettigrew in the larger department stores and perhaps have tea at the new Lyons Corner House at Marble Arch.

An hour and a half later, she was sitting downstairs at Montfort House, enjoying a well-cooked supper with the London staff gathered around her at the servants' hall dining table.

Mrs. Jackson was a conservative individual and, as she was fond of saying, she observed the old ways when it came to the conduct of servants in a great house. This was her first visit to Montfort House in many years, and the upper servants were known to her only by name. Within ten minutes of taking her place at the table she had formed the opinion that the present staff in the house got away with murder. It was evident that Lord and Lady Montfort were dining out this evening, but it was quite unorthodox, in her opinion, for the butler and his footmen to be sitting around downstairs at this hour, instead of in waiting upstairs. If Lord or Lady Montfort needed anything before they left for the evening, they would have to ring and wait for a footman to come up from the servants' hall. Iyntwood's butler, Mr. Hollyoak, would have been appalled at such laxity and quite rightly, too.

She lifted her eyes from her plate of food and noticed that there were several pairs of curious eyes fixed on her. Their communal scrutiny did nothing to alter her composure. She knew that they had all been guessing why Iyntwood's housekeeper had been called up to London from the moment they had heard she was on her way.

The new cook, a pretty and dashing young woman who could be no more than twenty-six if she was a day, was particularly attentive and full of questions. There was no housekeeper at Montfort House; the cook was second-in-command and fulfilled both roles in the house. It was natural for her to be curious as to why Mrs. Jackson was on her turf, but it was not Mrs. Jackson's habit to explain herself. The butler—and one glance told you he was far too young to be a butler, she thought—having accurately guessed his age at close to her own, would take several more years to acquire the gravitas of demeanor so necessary in a good butler to a large London establishment. *Oh well,* she sighed to herself, *London ways; everything happens at such a fast pace in the city, no wonder Edna Pettigrew always returns with tales of chaos in the servants' hall at Montfort House.*

Listening to the bright chatter around her, she noticed that, except for the cook, they were all Londoners, another mark against them. Mrs. Jackson, like many provincials, was a little narrow in her view about Londoners. Country-bred people remembered their place and looked up to the old and august families they worked for. City-bred servants were far too independent and unreliable, always ready to turn things to their own advantage. This opinion had been formed years ago, when Mrs. Jackson had started her career in London as a lowly housemaid at Montfort House, and had been reinforced by reports relayed by Miss Pettigrew when she returned from trips to London with her ladyship. "If that Mr. White was offered a job by some rich American he would be off like a shot," was a pronouncement often made by Miss Pettigrew when she came back from London brimming with information on new fashions, society scandals, and the inevitable report on Montfort House servants' hall, which was kept confidentially between the two of them.

Mrs. Jackson politely answered the Montfort House servants' questions and gave no further information as she ate her supper.

She had to admit the food was delicious: a stew of pork, bacon, and white beans, a cassoulet, the cook had been proud to tell her, that must have cost a fortune in ingredients. *No shepherd's pie made up from yesterday's leftover roast mutton from upstairs dinner in this servants' hall,* she thought as she finished her meal in silence.

"Her ladyship asks that you go up to see her soon as you can, Mrs. Jackson. You've plenty of time to finish your supper as they are leaving at eight o'clock. She's in the large drawing room." Mr. White certainly was a good-looking man, standing tall at six foot two, nicely proportioned, and perfectly attired with a pleasant, well-modulated voice.

"Very well, Mr. White. Thank you, Cook, that was an interesting dish, perhaps you will share the recipe with me before I leave." And without a backward glance she was on her way upstairs to the drawing room, hearing as she went an elevation in the hum around the servants' hall table.

Mrs. Jackson climbed the back stairs to the fourth floor of the house, to the old nursery and schoolrooms. When she opened the door, the rooms brought back a flood of memories of her first days as a housemaid in Montfort House, fifteen years ago, when the children were young and Nanny was still able to run after them, in the days before she got too stout to be really effective. The schoolroom was now used for storage, and the furniture that crowded the nursery was covered in dust sheets. But a fire had been lit in the grate and Nanny's old room was warm and comfortable, with familiar sagging easy chairs, tables and bookshelves filled with classics from bygone days. On the wall was a print of the late King Edward VII and, farther along, another of Queen Victoria when she was a young woman.

The prospect of the old nursery did a good deal to soften

Mrs. Jackson's stern countenance. Her handsome, classic profile had acquired rather a frigid cast since she had left Lady Montfort a few minutes ago, and her shoulders were still expressing some of the exasperation she had felt toward the end of their conversation. She had dropped all her Christmas and New Year preparations for the season, left her plans for the Iyntwood hunt ball dangling, to come up to London to help Miss Kingsley rescue her charity evening from disaster. Now she had discovered that this was not the only reason why she had been summoned.

She swung her suitcase up onto the bed, flipped open the lid, and removed two gray-and-black pinstripe skirts and a smart, well-made black bombazine silk dress, which she snapped briskly to expel any dust from the journey and then carefully brushed and hung in the wardrobe. She pulled open two drawers in the dresser and laid a sheet of lining paper inside each one. She next unpacked a stack of starched white cotton blouses, her underclothes and stockings, and a black full-length apron that she wore if she had to do something extremely messy, like arrange flowers. She laid her clothes carefully in the drawers and slid them closed. She placed her felt slippers underneath the bed and slipped a flannel nightgown under the pillow. Finally, she took out her rose-pink, woolen dressing gown from the bottom of the suitcase, a Christmas present from Lady Montfort last year, and hung it from the hook on the back of the nursery door.

As she was arranging her hairbrush and toilet articles next to the washstand she caught sight of herself in the looking glass and noticed that her expression was rather severe.

Now, Edith, she told herself, *you had better lose that look before you go over to Miss Kingsley's house tomorrow. Lord knows what you will find there.*

After considerable thought on the matter, she decided against acting on Lady Montfort's suggestion that she discover as much as she could about what was going on in Miss Kingsley's house—in other words, snoop. She would do nothing of the sort. She would be pleased to organize the charity evening, and do all she could to make it a success, of course she would, and she would enjoy it, too. And when she wasn't doing that, she would pop over to Selfridges in Oxford Street. Do a bit of shopping, and perhaps talk Miss Pettigrew into accompanying her to the Victoria and Albert Museum, or the National Portrait Gallery. Other than that, she had no intention whatsoever of getting herself involved in another one of her ladyship's inquiries. Their combined investigation into the murder of Mr. Teddy Mallory last year has been for a very good reason indeed. Lady Montfort's son, Lord Haversham, had been in danger of being arrested for murder. So it had been right and proper for her to help her mistress in any way she could. But the murder of Sir Reginald was not their business, and if Miss Kingsley was not discussing the sordid death of her friend, then Mrs. Jackson certainly did not believe it was her place to bring it up. As soon as her ladyship had recovered from the shock of finding a dead man at the dining table, she would be quite happy to leave things to the police. With this in mind, she left Nanny's room and walked across the night nursery to the day nursery and the bathroom next to the nurserymaid's old room.

She would take a nice long bath and then pop into bed with her hot water bottle, her cup of cocoa, and a good book. She was halfway through *Middlemarch* and everything she had read so far confirmed her opinion that marriage wasn't all it was cracked up to be. As she leaned comfortably back among her pillows and flipped the book open to her marker, she idly wondered if Ernest Stafford ever had time to come up to London.

Chapter Seven

Clementine left early the next morning to take Mrs. Jackson over to Miss Kingsley's house. It was a perfect late-autumn day with clear blue skies and the sort of snap in the air that encourages bracing walks along the embankment, but a wind coming down from the north told a different tale for the afternoon. They made the drive in silence, which did not bode well for Mrs. Jackson's compliance as an amateur detective's trusted assistant, thought Clementine, as she settled her gloved hands into her muff and gazed out of the window with a placid expression on her face. Mrs. Jackson had hardly rallied around the flag yesterday evening when Lady Montfort had briefed her on Sir Reginald's murder. Her manner had been quite correct, but a shade too detached and distant, and her responses had been negligible to say the least. Clementine fully comprehended how deeply conventional her housekeeper was, and though most loyal in her duty to the Talbot family, she probably did not consider the murder at Miss Kingsley's house to be something she must involve herself in—on anyone's behalf. She glanced across at her housekeeper's face. Mrs. Jackson appeared to be quite composed and relaxed, but Clementine suspected that she was probably fuming. Her enthusiastic suggestions to do a little careful investigation of their own at Chester Square had been received with respectful but chilly silence.

If she had offended her housekeeper's sense of dignity Clementine was truly sorry. But at the same time she was quite sure that once Mrs. Jackson was settled in Miss Kingsley's house and had met Miss Gaskell, her instinctive curiosity would be piqued and then they would see what she made of things.

When they arrived at Chester Square, Clementine noticed that the door was opened for them by the Clumsy Footman instead of the butler.

"Mr. Jenkins is with Detective Inspector Hillary, in the library, m'lady. But Miss Kingsley is waiting for you in the drawing room." The man said and on cue, the drawing-room door opened and Hermione walked into the hall. The presence of Scotland Yard's Detective Inspector Hillary and his sergeant in her house clearly didn't suit her; she was at her most austere and quite stiff with indignation. Starch aside, she was nonetheless courteous in her welcome to Mrs. Jackson.

"I am so grateful Lady Montfort can spare you from your duties at Iyntwood, Mrs. Jackson. Your reputation has preceded you and we are indeed fortunate to have your help. I am sure our charity evening will only benefit from your guidance. I will not introduce you to Miss Gaskell today, as it is important she has her rest. The butler will take you to her little office where you will be able to work undisturbed with the help of Miss Gaskell's records of previous events for the charity. And if you need to use the telephone, you will find it in the library. That is of course if we are lucky enough to be able to use *that* room today." She glanced toward the closed door of the library, her mouth tucked down in the corners in distaste.

She's as sour as lemon barley water, thought Clementine, confident that her housekeeper was more than a match for the old lady's iron rule over her household and her determination that not one word of what had occurred in her dining room would be uttered at Chester Square.

At that moment Inspector Hillary came out of the library, followed by a remarkably flustered Jenkins. The old man looked as shamefaced as if he had confessed to at least a dozen heinous acts, and was careful not to catch his mistress's eye. Evidently in both their minds he was guilty of disloyalty simply by being in the same room as the policeman.

"Finally, Jenkins. I was wondering where you might be." Hermione did not acknowledge Detective Inspector Hillary, her gaze was fixed somewhere over the policeman's head as she addressed her butler. "Now, this is Mrs. Jackson." Without turning her head, she gave an imperious wave toward the area in the hall occupied by Iyntwood's housekeeper. "She is here to organize the charity evening. I have told her to use the library telephone rather than the one in the butler's pantry, so she won't get in your way. She will be returning to Montfort House at seven o'clock this evening, so please make arrangements with Cook for her midday dinner and her tea. Perhaps you would show her down to the between-stairs office, if you have quite finished here." And turning to Clementine: "I will send Mrs. Jackson back in my motorcar, and Macleod will collect her tomorrow morning at nine o'clock sharp."

Hermione, having made all the arrangements she deemed necessary, was about to make her farewells when Hillary spoke.

"How fortunate you should arrive at this moment, Lady Montfort. I was wondering if—" But what he was wondering was interrupted by Hermione, as if he simply weren't there.

"My dear Clementine, I must say goodbye. Now my library has been made available to me, I can get on with my morning, what is left of it." Ignoring the policeman, she walked past him into the room he had vacated.

Clementine turned to Inspector Hillary and smiled to make up for Hermione's snub, but he appeared not in the least perturbed by the elderly woman's dismissive behavior. "I was hoping that I might call in on you, Lady Montfort, it would be helpful to resume our conversation about last night. Would it be convenient to follow you home, and might Lord Montfort also be available?"

The library door closed quite audibly as Clementine replied, "Yes indeed, Inspector. If we leave now, we might perhaps catch Lord Montfort before he leaves for his club."

Clementine would never have admitted to anything of the kind, but she was a natural for detective work. She possessed considerable intuition and had an inborn gift for timing, and once she had corralled her natural enthusiasm and vital energy, she knew when to inquire, and when to hold her counsel and let others do the talking, but most of all she knew when to prod. An endless fascination with people and what drove them to do the things they did had given her great insight into the oddities of human nature. She was naturally sociable, a practiced conversationalist, and had such easy manners that her company was much sought after in polite society. As a consequence she was invited everywhere, and there was no one in the Metropolitan Police, not even its commissioner, Sir Edward Henry, who had an address book to equal hers.

"Inspector Hillary, please sit here by the fire. White will bring you a cup of coffee and Lord Montfort won't be a moment. I am so glad I caught him before he left the house." And then, as if their visit were entirely social: "I do hope you will stay for luncheon," and by way of letting him know that luncheon was imminent and Lord Montfort would not expect to be kept waiting: "Our son Harry will be joining us—should be here at any moment."

"Thank you, Lady Montfort, how kind, but I have to rush off

to another appointment, there is always so much to do in the early days of an inquiry. But I would appreciate a few words with his lordship before you all go into luncheon." And with no more ado he waded in.

"I understand that you were seated next to Sir Reginald at dinner. Did you sense anything unusual or different in his manner?"

Clementine cast her mind back. "He was quite as usual. He talked about the New Year's Honours List. He expected to be elevated to the peerage for his efforts on behalf of the charity, which were considerable. He has done so much good work for East End orphans and the children of the impoverished. He and Miss Kingsley have positively slaved for the Chimney Sweep Boys over the years."

"Yes, the charity, it's an original name, and of course I have heard of it, who hasn't? Is it solely for the benefit of chimney sweeps' orphaned sons?"

This was a common mistake among those who were not bullied regularly for charitable contributions by Hermione's dedicated fund-raisers. And Clementine, who regularly beat the bushes in the county on behalf of the charity, was ready for him. "It has been Hermione Kingsley's life's work to fund an institution to take bright, promising boys, abandoned by impoverished parents, from orphanages and workhouses and give them an opportunity to become useful in the world. There are almost two hundred boys living at Kingsley House in Dulwich, with an additional forty or fifty who are at boarding school. But Kingsley House is home to all boys until they come of age. Miss Kingsley is proud that there are three Royal Navy officers among her earlier boys, a director of the Bank of Scotland, and several young men who have joined the Indian Civil Service. Some of her boys have grown up to achieve great things throughout the world.

"The name by the way honors Miss Kingsley's uncle, Charles Kingsley, who was a tremendous social reformer, sympathetic to the plight of working children. He wrote *The Water-Babies,* in which the main character, Tom, is a chimney sweep—hence the charity's name." And to herself: *I should be one of the directors, I think I put that all rather well.*

"Yes, I remember the book from my childhood—a cautionary tale, strong on ethics and morality; Mrs. Doasyouwould-bedoneby and the Golden Rule." Most policemen, thought Clementine, would have never have heard of the book, let alone remembered it as an instructive tale.

Inspector Hillary took an appreciative sip of his coffee. "Miss Kingsley is most anxious that our inquiry does not interfere with her annual charity evening and I have assured her it won't. Mr. Churchill has instructed that this investigation is to be conducted with the utmost discretion, no newspapers, no fuss of any kind. We will do what we can of course, but people do talk."

Clementine laughed and said yes they certainly did. And it occurred to her that one of the reasons this amiable and pleasant-mannered young man was conducting this inquiry was probably that the ex–home secretary, Winston Churchill, had requested he do so. As Lord Montfort had already pointed out, Detective Inspector Hillary was a far cry from the ham-fisted individual they had been lumbered with for the Iyntwood murder.

She was just relaxing into what she had mistaken for a conversation when she was subjected to a swift change of tack, so startling in its speed that she had not sensed it coming.

"Apart from the butler, you were the first person to enter the dining room that night. Why was that?"

"Miss Kingsley heard a cry from downstairs, we were sitting by the salon door, and before I knew it we had run downstairs to see what was going on. Miss Kingsley stopped to tend to her butler, poor Jenkins was suffering from shock. And I went on into the dining room."

"Now tell me exactly what you saw. Please take your time, no detail is unimportant, and remember all your impressions are valuable." He did not look at her but down at his notes, his pen poised.

She described her entry into the dining room and her realization as soon as she saw Sir Reginald that all was not well. She then went on to describe Miss Kingsley's reaction, and how she and Jenkins had taken her from the room.

"After that it was all hubbub and confusion," she said. "And it was then I realized exactly what had actually happened—that he had been murdered."

"Delayed shock," he said with some sympathy.

"Yes, something like that." She made herself sit back in her chair and unclench her hands.

"When you were standing in front of Sir Reginald, you say Miss Kingsley shook him and that was when you saw . . ."

"The blood on his suit and shirtfront, and on the edge of the tablecloth." She insisted on saying this herself, because every time she did so, the image receded a little and lost some of its ugly power.

"What did you do then?" He looked up at her, his pen still poised to write.

"I bent down and could see the knife handle sticking out of the middle of his chest. A little to his left perhaps. It was in quite deeply, I couldn't see the blade, but I knew it was a knife." She was amazed that she could say this now without a trace of a wobble in her voice.

"And then?"

"When Miss Kingsley realized that he was dead, she became

ill. She was half fainting, so I took her from the room." He wrote for a few moments and then looked up at her.

"She was on the other side of the table, you said. So how did you get to her?" He narrowed his eyes as he waited for her reply, and Clementine straightened in her chair,

"I walked around the back of Sir Reginald. He was seated at the top of the table."

"So you walked between the back of his chair and the dining-room window?" He was busily writing all this down, and she craned to see if it was in a column. It wasn't; his columns were on the other page, filled with neat, precise writing in timetable form, like a Bradshaw train schedule.

"Yes, that's right."

"And were the curtains closed or open?" Again that direct, intent gaze.

"Closed." *Had the murderer come in through the window?* This had not occurred to her before.

"You are sure of that?" His eyes, a mild, cool gray common in most fair Englishmen, were steady and unwavering.

"Yes, quite sure," she said, and she was.

"And you didn't suddenly feel cold, find the window open, and close it?" He was watching her closely and it made her feel she should doubt herself.

Clementine didn't answer for a moment. She cast her mind back to the dining room and briefly closed her eyes, the better to envision the scene. She had been standing behind the chair she had occupied at dinner. She hadn't felt cold during the meal, but as she stood in front of the body of Sir Reginald; there had been a distinct chill in the air.

"I do remember that it felt cold in the room, not when I came in, but at the far end of the room. I assumed that it was a reaction to what I had found. But I am quite sure I did not close the window."

"So you think the window was open behind the curtains." It was not a question.

Clementine felt a shiver ripple up her arms.

"I have no idea . . . Was it . . . ? Open, I mean?"

"When I checked the room it was closed, but the catches that lock the window were undone, and the butler is quite sure that all windows in the house were locked, and that those on the street side of the house on the ground floor are never opened or unlocked."

"So someone came in through the window from the street?" She had blurted this too quickly and he lifted his head from his notes.

"Too soon to be sure, but it is possible." He had stopped taking notes and sat back in his chair.

"And that would mean that the man who killed Sir Reginald was not one of us, not one of us in the house." Clementine had questions of her own, but she knew she must be careful not to be too impetuous.

"It certainly might look that way, but again it is too early to say. But, let's go back to the other evening. You said last night that Miss Kingsley and Miss Gaskell both left the salon at a critical time." He smiled, and Clementine realized that he was fully aware of her interest. Her curiosity had given her away; this was not a good thing. She got up and poured him another cup of coffee.

"I doubt if either Miss Gaskell or Miss Kingsley was capable of killing Sir Reginald," she said as she handed him his cup. It sounded quite ludicrous, she thought, like something from Oscar Wilde's story "Lord Arthur Savile's Crime."

"Yes, of course, it's highly improbable, they were all such close friends." It was a statement but he was asking a question. He took another sugar lump and stirred his coffee as he waited for her answer.

"Miss Kingsley and Sir Reginald certainly were good friends, for many years. Miss Gaskell is Miss Kingsley's paid companion and has been with her for three or so years. But after dinner there were several opportunities for Miss Kingsley's guests to be anywhere in the house, the men especially came up to the salon in twos and threes, some of them stayed downstairs for quite some time. Mr. Churchill was down there for . . ."

"Mr. Churchill was in the library, he was on the telephone to his secretary at Admiralty House." There was no change in his tone, he made this statement in an almost matter-of-fact voice, but it was clearly made as a point. Mr. Churchill was off-limits as a suspect, full stop.

"So Mr. Churchill has an alibi," Clementine observed to her hands folded in her lap.

"Yes, Lady Montfort, he does, so you can cross him off your list." She looked up to find him looking at her, his lips curved in a smile of indulgent amusement. "I'm sorry, this is not fair of me, I should have told you before when we first talked: Colonel Valentine is my uncle."

She felt like a guilty child. *Here's a pretty situation. Why on earth didn't someone tell me Detective Inspector Hillary was related to our chief constable, the man who so carefully tied up the loose ends in that little matter of our Iyntwood murder?*

"Might I say this, Lady Montfort, without offending you?" All traces of the policeman were gone; he was a nice boy from a good family, being considerate. "I want to add that this murder strikes me as both audacious and brutal. And I have been instructed that the inquiry is to be carried out with as much discretion as possible, which means that there are people in the government who are concerned about Sir Reginald's death. I think your interest in the events surrounding the murder might best be confined to—how shall I put this?—let's say academic interest. Do I need to be plainer than that?" His voice was pleasant, gentle even, but his face was expressionless and he nodded slowly, as if eliciting complete agreement from her.

Good grief, thought Clementine, as she gazed across at the serious face in front of her, feeling embarrassed and thoroughly caught out. *You would think that I had asked all the questions just now.*

Chapter Eight

Clementine was enjoying the company of her son, Harry Talbot, Viscount Lord Haversham. They were sitting in deep, comfortable chairs on either side of the fireplace in the drawing room, waving their glasses of sherry in the air and interrupting each other, amid exclamations of astonishment from Harry, when Lord Montfort came into the room after his brief session with Detective Inspector Hillary.

"Poor old thing, it was such a terrible shock, she is actually carrying on as if nothing . . ." Clementine broke off as her husband joined them. "Well that was awfully quick! Did he ask you anything at all?" She laughed; Harry's arrival had lightened the mood in Montfort House considerably.

"He asked me a lot of things, but *I* manage to keep my answers to a simple sentence. My business with Hillary is concluded and, unlike you, I am allowed to leave town whenever I wish to." Lord Montfort not only sounded smug, he looked almost pleased with himself. He nodded a greeting to his son and turned to accept a glass of sherry from the butler. "Good to see you, my boy." He raised the glass to his lips and took a sip. "I can tell that your mother has filled you in on this awful business. We are of course not talking about it, as specifically requested, aren't we, darling?" He smiled at his wife.

Clementine had just reached the part in her story when she had taken Hermione from the dining room, and Harry was hanging on her every word. Lord Montfort found a comfortable chair between the two of them and sat back, savoring his Fino, the better to enjoy his wife's animated recounting of Hermione's disastrous dinner party and interrupting her only occasionally to add his own perceptions of what had occurred there.

"Now, Harry, not a word outside the family. You understand the importance?" After recounting the horrors of their evening with evident relish, Clementine now unfairly prevented her son from enjoying the same experience.

"Yes, Harry, it's being kept hush-hush." Lord Montfort was quick to back up his wife. "Hermione's charity evening for the Chimney Sweep Boys is a week away. It is vital that this lamentable business does not become a topic for the newspapers, and the endless speculation and gossip that follows." He could have added, thought his wife, that the less that was known to the public, the better for all Hermione's guests, especially Mr. Churchill.

"Yes, of course, sir." To his credit, Harry didn't bristle at being lectured on discretion. "But who on earth would murder that pompous old windbag? Surely you don't bump someone off because they're a crashing bore. And what I can't quite take in is that this all happened at Miss Kingsley's birthday party for Mr. Churchill. It's like something out of a farce." Their son was apparently oblivious to the fact that murder had been done in the house of a close friend, causing everyone there acute embarrassment, not to say shock and grief, and putting Miss Kingsley and her household in an unpleasant position. Like his parents, he'd had no real friendship with Sir Reginald, who was a friend of a friend and someone he would perhaps vaguely recognize if he bumped into him in the street.

The farcical aspect of the murder aside, Harry was enjoying the situation far too much, thought his mother, but it was understandable because he had not been a witness to the hideousness of the thing. She was glad when he turned to his father to catch up on Iyntwood news, as she was still trying to decide if the fact that Detective Inspector Hillary was Colonel Valentine's nephew might be useful or a stumbling block in her inquiry. She had been unable to gauge from the policeman whether he disapproved of her participation in the Teddy Mallory affair. She glanced across at her husband, who, in an effort to distract her son from the melodrama at Chester Square, had involved him in a discussion about the new Purdy shotguns Harry had bought for Iyntwood's shoot in a fortnight.

I must be careful, Clementine thought, *not to appear to encourage Hillary to involve me. I must advise only if asked and save up my questions and favors for when it counts and not willy-nilly as they occur to me, otherwise I will annoy. I can perhaps make certain observations, might even guide conversations with Hillary to areas I need to know more about, but absolutely no more than that.* She returned her attention to the conversation between her husband and her son and was immediately aware that its mood had changed.

"Well actually, I have some news of my own . . ." Harry was saying as he leaned farther back in his chair, stretching his legs out in front of him. When her son and his father were together these days she was continually reminded how alike they had grown in the past few years. They were tall men, athletic in build, with the Talbot dark hair and blue eyes. They were at ease in their world, quietly confident and comfortable with who they were. Even their voices were similar in quality and cadence. Harry had never looked more like his father than he did now.

"I met with Captain Vetiver at the Admiralty this morning, it was a brief meeting, and not a word of what happened at Miss Kingsley's by the way. He has asked me to join the Royal Naval Air Service. I would be headquartered at the flying field out at

Eastchurch." Clementine noticed that Harry was speaking to the space between where she and Lord Montfort were sitting, his manner was slightly guarded, and the announcement sounded overly rehearsed. "But of course I would not be in uniform yet . . ." He added hastily, glancing at his father, "Not until that is . . ." He did not look at his mother, anticipating a flood of objections from her.

Clementine had already heard of Harry's hoped-for involvement with the RNAS from Captain Wildman-Lushington at dinner last night. With this information tucked away, she had rather hoped that her husband would continue on to luncheon at his club after his interview with Detective Inspector Hillary, so she could find out from Harry just how involved he was with Mr. Churchill's Royal Navy Air Service, in case she needed to square him. Now here was Harry blurting out his news, and inviting another family storm. *Perhaps it's for the better*, she thought. *Now we can honestly air our opinions, since he has obviously decided to make flying his future and stop dillydallying around a subject that makes us anxious.*

"Has it occurred to you that you are not yet of age?" Lord Montfort's voice was severe, and he looked at his son from underneath frowning brows, not an auspicious sign.

"Well of course it had, but I didn't think it was somehow relevant, it's just a few months after all. I am sorry, sir; do you object to my joining?" Harry could be disconcertingly contrite with his father, and always at the right time, Clementine thought with admiration. But however penitent his outward manner, it didn't appear to have its wished-for effect.

"Of course I object to your joining, my boy. It's a damn silly and irresponsible thing to do and certainly not expected of you, or your position. We are not at war! I know Churchill is eager, but there are those in the government who will do everything in their power to prevent us being embroiled in a war with Germany, and our foreign secretary is one of them. If you want to lead a useful life until you inherit, there is a constituency being kept warm for you in the county. Politics is the only real job for people like us, that and the stewardship of our land." His frown deepened and he put his sherry glass down on a side table with more force than was necessary. "And anyway those machines are death traps."

Oh dear, not that tone, Clementine thought; and she saw her son's face take on exactly the same expression as his father's, brows down, chin up. She rushed in to say, "I met Captain Wildman-Lushington at dinner the other evening, he's Mr. Churchill's flying instructor, and you know he was quite reassuring about the *new* aircraft. Did you get a chance to talk with him, Ralph? You didn't? Oh, well he said the Farman biplane was quite stable, it's the twenty-third edition of the first one, by the way. And if Mr. Churchill can fly a plane . . ." She left it for them to draw their own conclusions. Her husband shot a look of such reproach in her direction that she felt disloyal and hurriedly added, "Nonetheless, Harry, you have a duty to your position in the family, first and foremost."

"And you can't assume your duty with a broken neck. You are my only son. Your job is to inherit and take your place in the Lords, not join the military. There it is. Your duty as a Talbot comes first, Harry."

"So am I to take it that you are forbidding me to join the air service?" Harry asked, rather taken aback that his summons from Mr. Churchill had not gone down quite as well as he'd hoped.

Silent, Lord Montfort lowered his head and considered, his lips pressed together. After a good interval he looked across at his son, his face still stern. "Why should I forbid anything? I haven't been asked yet to give my consent."

"I'm sorry, sir, that was rather shabby of me." Harry met his father's gaze.

"Well then?"

"Well then, Father, I would like to be involved with the Royal Naval Air Service, it would be off-the-record for a while, and if it were to become official I would be offered a commission and accorded the rank of captain." Harry's voice was no longer nervous, and his face shone with the zeal of the already converted. "I believe that we will be drawn into a fight with Germany before too long, and if so, air reconnaissance would be an important element to an expeditionary force in achieving a quick resolution. I can be of real value, you see."

Clementine heard her son's sincere need to be of use, of value. She understood that ache to have a real job, a useful purpose in life. When she was younger, she remembered, she had often felt quite frustrated that her role consisted of producing an heir, acquiring a fashionable wardrobe, and running households in town and in the country already run by a staff of well-trained servants. As the years had gone by she had found distractions: her orchid house and designing Iyntwood's new gardens. She had truly enjoyed her young children without completely usurping Nanny's regime in the nursery. But often she had found herself needing so much more. It was different for her husband. He had his estates to run, which consumed the greater part of his time. He took an interest in the magisterial duties of the county and, even though he was not active in politics, took his seat at the House of Lords whenever government became too radical. And he was actively engaged in all country life and its sport and had bred an excellent line of hunters from his stallion Bruno. But if Harry felt the need to be useful then he should run as member of parliament for Market Wingley until he inherited his father's title, when he would move up into the Lords. *It isn't a question of what we want to do; it is a question of what we have to do, our generation understand this, why doesn't Harry's?* She remembered her husband as a younger man steadfastly learning from his father the duties that came with owning land, and the massive responsibility that burdened it. *We are far more dutiful; we never questioned our lot in life but continued where our parents left off, most of us with less money.*

But Harry's apology had its effect. She knew her husband was willing to try to understand his son's fascination with aircraft. His wish to join the RNAS did not come as a complete surprise, as both of them had been worn down by Harry's persistent fascination over the years with any form of transportation other than the horse.

"Harry, you have had this obsession with machinery ever since you were a boy. First it was motorcars and now it's aeroplanes." In her husband's mind, flying was the sort of thing only the foolhardy did, and would keep on doing until it was finally accepted that man's natural element was firmly on the ground and not in the air. "I think there is nothing we can do about it, unfortunately, as it seems to be a part of who you are. What does Vetiver have in mind?" *He sounds almost resigned,* Clementine thought.

"It's an idea of Mr. Churchill's actually—he wants me to help set up a training program for flyers and to bring in aircraft that would be useful when we go to war. I'm working with Tom Sopwith right now on a machine—" He stopped himself. "Actually, shouldn't really talk about it. You understand how things are." He looked embarrassed.

There couldn't have been a more unfortunate answer, Clementine thought, *that this was Churchill's idea.*

"I would like to think it over, Harry," was Lord Montfort's only response, and both his son and his wife understood the wisdom of allowing this to close the subject.

"Luncheon *is* ready, m'lady." A slight whiff of reproof from White; Ginger's delicious food must not be kept waiting.

But as it turned out, the day's events were on Harry's side. When Clementine went upstairs to dress for dinner at the Waterfords', Harry received a telephone call from the Admiralty. Later, when she joined her husband in the hall to wait with him for Harry to finish, so that they might all leave together, their son came out of the library. It was clear that his conversation with Captain Vetiver had not been a pleasant one, for Harry looked quite shaken.

"Great Scott," Lord Montfort exclaimed when Harry drew him to one side and related his conversation with Captain Vetiver. "The boy was with us only two nights ago at dinner. What can have happened?"

Harry reluctantly turned to include his mother with news that did not advance his cause for the RNAS. "Captain Wildman-Lushington was flying this afternoon, and his plane went out of control as he was coming in to land. It hit the ground, both pilots were thrown clear."

"Oh, thank God he was thrown clear . . . but is he badly injured?" Clementine could hardly believe what she was hearing.

"Unfortunately, Wildman-Lushington was killed."

It took some moments before Clementine could properly take in what her son had said. She heard the words, but fear that had started as a far-off flutter now gathered force and threatened to submerge her understanding. She was aware that her voice was barely audible even in the stillness of the hall. It was a whisper, a croak.

"Surely not," she said. "Surely he survived?" Neither of the men answered her, and her heart rate picked up. *There must be some mistake; why, only two days ago he was standing in Hermione's drawing room, taking immense pains to reassure me that flying did not present the dangers it did a year ago. Marvelous innovations all the time,* he had said, *safety a priority.* She sought reassurance that she had misunderstood, but there was none. Captain Wildman-Lushington had been killed outright.

The panicky moment began to ebb, and in its place a dull sadness took hold and lay in her chest, heavy and unpleasant. She could still see the bright, eager young face and the slight swagger of pride as the young man had told her that he had taken Churchill "up" and that the First Lord of the Admiralty had taken over the controls and flown the plane himself under his instruction. Bits of their conversation floated back to her: his enthusiasm as he explained the difference between one sort of aeroplane and another; the pride he had taken in being part of a new navy elite; and the naïve enthusiasm of a young man with his entire life before him. She felt almost angry as she remembered him.

"Terrible news, Harry." Lord Montfort was as shocked as she was, and she waited for him to express his dismay that young men were foolish enough to put themselves in such danger. Lord Montfort walked over to his son and placed a consoling arm on his shoulder.

"Why was the Admiralty telephoning you?" he asked.

"I was invited to go out to Eastchurch tomorrow with Captain Vetiver. That was him on the blower. Captain Wildman-Lushington was one of the pilots I was going to talk with about the training program."

"Did he say why the captain's machine crashed?"

"No, he did not, but I'm afraid a lot of it is due to poor training. Pilots don't often have enough mechanical knowledge of the machines they fly. Each flying officer must be taught how to cope with his plane's idiosyncrasies, or at least learn to discover what they are so they can fly them effectively. The engineering experience I picked up at Sopwith can help with that. And I have to convince the navy that the Farman has had its day."

And then Clementine's husband said something rather surprising, the last thing in fact that she ever thought she would hear him say, and when she heard it she felt bleak despair.

"Well then, Harry, I think you should accept their commission if they offer you one. It seems your path is set for you, my boy." He clapped his hand on his son's shoulder almost in congratulation, and then wound his silk scarf around his neck. He took his hat from the butler, then turned to his wife and gave her his arm.

"We will not be back late tonight, White. Lord Haversham will be leaving in the morning; he has to go to Eastchurch."

Now that her husband had had time to adjust to the idea, and understood that his son had a skill that was needed, Clementine saw that it merely became in his mind the transference of duty.

Her mood was introspective as they left the house and climbed into their motorcar. She thought again of Captain Wildman-Lushington: what an appalling waste, and for what? What on earth was it about men that drove them continually to push against nature? These thoughts sent her further inward as she tried to understand the world she lived in. During her childhood in India, the fastest method of travel was on horseback. She was fifteen when she had seen her first steam engine. It wasn't until she was nearly eighteen and had come back to England that she had seen a motorcar—a loud, faulty thing that made more noise than progress. Now she could make the journey from London to Iyntwood in under an hour by motorcar, or in thirty minutes on an express train. Communication had become so sophisticated as the telephone had taken over from the telegraph; she often wondered if people would forget how to write a decent letter.

And now, because of the restless nature of mankind, in the past several years young men had taken to the air, or tried to take to the air, in flight. Her sense of alarm deepened the more she contemplated the wasteful death of a bright young man who, barely two years older than her son, had been killed in the pursuit of something that could be of no real use to anyone at all.

Later that night, as she tossed around in her bed, Clementine asked herself the same question she had been asking herself all evening: was Wildman-Lushington's plane crash an accident? Could an aeroplane be made to fall out of the sky on purpose? And if it could, was the young man's death in any way linked to the murder of Sir Reginald? She lay awake for a long time in the dark, running over the catastrophic evening at Hermione Kingsley's house. In the end, she got up out of bed and, sitting at her desk, took out her diary and in the back divided the double spread of pages into columns. Then she wrote down as best as she could remember exactly who had been where between the hours of eleven o'clock and when they had found the dead body of Sir Reginald. She paid particular attention to when the women had left the dining room, and in what order and at what time the men had arrived to join them in the salon. When she had done this she realized she had several large gaps in her timetable. Well, it was a start and she would continue to work on it, and hopefully over the next few days would build a complete picture of where everyone was when Sir Reginald had been murdered.

The clock chimed the half hour and looking up she saw that it was well past two o'clock in the morning. She had to be up in time to talk to Harry before he left for Eastchurch.

Chapter Nine

Mrs. Jackson had spent her first morning at Chester Square going over Miss Gaskell's notes for the Chimney Sweep Boys charity evening for the preceding year. It had been slow-going and tedious work, as the guest list was an untidy, incomprehensible mess. Names had been crossed off and then added again to the list farther down, some names marked with an asterisk, others with an exclamation point. Mrs. Jackson assumed the marks were code to denote important or unimportant guests, but she couldn't quite be sure which represented which. She opened the ledger for expenses and donations for the year before. Here there was some order at least. There was a long list of names and the amount donated entered in the credit column. The total was an extraordinarily large sum. The size of each contribution helped her to understand that an exclamation point on her guest list signified a generous donor, whereas the asterisk relegated the giver to the status of a minor donor. She calculated a figure that separated the generous from the sparing, and then, because she was nothing if not orderly and neat in her work, she compiled two lists, in alphabetical order: list A and list B. Pleased with her work at the end of the morning, she had two lists numbering a total of two hundred and forty guests. How on earth had they managed to cram that many people into the two salons?

Even with both double doors connecting the two rooms laid open, it would have been a crush. In the end, she went downstairs to talk to the butler.

Mr. Jenkins was presiding over the business of washing crystal; he was being particularly tetchy with the James, the second footman, the one who had been given the unfortunate name of Clumsy Footman by Lady Montfort. The butler stood up as she came into the room and suggested they repair to his pantry so their conversation would not be interrupted. He called for tea to be brought, fussed around to make sure she was comfortable, and made a little space on the top of his cluttered desk so she could put Miss Gaskell's ledger and her own notebook down among an untidy melee of brown wrapping paper, balls of string, pencils, sealing wax, old account ledgers, and half-finished lists that littered its surface.

Miss Kingsley's butler conformed completely to Mrs. Jackson's ideal of an upper servant of the old school, and she felt reassured by his courtesy as she settled herself in a small chair to the right of his desk. His manners were those of a gentleman and his bearing was upright and dignified. It would be both rewarding and pleasant to work with a man of his sensibilities. After they had chatted politely about the weather, it had started to snow, and he expressed his concern for her comfort in the small room that she had been given to work in, Mrs. Jackson asked her first question.

"I am unable to talk with Miss Gaskell until she is a little more recovered and I hoped you might be kind enough to enlighten me. What rooms do you use in the house for the charity evening for the actual recital? I know the small salon may be opened into the larger one, but over two hundred people would be rather a crush, wouldn't it?"

"The paneled wall at the back of the large salon opens up completely into the gallery, giving us plenty of room. The gallery and the conservatory below it were added to the house in the 1850s, about ten years after the house was built, so that the family might hold large formal balls on the first floor. I would be pleased to show you over the house at two o'clock this afternoon. Last year we used the dining room to serve supper. I am not sure if we can this year, though . . . use the dining room, I mean . . . Miss Kingsley . . ." Here he stopped, uncertain about going further.

"If Miss Kingsley prefers not to use that room"—Mrs. Jackson could completely understand why she would not wish to—"then we could use the drawing room for supper and the inner hall and perhaps even the conservatory for her guests to relax in. This would give us ample space for the buffet and plenty of room for people to mingle in the hall and even on the stairs, something I have observed they seem to enjoy doing. And if the conservatory is heated, sitting there might be pleasant for Miss Kingsley's guests." She was rewarded for her quick assessment and understanding of the situation with a positive beam from the old gentleman, who up until now had seemed perhaps a little preoccupied and rather distant.

Mrs. Jackson returned to her between-stairs office to spend an industrious rest of the morning, working through a series of menus for the supper so that the catering chef might start ordering food. She had her dinner sent up on a tray so she could continue with her work.

Some time passed and looking up from her lists she noticed that it was a little after the time that Mr. Jenkins said he would take her on a tour of the house. Patting her hair into place and stopping only to wash her hands, she went downstairs to find him. Two housemaids putting away the washed china from luncheon upstairs stopped what they were doing to see what she wanted.

"Is Mr. Jenkins here? I was supposed to meet with him at two o'clock and I'm a little late. Is he in his pantry?"

"No, he is not, ma'am." The youngest maid made a respectful

bob. *Really,* thought Mrs. Jackson, *how well trained and polite they all are in Chester Square; so refreshing after Montfort House and all that easy familiarity.*

"Do you know where he is?"

The two women looked at each other, and the younger of the two blushed, leaving the senior housemaid to take over.

"Mr. Jenkins is in the wine cellar, ma'am. He often spends his afternoons classifying some of the inventory. I will run down and fetch him up directly." It didn't take her more than two minutes to achieve this, and Mr. Jenkins arrived a little puffed, but as polite and accommodating as ever.

"Yes, how may I help you?" he asked.

"You were to show me the room arrangements for the recital, Mr. Jenkins."

"Yes indeed, of course, of course. But who are you, my dear? Did you make an appointment?" The elderly butler looked rather mystified as to why this nice young woman was here to see the house.

For a moment Mrs. Jackson was too taken aback to reply. She realized that the old man had completely misremembered who she was and had quite forgotten their appointment. She turned to look at the maids for confirmation of the butler's forgetfulness.

"Mrs. Jackson is here to organize the charity evening, Mr. Jenkins," the younger housemaid said in a gentle voice. "Of course you remember."

"I most certainly do, Eliza," he said with dignity. In an effort perhaps to cover his absentmindedness, he pulled out his waistcoat watch and after consulting it said, "I thought we had an appointment at half past three, Miss, er . . . Miss . . ."

"*Mrs.* Jackson," prompted Eliza quietly.

"Mrs. Jackson. But since you are here early, by all means let's go upstairs and I will show you around."

Still baffled by the situation in which she found herself,

Mrs. Jackson decided it would be a good idea to have a little chat with the first housemaid when she brought her afternoon tea up to her. It was important that she establish exactly what was going on here. Had the butler been sampling his inventory in the wine cellar? He seemed quite sober but that was no indication. She drew near and discreetly inhaled, and found only the pleasant scent of well-laundered linen and a faint aroma of bay rum from a close early-morning shave. Either the shock of a murder in his dining room had temporarily addled Mr. Jenkins's wits or, more likely, he was showing his age. At any rate she needed information, from someone other than Mr. Jenkins, that she could rely on and wondered when she could arrange a meeting with Miss Gaskell.

Before she followed the butler to the back stairs, she turned to the elder of the two housemaids and asked her name.

"It's Martha, Mrs. Jackson. I will bring tea up to your office at five o'clock if that would be a good time for you." Another bob and she gave Mrs. Jackson the sort of look that made it clear she understood her dilemma.

Now that he had been recalled to his duty, Mr. Jenkins was determined to more than make up for his earlier mistake. He embarked on what turned out to be a most thorough and edifying round of the house; her official escort on a guided tour, as if she had just paid sixpence at the door.

They took in the principal floors of the house, which included a well-curated library, the pretty little sitting room that looked out over the garden with its Adam fireplace and mantel brought in, Mr. Jenkins told her, from the old Kingsley rectory before it had been demolished.

"Like many of the grand houses in the area, this house was built with its neighboring houses by Thomas Cubitt in the late 1820s," he explained, as he led Mrs. Jackson up the wide central staircase from the spacious inner hall, instead of the back stairs, so that she might better understand the layout of the house. "These gracious buildings still remain in the hands of those who originally bought them, nearly a hundred years ago now." Mrs. Jackson, who worked in a house that was more than three hundred years old and looked nothing like those of its neighbors, nodded, as if she was impressed.

At the top of the stairs they crossed the wide landing to their right and Jenkins opened a pair of double doors into a comfortable, well-lit apartment that faced the street on its north side and to the west the neighboring house, which bridged the top of the square just discernible through the trees.

"Two pairs of double doors separate the small salon from the large one," the butler explained as he opened them up to reveal the larger room. A handsome grand piano stood in the larger of the salons in front of two pairs of windows on the room's west side. Then, with all the pride of revealing an ancient architectural secret, the old man walked to the paneled south wall of the large salon and, releasing a concealed catch, slid one side of half of the wall to the right and the other to the left, revealing a lovely room with graceful proportions that looked out over the gardens at the rear of the house. The walls, covered in dull gold brocade, were hung with old portraits and landscapes and had the faint musty air of a place that was rarely used. The furnishings were of a period that Mrs. Jackson recognized as George III, with graceful lines and gilded wood frames.

"When these three rooms are opened up into each other we have a large area indeed, Mrs. Jackson." Jenkins turned to survey the three rooms almost with the complacency of ownership, she thought. "And there is plenty of space to seat everyone quite comfortably. The two rooms across the upper hall can of course be used as well to entertain our guests during supper. Miss Gaskell usually has the piano set here, just so." He used his hands spread slightly apart, palms facing each other, and swung his arms to indicate the position the piano would be moved to. "And then everyone has a perfect view." He smiled with pride. "Miss Gaskell says the rooms provide more than adequately for any singer or pianist to be heard perfectly well throughout. Almost as good, she says, as a concert hall." He waved airily to take in what was in fact a large area indeed and one that could more than comfortably seat a gathering of the number invited.

Perhaps to atone for his earlier mistake in forgetting who she was, the elderly butler became almost garrulous. "The other evening we had some music in here for a few of the ladies and gentlemen. It was only necessary to use the small salon." He shrugged off the smaller room as merely a parlor, thought Mrs. Jackson, when it was of a grand size. "Of course we had to open up the larger salon behind it to allow for the power of the pianoforte, which is of similar scale and dimension to that used in the Royal Albert Hall."

Mrs. Jackson wondered if anything could be heard outside the room if someone was playing the piano. *Possibly not,* she thought, then caught herself. No, she would not walk down that path, she would not be drawn.

She walked over to the windows of the gallery that looked out over the gardens. Two or maybe even three inches of snow lay over the shrubs and trees below, covering the garden and the world beyond it in a glittering blanket of faerie. She fleetingly felt a pang for Iyntwood and her missed country walk, the country was always so beautiful under snow. She had promised herself a trip to Selfridges to do some shopping tomorrow afternoon, but even shoveled clear the pavements would be slushy and the going treacherous. She sighed. It would take little of her time to arrange this charity evening and then she was not quite sure what she would do with her days.

She turned into the room as Mr. Jenkins was explaining how the chairs were set in straight rows around the piano, but not too close to the instrument, he cautioned, because of the power of its sound. She couldn't imagine why the audience had to sit in rows. Surely there were enough comfortable chairs and sofas for guests to sit in groups so that they might relax and enjoy the music, rather than arranged in tight ranks like children in Sunday school.

"Would you like me to talk to the butler at Montfort House about helping you out on the night?" she asked Mr. Jenkins, and was instantly gratified with a sweet smile as the old man's mild eyes quite lit up.

"If it wouldn't be too much of an imposition, I would be most grateful," he said. "It is becoming more difficult every year to acquire good servants. Our first footman left us quite abruptly a couple of days ago after some several years, and it has been the dickens of a job trying to find a replacement. The one I ended up with"—he made the luckless footman sound like an unsatisfactory new hat—"simply doesn't fit at all. He is awkward and even though he came with a good reference I can hardly believe how badly trained . . ."

"What happened to the one who left you?" She was only making polite conversation but his reply was rather startling.

"Why, nothing at all, and that's the puzzle of it. He just up and left us one day, for no good reason at all, and he didn't even trouble to give notice even though he had been with us for quite some time. But that's the way of young men in service today, such regrettably selfish behavior."

But Mrs. Jackson was only half listening; she turned and looked over the rooms again. With the chairs they already had in there, she rapidly counted places; they would need only to bring in chairs and sofas from the other reception rooms in the house to make seating quite comfortable, and with the help of Montfort House servants it would be simplicity itself to organize a perfect evening for the charity. An evening that offered the finest things in life, without being overdone and fussy; delicious food with good wine in rooms filled with flowers and a salon arranged so that everyone would be comfortably seated to listen to the superb voice of Nellie Melba. She mentally cast around the room so that she could make plans for the set-up of sofas and chairs. That immense potted palm would have to be moved to the far corner and the cumbersome Chinese screen taken out completely, as they both took up far too much space around the window. There were several other large and awkward pieces that perhaps could be moved altogether, she thought, as her gaze rested on a four-foot, Imperial-yellow Chinese water jar that squatted in front of the screen.

The walls of the two salons were done in fresh greengage silk damask, and Mrs. Jackson decided to arrange white roses around the piano and then send to Iyntwood for some bronze chrysanthemums and the creamy-yellow Crown Princess Victoria, a particularly beautiful Bourbon rose, from the hothouse if there were none to be had in the city. Feeling she had made tremendous headway with her plans, she turned to the butler. "Thank you for your time, Mr. Jenkins, you have been most helpful." And off she went to enjoy a nice cup of tea in the little office and to ask Martha to enlighten her on the peculiarities of Miss Kingsley's servants' hall. Edna Pettigrew was right, the servant problem in London was a nightmare. She was quite looking forward to an evening with her old friend when she returned to Montfort House, so that they could be outraged together on the shortcomings of London servants.

Chapter Ten

When Mrs. Jackson was called for the following morning, she found her ladyship dressed and busy at her writing desk. Mrs. Jackson had thought long and hard about Lady Montfort's request to find out as much as she could about the goings-on at Chester Square and felt she was already part of a fait accompli, which caused a twinge of resentment. She decided it would be best if she spoke to her ladyship of her reluctance to involve herself in Miss Kingsley's business right off the bat, so that they might avoid any misunderstanding going forward. But speaking out to Lady Montfort was difficult since the housekeeper rarely revealed misgivings and had certainly never actively disagreed with her ladyship.

So her opening words were rather stilted and to her own ears sounded uncouth and unwilling, making the rest of what she had to say come out awkwardly too: "I know you appreciate it when I speak plainly, m'lady."

And Lady Montfort said she did, and turned in her chair to give her full attention.

Mrs. Jackson consciously relaxed her hands at her sides and took several slow, measured breaths, and since looking at her directly was not the proper way to address her ladyship, she fixed her eyes on a point a little above Lady Montfort's head. And then with a final, steadying breath she said, "I have every desire to be of help to Miss Kingsley after what happened in her house, but I think it would be best if I were to concentrate my efforts on the charity evening only." She paused for this to sink in and was rewarded with a sympathetic nod of understanding from Lady Montfort, which had the effect of making her feel ungracious. She managed the last piece with a calm voice: "I do not feel it is my place to involve myself in making discoveries about the murder at Chester Square."

There I sound like a scullery maid with a grudge.

"Yes, I see, Jackson," Lady Montfort said. "Completely understandable, thank you for being so candid. Have you by any chance met with Miss Gaskell yet?"

Mrs. Jackson said she had not, but that she hoped to meet Miss Kingsley's companion this morning. Miss Gaskell, although still far from well, was thought to be a little improved and certainly not contagious. *What a relief, of course she understands! So much better to have things out in the open.*

Lady Montfort nodded again and said nothing, and Mrs. Jackson somehow knew, with a sinking heart, that this part of their conversation was far from over. Having said her piece made her feel less of a paid spy in Miss Kingsley's house, but she sensed the matter was not quite resolved between them.

"Very well, Jackson. I will be here when you get back from Chester Square this evening; I plan to have a quiet evening in for a change. Will you look in on me before you retire? I have some ideas for the hunt ball at Iyntwood that I want to run by you."

And with that their little talk ended.

As Mrs. Jackson was driven through the snowy streets to Chester Square she still felt disconcerted by her situation and was a little unsure how to proceed. Like many people of her background who worked diligently to attain a higher position than the one into which they were born, she guarded her status as an upper servant to a family of consequence carefully and, because she knew what it was like not to have them, set great store in the importance of dignity and self-respect. She felt almost trapped; something was looming on her horizon and Lady Montfort knew what it was. When the chauffeur drew up by the area steps that led down from the street to the servants' entrance to Miss Kingsley's house, Mrs. Jackson hoped that she would be able to meet with Miss Gaskell soon, so that she could get things moving on the charity evening. And most of all she prayed that Mr. Jenkins would remember who she was today.

As she was taking off her hat in the stuffy little between-stairs office, Martha arrived to inform her that Miss Gaskell was much improved and would be pleased if Mrs. Jackson would step up to her room when she had the time.

An hour later, when she was ushered into Miss Gaskell's bedroom by Martha, she was completely unprepared for the sight of the young woman lying flat in her bed, in a darkened room. It seemed to her the patient was far from well.

She turned to the maid in the doorway. "Martha, are you sure Miss Gaskell is recovered enough to see me?"

"Yes, ma'am, she particularly said it would be best now rather than later."

"Yes, please come in, Miss Jackson. I am much improved and if you will make yourself comfortable I will do all I can to help you with our task." The voice that came from the bed was low and hoarse from coughing, not feeble exactly, but its owner sounded deeply cast down. Mrs. Jackson approached and took a seat in a chair placed conveniently close to the bedside. In the low light of an oil lamp burning on a table by the bed, Mrs. Jackson could just about make out a dark head lying quietly on the pillow.

"I am so sorry you have been burdened with my unfinished responsibilities, Miss Jackson. But Miss Kingsley assures me that the charity evening will benefit for the better from your organization."

"I am doing my best, Miss Gaskell, but I doubt I can improve on your original plans." How could Miss Kingsley have told this sick young woman that Mrs. Jackson would do a better job of what had been Miss Gaskell's creation in past years? She was embarrassed at the insensitivity of the young woman's employer and immediately resolved to include Miss Gaskell in all her plans, and to tread carefully in introducing any improvements for the evening.

She opened her notebook. "If I might ask a few questions to make sure the arrangements I have made are in keeping, hopefully toward the end of the week you will be well enough to refine what I have put in place."

They worked quietly together for the next hour, until Mrs. Jackson was aware that the voice in the bed was tiring.

"Perhaps a sip of something warm to ease the throat, Miss Gaskell," she suggested and got up from her chair to ring for the maid. After another fit of coughing that sounded tight and hard, Miss Gaskell struggled to sit up. She was bent almost double, and Mrs. Jackson was instantly at her side, supporting her upper body as she pulled in pillows and packed them up to provide a wall of support behind the young woman's shoulders. Then she eased her back, saying how important it was not to lie flat when one coughed. Miss Gaskell drew a breath, and Mrs. Jackson held a glass of what looked like rather dusty water to her lips and told her to take small sips. As the maid came into the room, she said without turning her head, "Will you please put the juice of half a lemon and a full tablespoon of honey into a cup, pour in hot water, and stir thoroughly to dissolve. Then bring it up here quick as you can, please."

She heard the door close and concentrated her attention on the invalid. Now that she was sitting up, Mrs. Jackson saw her more clearly. Miss Gaskell's pale face was a perfect oval, made paler by her illness. She had deep circles under wide gray eyes that regarded her with the frank interest of the young. Miss Gaskell started to cough again and Mrs. Jackson took the cushion from her chair to place behind the pillows to support the young companion more fully in an upright position. As she pulled the pillows forward to push the cushion behind them, her hand brushed against something concealed there. Looking down, she saw it was a small portrait or photograph in an ornate but inexpensive frame.

When someone keeps a portrait under the pillows in one's bed, it is usually for only one reason. A likeness concealed this way was not meant to be seen, and its owner would no doubt be embarrassed to have its place discovered. Mrs. Jackson, half bent over Miss Gaskell, had one moment to see that the figure in the photograph was a stolid, broad-chested individual with the sort of side-whiskers worn by the late Prince Albert. *No doubt it is a photograph of Miss Gaskell's father,* she thought as she rearranged the pillows, *but why would his photograph not take pride of place on the table next to her bed?*

The door opened and in came Martha with a tray bearing a large kitchen cup and saucer from which steamy puffs of citrus scented the chill air of the room.

"Well now, Miss Gaskell, hot honey and lemon, an excellent remedy for a sore throat. Thank you, Martha. Please bring a fresh cup every two hours." Lifting the thick cup and saucer from the tray, she said, "It has lost some of its intense heat in the time it took to bring it up, but little sips please, and tell me if it is too tart." She held the cup to Miss Gaskell's lips.

Cautious sips until Miss Gaskell finished the cup.

"How is that now, a little better?" Mrs. Jackson put down the cup on its saucer.

"Indeed it is, Miss Jackson, my throat feels so much better."

"Honey has that effect, and it's *Mrs.* Jackson, not Miss." And then in response to the young woman's fluster of apologies: "It's an understandable mistake since there is no housekeeper in the house. Even if a housekeeper is unmarried, which I am, we are given the title out of respect. I think last thing tonight we will add a little scotch whiskey to your honey and lemon, it will help you sleep."

She noticed that Miss Gaskell seemed to wear a habitual smile of apology. The hallmark of a class of young women who, lacking financial security or a family to take care of them, become useful only to elderly spinsters and widows. Poorly paid, severely patronized, and with few prospects of making a family of their own, a companion, like a governess, was perched precariously between upstairs and downstairs, their status ill-defined, their lives often lonely and narrow.

Miss Gaskell might not enjoy the fellowship of the servants' hall, where everyone knew his place and proudly worked with skill as part of a whole, but neither was she considered to be on the same social footing as the family she worked for.

Mrs. Jackson remembered the sense of family she had experienced when she was a young girl new to service; the whispered confidences shared at night in their cramped attic bedrooms, a group of lower housemaids and kitchen maids united in their pretended fear of the upper servants, and the excitement of fleeting crushes on handsome young footmen. After the parish orphanage, the servants' hall had been the first family life she had ever known.

As Mrs. Jackson took stock of Miss Gaskell it was easy to see that she had been and still was quite unwell. There was probably no one in the house who would look after her with the care that usually rallies most of us through our illnesses, she realized. Miss Gaskell had been fed at mealtimes if she rang for food, given a jug of water or a cup of tea when the maids could spare the time, but nothing had been done for her comfort. Her room was both stuffy and cold. It was a cheerless apartment without a fire, and dark and gloomy with heavy curtains hastily dragged across the window. She felt Miss Gaskell's forehead, it was quite cool so luckily no fever, but her hands were awfully cold. Annoyed with everyone in the house, Mrs. Jackson got up and rang the bell. This time it was Eliza who came into the room.

"Eliza, please light a fire in the grate and draw back the curtains. Bring up a jug of hot water, a clean face flannel, and fresh towels. Oh, and be a good girl and fill up a hot water bottle, Miss Gaskell feels quite chill." She turned in her chair to smile at the young maid; after all, who was she to direct the Chester Square servants' efforts? She was reassured by a deferential little bob, before the young woman hurried about her business.

Mrs. Jackson picked up a hairbrush and carefully unbound, brushed, and plaited Miss Gaskell's thick, dark-gold hair. By the time she was finished a fire was burning in the grate and a wintry sun was shining through the windowpanes. She washed Miss Gaskell's face and hands with warm water. And then she sat back down and they regarded each other for a moment before Miss Gaskell said, "I am never laid low, Mrs. Jackson, I usually have boundless energy." She laughed, showing even, perfect teeth, milk-white like a child's. Her manner was modest and gentle, thought Mrs. Jackson as she considered her patient. She was obviously from some respectable family. Her room was well organized, with little homey touches, and there was a library in one corner. Mrs. Jackson noticed that she favored the novels of Jane Austen, and there were anthologies by Byron and Wordsworth. *A romantic young thing,* she thought, *I expect her favorite book is* Jane Eyre.

"I am not surprised you are feeling so poorly, Miss Gaskell. Lady Montfort told me you were sick before the party here the other night and that you were required to attend." She kept her disapproval at bay.

"Yes, Mr. Churchill brought a guest at the last moment, but I was quite happy to make up the numbers."

"And then you had to play the piano." Mrs. Jackson couldn't help her stern tone. Who on earth would make someone who was unwell attend a dinner party *and* play the piano?

"Yes, I am sorry." Immediately she was contrite, and Mrs. Jackson was annoyed with herself for sounding judgmental and causing the young woman to apologize.

"Lady Montfort said you played beautifully," she said.

"It was an honor for me to play; Lady Ryderwood has a wonderful voice. I was brought up in a house that enjoyed music, you see. My father was a concert pianist and my mother was a singer. That was of course long ago, but I was lucky enough to be taught to play the piano, and music means everything to me."

That would explain her cultured air and appreciation of music and literature, Mrs. Jackson thought, and she wondered if the young woman's parents were still alive. She was always sympathetic toward those who struggled through childhood without parents, as she had had to make her way in the world at a young age. She approved of the young woman's quiet disposition and her willingness to see the good in life; so many companions were either bitter or abjectly cowed by the time they were thirty.

"Shall we continue with what I have arranged so far for the charity?" she asked, and together they bent over her notebook and Miss Gaskell explained her seating arrangements.

"After we have observed the order of precedence, and incidentally the dowager queen Alexandra will accompany the Marchioness of Ripon and her dear friend Princess Esterhazy, so we must reserve our best places for them; even though the princess is very stingy with her donations. Well once we have taken care of our royal guests, we always reward generous contributors with the best places to sit. I call them the dress-circle seats. And then we seat people who have made lesser contributions around the edges of the room and in the corners in what I call the stalls."

They spent a pleasant morning together, and it was well past one o'clock when Mrs. Jackson realized how long they had been working and how tired Miss Gaskell now looked.

"It's time for me to go downstairs for my dinner, Miss Gaskell. I'll arrange with Cook to send up some nice hot soup for your luncheon," she said.

"I hope all the servants are being helpful, Mrs. Jackson; they have always been accommodating to me." Understandably, Miss Gaskell did not want her to see the servants in a poor light.

Now was the time Mrs. Jackson thought to ask about Mr. Jenkins, since her little chat the other afternoon with Martha had produced no real understanding about the butler's absent-minded behavior. She started tidying away her notebooks.

"Indeed they have been most helpful, Miss Gaskell. Mr. Jenkins runs a nice servants' hall, orderly and well disciplined. He has been most helpful, if not a little absentminded at times." She kept any possible hint of criticism out of her voice.

"Well, he is getting up there in years, Mrs. Jackson. He is a true gentleman and has been with Miss Kingsley all his working life. Before that he worked for Miss Kingsley's parents. This house is the only one he has ever known for nearly sixty years. He started here as a hall boy when he was seventeen years old." She watched Mrs. Jackson do her arithmetic and nodded as she arrived at her sum.

Good heaven's above, thought Mrs. Jackson, *that makes the butler nearly eighty years old. No wonder the poor man is forgetful.*

She said nothing in response, and Miss Gaskell, accurately interpreting her silence, went on, "Mr. Jenkins is well past the age of retirement, but Miss Kingsley cannot bear to let him go, even though he has a lovely little cottage waiting for him in Boscombe

Bay, and a younger sister who is ready to look after him in his dotage."

Seems like he's in his dotage already, thought Mrs. Jackson, and she imagined Mr. Jenkins dressed in his formal butler's coat, trousers rolled up to the knee, as he happily pottered among the tide pools of Boscombe Bay, shrimp net in hand, or strolling along the front with his sister eating winkles with a pin. The image was incongruous. Perhaps Miss Kingsley felt that her butler should remain at her side, where he had always been, and continue to lead the dignified life that he was familiar and comfortable with.

Miss Gaskell continued, "Very luckily the lower servants are ready to cover for him when he forgets things, but unfortunately this is happening with greater frequency and sometimes the things he forgets can cause embarrassment. Lady Ryderwood came to call last week. He took her umbrella and coat from her in the hall, and when it was time for her to go, he simply couldn't find them. The entire staff searched high and low. In the end, the hall boy found both umbrella and coat in the coal cellar, hanging quite neatly on a peg next to the boiler room. We had to work like mad to brush off the coal dust. We couldn't understand what he had been doing in the coal cellar anyway." She stifled a little giggle, and Mrs. Jackson realized that she was, after all, a young companion barely in her twenties. With her face flushed from laughing, which had ended in a fit of coughing, and her two neat plaits, she looked awfully young and pretty. Why on earth wasn't this sweet young thing not married to some decent solicitor or bank manager instead of being shut up here in this grand old house, a paid companion to an autocratic elderly spinster who was demanding and probably not always particularly kind?

Chapter Eleven

Clementine was reading a letter from her middle daughter, Althea, who was enjoying a particularly enthralling trip up the Nile with her archaeologically inclined friends under the protective auspices of Dr. and Mrs. Alistair Campion, to join Sir Wilfred Shackleton's dig in Thebes. She would be away for the winter, returning hopefully sometime in the early spring. Clementine scanned between the lines of her daughter's ecstatic descriptions of her journey from Memphis to Thebes for signs of a homecoming date and found none. The wretched girl had shown no interest in her London season and had avoided all opportunities to meet the young men invited to its balls, picnics, and parties. Clementine's concern for Althea's determination to avoid the usual pursuits that would lead to a satisfactory future was not quite as acute as that which she felt for Harry. But her daughter's letter caused an exclamation of irritation before she put it to one side, feeling both helpless and resentful as she remembered the hours she had sat up for Althea at countless balls until dawn during this year's London season.

Their eldest daughter was far more conforming than her siblings. She was successfully married to a French aristocrat who doted on her, and who had provided her with a beautiful house in Paris and a castle or two in the Loire Valley. Monsieur le

Comte de Lamballe was extraordinarily rich, his family was extremely well connected, and without a doubt he was a devoted husband. Perfect in every way, except perhaps for his nationality, and generous to a fault to his wife, which did a great deal toward offsetting the disappointment that her daughter lived so far away.

Now why, Clementine asked herself, *couldn't the other two settle to more conventional lives?* It was at this moment that her son, having no doubt consumed a large breakfast with his father, decided he would honor her wishes by dropping in on her before he left for Eastchurch. He appeared in the doorway, and she immediately saw by the expression on his face that he expected a lecture from her on his appointment to the RNAS. She had to admit it *was* rather a sad state of affairs when her only son, her dear, amiable, well-meaning son, should be so wary when he was in her company. She resolved to keep to herself any advice she desperately wanted to offer. Lord Montfort had given his consent and she must not interfere.

"Harry, darling, good morning. Have you had a chance to find out about Captain Wildman-Lushington's funeral? I take it you will be going?"

"Yes, I'm sort of representing Mr. Churchill as he is unable to attend. I'm meeting up with Sir Hedworth Meux, Wildman-Lushington's commanding officer, and driving down to Eastchurch with him." And sensitive as always to the feelings of others, he went on, "This business is bothering you, isn't it?"

"Which business, the murder of someone we knew in the house of a friend, or the accidental and wasteful death of a young man with his life before him? What an ill-fated affair Hermione's party has turned out to be.

"I am wondering, Harry . . ." She paused. She was never quite certain how much Harry knew about her involvement in the investigation of his cousin's death—probably far more than he let on. "I am wondering if perhaps Captain Wildman-Lushington's death might be in some way linked to Sir Reginald's murder. Is it possible that an aeroplane can be made to crash?"

Made to crash? He must think I've gone quite batty.

He turned in his chair to face her directly and leaned forward as he considered her question. She was grateful to see that his expression was quite serious.

"Any engine can be made to malfunction," he said after a while. "But the question one would ask next is, why? And why would someone invited at the last minute to a birthday celebration, attended by people he had never met before, need to be done away with?" He wasn't the slightest disconcerted by her question.

"Well, I suppose it does rather sound unrealistic and ridiculous. But he might have witnessed something on that night that made the person who killed Sir Reginald decide it was necessary to remove him too." As it had occurred to her, it would almost certainly have occurred to Detective Inspector Hillary. She wondered if Hillary knew of Wildman-Lushington's death. He had probably been informed before anyone, as this investigation appeared to be under the vigilant eye of the Admiralty.

"I see you are thinking about a possible suspect for the murder of Sir Reginald and are now linking events." Her son's voice was noncommittal, and she realized that of course he knew about her investigation into Teddy's murder.

"If Wildman-Lushington saw something out of place on the night of the murder, that means the person who killed Sir Reginald and Wildman-Lushington would have to have had access to Eastchurch and to Wildman-Lushington's plane. And that someone would also have been at the dinner party, or connected to someone at the dinner party." Having decided to take her seriously, Harry was now playing the game.

"Exactly *my* thoughts! Captain Vetiver was both a guest at that dreadful dinner *and* has access to Eastchurch." She remembered that Vetiver had come into the salon after leaving the dining room alone and probably, according to the timetable that she had worked on last night, around about the time when poor old Sir Reginald had been bumped off.

Harry was aghast. "How can you possibly imagine Captain Vetiver could be involved? He is Mr. Churchill's right-hand man, completely trustworthy and extremely well thought of." After the murder of her husband's nephew last year, Clementine had come to the understanding that any human creature, no matter how well connected, well born, or utterly trustworthy, was capable of murder if he or she was put in a position where he believed he had no other choice. She took a little time to explain this to her son and ended with, "So you see, darling, we must always consider everyone at the scene of the crime capable of murder, until one has proved otherwise. All of us who sat down to dinner in Hermione's dining room on 30th November are suspects in the murder of Sir Reginald, until we can each prove that we were with someone or somewhere else at the time of his death, it's simply a fact."

But Harry was having none of it. "Yes, I've read Conan Doyle, Mama, I know all about alibis. Well, you can forget Vetiver. He had no real connection whatever with Sir Reginald. You have to look to the people whom Sir Reginald knew best, the people who shared his life." He was lightly drumming his fingers on the little table to his right, a nervous staccato rhythm, his chin sunk in thought. The drumming slowed until the tips of two fingers lightly beat a steady tattoo on the rosewood surface of the table.

"But it's funny you should mention that Wildman-Lushington's plane might have been tampered with." He stared off into the fireplace, watching the flames leaping in the grate. "You see, we have been noticing some odd incidents at Sopwith. Tom has a new aeroplane that he's designed, doing some test runs on it, I can't fill you in, because it's all a bit hush-hush and anyway I know you are not interested in machinery and engines. But we have suspected for some time that there might be a spot of snooping going on at the factory. And what *is* worrying is that information might have been stolen from us either by a competitor or, worse, by someone working for another government."

And by "another government" he meant Germany, of course. Clementine was aware of the country's obsession with war and the government's increased expenditure on armaments, submarines, dreadnoughts, and other colossal machines of naval warfare. A headlong race to keep up with Germany's astonishingly massive new navy, bristling with innovations and gargantuan battleships equipped with powerful guns had been all the talk at London dinners and luncheons this season. And with Britain's increased preoccupation for new war machines and inventions to destroy the world they lived in, she had never heard the word *spy* mentioned quite as much as she had during her last week in London. *German spies, double agents,* and *counterespionage* were terms bandied about liberally at dinner parties. Up until now, she had seen it all as the inevitable business of selling newspapers and sensational novels. She almost laughed, and her son caught her change of mood and was quick to join her. They both shook their heads and smiled at each other.

"I know, Mother, sounds like the worst of cheap novels, like *Dr. Fu Manchu.*" Harry's youthful fascination with Sax Rohmer's fiendish arch-criminal of cunning perception and devious methods had increased as he had read every one of Rohmer's novels.

"Or like Conan Doyle's *The Adventure of the Bruce-Partington Plans,* where German spies spend months gleaning information on British plans and then try to make a getaway on the evening before war starts. Doyle told me he made more money on that short story than on his entire series."

They fell quiet. And Clementine realized how incredibly fearful everyone was these days. Underneath the bright chatter at dinner parties there was an undercurrent of unease that be-lied the swaggering conviction that Britain held center stage in world affairs. Society continued to impress, to hold lavish costume balls, dinners, and parties, and invite one another to their coun-try houses where diverting entertainments were arranged on a scale that seemed to become grander with each passing month. Perhaps our distractions have become more extravagant and more outlandish to deflect us from our unspoken fears that we are dancing on the verge of war, and our country is being over-run by secret agents all on a mission to discover our expensive military secrets, and turn them against us. Harry and Tom Sop-with's concern about security at the Sopwith Aeroplane Factory did not seem quite so far-fetched after all.

"What are you and Tom doing about this snooper?"

"Well, I talked to Captain Vetiver, and he's arranging with navy intelligence to check out the factory and those who work for us or with us. If there *is* something going on, I hope we are not too behindhand." Clementine wondered if perhaps Captain Vetiver was involved in the Secret Service Bureau.

"Will you have an opportunity to look at Wildman-Lushington's plane when you are at Eastchurch?" She pressed home her op-portunity: "Because if you do, would you bear in mind my the-ory that he might have witnessed something on the night Sir Reginald was killed? And see if you can find anything that might point to someone tampering with the machine?"

Harry smiled and nodded that he would. Perhaps talk about espionage had made him feel that sabotage was not such an out-rageous idea either, because he said, "I'm not an experienced engineer, but I would know what to look for.

"Well, I should be going. What are you doing with yourself while you are in London?"

"We have plans for the opera and the ballet, Lady Ripon's ball for Nellie Melba at Claridge's, and I have promised myself an hour or two with Gertrude Waterford and Olive Shackleton at Madam Lucile." Clementine dutifully recorded the events that would fill her next days and realized that every single one of them provided an opportunity for gossip, and that gossip was the source of useful information.

Chapter Twelve

Mrs. Jackson's second day at Chester Square had ended far more successfully than she ever could have imagined. She had spent time with Mr. Jenkins, who was unusually alert and up to the mark and had assured her that the flowers she wanted could be delivered directly from Covent Garden market on the morning of the event. "We are all standing by, ready to be directed by you in our efforts, Mrs. Jackson," he had reassured her with his old-world courtesy.

She worked steadily through the day, organizing the last items on the menu, and by five o'clock she decided to take a tea tray up to Miss Gaskell and see how she was doing.

She found Miss Gaskell sitting up in bed, still pale but less restive than she had been earlier that day. Within, a fire was crackling merrily in the grate in a room that had seen the working application of the duster and the carpet brush; without, the sun was burning brightly, warming the air enough to reduce hillocks of shoveled snow to mere mounds of gray slush and providing at the same time enough light to make Miss Gaskell's room almost cheery. Mrs. Jackson had not had the opportunity to go for her customary walk for three days now, and she felt a claustrophobic need for fresh air. She walked across the room and lifted the sash a little to let some into the room.

"You seem to be a good deal better this afternoon, Miss Gaskell. How do you feel in yourself?"

"My headache has gone and my throat is less sore. But I still feel quite dreadfully tired." Miss Gaskell had slipped a bookmark into her copy of *Ivanhoe* and laid it aside on the table.

Mrs. Jackson came alongside the bed and automatically started the business of plumping up the pillows. As she did so, she peeked behind the cushion and noticed that the framed photograph was no longer there. Looking around the room, she saw that it had not been returned to any of the little tables and dressers that furnished the room with plenty of surfaces on which to exhibit this kind of memorabilia.

She poured a cup of tea for Miss Gaskell and urged her to try a little hot buttered toast. As the young companion sipped her tea, she ran over the success of her morning's arrangements, and when asked by Miss Gaskell what she could do to help, she handed over the job of writing place cards for the dress-circle seating.

"Everyone will come," said Miss Gaskell. "They always do, and as Miss Melba is singing we will probably gather some extra uninvited ones, who will come with invited friends. It's always the way."

"Have you head Miss Melba sing before?" Mrs. Jackson did not have an ear for music, not even for the popular music-hall songs that provided affordable entertainment of a far less formal kind. For years she'd been mistakenly under the impression that Nellie Melba was a dancer.

"Yes, I was lucky enough to go to the opera in my first year here with Miss Kingsley when Miss Melba was singing in *La Bohème,* her voice is sublime. It was my first visit to a real opera, such a thrilling experience."

"You did not go with your parents to the opera, or the concert house?"

"Oh no, my parents died when I was ten. They died in a train accident when they were quite young. I was brought up by my mother's much older sister; she was the only family I had. She was so very kind and we became the entire world to each other. But her health was not good and when she died I had to work for a living and so I am here. I have been most fortunate." She added this last hastily in case, Mrs. Jackson thought, she might appear ungrateful. Young women companions learned to demonstrate eternal gratitude for their meager lot in life, it seemed.

Mrs. Jackson wondered what it would be like to have enjoyed a full and happy family life and then been denied it. She preferred to think that she had been orphaned when in all probability she had been abandoned by parents who were either too destitute to keep her or simply uninterested in being parents. She had been taken in by a kindly neighbor who had brought her up in her large family and then when times became hard the woman had given her up at age seven into the care of the parish orphanage. She never dwelled on the orphanage years, they had been too painful. When she was thirteen she had been found a position as a scullery maid in the large house of a well-to-do middle-class family in Bolton. Determined to do what she could for herself, she had worked long hours, provided the cook with meticulous, hard work, and had been promoted to the job of housemaid. She felt great kinship with this nice young woman and her unpretentious and equable manner. But she couldn't help wondering about that photograph. It was certainly not of Mr. Gaskell, father of Miss Gaskell, killed when he was a young man. There had been no mention of the aunt's husband. So who, then?

This question came into her mind off and on for the rest of the afternoon and evening. At the end of the day she decided to walk home to Montfort House. Chester Square was only a mile or two away from Lowndes Square, and the route would take her through Belgravia's residential streets, crescents, and squares, their central gardens planted with sycamores and plane trees, providing a pleasant sanctuary of greenery in summer and privacy for its surrounding terraced streets. It would be a pleasant walk. The area was well lit and the streets were busy with the servants who worked in the houses of the families who lived in one of London's most affluent neighborhoods.

As she paced along the pavement she did not notice the familiar, grand white stucco houses united behind a continuous palace front, making each terrace look like a large country house. Wide marble steps led up to black front doors sheltered from the elements by pillared porticoes. Heavy black iron railings protected the front from passersby on the pavement and protected them from falling down in to the little yard below street level—referred to as the area—that led to the servant's entrance to belowstairs.

She was not alone in the quiet neighborhood. As motorcars pulled up to front doors, down the steps came gentlemen in top hats and heavy overcoats, with ladies swathed in furs to protect them from the cold; lamplight sparkled on the diamonds in their tiaras and in their ears. Other motorcars arrived to deposit similarly dressed individuals at neighboring houses arriving for a dinner party.

Along the wide pavements, servants returned from errands, swept slushy snow from front steps and pavements, or hurried home from a day off with friends or a visit to the Vaudeville Theatre. It was easy walking, the pavements were clear and dry, the air sweet and washed clean by days of wind and snow. Mrs. Jackson's step was light. She did not look up, immersed as she was in her thoughts.

The only blight on the day had occurred at the end of the afternoon. Martha had arrived in Miss Gaskell's room to inform her that now that she was a little better, Detective Inspector Hillary of Scotland Yard would be calling at the house tomorrow morning to ask a few questions of her. So would she please be ready to meet him downstairs in the little sitting room at ten o'clock?

The effect this had on Miss Gaskell was quite bewildering, Mrs. Jackson recalled as she crossed Minton Walk and turned left. On hearing this news, she had gasped and fallen back into her pillows, and a fit of coughing had overtaken her with such violence that it had been quite some minutes before she was able to speak. And when she was able to speak she seemed incapable of doing so without breaking down completely. When Martha left the room her back had expressed the scorn and disgust she evidently felt, and Mrs. Jackson glimpsed her face drawn into a tight grimace of disapproval. Feeling protective, she hastened to calm the frightened young woman.

"He only wants to find out what you saw that night that was unusual, to help him understand the events surrounding Sir Reginald's murder." Having determined not to speak of the incident in the house unless someone else did first, and no one had uttered a word since her arrival, Mrs. Jackson was aware that she was breaking an unspoken law when she coupled the words *Sir Reginald* and *murder*.

"But I know nothing, absolutely nothing!" Miss Gaskell wailed, revealing how overprotected her life had been and also, thought Mrs. Jackson, how unreasonably scared she was. *When someone is this emphatic they know nothing, they usually know a good deal,* thought the housekeeper.

"There, there. It will be nothing, you will see." Mrs. Jackson patted the young woman's shoulder; she was tired after her long day and in no mood to deal with hysterics, for this was where they were headed it seemed. "Just a few questions, he will put them to you quite clearly. Answer him directly and then it will all be over."

"Yes, but it won't, you see?" Another wail echoed up from the tousled head on the pillows. "Because I was not in the salon at the time he was murdered, I was downstairs searching for pure spirit. I had been sent by Miss Kingsley to find it. Miss Meriwether had spilled coffee on her dress . . . I couldn't find the bottle, I searched everywhere. I can't remember. I can't remember anything." She was getting herself quite horribly worked up, thought Mrs. Jackson. More coughing, more wailing.

"You simply must get a hold of yourself, Miss Gaskell." Mrs. Jackson bent and fixed her gaze directly into the young woman's face, hoping to pull her out of her imagined fears. "Simply tell the inspector what you know."

Miss Gaskell opened her eyes and stared back with such speechless horror that Mrs. Jackson almost recoiled.

"I can never do that,' she cried, wrenching away. No one would believe . . ." She threw herself facedown on the pillows, crying so bitterly that Mrs. Jackson was alarmed for her health and recognized with a bolt of intuition that Miss Gaskell's near bout with pneumonia had been nothing of the kind. Her reaction to everything in the house from the night when Sir Reginald had been murdered was one akin to fear. *Of course,* she thought, *how stupid I have been. This young woman probably knew Sir Reginald well, since he was so involved in the charity. She has been suffering from shock and grief. Why on earth didn't I see this before?*

As Mrs. Jackson walked head-down in thought along the pavement, reliving the exceedingly tense and dramatic moments in Miss Gaskell's room, she was unaware that she had taken the wrong turn, and looking up she realized that she was on Sloane Street. She crossed over, turned right into Harriet Street, and then back down Harriet Walk, which ran directly behind the houses on Lowndes Square. As she turned out of the main thoroughfare she caught sight of a familiar London scene at the corner of Harriet Street: a street hawker selling hot chestnuts. She smelled the sweet scent of roasting chestnuts even at this distance.

The man, wrapped in an old wool topcoat secured about his waist with twine, a heavy muffler around his neck, and a battered bowler pulled down over his eyes, was standing over a brazier, arranging chestnuts in a large flat pan balanced on top of the hot coals. A fat woman in a cheerful-looking hat adorned with a mass of dyed feathers and a small, thinner woman were counting pennies into his palm, and having concluded their transaction and clutching newspaper cones of roasted nuts walked off around the corner in Harriet Walk. No doubt to return to the servants' hall of one of the houses on Lowndes Square. Their laughter echoed back across the empty street toward Mrs. Jackson.

She crossed the street and, giving the man tuppence, held out her gloved hands for a cone of newspaper. The scent of roasting chestnuts and hot charcoal rekindled a time when she had first worked for the Talbot family at Montfort House as a housemaid. *How young and scared I was then*, she remembered. *How they teased me about going upstairs to do the fires when it was still dark in the early morning. How would I have felt in those years if someone had been murdered in the house? Terrified*, came back the response. *I would have been scared witless, petrified of being along upstairs in the dark of the house.* She saw herself huddled down in bed with Maisie the scullery maid in their shared room, too frightened to sleep, their eyes glued on the unlocked bedroom door. They would most certainly have been terrified of speaking to a policeman from Scotland Yard about anything they might have seen. But she was quite sure of one thing: every servant belowstairs would have been clamoring for information and gossip in that surreptitious, forbidden way that servants had. A torrent of talk and speculation would have helped to put the situation to rights and the scariness would have become thrilling, like a good ghost story on a stormy night. *That's exactly what is wrong with Chester Square*, she thought, as she sat down on a bench at the top of Harriet Walk and peeled back the charred skin of a chestnut. *Everyone has clammed up and the enforced silence feeds fear and suspicion.*

Her mind returned again to Miss Gaskell's reaction to being questioned by the police. It was so extreme that it almost smacked of guilt as well as fear. As she ate her chestnuts she wondered why Miss Kingsley had imposed such a restriction on her household, that none of the servants, nor Miss Gaskell, dared even to mention Sir Reginald's name let alone his death. The entire household was in thrall to an elderly lady who was determined that the murder in her dining room simply hadn't happened.

And why, she thought as she stood up and brushed bits of charred chestnut from the front of her coat, *has Miss Gaskell been confined to her room with this exaggerated illness? Yes, the girl has a severe cold, but not so severe that she has to be quarantined in her room. Is it perhaps to keep her from the police, from answering their unwelcome questions?*

That day, Clementine had lunched at Claridge's with Olive Shackleton and Gertrude Waterford, and had then gone on with Gertrude to Lucy Duff-Gordon's fashionable and extraordinarily expensive salon in Hanover Square for a fitting. There had been a fashion show, something Lucy had dreamed up to better show off the lovely clothes she had designed for spring; this was an experience that Clementine found altogether fascinating.

The main room of the salon was full of tall, elegant young women floating around in a collection of Madame Lucile's recent creations; each lightly clad in thin, drifting layers of richly colored silk as they wandered past her in an exotic and languid procession. A particularly exquisite model, with fairy-bright silver hair and almost transparent white skin and wearing a rose-pink silk dinner dress, caught her eye. One of Lucy Duff-Gordon's assistants, noticing her interest, whispered in her ear, "It's called

'Heaven in the Circle of Your Arms,' Lady Montfort; Lady Duff-Gordon must have had you in mind when she created it!" Clementine had needed no further encouragement and had penciled an emphatic tick next to the dress on her card.

She had then spent the balance of the afternoon justifying to Pettigrew why she had chosen a dress in rose-petal pink, a color her maid thought would not work well with her coloring; it would make her look sickish: her ladyship's skin tone required rich, deep colors, not pastels.

When Mrs. Jackson came into her drawing room, it struck Clementine that her housekeeper was looking particularly handsome, and guessed she must have walked home. Mrs. Jackson's cheeks were flushed from cold air and exercise, her blue eyes had a positively steely gleam, and little tendrils of wavy auburn hair had worked themselves loose from the plaited bun secured severely at the nape of her neck. She presented a picture of youthful vigor but most of all she radiated intention, Clementine noted with satisfaction, and was far lovelier than any of the languid young women she had seen modeling those exotic creations this afternoon.

"Long day, Jackson?" she asked as she indicated an upright little chair next to her. They had crossed a line somewhere last June during their investigation into the murder of Teddy Mallory and the net result was that even though they still observed the formal arrangement of mistress and servant, there was a greater and deeper understanding between them; it was nothing quite as egalitarian as friendship, because that would have made them feel a bit uncomfortable, but something akin to it. Their appreciation and respect of each other's perspicacity and intelligence had grown considerably and their interactions since then had been those of two women who equally respected and liked each other.

Mrs. Jackson took the seat indicated, neatly shod feet together, hands in her lap, and back erect. She turned her handsome head attentively toward Clementine.

"How are things at Chester Square, servants cooperating and helping out?" Clementine asked.

"Oh yes, m'lady, they are a nice bunch; professionals every one of them and properly trained; the butler is a little elderly, but . . ."

"Looks pretty past it to me," Lady Montfort observed, and Mrs. Jackson realized she was being carefully pushed into conversation about the inmates of Chester Square servants' hall. In a sudden rush she gave in. *Why fight it? She knows something's up, and she's planted me there to find out what. So give her what she's after and be done.* But she held out a little longer, the last refuge of the truly obedient, and remained silent.

"And poor little Miss Gaskell looked so unwell on the night of the dinner party. How is she faring, can she be of any help to you at all?" Lady Montfort probed, her eyes fastened intently on her housekeeper's face.

"She's rallying nicely, m'lady, but she's quite reduced by what happened."

"Reduced?" prodded Lady Montfort. "If she is rallying, what could have reduced her?"

"She was doing quite well until the senior housemaid informed her that a policeman from Scotland Yard, Inspector Hillary I think she said his name was, would be coming to ask a few questions about the incident in the house."

"You must be referring to the murder of Sir Reginald Cholmondeley."

"Yes, m'lady . . . the murder." Mrs. Jackson suppressed a smile. "They don't speak of it at all at the house, the subject is definitely out-of-bounds. When Miss Gaskell was told that the police wanted to question her, she fell to pieces, carried on quite dreadfully."

Mrs. Jackson was quite aware of the particularly penetrating gaze her ladyship adopted when she was especially interested in an idea. And she set about the business of updating her on every single thing that had transpired since her first day at Miss Kingsley's house: the no-talk policy on the subject of the murder, the inability of the butler to remember who she was from one hour to the next, and the framed photograph that had been hidden behind the pillows of Miss Gaskell's bed in the morning, which had disappeared completely by the afternoon. She rounded this off with a description of Miss Gaskell's near hysteria before she had left.

"That is all remarkably interesting, Jackson. Who was the man in the photograph, I wonder?"

"He was of late middle age, maybe forty-five, barrel-chested, fashionably dressed, with the sort of side-whiskers worn by the late prince consort." She could see the image quite clearly in her head.

"Oh really, side-whiskers? How delightfully old-fashioned! Great heavens, Jackson, I think that was a likeness of Sir Reginald Cholmondeley. No one really wears side-whiskers anymore, unless of course the photograph was taken over twenty years ago. But you say he was dressed in an up-to-date fashion." And when Mrs. Jackson acknowledged that he had appeared to be, Lady Montfort jumped to her feet, clapped her hands lightly together, and then held them. "Jackson, I'm sure that photograph is of Sir Reginald! Now I must go in to dinner, but afterwards will you please come straight back here. Oh very well done, Jackson, very well done indeed!"

Chapter Thirteen

The servants' supper belowstairs at Montfort House that evening was a convivial affair, with Cook presiding from the head of the table. *Convivial?* Mrs. Jackson thought not. *Boisterous* was a far more apt description for this racket. The noise around the table was considerable with high-pitched shrieks of laughter from the roundly pretty second housemaid. Both footmen had joined them after serving upstairs dinner and were shouting each other down to gain the girl's attention. Mr. White was still upstairs waiting on Lady Montfort and would no doubt have seriously have disapproved of this din. But if Cook thought their behavior inappropriate, she did nothing whatsoever to call them to order.

Mrs. Jackson, constitutionally more phlegmatic than Miss Pettigrew, whose face wore a pinched look of disapproval, lifted her spoon to eat her fish soup. It was good: robust, complex in flavor, and fragrant with herbs, served with thick slices of crusty homemade bread. Mrs. Jackson lifted her voice above the roars of laughter.

"This soup is delicious, Cook, such flavor, but tomatoes at this time of year?"

"Thank you, Mrs. Jackson, I'm glad you are enjoying it. The stock is made from fish heads and bones with onions, simmered all day. Tomatoes dried and preserved in oil, from the end of the summer. The rest is plain old North Sea cod, such a nice fish for a soup like this." And the cook turned to laugh at the second footman's joke about a one-legged jockey.

Mrs. Jackson had to secretly applaud the energetic resourcefulness of a young woman who had the time to make such an excellent meal just for the servants' supper, as well as produce a six-course dinner for the upstairs dining room, even if it was beyond her to keep the lower servants in order.

Another gale of laughter ended in a piercing shriek when someone at the table, more than likely the plump housemaid, was pinched by the second footman. Sensing that Pettigrew was about to fall apart, Mrs. Jackson bent a look of stern censure on the first footman, who had the grace to lower his voice and nudge his second-in-command. For a moment there was a lull in the uproar. Mrs. Jackson remembered her appointment with her ladyship and rapidly spooned down the last delicious drops of soup.

Lady Montfort had picked her way through a few of the superb courses laid before her and was sipping a small glass of brandy when Mrs. Jackson returned to the drawing room.

"Now then, Jackson, sit down there on the sofa because I want to show you something." And Lady Montfort put into her hands a sheet of foolscap paper that when turned sideways showed a series of vertical columns, each headed by a name. The names, Lady Montfort explained, were those of everyone in the Chester Square house on the night of the murder, both upstairs and down. On the left-hand side was a list of hours and minutes. It was just like a Bradshaw's train timetable.

"Look at this, Jackson." She pointed to the column on the far left. "The women left the dining room at the end of dinner, at ten o'clock, to leave the men to their port. All of us went upstairs to the salon, they call it the little salon I think, but the doors to the large salon were open because Lady Ryderwood was to sing for us.

"And here is the interesting part." She tapped the next column. "Not all of the men came up to join us at the same time when they left the dining room. Here are Lord Montfort, Captain Wildman-Lushington, and Sir Henry Wentworth." Her finger moved to the corresponding columns. "They were first to join us in the salon at about a quarter to eleven; I know this because Lord Montfort remarked that perhaps Lady Ryderwood would not sing for too long and mentioned the time to me as he was anxious about the weather and getting home as soon as possible. They were followed by Sir Vivian Hussey, a good five minutes later." A long index finger tapped to indicate Sir Vivian's arrival in the salon.

"Now look here, this is interesting. At eleven o'clock, or close to it, Captain Vetiver arrives; mind this is twenty minutes *after* the men have started to come upstairs, Jackson. He reminds Jennifer Wells-Thornton that Miss Kingsley's nephew, Mr. Tricklebank, is waiting for her in the outer hall, as they are going on. She says her thank-yous to Miss Kingsley, and leaves. Nota bene, by the way, Jackson, what was Trevor Tricklebank doing all that time after everyone started to leave the dining room?

"Then there is a little calamity in the salon: the footman spills coffee over Marigold Meriwether's skirt and there is a big bustle in response." Her finger traced back to the columns for each of the women. "Miss Kingsley sends the footman off for vinegar to stop the stain spreading, and then she sends off Miss Gaskell for some pure spirits. Then, on Lady Wentworth's suggestion, Miss Kingsley leaves to get Epsom salt or baking powder. All this to-ing and fro-ing goes on for about fifteen, maybe even twenty, minutes. You see? At this time I seem to remember Mr. Greenberg comes up from downstairs, having kept Mr. Tricklebank company, so he tells us, as he waits for Miss Wells-Thornton in the outer hall. And a minute or two later, Miss Gaskell returns with the white spirit and is told to leave the skirt alone, as it is time for music." Lady Montfort took a moment to sip her brandy and marshal her thoughts.

"So here we all are, gathered in the salon. We take our seats, and this must have been between fifteen and twenty minutes past eleven. Lady Ryderwood sings her first and, as it turns out, her only song. I have checked my libretto for the opera and Lady Shackleton's score for *Madama Butterfly* and the song lasts about four minutes, which is not a long time when you are listening to a voice as richly perfect as that of Lady Ryderwood. Then at the end of the song or nearly at the end, in comes Mr. Churchill, who has apparently been speaking on the telephone in the library all this time to his secretary at the Admiralty. He arrives to interrupt the evening's music, and at this time Miss Kingsley and I hear the butler's loud cry from the hall. And off we go." She paused to allow her housekeeper to take this all in.

Mrs. Jackson realized that all the time she had been busying herself with the charity event at Chester Square, Lady Montfort had been working away at this list of where everyone was on the night of the murder, and had made this beautifully organized little chart. *She was doing this as she waited for me to join her in an investigation*, thought Mrs. Jackson, and she felt a guilty little thrill of pleasure, because this is exactly what they were doing. She quickly ran over the times again and then she looked up at Lady Montfort, who was positively beaming down at her, hands clasped, as she hovered over her housekeeper expectantly.

"Miss Gaskell was absent from the room for over fifteen minutes," Mrs. Jackson said.

"Yes, more like twenty, and Miss Kingsley was absent from the room for several of those minutes, too."

"Would that give Miss Gaskell time to go downstairs and kill Sir Reginald?"

"I would have thought so."

And here Mrs. Jackson finally acknowledged to her ladyship that she had joined her in what was to be their second murder investigation together. "I could time myself, m'lady," she said. "Tomorrow morning I could time myself leaving the little salon to go down the stairs, enter the dining room, wait there, and then walk back."

"Sir Reginald was seated at the bottom of the table, Jackson, at the far end," Lady Montfort reminded her. "And don't forget the search for white spirit."

"Yes, m'lady, I could wait in the dining room for a while to account for the time. I wonder how long it takes to stab someone?"

"Not long, done in the blink of an eye." This came too quickly for Mrs. Jackson's comfort.

"But wouldn't the murderer have blood on them, m'lady?"

"Not if you were quick! Well actually I really don't know!" Lady Montfort had the grace to look embarrassed.

If someone was stabbed in the heart, surely there would be blood everywhere? Mrs. Jackson asked, "Was it all over the dining room, m'lady?"

"The front of his evening clothes had a saturated patch around the handle of the knife, not as much as I would have thought."

"Was there blood on the walls and the carpet, m'lady?"

"Good heavens no, Jackson," Lady Montfort exclaimed at the splashy vulgarity of the idea. "And no sign of a struggle either. All this is beside the point really; perhaps we are getting ahead of ourselves.

"What we need to find out is why Adelaide is so frantic about talking to a policeman. Why she concealed a photograph of Sir Reginald under her pillow, if it was Sir Reginald, and why it took her twenty minutes to go downstairs, pick up a bottle of white spirit, and return to the salon. And also," she pointed to her timetable, "we need to know exactly where the servants were between a quarter to eleven and half past eleven. You see I have gaps here for the servants, except for the Clumsy Footman and the butler. And we really should fill them in."

Mrs. Jackson could quite see why Lady Montfort wanted to know these things; she wanted to know them too. But the little she knew of Miss Gaskell had made a strong impression.

"Is it possible that someone as young and scared as Miss Gaskell would have what it took to stab her employer's oldest and closest friend in the middle of a dinner party, m'lady?" she asked.

"Perhaps she had fallen for Sir Reginald and he wouldn't have her, which might explain the photograph under her pillow. Although how a lovely young thing like Adelaide could be interested in a dull as ditchwater old fogy like Sir Reginald rather eludes me at the moment," Lady Montfort said.

Completely missing the point, thought Mrs. Jackson, *that Sir Reginald was exceedingly rich and without a wife, whereas Adelaide Gaskell was exceedingly poor with only the prospect of a life of servitude and devotion to one old lady after another to look forward to, unless she married.*

But Lady Montfort needed her attention: "And now I come to the strangest part of this situation, and something which might or might not have anything to do with this distressing business. Captain Wildman-Lushington, who was also at the party, if you remember, Jackson . . ." her fingertip beat a rapid little tattoo on the chart next to his name, "was killed yesterday when he was trying to land his aeroplane. He was thrown clear, but his body was found yards away with a broken neck. But we'll leave that aside for a while until I hear from Lord Haversham about the aeroplane and whether it was tampered with. I merely wanted to keep you informed that there might be another murder."

Quite likely this aeroplane crash was just an accident, thought Mrs. Jackson. Opinion among her fellow servants at Iyntwood was loud and sure on this particular point: flying was dangerous. "Did," she ventured aloud to her ladyship, "the flying accident tie in with the murder?"

"I'm not sure at the moment. It might perhaps be a cover-up, especially if the murder had been observed by Captain Wildman-Lushington.

"Now to work, Jackson. Let's divvy up our tasks. Did you bring your notebook? Well then, here is paper and pencil. Let's assign what each of us must do."

And with all the youthful enthusiasm and gaiety of someone who is about to play a parlor game, Lady Montfort was up out of her seat and produced the necessary materials for their list-making.

"I am to find out whether Mr. Greenberg and Mr. Tricklebank provided an alibi for each other downstairs in the outer hall after they left the dining room. Then I have to think a bit more about Captain Vetiver, as he is the only person with a connection to Miss Kingsley's party, Eastchurch, and the RNAS, except of course for Mr. Churchill, and he doesn't seem to count in this investigation.

"It would be useful to find out about blood. As you so sensibly pointed out, wouldn't the murderer be covered in it? Perhaps I should ask Detective Hillary when I have the opportunity."

On occasions like this, Lady Montfort always reminded Mrs. Jackson of a little bird. Propelled by the energy of her thoughts, she moved lightly about the room as she discarded ideas and picked up on the threads of others. Every so often she stopped short and seemed almost to burst into song when she had a breakthrough in her thinking.

"Now, Jackson, what about you?" Lady Montfort alighted next to her on the sofa. Mrs. Jackson was pleased that she wasn't being told what to do. *At least I may come up with my own list then*, she thought.

"Well, m'lady, I will find out how Miss Gaskell's morning with the police inspector went, and perhaps I can get her to talk about that photograph and find out if it is actually Sir Reginald. I will also check how long it takes to go between the salon upstairs and the dining room. I wonder too about Miss Kingsley at that time, as they were both away from the salon together for about five minutes.

"And then tomorrow afternoon I have to go to Kingsley House in South London and meet with the matron there. Several young boys are selected each year to be pages for the charity evening and it is usually Miss Gaskell's job to interview them and choose three or four. But I am to do it in her place, so that might be useful." Mrs. Jackson was quite pleased with her list. She paused, pencil poised, to see if Lady Montfort had anything to add to it.

"Oh indeed it will, Jackson. Do you think you can possibly find out where all Miss Kingsley's servants at Chester Square were at the crucial time? Will it be difficult if they don't talk about what happened?"

"Well, I'll do my best. This might take a bit longer, m'lady, as I don't want to upset anyone. They are such a closedmouth lot," she said as she added a note to her list.

They both studiously jotted down their directions to themselves. And Lady Montfort said, more to herself than to her housekeeper, "This is all very jolly." She did some underlining and then looked up. "And I'm going to the Royal Opera House with Lady Ryderwood and Mr. Greenberg tomorrow evening. We will be in Lady Shackleton's box, so nice for us. It will be interesting to have a little talk with them and see if they can remember anything unusual about that evening."

"Is Miss Melba singing, m'lady?" Mrs. Jackson wanted to show off her newfound knowledge.

"Sadly not, she rarely sings at the Royal Opera House these days. She's in London en route to her native Australia to settle in

Melbourne. No, it's Luisa Tetrazzini singing the soprano role, and we are all thrilled to bits because Enrico Caruso is to be 'Pinkerton.'"

"What opera are you going to, m'lady?" Mrs. Jackson wondered if one saw or listened to opera.

"*Madama Butterfly,* so there won't be a dry eye in the house."

Chapter Fourteen

The comfortable circumstances of the Chimney Sweep Boys charity were apparent in the well-kept grounds surrounding Kingsley House and its warm, clean, and well-furnished interior. Mrs. Jackson, who was a snob about architecture, living and working as she did in one of the most gracious Elizabethan houses England had to offer, could think of no better purpose for the overly ornate and architecturally hideous redbrick house than to house the young people lucky enough to be rescued from the degradation and fear provided by a life of poverty. It had been built in the neo-Gothic style so popular in the mid-1800s to gargantuan proportions, according to Miss Gaskell, for a retired West Indian sugar baron who had drunk away his fortune.

The resident matron for the charity was waiting for her in the heavily paneled hall. She was a tall, wide woman, with a well-fed red face and big arms crossed tightly in front of a bosom as wide and as deep as a bolster. She was tightly constrained within a navy-blue serge dress and a crisp white apron. For some reason she had chosen to include, as part of her uniform, a complicated white-starched and winged wimple of the sort worn by hospital nurses in religious houses, which stood out in crisp wings around her large head.

The matron introduced herself as Miss Biggleswade. As she

pronounced her name she gave Mrs. Jackson a thorough once-over, her deep-set eyes taking in every detail from Mrs. Jackson's elegant but simple hat to the quality of her neat little boots. *No doubt she has accurately pigeonholed me precisely for what I am,* Mrs. Jackson thought, *a working woman in the employ of a rich and established family.* She bore the matron's scrutiny with her customary poise and felt a pang of sympathy for whoever had to work for the woman.

"Just call me Matron, Mrs. Jackson, everyone does here. I am solely responsible for the boys' welfare in Kingsley House," Miss Biggleswade explained as she labored up the well-worn, oak staircase. "I am responsible for the domestic side of things, and the boys' behavior once they are finished with their schoolwork. With one hundred and ninety young boys, I can assure you I have my hands full with the little scamps." She lowered her voice to a more confiding tone: "And what with all this bother over Sir Reginald's accidental death and policemen talking to the headmaster and his staff, I am behindhand this morning, dear. So it's take us as you find us, I'm afraid."

Matron toiled up another flight of stairs; her corsets creaked ominously as she reached the penultimate step and paused to catch her breath, the crisp angles of her wimple shaking from the effort of her climb.

"All the boys are at their lessons on the ground floor of the house for the rest of the morning. So we can catch our breath and get to know one another." And on she lumbered to open the door of her room.

"Please come into my little home away from home, and we will have a nice cup of tea, dear. Then I'll call in the boys who have excelled both in their schoolwork and their good conduct and you can talk to them in turn." She ushered Mrs. Jackson into a comfortably sized room so stuffed with furniture and whatnots supporting a mass of bric-a-brac and curios that Mrs. Jackson felt stifled the moment she set foot in it. Matron, now quite star-tlingly short of breath, nevertheless talked on, pausing to inhale in great wheezing gasps, her face red and mottled from the exertion of her climb.

"Miss Gaskell always made what I thought were the strangest choices in her selection of pages for the charity evening." A deep sniff of disapproval. "But I can see you are a sensible woman." And Mrs. Jackson understood that her conversation with Matron if handled with the right touch would be as informative as anyone could hope for.

They settled themselves in lavender and pink chintz chairs with deep flounces, and tea was brought to them by a young maid. Matron poured milk into teacups, and had yet to pick up a large teapot adorned with lurid pink roses, when something occurred to her.

"Oh, just one moment, please excuse me, dear. I almost forgot." She thrust herself out of her chair, trundled across the room, and opened the door. Leaning through its embrasure, she called up the corridor, "Symes, Symes? Come here, boy." And after a moment a small, nervous, and sharp-eyed little boy appeared in the doorway and stood dutifully to attention before her, his thin, mouse-color hair, skinny arms, and knock-knees assurances of an early life of deprivation.

"You can cut along to your classroom, Symes, and if I catch you running in the dormitory corridor again it will be bread and water for a week." She reached out a sturdy arm and pushed the boy in the direction of the stairs, and with a fearful nod he set off as quickly as he could without breaking into a run.

"Have to have my eye on them all the time, you see, Mrs. Jackson. It takes some of them a long time to understand the importance of obeying rules, coming from their disadvantaged beginnings. It will be the third time this week I have had to put that boy in the corner for running. We never beat boys in Kingsley

House." She went on virtuously and Mrs. Jackson was careful to keep her face impassive. "A good whipping never works with their kind. But most of them learn to toe the line quickly if you deprive them of the one thing they count on here: three square meals a day and hot milk at bedtime. Now where were we? Ah yes, this sad business of Sir Reginald. Were you there, dear, at the time I mean?"

It had been a long time since anyone had dared to call Mrs. Jackson "dear" and Matron had committed this blunder several times, but Mrs. Jackson chose to ignore her presumptuous gaffe. "No, I wasn't, Matron, I am just . . ."

"I heard all about it from the chauffeur; Macleod is a terrible old gossip, all chauffeurs are of course. But that's servants these days. Now, how is Miss Gaskell? I heard she had been taken quite ill."

"Nearly recovered, she . . ."

"Not a robust girl, I'm afraid, which makes extra work for poor Miss Kingsley. I advised Miss Kingsley not to employ such a young and flighty girl as a companion. Choose someone solid, I said, someone dependable, not some flibbertigibbet, always making eyes at the gentlemen." She put four sugar lumps into her teacup.

"She is certainly a pretty girl," Mrs. Jackson managed to contribute.

Matron made a loud, derisive sound as she turned her immense, creaking bulk in her chair toward the tea tray and seized a plate of iced fairy cakes. "Ah yes, most conscious of her appeal is Miss Gaskell, always on the lookout for an opportunity, that one." She waved the plate toward Mrs. Jackson.

"Not for me, thank you. Yes, I suppose that is a risk with employing young and pretty girls." Mrs. Jackson felt disloyal to Miss Gaskell as she offered encouragement to a woman who needed none at all where her judgment of the young companion was concerned.

In between delicate bites of cake, the offering of sandwiches, and the cutting of a large Victoria sponge cake oozing raspberry jam and cream, Matron recounted a seemingly endless catalog on the unsuitability of Miss Gaskell as a companion, listing all her faults and finding nothing to recommend in her.

". . . Now of course with Sir Reginald being murdered under the poor lady's nose, where is Miss Gaskell to help and comfort her mistress, I ask you? Upstairs in bed with a cold, so I have been told. Well I'm sure she is cast low; she had such high hopes for Sir Reginald and now they have been dashed once and for all."

"Indeed, Matron? I had wondered . . ." Mrs. Jackson tried not to lean forward.

"Oh yes, she had plans there all right; all wide eyes and demure little gestures, all 'yes, Sir Reginald, no, Sir Reginald.' It was sickening to watch. Of course he was far too busy to pay attention. But that little miss was always finding an excuse to come here when he was at Kingsley House on business. Little errands to run for Miss Kingsley, all of them made up, I'm sure. Then I understand from Macleod that she was the talk of the servants' hall in Chester Square, always thrusting herself forward when Sir Reginald came to call on Miss Kingsley."

"Sir Reginald didn't return her interest? I mean, Miss Gaskell is an attractive young woman with a pleasant manner . . ."

Matron shot her a shrewd look and pressed her lips together. "Sir Reginald was embarrassed for her," she finally said. "His only interest lay in the welfare of the boys and helping the brightest and ablest of them to make a useful life. He was a good Christian gentleman, devout, and with a strong sense of right and wrong . . . and morality. That is our purpose here at Kingsley House, Mrs. Jackson, first and foremost, to instill in these young heathens a sense of right and wrong, and to help them take their place in the world. No, Sir Reginald was polite but remote with Miss Gaskell.

"And now perhaps you had better meet with the boys. There are six of them this year, chosen by Sir Reginald himself just last week." She pulled out a piece of crumpled paper from under her apron, glanced at it, put it down on the tray, got to her feet, and waded across the room.

Mrs. Jackson had no intention of talking to the boys with this old busybody evaluating her every word. "I think I would like to meet with them individually and alone, Matron. It is always interesting to see how boys do with complete strangers, away from the people they know. I have some specific tasks in mind for the charity evening and I want to make sure that the young men we choose are able to fulfill them." This was her longest speech so far, and Mrs. Jackson realized that if Matron had underestimated her when she first arrived, she did not do so now. She was evidently displeased to be deprived of the opportunity to meddle in her interviews, but Mrs. Jackson had been sent by Miss Kingsley, and Miss Kingsley was God in this house, too, of that Mrs. Jackson had no doubt.

"Very well, I will put you into the sick bay, as I have to get on with my inventory of the laundry here. Just tell me when you are finished and who you have chosen."

Mrs. Jackson was taken down a wide corridor and shown into an empty room with twelve beds ranged in two lines of six on either side of the room. A strip of India drugget ran down the center to a large white-painted desk at the end. Matron pulled forward a wooden chair that had been standing by the door and set it in the middle of the room, and then puffing with exertion left her to it.

Mrs. Jackson walked to the window and looked out onto the stark lawns and tidy flower beds, cut down and mulched for the winter and scattered with the remnants of fast-melting snow.

Despite the dull gray winter sky, the sparse winter landscape, and the scarlet brick, Kingsley House was on the whole a reasonably agreeable place, better by far than a parish workhouse or orphanage, thought Mrs. Jackson. There was a knock on the door and she called out to come in.

The door opened and a pleasant-looking boy came into the room; he was perhaps the same age as Symes, but there the similarity ended. Whereas Symes was a thin and weedy little specimen, this boy was tall for his age, with clear, fresh skin and a glossy, well-set-up look about him.

"Matron asked me to come straight in, but I thought I had better knock." He walked into the room and introduced himself as Daniel Phelps, and then he stood in front of her, his large brown eyes fixed on her face, alert to what she might need from him.

"There is nowhere for you to sit but on the bed," said Mrs. Jackson.

"I'll stand—we are not allowed to sit on the beds, ma'am." And he stood with his hands at his sides and waited.

Mrs. Jackson was not at all sure what she should be asking this polite young man. "How long have you been here, Daniel?" she finally ventured.

"Since I was six. I will be nine next month." His body was still but his eyes flitted to the corner of the room as if he expected to see someone there.

"Matron says you are a good scholar, and that you work hard at your lessons."

The boy nodded and shifted his weight.

"Who is your schoolmaster?" she asked in slight desperation.

"Mr. Crosby for mathematics, Mr. Carruthers for French and Latin, and Mr. Newhouse for geography, history, and English." The young eyes were watchful but not unduly so.

Mrs. Jackson drummed up another inane question: "And I suppose you will go away to school soon?"

"Yes, ma'am, I have been accepted into Saint Austin's. Sir Reginald particularly wanted me to go there." There was no evident pride in his voice, it was a statement of fact.

She felt unsure what to ask next and then inspiration struck. "What do you want to do when you leave school?" It was the right question, and he answered with real enthusiasm, the first he had shown.

"The Indian Civil Service. I am hoping to take Hindi next month if they can find a tutor." This was the most animation she had seen in him. He was strangely docile, she thought, there was no real spark there; just a nice, dutiful middle-class boy, with not a trace of the East End in his carefully formed vowels and consonants. She would have given anything to know more about his previous life and how he had come here. But she didn't trespass and cause embarrassment. She knew how hard it was to acknowledge the lack of parents and the awful shame children felt at being abandoned.

"Are you familiar with Miss Kingsley's charity event, the one she holds at her house every year?"

"Yes, I am familiar with it."

"Then you know we like to have some of you young men to meet the people who are interested in the charity. To help the butler take coats and hats, show our guests to their seats in the salon, and help out all round. Do you think you would enjoy that?" She saw the slightest hesitation, his fair skin flushed and his young face wrinkled in concern.

"Do you tell us exactly what we are to do? I would hate to make a mistake and ruin things."

"Oh, it is not a difficult job at all. But you might find it interesting. Don't worry about the details too much, everyone is there to have a pleasant evening and that includes you young men."

She interviewed the next five boys and found there was not

much difference among them; all were well-mannered, scrupulously clean, with none of the blots, scrapes, bruises, falling-down socks, and ink-stained fingers that Lord Haversham had exhibited when he was that age. She was talking to the same boy over and over again, she thought, as if they had stepped off a conveyor belt in a manufactory, newly made in one another's likeness. They were all extremely polite and attentive, and every one of them exhibited concern that they do a good job at the charity and "not let the Chimney Sweep Boys down." Afterward she wondered if any of them were ever unruly or broke rules, if they shouted, whistled, and threw stones. It didn't matter how different their backgrounds had been before they arrived here, as they were now neatly institutionalized. She wished she could observe them in their common room, away from adult supervision.

When the last boy was about to leave, she took a risk.

"Tell me, Edwin," she said, and he turned back to her at the door. "Was Sir Reginald Cholmondeley a kind man to you all?" She was instantly rewarded with a look of consternation—a rabbit in the entrance to its burrow when it emerges and finds a stoat waiting there. Transfixed, he gazed at her silently.

"Sir Reginald took a good deal of interest in how well you did here. He must have been like a . . . father to you boys."

Edwin didn't answer.

"Did he spend a lot of time with you?"

"Sometimes," came the cautious answer, and he reached for the door handle.

Into her mind flashed something she had seen briefly at the top of Matron's list of the boys she was to meet that morning, the word *Chums* and then underneath it the six names. It had taken her a moment to make the connection: *Cholmondeley* written thus was pronounced "Chumley," and this group of perfect boys must have been referred to as Chums.

"Were you one of the Chums?" she asked before she could

stop herself, and then with a flash of intuition: "That was Sir Reginald's society for boys who excelled, wasn't it?"

"Yes, it was." His hand closed around the door handle, but he did not open the door.

"What sort of activities did you excel in? Sports, literature prizes, that sort of thing?" Now she was sure what questions she wanted answered.

"We have to excel in everything: academics, sport, comportment, and doing our duty to the school and the governors." It was a mechanical answer, but his eyes were watchful and he did not take his hand away from the doorknob.

"That must have been taken a lot of effort to accomplish; you must be a hardworking boy.

Edwin turned around and gave her a thoughtful look. "Yes, we have to work hard here. We want to be a credit to the charity."

"I am sure you are," she said, hoping to reassure. And she saw the relief on his face as he left the room without a backward glance.

Mrs. Jackson sat on in the sick bay with its rows of empty beds and thought about the boys she had interviewed. It didn't matter in the slightest which ones came to help at Chester Square, they were all equally acceptable. But she thought Edwin, Clive, George, and Albert would probably more than adequately fit the bill for taking hats and coats and helping during supper. She did not doubt for one moment that they would do a thorough job, far better than Jenkins's luckless and ill-trained Clumsy Footman. She sighed and stared across the room. They were all such earnest boys, extremely conscious of their duty to the charity, and so careful with their answers.

When Mrs. Jackson returned to Matron's parlor she found her sitting at a desk, working on her laundry inventory. She was running a pencil down a column of figures and obviously performing rapid mental arithmetic; the tip of her tongue protruded from between large yellowing teeth and she was breathing quite heavily. Her small, deep-set eyes lifted from her work as Mrs. Jackson came into the room and in one smooth movement she closed the book and slid it under a stack of bills skewered on a spike to the left of her on the desk. She got to her feet and came around her desk.

"Got what you came for, did you?" Her belligerence was palpable. "Yes, I wondered why you wanted to talk to the boys on their own, and so I spoke to Edwin when you had finished questioning him, and what I want to know is why were you asking about the Chums, ay? There are no favorites here, Mrs. Jackson, all the boys are treated the same." Matron came toward Mrs. Jackson, her head down: a large sow protecting a farrowing house full of piglets. Mrs. Jackson fully expected the woman to butt her in the stomach and she almost took a step backward.

"Matron," her voice was cold, "Sir Reginald Cholmondeley often talked of the Chums. He said they were his most promising boys. Naturally, I needed to know if his death had upset them. If they are distressed about the death of Sir Reginald, it would not do to bring them to the house where he was murdered. I am sure you understand the necessity of my questions, now."

She had stopped Matron in her tracks, but the woman was still uncomfortably close. Angry eyes were staring intently into her face. Mrs. Jackson felt a momentary surge of alarm and an irrational fear that at any moment Matron might lift a mighty arm and hit her. *Don't be so ridiculous,* she told herself, *she's just a mean-spirited woman who bullies little boys. But why does she care so much about my questions?* She stood her ground and began to pull on her gloves to disguise the fact that her hands were shaking a little.

"Now, you listen to me, dear," Matron said. "I know a snoop when I see one, and you can tell Miss Kingsley from me that all the boys here are doing well, even with the terrible loss of Sir

Reginald. And," a large, hard finger came up and thrust itself under Mrs. Jackson's nose, "there is no need for you to return to Kingsley House. Send a note with Macleod as to which boys are needed and they will be sent over promptly."

She makes them sound like chattel, thought Mrs. Jackson. Obviously in Matron's view the Chimney Sweep Boys were from the gutter and any of them who did not conform could just as easily be returned there. How could someone so coarse and mean in spirit have charge over children in an institution that prided itself on producing gentlemen?

Matron took a step back and Mrs. Jackson turned toward the parlor door. "There is no need for you to come downstairs with me, Matron, I can find my own way out." And she left the room and walked down the corridor with the slightly shaky feeling that always comes when someone large and nasty has revealed true spite and malice for no understandable reason.

As Mrs. Jackson came down the last three steps into the hall she turned and saw standing in a corner at the top of the corridor the small outline of Symes, his face to the wall.

Poor little chap he must have been running again. She walked over to the boy. "Hullo, Symes. Do you often have to stand in the corner?"

He turned and regarded her solemnly. "Yes, often, I'm afraid. It's for running in the house. I am always trying to catch up, you see."

"Have you practiced fast walking? You concentrate on keeping just under the run, and if you keep your arms straight by your sides you can't break into a run and it looks just as if you were walking no matter how fast you go. You will find you get there just as quickly and no punishments! Housemaids do it all the time." She smiled at the pale little face looking up at her, as he nodded.

"So you are not one of the Chums, then?" she asked.

He looked worried, and then taking her on trust, he said, "No, I'm good at lessons but not in doing my duty because I am always late. I'm not much good at sport either. The Chums," he added, "are different. They are the brightest boys here. It doesn't do to cross one of them though, because they can be mean to new boys. They have special privileges. They can give you a flogging if you break the rules. And if you break rules and cause trouble you are for the high jump all right and can get sent away to . . . an orphanage." A look of dismay, and Mrs. Jackson realized that talking to her when he should have been standing facing the wall was certainly breaking a rule.

"Would you like to be a page at Miss Kingsley's charity evening?" she asked, and watched his face light up for a moment and then fall.

"She wouldn't let me," he said.

"Oh yes she would, Symes, if I asked for you. And I think you are a nice, bright boy, the sort of boy who would make an excellent page—as long as you can remember to fast-walk and not run. What do you say?"

"I say, yes please, miss," said Symes.

"Good. Now what's your first name, your Christian name?"

"Arthur."

"Very well then, Arthur Symes, I am putting you on the top of my list."

She was about to walk away when she looked up and saw hanging on the far wall of the hall a large oil painting heavily framed in ornate gilt. It was a portrait of a middle-aged man with side-whiskers and a balding head; he had his arm ponderously resting on the shoulder of a small boy who was steadfastly looking toward a glowing future and was undoubtedly a Chimney Sweep charity boy. She turned back to Arthur Symes.

"Who is that in the painting over there on the wall, Arthur?"

The boy turned his head and said without hesitation, "Sir

Reginald Cholmondeley, and that one over there, the lady, is our benefactress."

And on the far wall of the hall facing Sir Reginald Cholmondeley was Miss Kingsley, gazing across the room with calm confidence at her oldest and closest friend.

Chapter Fifteen

Triumphantly gloating over her correct identification of Sir Reginald in Miss Gaskell's photograph and her conversation with Arthur Symes and her interesting, if unpleasant, conversation with Matron, Mrs. Jackson stepped over the threshold of the Chester Square scullery into an air of gloom and despondency. Instantly, all feelings of accomplishment were forgotten.

Both the maids and the second footman, James, were in the servants' hall. From the kitchen she heard Cook calling out instructions to her silent crew of kitchen maids.

"Good afternoon, Martha. Is something wrong?" Mrs. Jackson said as she unwound her scarf from around her neck.

"Mr. Tricklebank's in trouble with the pleece, an' Mistress was took so bad she's upstairs under the doctor."

"What?" Mrs. Jackson was aghast. "Miss Kingsley is what?"

"Under the doctor; under Dr. Brewster's care I mean. Took a turn for the wuss when she 'eard of Mr. Tricklebank's arrest." Martha was so undone by what had happened that all her carefully learned King's English had disappeared and her cockney origins were reasserting themselves more strongly by the moment.

"Arrest for what, Martha?"

"For lying abaht where he was on the night of the murder,

course." And then realizing she had broken a cardinal rule that the fateful evening must not be referred to, she turned away, her face set as she started banging down plates and cutlery on the table.

Mrs. Jackson took off her hat and unbuttoned her coat and handed them to Eliza, who was taking in all this information, her eyes large and bright with excitement.

"And where is Mr. Jenkins, in his pantry?" she asked, and Martha nodded.

"Mr. Tricklebank is probably not under arrest, Martha; he is just helping the police with their inquiries."

Martha shook her head to this. Overburdened by the truth of the situation, she was driven to reveal it: "Mr. Tricklebank was 'ere for 'is tea with Miss Kingsley. Then that Inspector 'Illary from Scotland Yard arrived and there was 'ell to pay. Mr. Jenkins was in the drawin' room and 'eard everything. I don't know what this 'ouse is comin' to."

"Very well then, I will go straight into Mr. Jenkins." Mrs. Jackson simply couldn't take any more muddled explanations. If Mr. Jenkins could actually remember the incident, he would be perfectly capable of explaining the situation in understandable English.

She found the elderly butler sitting at the desk in his pantry looking quite exhausted, but he recognized her instantly and seemed to be aware of what had happened that afternoon.

"Mr. Jenkins, I am so sorry, it sounds as if this has been a difficult afternoon. Martha says Mr. Tricklebank was arrested. Is this true?"

The old man sighed and shook his head, not in answer but in despair of comprehending Mr. Tricklebank's predicament with the police.

"As good as, Mrs. Jackson, as good as arrested. You see he lied to the police *and to his aunt*." Mr. Jenkins's tone implied that lying to Miss Kingsley was the far worse crime. "About where he was after dinner on the night of . . . the night of . . ."

"Sir Reginald's murder." Mrs. Jackson was in no mood for pretense or evasion.

"Yes, *that* night. Mr. Tricklebank said he was going on with Miss Wells-Thornton to her cousin's party, but when they got outside he put her in his motorcar and sent her off to the dance, and then he walked off down the street. Now he is unable to account for his whereabouts for a couple of hours. He originally said he was at his club, the Pheebles, but the porter there says he didn't arrive until one o'clock in the morning. So his time is unaccounted for, for several hours, and of course it *looks* bad. Miss Kingsley was so upset when the police took him away that she had a fainting spell and is not doing well." The old man looked quite done in himself, Mrs. Jackson thought, as he went on, "Dr. Brewster is with her now, and Miss Gaskell is up and dressed and looking after her when she should still be in bed."

"I am sure Miss Gaskell will be quite all right," said Mrs. Jackson, trying to reassure the old man.

"Miss Gaskell should *not* be up and about. She has been unwell this afternoon, and I heard her coughing all morning. Dear, dear me, as if Miss Kingsley hasn't enough to worry about." Mrs. Jackson made sympathetic noises, providing the elderly butler with a concerned and listening ear.

"I think Miss Kingsley might disinherit Mr. Tricklebank. She threatened as much this afternoon. He has always been a heedless young person, with his gambling and his feckless ways. But underneath all that silliness, there is a sweetness and a goodness to him. You see, I've known Mr. Tricklebank since he was a baby, Mrs. Jackson. I'm worried that this is most likely the end of him with Miss Kingsley. We live in such difficult times these days, young people are ever so . . . and Miss Kingsley has high standards, as she most certainly should." He lifted the cup of hot sweet tea she had brought for him to his lips with shaking hands, and Mrs. Jackson was troubled to see how frail and aged he looked.

"Once Mr. Tricklebank has set his evening straight with the police, everything will smooth itself out. There is bound to be a perfectly good explanation." She did her best to soothe, but the elderly man was shaking his head, and Mrs. Jackson did not doubt that Miss Kingsley's threat had not been an empty one.

She left the butler to worry over the perplexities of the age he now found himself living in, and went in search of the first footman, John. She found him with exasperations of his own: it seemed that the Clumsy Footman had somehow managed to break two cups and a soup plate—all of them Dresden—merely by carrying them into the china pantry on a tray.

Mrs. Jackson waited outside the pantry door until John's outrage at the second footman's ham-fisted handling of priceless porcelain had abated a little. It sounded as if the first footman's family of origin were East End costermongers, since most of the words he was using were Anglo-Saxon epithets of the harsher kind.

". . . Bleedin' chips on every ruddy cup. An' another thing . . . drop one more of them buggers . . . have your guts for . . ." wafted out the pantry door. Mrs. Jackson waited for a lull, and when it came she cleared her throat. John put his head out of the pantry door, saw her, straightened his waistcoat, ran a hand over the top of his smooth head, and said quite pleasantly, "Yes, Mrs. Jackson, how can I be of help?"

"I think it would be a good idea if you were ready to stand in as butler tomorrow, John. Mr. Jenkins seems all in, and I think it a good idea if he takes things easy for a day or two. I will ask Martha to help you with the day's duties tomorrow. Once Mr. Jenkins has had a nice rest we can resume a normal routine." *Whatever that is in this house.* She was a little concerned that John might bristle at her assuming a command position and was relieved by the respectful bob of his head.

"I will just pop upstairs for a moment and see how Miss Gaskell is faring, and then Macleod can drive me to Montfort House. Please ask him to stand by with the motorcar."

Miss Gaskell was up and dressed. She was sitting in her window with a shawl wrapped around her shoulders, looking out onto the darkening night.

"How are you, Miss Gaskell? I heard from Mr. Jenkins the awful news of Mr. Tricklebank."

The girl turned a blank, pale face toward Mrs. Jackson and nodded. "Awful, isn't it? But it's madness to imagine him harming anyone. It isn't in his nature."

Any more than it is in yours, Mrs. Jackson thought. "In that case I'm quite sure that the police will not detain him for long, as soon as he has been straight with them."

"Yes, but you see we all know where he probably was, it's not the first time." Miss Gaskell coughed—not a chest cold sort of cough but the sort of little *ahem* when a point is made. Mrs. Jackson understood the signal and took it that Mr. Tricklebank was not only irresponsible but probably had a weakness for all the usual vices of the young man about town: wine, cards, and of course, women. Every family had a Mr. Tricklebank, it seemed.

"I had a most interesting visit to Kingsley House today, as a matter of fact."

Miss Gaskell had turned her head away to resume her study of the empty street, but this remark caused her to turn back from the window immediately. "Interesting?" she quavered, as well she might after all the horrid things Matron had said about her.

"Yes, it is a most impressive and Christian charity." Miss Gaskell's eyes flickered briefly. "I have a list of the boys who would be suitable for the evening. Shall you write or shall Miss Kingsley write to Matron?"

"Miss Kingsley; then Matron will do as she is told, otherwise . . ."
Mrs. Jackson could only imagine how difficult Matron had been
to work with for the young companion.

"How long has Matron been at Kingsley House?" she asked in
what she hoped sounded like an idle question.

"Oh, quite a few years, maybe as many as ten; she was the matron when I came here. Was she very difficult?"

"Oh, she was most helpful in her own way, but not a particularly pleasant woman in her manner."

"No, Matron reserves her good manners for Miss Kingsley and
the governors." The companion fell into a brooding silence, and
Mrs. Jackson asked her, "How did your interview go with the
police, Miss Gaskell, nothing to worry about after all?"

The young woman laughed and said how silly she had been and
that the interview with the police had not been as frightening as
she had thought. Mrs. Jackson wondered what they had said
about the fact that she had been roaming around the house without an alibi at about the time Sir Reginald had been murdered.

"I can't imagine what you think of us all . . ." Miss Gaskell
tailed off rather listlessly.

"Well, I think there has been a murder in the house, Miss
Gaskell, and you are all still in considerable shock. And I think
you are all protecting Miss Kingsley's feeling about the murder
of her close friend by not referring to what happened. Sometimes it is a good thing to talk things over, it helps us find our
feet again." She let this one lie and watched Miss Gaskell closely.

"Miss Kingsley has expressly forbidden us to discuss the
events of that evening, Mrs. Jackson. I believe the servants are
quite happy to go along with her wishes." Miss Gaskell resorted
to being sniffy and missish, but it did not disguise the anxiety the
young companion evidently felt and which pervaded throughout the Kingsley household.

Mrs. Jackson moved to the window to draw the curtains

against the night. Looking down to guide the heavy fabric around the wastepaper basket, she saw something there that made her almost giddy with excitement. For lying at the bottom of the basket, and almost concealed by balls of screwed-up writing paper, was the corner of a photograph that had been ripped in two. Coyly peeking up at her from behind a crumpled list of contributors to his charity was the whiskery face of Sir Reginald Cholmondeley, whose photograph hitherto had been kept in an elaborate frame and concealed underneath Miss Gaskell's pillow.

Well now, thought Mrs. Jackson as she said good night to the young woman, *what a good day it has been for discovery.* She went downstairs, put on her hat and coat, and left the house feeling as if she were escaping from a tomb.

Chapter Sixteen

While Mrs. Jackson was tucked up with a good book and a glass of hot milk in the old nursery, recovering from her day of triumphs and revelations, Clementine, dressed in her best Fortuny evening gown, was taking her seat in the Shackletons' box at the Royal Opera House.

Lord Montfort had offered to accompany Olive Shackleton and his wife to the opening night of *Madama Butterfly* on his last evening in town before he left for Iyntwood. It was a deeply generous act on his part and Clementine went to great lengths to thank him for this kindness. She knew the opera was a close equivalent to an evening spent in hell for her husband. In his own words he could never quite appreciate the appeal of listening to a contest between the bellowing of solidly overweight men and the shrieking of large women, often at the same time, in a hot auditorium crammed with people, all of whom he believed were there because they had nothing better to do. Yet here he was with all the appearance that the evening held nothing but delight for him.

They were accompanied by Lady Ryderwood and Aaron Greenberg, and after Lord Montfort had settled Lady Shackleton and Lady Ryderwood on either side of his wife at the front of the box, he took a seat at the back of it next to Aaron Greenberg, where they fell into quiet conversation.

Sandwiched between two devotees of Italian opera, Clementine felt rather like a fraud. For her, the appeal of a first night was watching fellow opera-goers at play before the curtain rose on an extravagant production with ornate sets and lavish costumes. The singing, which she enjoyed for the most part, was a rather secondary appreciation. Leaving Veda Ryderwood and Olive to discuss the merits of various sopranos most suited to the role of Butterfly, she gazed down at the packed auditorium to watch society's overture to the performance.

The Royal Opera House had undergone a tremendous change in the last few years and had been thoroughly refurbished. Tonight it reminded Clementine of a great gilt-and-plush jewel box. The red-velvet tiers were festively swagged with glossy green foliage, bright with autumn berries, entwined with winter-flowering jasmine and hothouse lilies to scent the soft, rarefied air. Gathered below and on either side of her were London's beau monde: women, sumptuously dressed, shone like stars in their jewels, accompanied by meticulously tailored men who provided a perfect black-and-white foil for the brilliant oriental colors in fashion this year inspired by the exotic sets and costumes of the Ballets Russes.

Clementine nodded to friends among the glittering, shifting crowd below as she watched them greet one another: the younger women with little cries of surprise and exclamations of delight at a particularly magnificent dress; the older with stately inclinations of the head before, barely moving their lips, they fell into a long, murmured exchange of information and gossip. In boxes on either side of her, a more illustrious crowd fluttered fans to cover whispered assignations and the more scurrilous news of the day, causing heads to be thrown back in trilling laughter and bright, malicious eyes to flash. Handsome young men regarded the throng through half-closed, insolent eyes, exhibiting habitual boredom, or brayed with loud foolish laughter, as they waited to be released for the real business of the night's pleasure at the card tables of their clubs. Standing apart from the distraction created by life's partygoers, England's politicians, industrialists, bankers, and landowners talked among themselves. Their faces betrayed nothing but polite, well-bred interest, that particular air of the patrician Englishman for which he is renowned, the reserved demeanor the Germans called arrogance and the French sangfroid. They talked of war, they talked of cabinet placement, and they talked of money. Clementine noticed them in their familiar groups and her gaze traveled onward until it alighted on the tiny, birdlike figure of Lady Cunard, who was busily making the rounds among the especially rich and highly titled, darting from box to box, disappearing and reappearing like a marionette in a puppet show. Clementine turned to Olive to indulge in a little information-gathering of her own.

"What were you telling me about Maud Cunard the other day, Olive?" Olive Shackleton spent most of her time in London when her husband was in Thebes on his archaeological dig, and was far more au courant with London's more salacious gossip than Clementine was. "She was at dinner with us the other night, I could only suppose it was because of her success in drumming up funds for the opera house. Hermione was possibly hoping Lady Cunard would divert a little toward the Chimney Sweep Boys." Clementine had been surprised to see Maud Cunard at Chester Square, as Hermione though well connected was hardly considered fashionable.

"Not remotely possible, real acts of philanthropy are not Maud's strong suit. She has taken to inviting her friends to call her Emerald, by the way." Clementine immediately thought of her cook Ginger. *What,* she wondered, *is the appeal of concocting a persona by renaming oneself?*

Olive went on, "She's made short work of London; it has become chic to be invited to her salon. *Everyone* goes, at least once. But it is not for the fainthearted. Maud loves to serve people's frailties up for luncheon as a special treat. Asquith actively discourages his senior ministers from going to her parties, after she put Sir Edward Grey completely on the spot about foreign policy. She actually made the poor man admit that whether he liked it or not, his hands were tied by the terms of the Entente Cordiale when he muffed things so badly in the Agadir Crisis. I try to stay clear of her, and so should you, Clemmy, she can be positively dangerous. Ambition doesn't come close to describing . . . and I think Sir Thom," Olive was an old and intimate friend and she giggled as she used the Talbot's pet name for Lady Cunard's lover, "is rather scared of her. He does, by the way, have a bit of a thing about . . ." She nodded toward the Marchioness of Ripon, who was seated in a box across the opera house.

"Everyone has a bit of a thing about Lady Ripon. Perhaps it's her height." The Marchioness of Ripon was easily six feet tall, always splendidly dressed and extraordinarily charismatic. "I thought Maud was done for after that business with the window cleaner." Clementine remembered the unfortunate incident of Sir Thom and Maud Cunard caught in flagrante by a window cleaner at her husband's country house, Neville Holt, threatening scandal for months.

"Oh good heavens, yes, so did I." Olive shook her head in silent laughter. "What a to-do! Can you believe the man—he was a laborer from the estate, *not* a window cleaner—saw them both tucked up together as clear as day. If it wasn't for Bache Cunard's immense influence in squashing that newspaper story, Maud would be twiddling her thumbs on the Continent somewhere, just like poor old Daisy Warwick." Everyone understood that infidelity, one of the unrecognized pastimes in society, if kept under wraps was acceptable, but revealed to the world in newspapers or divorce courts was quite unpardonable and resulted in the culprit's being ruthlessly excised from society, until it chose to forget.

Clementine watched Maud Cunard making the social round and realized that by the end of the night everyone in London would know of Hermione's calamitous party for Mr. Churchill. Another thought occurred to her: Maud was an observant woman, who understood human nature well. Clementine made a mental note to see if she might glean some of her observations on the night's events at Chester Square.

The muted murmur behind her grew in intensity and glancing over her shoulder she was pleased to see her husband was still immersed in conversation with Mr. Greenberg, who appeared to be explaining something of great interest. Every so often Ralph would nod slowly with his lips pursed, a sign he was being extra attentive.

Clementine had met Mr. Greenberg on many occasions and had found him intelligent and well read, a thoughtful and considering man with the careful, cultivated manners of an arriviste, albeit one with an established provenance, as Mr. Greenberg had been a close friend of the late king. *He is one of those men,* she thought, *who enjoys society to its fullest extent, but never betrays a confidence and is always ready to play the role of financial adviser.* Neither was Mr. Greenberg ever seen to embrace the vulgar or outré interests of the more jaded members of the exceedingly rich. He was a paragon of restraint and virtue. And he had to be, she realized. Aaron Greenberg was welcomed into society—everywhere. He was gifted with the ability to recognize a potentially lucrative investment and so was on everyone's guest list, but Aaron Greenberg was not of society nor ever would be. No matter how many august families invited him to dine, to shoot, to dance and flirt decorously with their wives and daughters, there his connection with them ended. He might watch his

Thoroughbred win the Derby, sail his yacht at Cowes, and single-handedly fund the opera season after season. He might well be taken into the confidence of princes, dukes, and earls, even kings, but as a Jew he could not marry one of their daughters. Clementine, as the mother of an unwed daughter, thought it was regrettable that race counted for so much, and it was certainly an indication of how hidebound the English aristocracy continued to be—even those of them who were still struggling to support estates that had leached their fortunes decades ago. But having been brought up in India, that outpost of the British Empire where race and religion set unbreakable lines among the three million people the British referred to loosely as Indians, she knew only too well the cultural and societal importance of not breaking caste.

There was a smattering of applause that gradually grew in strength as Sir Thomas Beecham strode out into the front of the opera house. He stopped and glanced up at the royal box, but as always it was dark. *What a disappointing king George has turned out to be,* Clementine thought; *he is probably busy spending the evening sticking stamps in his album, before retiring for the night at ten o'clock.* She felt a stab of nostalgia for dear old Bertie, who never missed an opening night, always accompanied by the beautiful wife of one his closest friends and a lively procession of coming and going amid clouds of cigar smoke and laughter, before he discreetly disappeared during the entr'acte.

Sir Thomas bowed his head and waited before them to be feted. He bowed again and the applause grew. Satisfied with his welcome, he walked down into the orchestra pit and inclined his head toward his first violinist, to be rewarded by more applause. Finally, taking his place at his conductor's podium, he turned once more for a final round of adulation before he picked up his baton and with arms extended turned toward his orchestra, inviting them to stand and acknowledge the house.

"Great heavens, is he ever going to *play*?" murmured Olive Shackleton, who had been in love with Sir Thom for years and had almost given up on him, being neither young enough, beautiful enough, nor rich enough for the great impresario. And great impresario he most certainly was, Clementine thought, as she watched him nod his handsome head at the adoration he expected to receive. Undoubtedly a fine musician and tremendously gifted, he was also rich enough to have his own symphony orchestra and he held absolute sway over both His Majesty's Theatre and the opera house. He also held absolute sway over the hearts of many of its financial contributors too. Successful and handsome as he was, Sir Thom was not to Clementine's taste; she disliked conceited men and though she admitted that he had immense charm and could be tremendous company, she preferred men who appeared to be disinterested in their appearance and if they flirted did so with dignity.

Veda Ryderwood, sitting quietly on Clementine's right, fixed her large dark eyes on the stage, her lovely face expectant, her hands resting quietly in her lap, waiting. The murmured voice of Mr. Greenberg behind Clementine stopped its instructive conversation and said, "Ahhh," in anticipation. Out of the corner of her eye Clementine noticed that Mr. Greenberg had fixed his attention forward, whereas her husband had settled back in his chair, arms crossed on his chest and chin dropped down onto the starched front of his boiled shirt.

The curtain rose on an elaborate version of a traditional wood-framed Japanese house, with paper walls and a blue-tiled roof, set amid a garden frothing in pink cherry blossoms and suffused with golden light from a glowing backdrop of Mount Fuji at the peak of a splendid sunset. There was a deep sigh from Lady Ryderwood, probably not in appreciation of the splendors of the set but because Enrico Caruso had strolled onto the stage, dressed in an American navy uniform with his hat tucked under his arm.

Despite his girth, or perhaps because of it, Caruso was, thought Clementine, undoubtedly impressive. She lifted her opera glasses and along with several hundred other women examined the handsome, dark features of the famous tenor as he stood center stage to bask in their approval. She glanced again at Veda Ryderwood and saw on her face such wonder and reverence that she felt a small shiver, which intensified as Caruso filled his powerful lungs and the opera began.

As Butterfly's tragic story of enduring faith in a man who has every intention of abandoning her unfolded, Clementine found her mind wandering at times between arias. She found the set and costumes both sumptuous and exotic, and there were parts of the opera that were extraordinarily moving, but she privately agreed with her husband that sometimes it was hard to keep up with what was going on, especially when everyone sang together at once. And although Luisa Tetrazzini's voice was remarkable in its power and thrilling tone, her short, buxom figure simply wasn't set to its best advantage in a kimono, especially with that large, flat bow-tie arrangement in the back.

As Tetrazzini began her aria "One Fine Day," Clementine found herself comparing her quality with that of Lady Ryderwood the other evening, and decided that she preferred Lady Ryderwood's version. There had been more determination and thrust to Lady Ryderwood's performance, she thought. Lady Ryderwood's Butterfly would never give up on reuniting with her errant husband, whereas she felt Tetrazzini's Butterfly was lying down somewhat on the job and was all for throwing in the towel.

Then, with the shocking suicide of Butterfly, which left the audience feeling breathless and some of the less sophisticated in tears, the opera ended in a storm of applause from the stalls, as those in the dress circle and boxes turned to one another, patting gloved hands together politely, smiling and nodding their approval, most of them already thinking about their champagne and lobster salad for supper.

It took a while before Lady Shackleton's party actually left the opera house. There were so many little farewells to be made, and Clementine sensed that her husband was not only hungry but bored with waiting. She put her hand on Lady Ryderwood's arm and said, "Should we leave for the Savoy now? I think Lady Shackleton still needs to talk to a few people."

Aaron Greenberg must have felt the same because he was holding out Lady Ryderwood's opera coat for her, and Olive Shackleton, who was stuck like a burr to Lady Busborough's side, must have noticed them wrapping themselves up, because she said, "Oh yes, do go on. We won't be long, we just need to . . ." And once again she was drawn into another group of exclaimers, all chattering brightly and gathering around Lady Cunard like moths to the flame. This gave Clementine the opportunity to say something to Maud Cunard about recovering from the upheavals and shocks of the last time they had met, hoping to draw her in. But Maud turned a blank face to her, thin brows arched in surprise, and after staring vacantly at her for a moment drawled, "I had a perfectly lovely evening, Lady Montfort. What an extraordinary voice Lady Ryderwood has, you would think she sang for a living." And having delivered both a barb and a snub, she turned back to join her group of friends.

How interesting, thought Clementine, *someone has made an indelible impression on Maud Cunard about the importance of not discussing Sir Reginald's murder. Of course we were all warned off, but I thought Maud Cunard was irrepressible. What a surprise.*

Supper at the Savoy was far from fun as Lord Montfort put his foot down and declined an invitation to join the Marchioness of

Ripon's larger party. The six of them took a table on the edge of things but with a good view of the fashionable world at supper.

They were joined by Lady Shackleton and Clarence Tavistock, and right behind them was Sir Thomas Beecham, urbane and consciously unaware that all eyes in the dining room had turned to him. On his arm was Lady Ripon, who positively towered over him; dazzling and glossy, her flawless white shoulders and magnificent bosom were perfectly displayed by a garnet-red dress that clung to the edges of her superb figure. As they passed, a flurry of talk and excited whispers followed them.

Goodness me, thought Clementine, *how exhausting it must be to be so sought after and invited everywhere.*

And then turning in her chair she found Mr. Churchill standing at her elbow, bowing and smiling and saying dear lady.

But it was not for Clementine that he had come to their table. As soon as he had greeted her, and he did so with his habitual expansive geniality, he took Lady Ryderwood's hand in his and bent over to kiss it, unashamedly showing off his balding crown.

Interesting, thought Clementine, as she took this in. *It seems Lady Ryderwood has a distinct crush on Mr. Churchill, or maybe it's the other way around. I hope she is aware how fierce Mrs. Churchill is about these little things.* She took in the rosy flush to Lady Ryderwood's cheeks and noticed that her large, dark eyes were quite brilliant as she looked up at the man bending over her chair.

Lady Ryderwood was too restrained in manner to behave like an obvious flirt. During her brief conversation with Mr. Churchill she turned her head up to look at him and listened gravely without a trace of affectation to what he had to say. But her responses were made with emphasis, and she looked directly into Churchill's eyes, her own bright and alive with interest. Clementine was impressed. *There is certainly a difference between flattering a man with ready laughter and breathless chatter and the direct, unswerving interest that Lady Ryderwood is bestowing.*

And it had its effect. Mr. Churchill eventually straightened up with demonstrable reluctance and must have said something amusing, because Lady Ryderwood opened her delighted mouth and laughed, showing pretty white teeth. And then with her characteristic composure she said good night to Mr. Churchill and turned to Lord Montfort as she lifted a glass of champagne and took a sip.

Clementine transferred her attention to Mr. Greenberg, who was seated to her right. He was such an unpretentious man, with an agreeably light and playful manner, that she found it easy to enjoy their chitchat about the opera: whether Sir Thomas would ever welcome Nellie Melba to sing at Covent Garden again, and if he did, would she accept?—since their feud was of a long-standing and bitter nature. When they had finished with this diverting topic, she thought it time to direct their conversation to what had happened on the night of Hermione's dinner party.

"It must have been the most terrible thing to discover, Lady Montfort." There was no prurient interest but genuine sympathy from Mr. Greenberg when she referred to the untimely and shocking death of Sir Reginald.

"Yes, it was actually, quite awful. The image is beginning to fade, but . . ." She lifted her hands palm-upward in resignation. "There are other parts of the evening that I find have stuck quite vividly in my mind and others that are a complete blank, which makes the experience rather disconnected and troubling. Do you mind if I ask you something about that time? You see, I find if I talk about it a little, it takes away some of the dread." She waited to be snubbed, but Mr. Greenberg, although no doubt cautioned as they had all been not to gossip, played by his own rules.

"No, I completely understand." He took an oyster, neatly lifted it off its shell and popped it into his mouth. He closed his eyes briefly and said, "North Sea, Orkney probably; always so much brinier than those from the south coast."

"Is there a discernible difference?" She took an oyster. "I can never tell."

"Yes, a considerable difference; try eating them without the mignonette, or lemon or all those other bits and pieces, then you will taste the oyster. Now what were you saying about the other evening?" He consumed several oysters with his eyes closed and then opened them and turned courteously to her.

"Well, when you left the dining room the other night, can you remember where everyone was, all the men I mean?"

"No, not really, but I will try. I think your husband, Sir Henry, and that young flying officer walked straight up the stairs to join you in the salon. I know Mr. Churchill hurried off to the library to use the telephone; he was the first to leave us. And Captain Vetiver stayed behind in the dining room to talk to Sir Reginald. I spent a little time in the hall with Sir Vivian Hussey, he wanted to talk about Royal Opera House business; have you any idea how expensive that place is to run? It's outrageous . . ."

Clementine did not want to hear about the Royal Opera House or its business, as she had spent nearly three hours in it and that was more than enough.

"But you didn't talk to Sir Vivian for long, because he came into the salon after my husband."

"Yes, that's right. So what did I do then? Oh yes, now I remember, I talked to Tricky."

Clementine smiled, what a perfect name for young Trevor Tricklebank.

"Tricky? Oh good heavens, is that what he is called? Tricky! It is a perfectly splendid name for him. I wonder if Hermione knows!" Clementine laughed at the thought of Hermione's affable twit of a nephew, with his continual ability to charm the old lady and at the same time make no effort to fulfill his obligations as her only surviving family member.

"I am quite sure Trevor has been called Tricky ever since his days at Harrow. We talked of money, what else?" He laughed, sharing the joke with her that he was sought after because of his prowess for making lots of it. "Everyone is worried about money these days, thanks to the exorbitant taxes we pay."

"I don't know how they manage their allowances at all, these young men with their highly expensive way of life" said Clementine, carefully guiding the conversation back to Tricky.

"Well, they gamble a good deal, a big win here and there. Hopefully they don't touch their capital." Mr. Greenberg shook his head at the profligacy of the financially unenlightened and ate another oyster.

"So you stayed downstairs with Tricky, sorted out his financial affairs, and kept him company."

"Until Miss Wells-Thornton came down so they might leave for another party together." He smiled at her and she thought for a moment that he winked an eye.

"So you *saw* them leave, then?" Clementine knew she was now pushing the limit, but Mr. Greenberg seemed not in the least put out.

"Yes, I saw them leave. I walked outside with them to get a breath of air. Mr. Tricklebank put Miss Wells-Thornton into his motorcar and told the driver to take her on to her party. And then he said he would hail a taxicab, and off he walked into the night."

"But surely he was supposed to be going on with Miss Wells-Thornton!" Clementine pretended to be shocked.

"And that is why he is called Tricky, my dear Lady Montfort, because that is what he told his aunt so he could leave what was doubtless a boring evening for him, and go off and enjoy the town in his own way." It was quite clear that Mr. Greenberg approved of Tricky's tactics, and he laughed in approval of his naughtiness to his aunt, and Clementine laughed, too. It was so entirely typical that an aging old lady who controlled the lives of countless people could be so easily duped by the one person she doted on.

"What about Captain Vetiver? Was he still in the dining room alone with Sir Reginald?"

"I have no idea at all about Captain Vetiver." Clementine distinctly got the impression that Aaron Greenberg had no interest at all in the captain. "The dining-room door was closed and one of the footmen said that Sir Reginald had made it clear not to disturb them until he rang."

A waiter filled their glasses with champagne and they thoughtfully sipped for a moment or two.

"The footman said 'them'?"

"Yes, the footman said 'them.'" He caught her eye and shook his head. "But Vetiver is not the type, my dear Lady Montfort, to do something as distasteful as stab a guest in someone else's house—he is far too nice for that. It was an act of brutality, and Vetiver is too correct, too clean, too much of a hand-washer." Mr. Greenberg laid down his fork and lifted his glass.

"Well, who then?" Her straightforward question made him laugh.

"Now don't try to lure me into playing *that* game—you remember, my dear Lady Montfort, we have been told we mustn't chatter about what happened that night. Of course I am assuming *they* meant talking to people who were not present at Winston's birthday party, otherwise we would be guilty of doing something like breaking the Official Secrets Act." He took a contemplative sip from his glass. "No, I think some socialist got in through the dining-room window. Hermione should have hired a porter for the front door, a big brawny chap with a nice stout truncheon. A shame all around really. Lady Ryderwood's voice is superb and we were only treated to one song, and Miss Gaskell's playing was so simpatico."

Mr. Greenberg popped another oyster into his mouth, and said more to himself than to her, "Mmm . . . like kissing the sea on the lips." And Clementine, for the first time in years, blushed.

Chapter Seventeen

Clementine was feeling a little jaded, as she had drunk far too much champagne the night before and had come to the conclusion that getting into bed at three o'clock in the morning several nights in a row was regrettably a thing of the past. *Really, time spent in town is sometimes such hard work,* she thought crossly as she sipped black coffee with lots of sugar, in the hope of stilling her pounding head. *I almost wish I were returning to the country with Ralph.*

If she had not had quite so much champagne, the evening would have been perfect. Both Aaron Greenberg and Veda Ryderwood were wonderful company. Mr. Greenberg, a deft and witty raconteur, had kept them entertained with lively tales of his early banking days in Istanbul and Paris, his handsome head thrown back to laugh at his youthful naïveté at the hands of the world's most formidable banking sharks. And surprisingly Lady Ryderwood, in her own gentle, unassuming way, had recounted stories from her earlier life in the Balearics, of trips to Seville in Andalusia for the gypsy festivals.

With the onset of a headache that would accompany her day, Clementine remembered she had made a rash promise to ride with Lady Ryderwood the following morning and was beginning to regret the thought of getting on a strange horse and cantering up and down Rotten Row with possibly the entire Household Cavalry for company. *What could she have been thinking?* She looked across the room at the upright figure of her housekeeper, who had arrived with her coffee and was standing by the door with ill-concealed zeal as she waited for Clementine to begin their meeting.

Mrs. Jackson, alert and well rested, had the clear-eyed intensity of one who has enjoyed a full eight hours of untroubled sleep and is obviously brimming with information. *Let her go first then,* thought Clementine. She finished her coffee and nodded a world-weary head at her housekeeper. "Go on, Jackson, I can tell your visit to Kingsley House must have been a good one."

"Yes, it was indeed, m'lady, most informative. My visit was primarily with Matron, but I had an opportunity to talk to several of the boys." Here she looked down at her hands, and Clementine suspected that things with Matron had not gone smoothly. Mrs. Jackson rarely revealed her feelings, but in Clementine's considerable experience her housekeeper's rigid demeanor was easily translated into one of distaste.

"And what is Matron like?" Clementine encouraged her housekeeper to elucidate.

"She is a rather interesting individual, m'lady. The place is well run, but the boys are scared of her. At the end of my visit she was rather challenging, accused me of snooping, which of course I suppose I was. It was altogether rather unpleasant."

So that's it, thought Clementine, as she picked up on the faintest note of contempt in her housekeeper's voice. *Matron is a bully, a fault that Jackson finds unforgivable.*

"She was challenging, Jackson? Now that's interesting. So she is sensitive about people knowing what's going on in her bailiwick, is she? Do you think she was concealing something?"

"Perhaps a *little* overprotective, m'lady, but more usefully she is a gossip. She made it clear she believes that Miss Gaskell is out to catch a husband in Miss Kingsley's house and that she had set her sights on Sir Reginald. Who, as Matron made quite clear, was dedicated to his position as governor on the board of the charity and with no time for Miss Gaskell at all. But I was also able to confirm that the photograph under Miss Gaskell's pillow was indeed a likeness of Sir Reginald Cholmondeley, as there is a portrait of him hanging in the hall of Kingsley House."

She went on to fill Clementine in on her conversation with the candidate pages for the charity evening and her final conversation with Arthur Symes, winding up with a brief account of Matron's aggressiveness at what she perceived was Mrs. Jackson's unorthodox questions of the boys she had interviewed.

"And that's not all, m'lady. Almost as soon as I got back to Chester Square I was told Mr. Tricklebank had been taken off by the police, because he had lied about where he had been when Sir Reginald was murdered."

Suffering as she was from a liverish condition, Clementine was only mildly enthusiastic for her housekeeper's good work.

"Well done, Jackson, you are extraordinarily on top of things. I learned last night that Captain Vetiver remained in the dining room with Sir Reginald, with the door closed, and the butler outside so they might not be interrupted. Interesting, don't you think?" Her housekeeper acknowledged that indeed it was.

"And, I heard about Mr. Tricklebank's lie too. I wonder if he is under arrest? Let's talk about that in a moment, Jackson. Please sit and make yourself comfortable, so we can concentrate on all we have learned, and work out our next steps. It seems we have been awarded some possible suspects.

"So, Miss Gaskell with her unaccounted-for twenty minutes has put herself at the top of our list, and now this connection with Sir Reginald makes me very suspicious. What d'you think, Jackson?"

"I am not too sure about . . ."

"It appears she has a motive. She was dangling after an independent man, an ideal marriage prospect for her. He obviously reciprocated in some way; perhaps he gave her a photograph of himself, which she kept hidden. Right there a red flag is waving away at us. Then perhaps he decides Miss Gaskell is not an appropriate wife for a newly appointed peer and he backs away. He tells her as much on the evening of the party. She finds herself downstairs alone with him, they quarrel, and she kills him."

She turned to her housekeeper, who was watching her closely. The expression on Mrs. Jackson's face was quite neutral, but there was a decided frost in the air at her end of the room. *Jackson doesn't think it is Miss Gaskell.*

"Who else then, Jackson? Come on, tell me your theory, I can tell you have one." She laughed at her housekeeper's determination always to remain circumspect and never to thrust an opinion forward until she was good and sure of herself.

"Far be it for me to comment, m'lady, but I do not favor Miss Gaskell as the culprit. I agree she had the time and the opportunity. But I am not sure whether she is capable of murder. I find her to be timid, and the method of murder was so brutal . . ." She almost wrinkled her nose. "And required close physical proximity."

Mrs. Jackson went on to describe finding the torn photograph in Miss Gaskell's wastepaper basket. "If there had been an understanding between them, his death certainly crushed her hopes for the future, but I do not see her killing him in that way."

"He jilted her?" Clementine put in, and then she nodded encouragement for Mrs. Jackson to continue with her train of thought.

"He might not, m'lady. They might have planned to marry, which would explain her grief. If you saw Miss Gaskell at this moment, m'lady, I think you would agree that her behavior is one of despair, rather than fear that she might be caught as a murderess . . . it's just a feeling I have. She has been brought low by Sir Reginald's death."

Clementine decided that strong black coffee had only made her headache worse. "Right, Jackson, I'm with you so far. But don't let's forget: *hell hath no fury* . . . and all of that, and what about the photograph torn in two! If you are grieving for a lost fiancé you don't tear up the only image you have of him. Sir Reginald throws her to one side, and she kills him. As she lies in bed stricken with fear at being discovered, she takes the photograph of Sir Reginald out of the frame, tears it up, and throws it away."

"Yes, m'lady, if you say so, but she threw it in her wastepaper basket for the maids or anyone to discover. She could have thrown it on the fire . . ." Frost was gathering again.

"A good point. So she was angry with him for throwing her over, hence the torn photograph, but not bold or angry enough to kill him. But I think it is important we continue to discover more about her relationship with Sir Reginald.

"But didn't you say Matron told you that Adelaide was out for *any* of the men in the house. What about Mr. Tricklebank? Miss Kingsley is immensely rich and Mr. Tricklebank will inherit the lot, unless he misbehaves and his aunt leaves it all to the Chimney Sweep Boys. And that's been done before by elderly spinsters, think about all those well-endowed cats' homes in Surrey.

"So perhaps Miss Gaskell was involved with Mr. Tricklebank. Together they eliminated Sir Reginald to clear the way for Mr. Tricklebank to step into a plum position with the charity and an increased allowance from his aunt." Clementine felt a surge of energy overtake her precarious stomach.

"But Miss Gaskell did not have a photograph under her pillow of Mr. Tricklebank, m'lady. And I think Miss Kingsley would disinherit her nephew if he were to marry her paid companion. He is expected to marry Miss Wells-Thornton." Mrs. Jackson's tone was without emphasis, but she straightened in her chair, her back determinedly defending her position. And Clementine wisely rushed in to agree with her, mindful that she must be respectful of her housekeeper's opinion after she had so definitely asked for it. Mrs. Jackson's hunches had been spot-on in the past, she reminded herself.

"Let's concentrate on Mr. Tricklebank as a solo suspect, because of his lie. I wonder where he went after he left Chester Square. You said that he didn't get to his club until one o'clock. That leaves two full hours unaccounted for. Oh good heavens, I just remembered that the window in the dining room was unlocked, and I am wondering if it could have been unlocked by Mr. Tricklebank. I think Mr. Tricklebank might easily have returned to the house after he left, through the dining-room window. He is tall and quite athletic enough to stand on the portico balustrade by the front door and get onto the window ledge from there. He leaves the house with Jennifer Wells-Thornton, having said they are going on to another party. Off she goes, leaving him to reenter the house from the dining-room window, unnoticed."

Quite pleased with herself, Clementine got up and walked to the drawing-room window and looked out onto the street, trying to gauge the distance from the sill to the railings on the edge of the pavement, headache quite forgotten.

"Yes, the gap between the pavement and window sill is too far to breach, but not from the front door to the windowsill. Will you please check that, Jackson? Will you see if you can measure the distance from the portico balustrade to the windowsill at Chester Square and see if it's possible?" She turned from the window and looked down at the floor in concentration.

"Mr. Tricklebank was living above his means. If Sir Reginald was out of the way, he could step in to his place on the board, to a greater annuity from his aunt. I think we're onto something, Jackson, I really do! If you will check the dining-room windowsill in relationship to the front door, I will go further into the alibis of the other two men who were downstairs at the crucial time: Mr. Greenberg and Captain Vetiver. And you will hopefully find out where the servants were then, and keep tabs on Miss Gaskell. Is there anything else we should talk about, have we covered all points?"

"Yes, we have, m'lady." Clementine was relieved that Mrs. Jackson's enthusiasm had returned during the last few moments; she evidently approved of Mr. Tricklebank as the chief suspect. But now she noticed that her housekeeper was looking regretful, an expression she had become familiar with over the twenty years she had been in her service.

"There is something else I feel I must tell you, m'lady, and it's not about Chester Square. It's about Montfort House." Clementine experienced a sinking feeling and it wasn't from a hangover. "I am rather surprised that the new cook makes such elaborate meals for the servants. I know they are not hard-pressed in the kitchen, as you and his lordship have been dining out so often. But it's not right in my opinion for a cook to serve up Coquilles Saint Jacques for a servants'-hall supper, even if, as she says, they would have gone off and had to be thrown out. It seems an unsuitable way of doing things, to my mind. Blurs the lines of propriety and causes confusion."

Clementine closed her eyes. *On no*, she thought, *not after months of interviews and dissatisfactory meals prepared by talentless kitchen maids.* If there was one thing her husband would not forgive, it was bland and unappetizing food. In her mind she saw Montfort House up for lease, and that would never do.

"Well, Jackson, better keep an eye on things down there. Quite frankly, I am not too concerned if Cook is being a little overgenerous with our food. Lord Montfort thinks her cooking is superb and that's all I am concerned about for the time being. Did you speak to White and the footmen about helping out at Miss Kingsley's charity evening?"

"Yes, m'lady, he is happy to be of help."

"Good, and let's hope that we can sort out this Ginger business in a satisfactory way before we all go back to Iyntwood." She had thoughtlessly referred to the cook by her sobriquet and it was pounced on.

"'Ginger,' m'lady?" Mrs. Jackson's face for the first time in their many years together betrayed not just surprise but outrage.

"Yes, that's what she likes to be called. Didn't you know?"

"I most certainly did not, m'lady. I am genuinely shocked by such indecorous behavior."

"Pettigrew puts it down to her being a Londoner." Clementine wished she had not brought up the subject.

"The cook is from Lancashire, like myself, your ladyship. I can't imagine what she thinks she's playing at. 'Ginger' indeed."

Chapter Eighteen

It was a particularly fine early-winter morning; the sky was the palest of blues, a light frost spangled the grass, and the air smelled like freshly washed laundry. It was, thought Clementine as Herne drove her over to the Knightsbridge Barracks, a perfect day for a ride *and* the kind of weather that makes high-spirited horses friskier. She prayed the mount Lady Ryderwood had for her was well behaved and not some overwrought young mare that had not been out for days.

She need not have worried about the temperament of the horse she was given to ride. Lady Ryderwood was hardly the most athletic of women and her horses were calm and well trained. The dark bay, saddled and waiting for her, was a gentlemanly gelding kept for the sole purpose of providing a mount for any friend of Lady Ryderwood to accompany her early-morning rides.

Sir Francis Ryderwood must have had considerable clout with the Household Cavalry after his heroic participation in the Boer War, for his wife had miraculously secured stabling at the Knightsbridge Barracks for the year. Both horses were gleaming with health and the sort of grooming that could be achieved only by cavalry discipline: the tack was immaculate, bits and stirrup irons gleamed, and Clementine was reassured by the friendly young lance corporal of the Blues who helped them up onto their horses. And then off they went out into a bright winter sun, still low on the horizon, and turned left onto South Carriage Drive.

"What a wonderful idea, Lady Ryderwood, it's a perfect morning for a ride." Clementine relaxed as they walked their horses up the wide tree-lined avenue that led from Hyde Park corner toward Serpentine Road.

"How is Bellman for you, Lady Montfort? He's a nice steady boy, but I can tell he is quite ready for a little run."

"Then when Bellman and I have had an opportunity to get to know each other, let's give him one." Clementine leaned forward and smoothed her gloved hand down the arch of the gelding's neck.

"I haven't been out much in the past week," Lady Ryderwood continued. "But the trooper at the barracks is happy to exercise the horses, so they are not too skittish. Life in London can sometimes be demanding, and an early-morning ride stops me from feeling seedy when I have been spending too much time in drawing rooms and theatres."

Clementine noticed that Lady Ryderwood rode much as she had expected: she sat well on her horse, did not fidget, and had quiet hands, but she was certainly a passenger on a pretty little mare as delicate and beautifully mannered as her rider. *Someone has spent a lot of time training these animals,* thought Clementine, *and has done a good job of it indeed.*

"Did you ride much in Ibiza?" she asked.

"Yes, we did. My husband lived for his horses, he chose and trained both of these sweet-tempered beasts; I just accompanied him on short rambles. This little girl," she leaned forward and patted her mare's neck affectionately, "is part Connemara and a wonderful jumper, but I am afraid I am not an awfully courageous horsewoman."

"You were not lonely for society in Ibiza?" Clementine thought the cultured Lady Ryderwood far more suited to town life than to an outdoor life in the Mediterranean.

"I had my music, and my teacher would come and spend weeks with us in the summer. He found it restful after the fast pace of Milan." *She must mean her voice teacher,* thought Clementine.

"I was so disappointed that we only had one song from you the other evening, but that one was quite beautiful, you have a wonderful voice."

"Thank you." This was gravely said, without any trace of conceit or false modesty. "I wanted to sing professionally when I was younger, but of course it was out of the question, and then I met my husband . . ."

They rode on for a few moments in silence, the only sound was birdsong and the distant hum of traffic. *We could be in any country-house park,* thought Clementine, as she watched a fat gray squirrel drop its acorn and run for a tree at their approach.

"Lord Montfort told me of Captain Wildman-Lushington's terrible accident the other day," said Lady Ryderwood. Clementine knew it was unusual for her husband to pass on this kind of information to someone he barely knew. This indication that he already considered Lady Ryderwood to be "one of us" did not surprise her; Lady Ryderwood's unaffected manners and quiet dignity would appeal as much to her husband as they did to her.

"We heard the news quite quickly because our son is thinking of joining the Royal Navy Air Service. I am horrified that such a wonderfully bright and promising young man could have died so tragically." The murder of Sir Reginald had not moved Clementine quite as much as the loss of the younger man's life, she realized, and went on, more to herself than to her friend, "Flying is such an awfully dangerous business, but Harry's enthusiasm knows no bounds ever since he spent a summer with his friend Tom Sopwith, who designs and makes these wretched contraptions."

"It is the way of young men, to take risks." Lady Ryderwood made this statement quite matter-of-factly. "It is in their nature."

"Yes of course, but I don't understand the merit of flight. We already move at breakneck speed in our motorcars and trains. Flying seems to me an impractical and quite useless innovation." She turned to look at the young woman riding beside her. "They never seem to be able to get the wretched things down safely, once they have achieved the business of being up there."

"I have no children, but it must be troubling to believe one's child is in danger."

Clementine looked ahead. She was not sure she wanted to discuss her fears with someone she had known only a couple of weeks, and she rarely brought up her concerns with Harry's flying to her close friends.

"Have you ever been up, Lady Montfort?"

Clementine was so startled by this unusual suggestion that she blurted, "No, nor do I ever want to," far more sharply than she intended.

"Neither have I, but I understand it to be the most wonderful experience to fly over the country toward far horizons and view our world from above; godlike, almost. Unimaginably exciting to see the edge of a city as you fly towards it and moments later look down on its rooftops and buildings, and watch people moving below you in the streets. I can't imagine anything more joyous."

Clementine was about to harrumph, but her natural consideration stopped her. She had never allowed herself to play with the idea of flight as joyful. She had been far too busy thinking the worst, since that was what was reported in newspapers.

"I never for one moment imagined that it would be a particularly pleasing experience. I find it hard to look out from the top of a tall building, it makes me dizzy and fearful." She loathed high places, they filled her with anxiety.

"Yes, I am the same way" Veda Ryderwood agreed. "But I understand that flying is a different sensation altogether; there is an absence of vertigo because the aeroplane is one with the air, you see. It must be such a freeing experience." This last was said in a quiet voice, and there was sadness here, Clementine realized.

Poor thing, she thought, *finding herself widowed so unexpectedly and so young has made changes in her life that must be hard to adjust to.* It occurred to Clementine that perhaps Harry's love of flight made him feel less hemmed in by expected duty to a large estate in an age when it was more of a burden than the pleasure it had been for his forebears.

"I think my son might love that most about flying," she said. "Liberation from the must-dos of life, and the burdens of our earthbound existence, I had not thought of it that way." She turned in her saddle and found Lady Ryderwood ambling along on her horse and smiling at her with such kind understanding that it was almost too close, too intimate for her.

"Canter?" she asked, and then a little later, when the horses politely responded with a restrained push forward, she glanced back to see that Lady Ryderwood had fallen behind and had returned to a more gentle pace. Clementine urged the gelding to pick up the pace, knowing Bellman needed the exercise. She galloped on to the end of the drive, turned, and came back to find her friend decorously trotting up the track toward her. She waved her hand as she drew alongside Clementine.

"Well, Bellman thoroughly enjoyed that. I think he believes he has just won the Derby!" Lady Ryderwood exclaimed. "You ride well, Lady Montfort; I wish I had so secure a seat."

They rode toward the barracks in silence. Clementine's gallop had soothed her fretful mind and she relaxed in the loveliness of the morning. As they came down toward Hyde Park Corner they saw that other riders were now out, all trotting or walking their horses in the correct way of riding in the Row; only occasionally would a pair break into a sedate canter. She called out a good-morning to a few acquaintances. She waved to Lady Marchmaine, who was out with her two daughters on their ponies, and confirmed a luncheon engagement for next week with another old friend. And on they went.

Clementine looked across at the young woman riding next to her. Her face showed nothing as she gazed tranquilly ahead, but perhaps sensing that she might have intruded, she turned her head and caught Clementine's eye.

"I hope I did not offend you, Lady Montfort, about the flying I mean. I would be furious with myself if I had."

Clementine hastily assured her that she was not upset. Privately, she had been initially irritated at what she felt was rather an intrusion, but Lady Ryderwood had sought only to pose an understandable reason for her son's daredevil interests.

"I am grateful to you; it had never occurred to me to think of flying as an enjoyable experience. Great heavens," she said, laughing, "you might even talk me into going up."

"If you decide to do that, please let me know and I will come with you. After all, if your son is actively involved at Sopwith, you have all the opportunity in the world!" And they both laughed as their horses pushed forward into an eager trot back to their stables and oats. Clementine decided that she was pleased indeed to have met this young woman.

They returned to the Knightsbridge Barracks as a splendid dark-bay stallion was being led out of the covered riding arena toward the stalls where Lady Ryderwood's horses were kept. He was superbly muscled and had a strong, arched neck and large eyes bright with intelligence. He had obviously been put through his paces by the young cavalry officer who was leading him, as the veins were standing out on his glossy skin, but he was barely winded, unlike the young man perspiring at his side and almost running to keep up with him.

"What a beautiful animal." Clementine quickly got out of the way, as the horse was dancing sideways on the spot, nostrils flared, hooves striking the cobbles, filling the courtyard with his immense size. He was being led with a stud chain across his nose but was still trying to throw his head in the air as a prelude to a full rear, and the young officer leading him had to jerk smartly downward on the lead rein.

"Whoa there, Lochinvar, behave yourself." The officer's voice was firm and the horse steadied and dropped his head. Sensing that he had settled, Clementine walked forward, lifted her hands, and cupped them below the horse's chin. The horse immediately lowered his massive head and snorted fiercely into her palms, searching for a treat. "What is he?" She was enchanted by his size and power and, now that he was calm, by the gentleness of his lips searching in her hands.

The young officer looked over at Lady Ryderwood, who said nothing, so he answered, "He's a Hanoverian: intelligent, strong, hardworking, and lovely to look at. He was a good boy today, I think you'll be pleased with him." He looked over at Lady Ryderwood, who nodded and moved to one side, indicating with her hand that he should continue on. As Clementine watched the horse and its rider walk on, she thought there was something superbly majestic about the horse's gait, as he moved forward effortlessly and with incredible lightness for his size.

"Your horse, Lady Ryderwood? What a beauty!" The mettlesome animal seemed not to fit with this dainty little creature standing there holding the reins of her docile gray mare, this walker and trotter of placid, perfectly trained horses, who might find the courage to follow the hunt at a sedate pace when she came down to join them at Iyntwood.

"Lochi belonged to my husband; he was a two-year-old when he bought him. He is a superbly athletic animal, but he has an opinion as you can see. I'm lucky the young officer enjoys riding him, as he is far too much horse for me. I should let him go, but I can't bring myself to sell him. Francis loved him so much." She turned to the stable lad and handed over the reins of her mare.

How sad that would be, thought Clementine. *I would never let Ralph's horses go to someone else.* "I hope you don't sell him, Lady Ryderwood, he is quite splendid, and thank you for inviting me to ride with you. I needed to blow away the cobwebs, after the terrible thing that happened at Hermione's party." Lady Ryderwood hesitated, and then with a slight frown on her face said, "It was quite a tragedy, Lady Montfort. I have been quite unable to sleep since that evening. What an awful business . . . and how particularly distressing for you to have been the one to . . ." She shook her head, finding herself unable to continue.

"Yes, I am still struggling to make sense of it . . ." Clementine was careful not to rush to a question. "The whole evening has become so confused in my memory. All that hubbub with Marigold's dress, I remember talking to you about the opera house, do you remember if . . ."

"Ah yes, I do remember, and then Sir Henry arrived and we talked about hunting. I was so delighted when Lord Montfort invited me to Iyntwood for your Boxing Day hunt, the other evening. Mr. Churchill says the Wingley hunt takes in some wonderful country. Perhaps I will see the Churchills there when I visit?" Clementine, who had been ready with another question about the Marigold Meriwether moment, almost laughed at the idea of her husband welcoming Winston to join his beloved hunt on Boxing Day, and was spared having to answer her by Herne opening the door of motorcar.

"Can I drive you somewhere, Lady Ryderwood? Perhaps we can drop you at your house?" she said quickly, before there was any more regrettable talk about Mr. Churchill swanning down to Iyntwood to join Lord Montfort for a few days in the country.

"Thank you, Lady Montfort, how very kind of you." And then when they were settled in the back of the Daimler, Lady Ryder-wood laid a gentle hand on her arm and said, "I can't imagine how frightful it was for you, Lady Montfort, finding the poor man like that. I admire your composure. Mr. Churchill told me that Inspector Hillary is one of Scotland Yard's ablest men—one of their top men in fact. He fully expects everything will be sewn up by the end of the week, especially if we cooperate by not discussing what happened." Leaving Clementine with no possible opportunity to ask any further questions.

One of Scotland's Yard's top men? thought Clementine rather bleakly. *Yes, that is* exactly *what we were told last time.*

Chapter Nineteen

Mrs. Jackson's morning had started with a surprise. She was awakened by a light tap on her door, when the second housemaid arrived with her morning cup of tea. As she struggled to wakefulness—it was seven o'clock and time she was dressed—she reached for a bracing cup of tea to help her focus. And there on the tray was a letter.

She recognized the distinctive writing in the address immediately, as it had adorned countless notes to her ladyship with lists of plantings for the sunken garden at Iyntwood. But it was the last thing in the world she expected to see on the envelope lying innocuously on her breakfast tray, and the sight of it did more to stir her senses than her first sip of strong Darjeeling. She felt herself blush with delighted disbelief that Mr. Stafford had written to her, and then, circumspect as always, she gave herself a moment to collect her thoughts and govern her reactions, and in that time found she was almost reluctant to open the letter.

Mrs. Jackson did not believe in racing into friendships of any kind. Her acquaintance with Mr. Stafford had been a long time in growing from its initial polite exchange on flowers for the house. It had reached the stage, this summer, of an occasional "dropping in" at Mr. Stafford's cottage in the village, always at *his* invitation, to admire the vivid array of plantings he toiled over in his back garden. Ernest Stafford was a sociable man; he was well thought of in the village and on the estate, highly regarded by Lord Montfort, respected and referred to by her ladyship, and positively revered by Mr. Thrower and his battalion of undergardeners. With all this popularity it was sometimes puzzling that he purposefully sought her company, she thought, as she regarded his unopened letter with mounting apprehension.

She turned the envelope over in her hands as if hoping to divine its contents without actually having to read them. Annoyed with herself for being a ninny about a little thing like a letter, she picked up her butter knife and slid it through the top of the envelope and pulled out the half sheet that it contained, a piece of drawing paper from the pad Mr. Stafford carried at all times to make quick sketches of his garden-design ideas. She transferred her annoyance from herself to Mr. Stafford. *Why didn't he use proper letter paper, for heaven's sake?*

Dear Mrs. Jackson,
Mr. Hollyoak told me that you had been called up to
Montfort House and I hope you are enjoying city life as a
change from the bitter northeasterlies we have had here
for the past two days. [A conventional enough beginning, a weather report was always acceptable in an opening paragraph; she breathed a little easier.]
I am up to London on Monday the 6th inst. to visit
David Prain at Kew. I don't know if you have visited the
gardens at Kew, but I thought you might enjoy the Palm
House and the Waterlily House, both lovely spots on a
winter's day.
Please drop me a line and let me know if this is
something you would enjoy. I can easily meet you at 11
o'clock at Kew Bridge Railway Station (there are plenty of
trains leaving from Waterloo but the 10:35 will have you

there by 11). Perhaps we might even have time for a chop
at the Lamb and Flag before our visit to the gardens.
    Yrs. Respect'lly
    Ernest Stafford

The sixth? That would be the day after the charity event; she would certainly be free to accept—if she chose to do so. But would it be a good idea? She was still a little unsure about Mr. Stafford, for he had a way of being perhaps a bit too outright at times. Not that she didn't appreciate his open and informal ways, now that she was used to them. She was almost resolved to reply immediately, to thank him and say no. But something made her put the letter carefully back in its envelope and set it inside the book she was reading. She would think it over and then decide. It did not do to rush things.

Grateful for the distractions of her working day, Mrs. Jackson was dressed and pinning up her hair within thirty minutes of the letter's arrival. She went about her morning routine at Chester House with her customary efficiency, giving considered and intentionally focused thought to *everything* she did, but thoughts of the letter and its invitation intruded on her day more often than she welcomed.

She was grateful for the distraction of recalling what she could of Mr. Tricklebank, whom she had seen only once, on her second day at Chester Square. He was a tall man in his late twenties, of light build, with a slightly round-shouldered stoop and soft, fair hair. She had been on her way to the library to make use of the telephone and noticed Mr. Jenkins helping Mr. Tricklebank into his topcoat. The younger man had turned for his hat and cane as he chatted pleasantly with the butler, leaning casually on his stick as he waited for Mrs. Jenkins to open the front door. Then with a neat twirl of his wrist he set his silk top hat at an angle on his head, lifted his cane to rest lightly on his right shoulder, and sauntered down the steps from the front door to the pavement. With a parting wave of his hand to Jenkins, he turned to walk up the street, and Mrs. Jackson had moved on to the library, thinking only that Mr. Tricklebank's manners were rather pleasant toward the older man.

But Mr. Tricklebank's awkward lie to the police and to his aunt had made him Lady Montfort's suspect, and after their discussion the other morning, Mrs. Jackson wondered if perhaps their investigation would be short-lived; it might not be long before the police made a full arrest. But surely a vicious murder in the house of his aunt with a salon full of guests upstairs was the last thing a gadfly like Mr. Tricklebank would be capable of, with his harmless empty chatter and the mild and unremarkable air of the seasoned idler. Mrs. Jackson had sensed that Mr. Tricklebank had all the vacuity of a tailor's dummy, and was far more likely to wait hopefully on the expectations of a healthy inheritance than actively to employ ruthless methods to gain it earlier. Surely the Mr. Tricklebanks of this world meekly married their aunt's choice of bride, collected their reward for doing so in a substantial inheritance, and then spent the rest of their lives at one of their many gentlemen's clubs.

On the other hand, Mrs. Jackson did not particularly fancy Miss Gaskell as a favorite suspect either. The more she found out about the young companion, the more she saw her as a victim of circumstance, and certainly not strong-willed or passionate enough to change the events of her life by violent methods. *But the facts*, Mrs. Jackson thought as she mentally traced Miss Gaskell's steps on the night of the murder, *must be established*. And the fact that the butler had been standing sentinel in the hall outside the dining-room door after dinner did not mean that Miss Gaskell could not have entered the room without his knowledge. Mr. Jenkins's memory was demonstrably unreliable, even if his commitment to duty was steadfast. And the photograph under Miss Gaskell's pillow was significant, as was its later appearance in the wastepaper basket; even more so in light of Matron's unkind gossip.

And what about the unlocked but closed window in the dining room—how did one account for that? She might, of course, put it down to another vague eccentricity on Mr. Jenkins's part, as he forgetfully caused quite a few small incidences of chaos in the course of his working day. But Mrs. Jackson was a woman renowned for her methodical thoroughness and she discarded the idea as sloppy thinking. Mr. Jenkins was absentminded, not irrational. This troubling little detail of the unlocked window pointing to Sir Reginald's killer having come in through the dining-room window did not weigh in Mr. Tricklebank's favor. Perhaps it had been made to look that way?

And it was with this thought in mind that she let herself out of the main entrance to the house at Chester Square, leaving the front door slightly ajar with the doors to the inner hall closed.

It was still bitterly cold outside and she was grateful for the protection of the portico, which projected from the face of the house, supported by four tall pillars with a low wall on each side surmounted by an ornate balustrade. With her back to the front door, Mrs. Jackson put her hands on the balustrade of the left-side wall and leaned over to gaze down into the belowstairs area a floor below. She had a straight line of sight to the steps leading down to the area from the gated entrance on the pavement. If she leaned out and craned down she could just about see the entrance door to the servants' hall underneath the portico.

She straightened up, turned, and, still with her back to the front door, faced the street. There were three wide stone steps down onto the pavement of Chester Square. Marching in a solid line, left and right, protecting the area below them from the pavement, were the ubiquitous, handsome black iron railings each surmounted by a finial spike, which formed such a feature of

Belgravia's smart, terraced mansions. If she turned her head to the right she could see the two other houses that adjoined Miss Kingsley's house stretching away to the corner, and to her left, since Miss Kingsley's house was on the corner of the terrace at the top of Chester Square, she could just see the beginning of tree-lined Chester Walk as it intersected with the square.

The distance between the railed edge of the pavement and the facade of the house was too great to span without the use of a ladder laid horizontally. She turned back to the left-side wall of the portico and gazed across at the windows on the ground floor of the house. There were three of them equally spaced apart, the window for the hall and then two dining-room windows. If Mr. Tricklebank was tall enough, which he was, and athletic enough, which he might be, he could step from the balustrade across quite a terrifying gap, since the area was easily twelve feet below, and make it safely to the first wide stone sill of the hall window. The sill was certainly wide enough for a man to stand on. Then with good balance and long legs he might sidestep from there onto the sill of the first of the pair of dining-room windows; it would be a stretch but quite possible. Anyone doing so would have to be reasonably fit, she thought as she looked at the distance and wondered whether Mr. Tricklebank was foolish or desperate enough to try this stunt on an icy winter night.

She stood there in the frigid morning air, her arms folded tightly across her chest as she took stock of the front of the house and its surroundings, and when she had committed all possibilities to memory she turned and went back inside.

Rubbing her hands up and down the outsides of her upper arms, she walked across the hall toward the back stairs. Matron had said that Miss Gaskell had put herself forward to be interesting to any man in the house. Maybe Miss Gaskell had unlocked the window so that Mr. Tricklebank could reenter the house and kill Sir Reginald. But surely if this unlikely pair had designs on the old lady's money they would have eliminated Miss Kingsley and not Sir Reginald.

Still shivering with cold, she hurried to the little between-stairs office, where she sat down at the desk and considered the possibility of Miss Gaskell as accomplice to Mr. Tricklebank, or directly in her own interests. But she got only so far before she decided it was time to cast around for further information, so she got up and went downstairs to the servants' hall.

"Martha, would you ask the kitchen maid to make some tea, and do you have time to take a cup with me?" she asked the first housemaid, who was standing over the table, mechanically turning the pages of the daily newspaper and barely reading what she saw before her. Of course Martha had the time for tea. Miss Kingsley was in her room, Miss Gaskell in hers, both of them undoubtedly picking through a light luncheon served to them on a tray. The servants dusted immaculate furniture, swept carpets that had not been trodden on, polished untarnished silver, rearranged the china cupboard, and argued over who was to take trays to the two ladies languishing in their bedrooms upstairs. After which they sat around the table in the servants' hall and drank endless cups of tea.

As they waited for the kettle to boil, Mrs. Jackson went through Martha's household duties for the charity evening. She purposely flattered Martha by asking her advice on table linen for the charity event, and when she felt thoroughly disgusted with herself for being smarmy she dexterously turned the conversation to Miss Gaskell.

"I am rather hoping Miss Gaskell will be well enough to come down tomorrow and take care of the last-minute details for the charity evening. I think it will help restore her to everyday life."

"Yes, that would be nice, but I doubt it." Martha, standing over the table, poured hot water into the teapot, covered it with a garish woolly tea cozy, and rattled two cups and saucers, the milk jug, and the sugar bowl onto the table in front of them.

"She still seems so low, depressed I would almost call it," Mrs. Jackson observed as they both stared into their empty cups, waiting for their tea to brew.

"You can say that again," said Martha, her plain face wrinkled up in scorn.

"'Grieving' I would have said, almost as if she was a part of Sir Reginald's family." Mrs. Jackson did not look up, as she did not want to see Martha's derision at her impudent suggestion.

Martha made an impatient movement of dismissal with the sugar tongs, snorted more disapproval, and asked her if she would be mother. Mrs. Jackson obediently poured tea.

"Well I am sure she worked with him on the charity, and no doubt he was rather like a father figure to her." Mrs. Jackson, dismayed at how Machiavellian she was being, felt like a spy. She hoped Martha needed an outlet from the imposed silence of the past few days and would welcome a confidante who was not part of the Kingsley family. She was rewarded.

"A father figure, my *foot*, Mrs. Jackson." Pushed beyond patience, Martha was compelled to set the record straight. "She wasn't looking for a father, not that one, a husband more like."

"Oh, there was an understanding between them?" Mrs. Jackson put down her teacup and turned to face Martha, her eyes wide with polite surprise.

"Well I don't know about *between them,* but there were certainly hopes on Miss Gaskell's part." Martha crossed her arms under her bosom in judgment and sank her chin down onto her neck as she pondered Miss Gaskell's improper optimism. "Not that we repeat that sort of thing, you understand?"

She cast an inquiring glance at Mrs. Jackson, who obediently said, "No, of course not. Poor young thing, to have her hopes dashed in such a sad way," in what she hoped was a spinster's voice forever commiserating with the lovelorn.

Another snort erupted from Martha. "Poor young thing, my *eye,* she's a scheming piece of work. Oh, the times I've heard that sweet voice cooing agreement as she sits down to play the pianoforte for Sir Reginald and Miss Kingsley of an evening, with that soppy, simpering expression on her face. Pure treacle she was. And then you catch her—always watchful, careful not to displease. Furtive, I call it. She was a right sly little madam. There, now I've said it." She paused. "And I'm not sorry for it neither."

Matron's gossip confirmed, Mrs. Jackson took it a step further. Hoping to discover if Martha suspected tender feelings between Mr. Tricklebank and Miss Gaskell, she decided to come right out and ask it. Martha's reply was quite definite.

"Oh good lord no, Mrs. Jackson, certainly not! If Miss Kingsley thought Mr. Tricklebank was romantically interested in her paid companion she would have sent Miss Gaskell packing immediately. No, Mr. Tricklebank is a lovely, kind gentleman, he may not be the brightest, but he's not *that* stupid. His purpose is to marry Miss Wells-Thornton and face up to his responsibilities to the charity, and I am quite sure Miss Gaskell understands that and wouldn't waste her time. And if I know Miss Kingsley, that is exactly what will happen. Mr. Tricklebank will marry Miss Wells-Thornton, just you wait and see."

She was interrupted by the first footman, John, as he came clattering down the back stairs.

"Where's James?" he asked, looking around for the Clumsy Footman.

"Polishing in the silver pantry and 'e's put a bloomin' great dent in the silver punch bowl; there'll be 'ell to pay when Mr. Jenkins finds out." Martha's dropped aitches were an indication of her embarrassment at being caught gossiping about the Kingsley family.

It seemed as if the second footman's job was continually to displease, thought Mrs. Jackson. He had had his pay docked twice for breakages, and still he managed to do something slipshod or hurried, attracting criticism and more exasperation from his fellow workers. She felt almost sorry for the pale young man who silently went about his work under a continual deluge of criticism.

"Send Eliza to look for him, he's probably having a smoke in the area, and for heaven's sake find Mr. Jenkins, because that policeman is here again." John swiftly ran a comb through his hair, put it back into the inside pocket of the coat, and turned to run back upstairs.

"Is he here to see Miss Kingsley?" Martha asked, getting to her feet. "Because she is having an after-luncheon rest, and shan't be disturbed. He'll have to come back."

"No, not for Miss Kingsley, he wants to speak to James, and it's not the inspector, it's his sergeant."

"He'll have to come down here and talk to him. Mr. Jenkins doesn't want the staff interviewed in the drawing rooms, so show him down." But John was already bounding up the stairs.

And as Mrs. Jackson was wondering why the police wanted to talk to the Clumsy Footman, Detective Sergeant Wilkins of the Metropolitan Police came ponderously into the servants' hall and stood before them, a short, stout man with an overly large head and shrewd eyes. He immediately noticed Mrs. Jackson.

"The Mrs. Jackson who works for Lady Montfort, isn't it?" His eye flicked over her. "How kind of her ladyship to offer your services to the household; I am sure Miss Gaskell is still far from well." Everything he said and how he said it implied disbelief and suspicion. He didn't wait for her reply but turned swiftly to Mr. Jenkins as he came down the corridor from the back stairs.

"Ah, Mr. Jenkins, good afternoon. I am afraid I must ask you, or your first footman, to come down to the city mortuary with me, because we think we might have found your previous first footman, a Mr. Leonard Crutchley."

There was a series of exclamations from all the servants, who had crowded into the servants' hall the moment they heard that a policeman was belowstairs. Kitchen maids drying their hands on tea towels cried out with shock, and Eliza, who had come downstairs with a bucket and mop, let them drop to the tiled floor with a crash, threw her apron up over her head, and burst into tears. *Evidently Mr. Crutchley was popular among the female servants.*

He did that on purpose, thought Mrs. Jackson; *he wanted to see their reactions. The police always do that, take people by surprise and shock them into betraying some emotion or blurting something out.*

The sergeant, pleased at the uproar he had caused, waited for it to die down before he started another one.

"The other person I want to see is your new footman, your second footman, working name of James, real name Eddy Porter— like to have a word with this young man first off." The sergeant's manner was genial, as if he anticipated a pleasant, informal chat with clumsy Eddy Porter.

Eliza piped up, "I think James is cleaning shoes in the scullery. I'll go and find him if you like."

"Yes, Eliza, if you would, please," Martha said, quickly giving her permission before she was upstaged by the policeman. "When you say 'mortuary' you mean that Len is dead, don't you, Sergeant?" She continued, not put off by the repressive look he gave her, "I mean you said 'mortuary,' so of course you think you have found the body of Mr. Crutchley. I am right, aren't I?"

The policeman ignored her and turned to Eliza, who had come back from a quick tour of all the rooms belowstairs.

"He's not down here. And he's not outside having a cigarette.

Do you want me to run over to the mews, Martha, and see if he's taking a break with Macleod?"

Martha nodded, "Yes, and please be quick about it, Eliza. The sergeant wants a word with him and we don't want to keep him waiting here too long." But when Eliza came back and said that James was not at the mews, and after she and John had searched through the house, they came back to report that James was nowhere to be found.

"His uniform is hanging up in his room, and his personal things have gone," said John, looking guilty, as if he had helped spirit the other man away.

"Then he's scarpered," said Martha. She turned to the policeman. "Don't s'pose you have another footman lying around in your mortuary then, Sergeant?"

The sergeant unbuttoned the top right breast pocket of his uniform jacket and pulled out a small notebook and a lead pencil.

"So you think it's Leonard Crutchley then?" Martha persisted. She was not going to give up, Mrs. Jackson thought with admiration.

"We have to have a formal identification first of all, miss, but certainly the man we have at the mortuary is a footman. He is wearing livery and it is exactly the same livery as the one this gentleman has on here." He glanced at John and then past him toward the butler.

"Mr. Jenkins, shall I take John here along with me for identification purposes?" The policeman was correct in assessing that the elderly man was going to slow his day down considerably, as the butler was holding out his waistcoat watch to show it was certainly not the correct time of day to identify bodies.

Mrs. Jackson was quite distressed for Mr. Jenkins. His direction of the servants seemed to grow more tenuous each day and she was growing accustomed to finding him gazing vacantly out a window in one of the many rooms in the house. At her approach hc would turn to her with a look of such frightened surprise that she was reminded of the White Rabbit in *Alice in Wonderland*. When she stated her reason for interrupting his reverie, he would pull out his waistcoat watch and without even looking at it say, "Really, my dear young lady, that's impossible, I believe I would have remembered." It sometimes took all her restraint not to reply, *Why, sometimes I've believed as many as six impossible things before breakfast,* a perception that she thought was not too wide off the mark.

Then, to Mrs. Jackson's relief, Mr. Jenkins pulled himself together.

"Absolutely not, Sergeant, I will accompany you myself. John, my overcoat, gloves, and bowler if you please, and while I am gone please make sure that Miss Kingsley is not troubled in any way. Now then, Sergeant, I am ready. And we will use the servants' entrance on our way out, and perhaps you would kindly remember to use that door when you come to this house next time." And correctly attired for cold weather, the elderly butler led the way to the area door.

Chapter Twenty

The servants sat on in the Chester Square servants' hall as they waited for Mr. Jenkins's return. John was sent up to retrieve luncheon trays. He returned and they ate their dinner in silence. Mrs. Jackson picked her way through an insipid mutton stew and idly wondered what delicacy had been served up in the servants' hall at Montfort House. *It certainly wouldn't be anything as bland and tasteless as this mess,* she thought, pushing aside a half-cooked dumpling and eating around watery, over-boiled cabbage. Now that they were gathered together, the tight-lipped silence among the Kingsley servants, which had prevailed when she first arrived in the house, returned. When Eliza's distress abated enough for her to ask through a stuffed nose what could have happened to the new footman Eddy Porter, Martha turned such a frowning look on her that she lowered her eyes and returned to her weighty treacle pudding and lumpy custard.

Mrs. Jackson decided that the moment Mr. Jenkins came back to the house and she knew whether he had been able to identify Leonard Crutchley's body, she would call it a day and return to Montfort House. She hoped that Mr. Jenkins had his wits about him, because livery alone would not be enough to identify a body that had been in the Thames for four or five days.

The kitchen maids cleared the table; their noisy chatter over the sound of running water and the clatter of pots and pans that accompanied washing up seemed even louder amid the expectant silence in the servants' hall as they waited on. John left for a cigarette in the area outside the servants' entrance, and Martha instructed Eliza to make tea. The racket in the scullery came to an end, and the kitchen maids came back into the room looking apologetic and sat down with them.

And finally the area door opened and slammed shut. Mr. Jenkins had returned. Every one of the servants stood up as he came into the servants' hall, but none of them spoke. Mrs. Jackson thought it said a great deal for their respect that they waited for the butler to speak first. His trip to the mortuary had obviously been harrowing: his face was gray and pinched with cold, and there was a look of miserable despair about him. If they all hoped to be informed whether he had been able to make an identification, they were to be disappointed. Mr. Jenkins nodded to them briefly and without saying a word walked down the corridor to his pantry and closed the door.

"Oh good Lord, it was Len," said Martha, and she put her large hands over her face. "What is the world coming to? This will be too much for Mr. Jenkins, I know it will."

"Make some tea for Mr. Jenkins please, Eliza," Mrs. Jackson said as she got to her feet and prepared to follow the butler. And to the cook who had poked her head out of her kitchen door: "Cook, will you arrange for someone to cut some sandwiches as quickly as you can, unless you have something hot and nourishing on hand, like soup. The chicken soup from upstairs luncheon will do perfectly. If there is any left, I will take it in to Mr. Jenkins." Mrs. Jackson wasn't going to have any more of this pact of silence and closed doors; she was far from being an impatient woman but she had no intention of waiting around for a couple of days for what had happened at the mortuary to reveal itself. She did not catch anyone's eye because she felt the looks that were being given one to another among them at her having instructed the cook to serve the butler soup made for Miss Kingsley. *Too bad if they don't like it*, she said to herself. *I'm not leaving here until I know, and that poor old man needs something a bit better than dreary reheated mutton stew inside him.*

When a tray was produced with a large bowl of soup, sandwiches, and a pot of tea, she carried it through to the butler's pantry to find Mr. Jenkins sitting at his desk, still wearing his bowler and scarf, his topcoat thrown carelessly aside over a chair.

Violent death had come to Chester Square not once but twice, and the stress was taking its toll on the elderly members of the household. Miss Kingsley was still shut up in her room and was not at home to anyone who called. Her butler, who after the death of Sir Reginald had been visibly fraying around the edges, after identifying the murdered body of his comrade was beginning to unravel.

It was distressing to see him sitting at his desk cautiously sipping a tiny glass of whiskey. Offering a cup of hot sweet tea seemed inadequate and silly at a moment like this. Mrs. Jackson cleared a space on the desk and quickly laid out a napkin and a spoon. Then she placed a bowl of fragrant chicken soup in front of him and a small plate of sandwiches next to the bowl.

"You've missed your midday dinner, Mr. Jenkins, so here, take a bite of sandwich and then eat some soup." And with that she sat down and waited. Severe shock often increased the appetite and she knew she must be patient and wait for him to eat.

He barely acknowledged her, but to her relief he took a tentative bite of his sandwich, grunted, and took a larger bite. He chewed voraciously and sipped his whiskey, and when he had finished that he picked up his spoon and started to eat the soup, taking an occasional bite of sandwich. Mrs. Jackson saw a little color return to a face that had been the color of putty.

"You may take the tea away, Mrs. Jackson," he said as she moved toward the tray. "I don't want any of that slop today." And he poured himself another whiskey. And still Mrs. Jackson said nothing.

"They always forget to put mustard on the ham," was his assessment of his sandwiches as he finished them off, and poured a third whiskey.

Mrs. Jackson judged that now was the time, before he finished off his glass.

"Were you able to make an identification of the man at the mortuary, Mr. Jenkins?" she asked.

"Yes, Mrs. Jackson, I was. It was difficult because the body had been in the water for several days; he had been washed downriver to Tilbury. He was found last night . . . poor lad."

"So it was Mr. Crutchley, was it?"

"Yes, it was Len, it was undoubtedly Len." His voice sank low and for the first time he allowed himself to express a little of the emotion he felt. "That boy had worked for me for ten years, from hall boy to second footman and on up. I trained him myself. He was only twenty-four."

Mrs. Jackson saw his sorrowing face and knew how terrible it must have been to identify the body of someone who had been part of the old man's family. *Those who work for us always become like our own,* she thought, as she remembered the housemaids she had trained, the cooks she had befriended, and the footmen who had come and gone in her life over the years. But however much she empathized with the tired, saddened old man sitting across the desk from her, grieving over the loss of someone whom he had been fond of, she had to know more.

"You say he was in the river; had he drowned?"

"No, not drowned. The police say he was dead when he went into the Thames. He had been hit over the head and his body thrown into the river. Thrown there like rubbish." Mr. Jenkins's hands shook and he finally looked up at her.

"He was murdered, Mrs. Jackson, waylaid on his way back to the house from running an errand, knocked out cold, robbed, and thrown away. And I thought, God forgive me, that he had run off. He was a straightforward, law-abiding lad with no vices. He worked hard, he was respectful to those he worked with, and a good son to his mother. I was training him up to take over my job when I retired. And I thought he had just run off. I never dreamt . . ." His voice trailed off and he stared across his desk at her, looking for reassurance that the world he knew was not crumbling away. But she had nothing to offer, so she nodded her reassurance that the shock would wear off and in time he would accept this loss. Then she noticed that his pale, watery eyes were losing focus, he was withdrawing into himself. The events of the last few days had been too much, this second murder had come as a terrible blow, and unable to find his equilibrium, he was staggering, reeling at the loss of a young man he had cared about.

Mrs. Jackson got up from her chair and walked around the desk. She took the glass from his hand, as whiskey couldn't help him now. She gently removed his bowler hat from his head, and he was hardly aware that she did so. She put a comforting arm around his shoulders. How long she stood there she didn't know, but after a while she rang for John. She met him outside the butler's pantry and told him to help the old man to bed.

"Light a fire in his room and keep him warm, on no account must he get cold. If you can, it would be a good idea to sit with him through the night, or at least check up on him, he has had a terrible shock. And yes," she answered his look of silent inquiry, "yes, it was Leonard Crutchley. Murdered. And now I want you to tell me something, John. Be quite straightforward about your answer, please."

She left Chester Square twenty minutes later, coat buttoned up tightly to her neck, her scarf wrapped up to her ears and her hat pulled down low over her brows. She walked rapidly and all the way she thought of nothing at all, she was aware only of her steps ringing out on the hard pavement and her breath clouding the air as she walked. It took her exactly fifteen minutes before she ran lightly down the area steps and through the scullery door into the servants' hall of Montfort House.

There was the usual clamor belowstairs at Montfort House, but after the repressive atmosphere at Chester Square, Mrs. Jackson welcomed the relaxed gaiety of the group. The second footman lowered his voice the moment she walked through the door, and the pretty little housemaid stopped talking in midsentence as she took her place at the table. Mrs. Jackson felt quite sad that she was the reason for their silence. She had evidently established a reputation with the younger servants as a crabbed old spinster.

Ginger, however, smiled and said, "Good evening, Mrs. Jackson, Percy and Annie are going out to the Picture Palace to see the new Mary Pickford film. It's come all the way from America, what's it called again?" She turned to the second footman, who glanced sideways out of the corners of his eyes at Mrs. Jackson before he answered.

"*Caprice*," said the housemaid, for him, and giggled.

"I am going to go with them of course; perhaps you would like to come with us?"

Mrs. Jackson was almost too startled to reply. She had never seen a film, but she had heard that the Gaumont Picture Palace was a grand affair with a Mighty Wurlitzer organ that played throughout the performance, but as to this Mary Pickford, or whoever she was, she had never heard of her, buried as she was in the Buckinghamshire countryside. She hesitated before she said with genuine gratitude for being asked, "How very nice of you to invite me, Mrs. Harding, but I am quite done in. And her ladyship has asked me to pop in and see her before she leaves for dinner." She was conscious of quick glances around the table. *I wonder if they think I am here to spy on them,* she thought. And just in case she was coming off as starchy and stuck-up she added, "I am really looking forward to my supper. It smells absolutely delicious."

"Be on the table in a tick, Mrs. Jackson." Ginger smiled and gestured to the maids to finish laying the table. "Call Mr. White, would you, Perce? And after dinner, Annie, you must help with the washing-up, if we are to be on time for the picture. I love Mary Pickford, she's called America's Sweetheart! Isn't that nice? And that Owen Moore is so handsome you would never guess he was a penniless tinker's son from Ireland!" She walked around the table straightening cutlery and smoothing napkins into place and the footmen and maids rushed to help her. There was the usual bustle of chatty activity, with Annie giggling and the footmen vying with each other to make her squeal. Mrs. Jackson was almost glad that Miss Pettigrew was upstairs engrossed in the many little duties she performed for her ladyship at this hour of the early evening, so she wouldn't have to catch her eye. They all came to the table and stood behind their places to wait for Mr. White, who said such a short grace that Mrs. Jackson was still standing waiting for more as the rest of them sat down.

She lifted her fork to her mouth, realizing as she did so that her mouth was watering. And then: *Oh good heavens above!* She filled her mouth with something hot and delicious in which there were spicy sausages cloaked in a thick, rich tomato sauce poured over some tiny little potato dumplings that were as light as tiny feather pillows.

"This is wonderful, Mrs. Harding," she said in deep gratitude that the new cook was a spendthrift with the Talbots' money. "What is it?"

"It's called gnocchi with a ragout sauce, Mrs. Jackson, a simple rustic Italian dish. I'm glad you like it."

Mrs. Jackson had never heard of such a thing, but dear Lord , she thought as she scraped her plate and wondered if it was politic to ask for more, it was tasty and satisfying and the flavors! In all her life Mrs. Jackson had never tasted anything quite like it before. Where on earth had this young woman learned to cook? It wasn't in the north of England and that was a fact.

She looked around the table at the shining faces of the Montfort servants as they ate their dinner and talked about their favorite films. The two footmen were leaning back in their chairs, outwardly flirting with the little scullery maid and the second housemaid. Mr. White was listening to Ginger as she told a funny story about the milkman, his face wreathed in such a delighted smile that his eyes had disappeared into two crescents. *Well, he's a goner,* thought Mrs. Jackson.

Clementine was about to take her bath before dressing for dinner when Mrs. Jackson came into her room. She had not expected to see her housekeeper until the following morning before she left for Chester Square, so hopefully Jackson had something vital to tell her. As usual, her housekeeper was standing in her doorway, quite composed, her face betraying nothing. *Really,* thought Clementine, *there is something almost inscrutable about her; I am never too sure what's going on in that bright mind of hers.*

"Do come in, Jackson, I was about to take my bath but it can wait. You are back early from Chester Square. Has something . . . ?" Her sentence remained unfinished since she realized it was always left to her to fill in the silences until Mrs. Jackson was ready to inform.

Mrs. Jackson remained where she was, simply looking at her.

"Something has happened, Jackson, come on out with it." And finally her housekeeper spoke, her tone perhaps a little flatter and less conversational than usual.

"Yes, m'lady, something has happened. And I am still trying to work out how it fits in to everything we already know."

Clementine sat down on her sofa and made herself wait. After a moment Mrs. Jackson took a breath and told her that Miss Kingsley's first footman, the one who had walked out two days before the dinner party, had finally turned up, and that the Clumsy Footman, whose real name was Eddy Porter, had done a bunk. As Mrs. Jackson talked, Clementine's mind went blank. And when Mrs. Jackson finished, her first thought was that everything that had gone before in their investigation now simply didn't make sense.

"What do we know about this Eddy Porter fellow?" she asked.

"Very little. I spoke with John, who is now the only footman at Chester Square, and he said this Eddy Porter had been sent to the house by Gibson's Domestic Agency. I telephoned the agency before I left Chester Square, and they haven't heard of him. They have no record of sending over anyone to Mr. Jenkins to interview. They said there is a shortage of well-trained footmen at this time of year."

"So the first footman Leonard Crutchley was murdered to get him out of the way. And the Clumsy Footman, this Eddy Porter, was planted at Miss Kingsley's house. But how does a *footman* fit in with the murder of Sir Reginald?" Clementine having finally straightened out the confusing array of footmen employed at Chester Square could not venture beyond these new facts and sat waiting for further enlightenment.

"I am not sure, perhaps because he was not a footman, m'lady. He *was* a strange-looking man, from the little I saw of him. Too tall, too thin, pitch-black hair, horribly pale skin, and washed-out blue eyes. It was eerie really. John told me he didn't know the first thing about waiting at table. I asked John exactly what had happened on the night of the murder, where all the servants had been from when the ladies left the dining room until Sir Reginald's body was found, and especially where this Eddy Porter was. And this is what he told me." She drew in a breath.

"Wait a moment. You have had a long day of it, Jackson. Come on, sit down here. That's better. Now, on you go." Clementine reached for her notebook and her pencil as her housekeeper assembled her thoughts.

"John said that when the ladies left the dining room to go up to the salon, Mr. Jenkins told the second footman, the Clumsy Footman to wait on them upstairs. Do you remember that, m'lady?"

And Clementine said yes, she remembered a footman, she did not know his name, but it was the clumsy one, the one who had spilled coffee. He had certainly been tall and his hair very black.

"Yes, well then he was sent by Miss Kingsley downstairs after the coffee accident. How long do you think he was gone for, m'lady?"

"Perhaps ten minutes, might have been more, I am not quite sure."

"John told me that while Mr. Jenkins was in waiting outside the dining-room door he was belowstairs, setting up some glasses to take up to the salon and the gentleman were all on their way upstairs to join the ladies. He told me that this Eddy Porter, the Clumsy Footman, arrived in the servants' hall and went outside into the area to have a cigarette. John didn't feel it was his place to say anything about him taking an unregulated break because Porter was an arrogant sort with an unpleasant attitude to the other servants. But John went straight upstairs to tell Mr. Jenkins and Mr. Jenkins came downstairs and had some stiff words with Porter. John said Martha told him afterwards that Mr. Jenkins stood in the servants' entrance into the area and was actually shouting at Porter to go back upstairs and take care of the gentle-men and the ladies in the salon. And Porter came inside, took his vinegar, and ran up the back stairs."

"Could he have—?" Clementine rushed in, but Mrs. Jackson ever so politely lifted her hand from her lap to indicate that she was almost but not quite finished.

"Here is the most interesting thing, m'lady. According to your timetable, Porter was outside in the area at about the time Sir Reginald was murdered, so if anyone got into the dining room through that window, then Porter would only have to look up to seen anyone climbing from the portico onto the dining-room windowsill. And this also means that Mr. Jenkins, who had been standing outside the dining-room door in the inner hall, left his post for as long as it took to go down to the servants' hall and deal with Porter and then come back up again, something we did not know about before." Mrs. Jackson having delivered this use-ful information sat back in her chair with a look that said, *Ask me to do something and you can be sure that I do it well.* And Clemen-tine thought, *Smug doesn't come close to it.*

"Then this Porter fellow came to the house to engineer the death of, or to murder, Sir Reginald. Has he already disposed of Leonard Crutchley and then presented himself as from Gibson's, complete with false references? Was he hired to murder Sir Regi-nald in this rather complicated manner? It's hard to understand why anyone would want to murder a Goody Two-shoes like Sir Reginald, but what motive would a footman have?" Having written down all her notes, Clementine was still grappling with the concept that another dimension had been added to her inves-tigation.

"Indeed, m'lady, but how did he get into the dining room? He might have gone up the area steps to the pavement and then to the front door, stepped from there across to the dining-room window, murdered Sir Reginald, and then climbed back out of the window and returned the same way to the servants' hall through the area. But somehow I think that would have taken longer than ten minutes, and he was standing in the area smoking a cigarette when Mr. Jenkins told him to get back upstairs, and why didn't he close the window afterwards, when he went back upstairs?"

"Because he didn't have time, because Mr. Jenkins discovered the body before he could do that. I don't somehow think . . ." Clementine thought about Adelaide Gaskell and her possible crime of passion. "Perhaps Miss Gaskell can shed some light on this, after all she was also running around the house at the same time as our clumsy footman, Eddy Porter; it doesn't do to ignore her at this moment, now that Porter has emerged as the possible villain. Perhaps this Porter and Miss Gaskell are linked in some way." Clementine, despite Mrs. Jackson's belief that the young companion did not have the courage it took to murder Sir Reginald, was reluctant to let go of Miss Gaskell with those unaccounted-for minutes, and the torn photograph.

"Oh good heavens, look at the time, I must run and take my bath. I'm off to the ballet with Lady Waterford and Mr. Greenberg as Lady Ripon's guest, so I mustn't be late. Looks like you still have your hands full at Chester Square, so carry on the good work." Clementine rustled to her feet as Pettigrew came in from her dressing room with her evening gown over her arm, and seeing that she was still engaged with her housekeeper, she disappeared into the bathroom, which was cloudy with fragrant steam. Clementine just had time for her last instruction to Mrs. Jackson: "I think it's time to get stern with Miss Gaskell, and if anyone can do it you can, but carefully, Jackson, carefully. If she is the murderess, she is certainly not what she seems. I really envy you, you know, I would give anything for two minutes with that young woman. How many days is it now until the charity evening, by the way?"

"Three, m'lady. Miss Kingsley and Miss Gaskell are going to have to come out of their rooms by then."

"Hopefully before, Jackson."

And off Clementine went to soak in her bath and ponder the endless possibilities that cluttered up their inquiry involving bogus footmen, unlocked windows, and geriatric butlers. And Mrs. Jackson went back to the Montfort House servants' hall for a cup of tea with Ginger before she left to chaperone her young charges to the Gaumont Picture Palace, and to hear exactly how that interesting young woman had come across such an incongruous culinary repertoire.

Chapter Twenty-one

Clementine spent what turned out be an anxious evening at His Majesty's Theatre and afterward decided that if she had to choose between an evening in the company of Constance Gladys Robinson, the Marchioness of Ripon, and the overactive Lady Cunard, both of whom numbered among Sir Thomas Beecham's many current paramours, hands down it would be Maud Cunard. At least you could squash some of Maud's more bullying and steamrolling traits, she thought afterward, whereas Gladys was like a powerful Eastern potentate from a fairy tale: splendid, implacable, and coolly assured that everything must go her way. And most certainly Gladys did not run around society referring to herself by her pseudonym, as did Maud, alias Emerald. Gladys did not run around at all. She was extraordinarily stately: easily six feet tall with marvelous deportment that made the energetic Maud with her tiny frame and her sharp features seem rather like a frantic hen.

Mercifully unprepared for what was to come that evening, Clementine found herself seated on Gladys's right in the best double box the house had to offer, second only to that of the royal box, which once again was completely dark. Clementine had been received with a languid smile and a gracious tilt of the head from the marchioness as she had indicated the seat that had been left vacant for her. As she took her place next to Gladys, Clementine was aware that she was among one of London society's most fashionable cliques. She could only assume that her invitation came to her through their mutual friend Gertrude, Lady Waterford, who had greeted her arrival with a pleased smile as Clementine had taken her seat between her and the marchioness. She nodded to those she knew: Hartley Fairfax-Hunter and his beautiful wife's best friend Lady Westmorland; the elegant Marque twins, first sons of Lord Acton Marque, twins in the family always muddled the line of succession; and the Princess Esterhazy. All gave her polite bows and smiled their good-evenings. The only people she knew well were Gertrude Waterford, and the ubiquitous Aaron Greenberg, who appeared to be on everyone's guest list this year. As the curtain rose on the ballet, the lively chatter around her dropped to respectful silence; the marchioness would not tolerate conversation in her box during a performance unless she instigated it.

Clementine, who was still reeling from her meeting with her housekeeper, spent the first part of the evening pondering the events at Chester Square as she idly watched the ballet. She remained absorbed in her thoughts until Nijinsky came onstage for his solo performances, when she allowed herself the luxury of paying attention.

As always, she was completely mesmerized by the intensity of expression in the Polish performer's dancing. Fashionable London ladies vied with one another to entertain the dancer at dinner parties and soirees, but Clementine refused to be drawn into the current fad among her more puerile middle-aged friends in forming a crush on the dancer. Nijinsky was clearly not a man who completely enjoyed the company of women, which made infatuation seem rather pointless. He was considered beautiful, and Clementine agreed that he was, but there was a disconcerting and rather feral look to him with his long muscular neck, on which was balanced a beautifully shaped head with a pale face, extremely wide cheekbones, and lips that were remarkably full. She had come to the conclusion, having once been introduced to the dancer, that there was something rather troubling about the expression in his eyes.

Up until now Clementine had been enjoying herself, and had felt almost flattered that Gladys had invited her to share her box, as the Ripon circle was decidedly a far more stylish set than that of the Earl and Countess of Montfort. And when during the intermission Gladys particularly expressed the hope that she would see the Countess of Montfort at her ball at Claridge's to welcome Nellie Melba back to London, Clementine had thought for one brief moment that she had become one of those women who were invited everywhere and had magically acquired a passport to cross all lines that separated the cliques that made up fashionable society. *My goodness,* she thought, as she gazed out across the theater from the best box in the house, *where will all this end up? If I keep straying from the tried and true I shall find myself sitting on a cushion on the floor of some uncomfortable little house in Bloomsbury discussing Postimpressionism with Roger Fry and sipping a glass of vodka.*

As Nijinsky finished his solo and bounded off the stage amid thunderous applause from the stalls, and the corps de ballet made their entrance the audience settled back to catch up on serious gossip. Gladys, without turning in her seat, said in her strange, one-note, flattened tone that seemed to come from the back of her throat, "Everyone is talking of nothing but Nellie Melba's only recital in London at Hermione Kingsley's charity evening at Chester Square. It will be such a coup for Miss Kingsley to host Miss Melba's only appearance in London this winter. How is she doing, by the way?" Gladys lowered her opera glasses and turned her large, diamond-crowned head to gaze at Clementine, her cool eyes casting a quick assessing glance over Clementine's dress, her fashionable hairstyle, and the exact sum her jewels would have fetched at auction. Clementine immediately understood that the marchioness knew of the murder at Chester Square and that she had been invited to sit next to her so that she might inform, as Hermione was still incommunicado.

"She is very well, and in her usual way completely underplaying all the terrific work it takes to put on an evening of such importance for her charity," Clementine replied, then she sent up a prayer that Mrs. Jackson was on top of everything and not neglecting this part of her duties.

"I hope the poor old thing is not *too* exhausted by it all. I was going to suggest she move the occasion to Claridge's, but Beecham says that the acoustics in Miss Kingsley's salon are quite adequate. I am sure the evening will be a complete success." And there it was, thought Clementine, as she caught the emphasis on the last word in Gladys's otherwise unemphatic drawl: a warning to be communicated through her to Hermione. Gladys had somehow heard of the Chester Square debacle and she was making it clear that her famous and personal friend Nellie Melba, whom she had no doubt encouraged to sing at Hermione's recital, must not be embarrassed in any way whatsoever. Gladys most certainly did not wish her reputation or her dear friends, the Princess Esterhazy and the dowager Queen Alexandra, who would, as Mrs. Jackson had already told her, be accompanying the marchioness to Chester Square, to be compromised in any way.

Clementine had far too much information about the state of affairs at Chester House to be able to respond without her pulse rate increasing significantly. Both Miss Gaskell and Miss Kingsley had shut themselves up in their rooms, the butler was on the verge of a breakdown, and all the Montfort male servants had been commandeered for the charity evening as Miss Kingsley's footmen were either dead or wanted by the police. She felt a flash of nervous panic at the thought of the charity evening going forward with all of London society invited to Chester Square and a murderer running loose in the house. What a mistake not to have worked harder on Hermione to postpone, she thought, and why was it always so damn hot in this place? Resisting the urge to open her fan to cool her cheeks, she sought to change the topic. But Gladys had not quite finished with her.

"I hear that Veda Ryderwood is also to sing at the recital, a couple of duets with Miss Melba. Have you *actually* heard her sing?" Clementine heard in Gladys's monotone the politest of suggestions, a well-bred query, the sort of inquiry someone floats up if you suggest a race between your talented but yet unheard-of two-year-old Thoroughbred against their three-time Derby winner. Clementine assured her that she had heard Lady Ryderwood sing and that her voice was quite superb—not as superb as that of Miss Melba, she hastily added—but still perfectly lovely.

"Yes, I heard she was quite good. Beecham thinks highly, says she has the dramatic coloratura range reminiscent of Velma Moser. Do you remember her remarkable aria as 'Queen of the Night' when she was a young woman, such an intricately difficult song. I think she sang with the Munich opera. Or was it Milan or Moscow? It started with an *M* at any rate." Clementine doubted if Gladys really knew who this singer was; she might be the doyenne of the Royal Opera and the woman who had brought the Russian Ballet to London, but she was really interested only in celebrating famous musicians and singers at extravagant parties, not actually listening to them perform. So she nodded and smiled as Gladys pressed relentlessly on, "I rather wonder if Lady Ryderwood might be a shade too pushing, don't you?"

Good heavens, thought Clementine, she is worried that Melba will be upstaged. Sir Thom can't stand Nellie Melba and he's putting the wind up Gladys about Melba's private performance. Stop it, she told herself, this is ridiculous, you are getting things completely out of proportion.

"Lady Ryderwood is a gifted amateur singer, Lady Ripon, honored to sing with Miss Melba; she is an unassuming young woman and her voice is quite delightful." Her reassurances fell on deaf ears, as Gladys had heard talk and needed further information and was also taking more than a moment to caution.

"Nonetheless, I do hope she will not try to *overpower* the evening—since I understand she has only just returned to London. It doesn't do to thrust oneself forward. I hear she has been almost continuously in the company of some of our senior cabinet ministers: Sir Edward Grey, Winston Churchill . . . and, unfortunately, that dreadful Mr. David Lloyd George, isn't that right, Gertrude?" This was said across Clementine.

Lady Waterford turned her lovely green eyes toward the marchioness and frowned, refusing to be drawn into Royal Opera House politics, or politics of any kind. If anyone knew how to stop this terrifying interrogation in its tracks Gertrude did, thought Clementine. Her closest friend despised common gossip and always refused to participate.

"It will be a pleasure to introduce Veda Ryderwood to you, Gladys." Gertrude's expression was neutral, her tone polite; she was not to be drawn. "She is a most unassuming woman and most likely feels quite overwhelmed by the thought of singing a song or two with Miss Melba. Her modesty is refreshing and I rather think it is for this reason that she is beginning to be invited everywhere."

Having effectively silenced Gladys, Gertrude turned back to not listening to Mr. Greenberg, and Clementine allowed herself a slow outward breath of relief. And then their attention was diverted completely by Nijinsky as he sprang onto the stage in a tremendous vertical leap and seemed to hang in the air for a moment to give everyone an opportunity to welcome him back in a storm of applause from the front row. Out of the corner of her eye Clementine noticed Gladys acknowledge this adulation with a queenly inclination of her handsome head, as if it was her the audience was applauding and not the dancer on the stage.

Clementine was particularly determined to find out more from Gertrude on this business of Lady Ryderwood and her apparent flirtation with a senior cabinet minister notorious for his pursuit of women. During supper at the Savoy she had the opportunity to do so.

"Tell me more about Lady Ryderwood, Gertrude. I find her delightful company, but what can this be about her and Mr. Lloyd George?"

"Oh it's the usual stuff, Clemmy, people love to gossip and speculate, and she has returned to England after years of isolation in Spain or somewhere equally hideous. The poor thing has to run the gamut of every mean old spinster and unattractive widow. You know how it is." Gertrude had pecked away at two tiny morsels of truffled foie gras and now sat back in her chair so that the waiter might take away her plate. Clementine resolved to tread carefully, Gertrude was the epitome of discretion and rarely repeated information, even if she spent her time with people who did. Her reputation in society was unsullied and she intended to keep it that way by never making enemies among those who were unsubtle enough not to keep their own affairs hidden from public scrutiny.

"I didn't for one moment think that she was involved with anyone, but Lady Ripon implied something otherwise," Clementine persisted, and she put down her fork; if she never ate lobster salad again it would not be too soon, she thought.

"Yes, and it's always the way with that crowd. Scandal is what they mull over with the morning toast and marmalade. You always rather avoided them I thought." There was a hint of reproof, as Gertrude expected her closest friend to remain above suspicion when it came to scandalmongering.

"We were invited to Chester Square for Hermione's dinner for Mr. Churchill. Sir Vivian Hussey and Maud Cunard were invited and it sort of went on from there. And of course Olive is so involved with the Royal Opera House." Mentioning their mutual friend Olive Shackleton somewhat mollified Gertrude and she said, "Well, unfortunately, Lady Ryderwood was invited by Lady Cunard to a dinner party, and Lloyd George and our Foreign Secretary, Sir Edward Grey, were there and found her company perhaps a bit too intoxicating for Emerald's taste." She smiled as she mentioned Lady Cunard by her self-given name. "So I imagine that is where all this came from. Lady Ryderwood is lovely and has her own particular brand of quiet charm, and of course all the old hens are spitefully jealous. Sometimes I get quite sick of it all. But I can assure you, Clemmy, Lady Ryderwood is not romantically involved with Lloyd George, or otherwise." Lady Waterford's slender white shoulders shivered with distaste at the mere thought.

Annoyed with herself for appearing to pry, Clementine decided that it didn't take long for a steady diet of London society to pall. She almost wished she were back at Iyntwood setting out on a nice country walk with the dogs tomorrow afternoon, instead of attending yet another fitting at Lucile's, where she must say no to the pretty pink dress that had garnered such disapproval from Pettigrew.

But Clementine did not go to Lucile's salon in Hanover Square the next day after all, because she was invited to tea with Hermione Kingsley, who had at last emerged from her bedroom. And as Clementine soon found out, as they lifted their teacups and said no to diminutive cucumber sandwiches, Hermione was in the mood to confide.

"I can't thank you enough, my dear Clementine, for your generosity. Mrs. Jackson has done a sterling job here standing in for Adelaide. I actually think she has improved on the arrangements for the charity evening. She suggested using Monsieur Devereux for the food, and the menus she has chosen look absolutely perfect and then..." Hermione recounted all of Mrs. Jackson's wondrous ideas, ultimately reassuring Clementine that she need not fear for the success of the evening, thereby avoiding ostracism and social damnation from the Marchioness of Ripon.

"Now, Clementine, my dear, I must talk to you about something important, and I am sorry to say distasteful." Hermione set down her empty cup and shooed the butler away with a quick, "That will be all, Jenkins." And Clementine put down her cup, too, and waited because she knew that what was to follow had been percolating in Hermione's head for days. However close she was to Sir Reginald, she must have brooded on the unfairness of his murder in her dining room and now she wished to unburden herself.

"I don't quite know how to tell you of Trevor's connivance and lies the other evening."

Clementine had to recover her wits. *We are to discuss Trevor Tricklebank. After everything that happened here? Trevor?* After a moment's reflection she decided it best to let Hermione tell all in her own way.

"I need your clever mind and your brave unwavering counsel as an old friend and I hope what I have to tell you will not shock you too much. On the evening of my little party for Winston, Trevor told me that he could not stay for Lady Ryderwood's delightful singing after dinner as he had promised to take Jennifer Wells-Thornton on to a dance for her cousin. As you know, Jennifer and Trevor are practically betrothed. Well, now I understand from a third party," Clementine took this to be the police, "that Trevor put Jennifer into his motorcar and told the chauffeur to take her on to her cousin's house. Then he took off for some unknown destination. He was gone two hours before arriving at that dreadful club he belongs to, where he proceeded to run up more gambling debts. And since Trevor will not say where he was, I can only assume it was at an insalubrious establishment. There, my dear, I've said it, and I am sorry if I have embarrassed you."

Clementine remained impassive. Silence lay between them for a moment.

"Trevor will be twenty-four next month and I feel that I must be firm with him in a way I have not been before. His affairs are in a lamentable state, he drinks too much, smokes too much, and I dread to know how he fritters away his allowance." Hermione paused, and Clementine felt as if she were listening to the late Queen Victoria complaining petulantly about Bertie's antics in Paris. She assumed an expression of sympathetic understanding, encouraging the elderly spinster to continue.

"I put it to Trevor this morning that his present way of life must end. He must marry Jennifer, give up all these awful gambling houses, and join an appropriate gentlemen's club. If it's too late for someone with influence to put him up for White's, then Boodle's will do. And he must prepare to take a seat on the board of governors for the Chimney Sweep Boys. Or . . ." and the querulous old voice became quite steely and the aging face screwed itself up so tightly that she no longer resembled a benign old tortoise but an ancient gargoyle made of ivory leather, "or I will disinherit him and appoint Mr. Aaron Greenberg as chairman for the charity's board of governors."

Clementine was fascinated; her speculations had been spot-on, it seemed. But she noted with interest that there had been no mention of Trevor's twenty-four-hour detention at Scotland Yard, and there probably never would be.

"What was Trevor's response?" she asked.

"Trevor said that he would be quite happy to be on the board for the Chimney Sweep Boys, but that he could not possibly marry Jennifer. That as much as he liked her, he was not fond enough of her for *that*. And then, Clementine," the old lady's voice shook, either with age or rage, it was hard to tell, "he told me that he couldn't marry Jennifer anyway, because he was already married!"

Clementine actually heard herself gasp, and though it wasn't a loud inhalation, it was enough to make her pull herself together. She made herself keep quite silent, bent a look of inquiry on Hermione, and waited.

"I told Trevor that he was a snake in the grass and that I was done with him." The old lady was so overcome that she relinquished her upright posture and actually sank back against the cushions in her chair and closed her eyes. *She is quite done in, poor old bat*, thought Clementine as she trotted over to Hermione and sat down next to her on a little footstool by her chair, in time to hear Hermione say under her breath, "It is enough to be double-crossed and fooled by Reginald, but to have one's own flesh and blood, and the last remaining member of my family, be so deceitful and treacherous, is too much."

Double-crossed and fooled by Sir Reginald? Clementine's mind positively shouted these words as she dutifully asked, "Did Trevor tell you whom he was married to?"

"No, my dear, he did not. He said that if I was done with him, then he had no further obligations to me." Her voice was faint, and Clementine decided that it was time for a little brandy; she got up and rang for the butler.

Chapter Twenty-two

Dancing until the early hours of the morning is always so thrilling when you are twenty, thought Clementine, as she crawled into bed after Gladys Ripon's fete for Nellie Melba, but when you have brought out two daughters in almost as many seasons it becomes quite punishing.

If only they could end these things just after midnight, she grumbled to herself as she fished around with her tired feet for her hot water bottle and shook her pillows to better support her weary head, it would be a far more pleasant experience.

I simply must decline a few invitations, otherwise I will be good for nothing, she promised herself when, still wide awake three hours later, she watched the gray light of eight o'clock in the morning lighten the edges of the curtains.

I am getting to that age when staying up into the small hours means I don't sleep at all. She sighed as the images of the evening receded and she dropped into a deep sleep.

It was after noon when she woke. The room was dimly lit by winter sunshine and she reached out a hand to the bell pull. Ten minutes later her breakfast tray was brought in, and propped up against a wall of pillows, she sat up in bed, sipped her tea, and wearily considered the night before.

The ball had been like all London balls at Claridge's, attended by everyone who was anyone. A profusion of flowers decked the great ballroom, the anterooms, and the smaller salons; hot and cold buffet suppers were offered in the dining rooms, champagne was served from start to finish, and a thoroughly modern band played a variety of tunes from waltzes to the fox-trot. An affair exactly like the previous ball she had attended there, almost down to the same flowers and the same food.

Clementine had stood up for one dance with her husband's old shooting pal Jack Ambrose, and then they had joined Gertrude Waterford, Mr. Aaron Greenberg, and a Mrs. Crawford-Beamish for a glass of champagne and a bite of supper.

Clementine, who had been listening with half her attention to Jack Ambrose quarreling gently with Gertrude about how obnoxious Germany had been in trying to muscle in on the port town of Agadir in Morocco, felt she couldn't take another evening dedicated to the belligerent kaiser's aggressive quest to snap up previously unheard-of tin-pot towns that no one could possibly find on a map.

"I was disgusted with our Foreign Secretary, Grey was a complete pansy about the whole thing . . . we should have gone in there and trounced the lot of them," Jack Ambrose said in summation of the Agadir Crisis; a career in the cavalry with active service during the Boer Wars had made him an addict for the glorious splendors of a full cavalry charge.

Clementine sighed and looked around for a distraction as Gertrude said coldly, "What nonsense, he did everything right and kept a cool head and Germany backed down. How could you say—?"

"All I *am* saying is that the Moroccans and the French were not saved by *Grey*, for God's sake, they were saved by the German financial crises, that's the only reason they went away." Jack's eyes bulged, and his face turned red. "I hope to God the man shows a bit more backbone when Germany starts throwing its weight . . ."

Oh for heaven's sake, thought Clementine, *more obsession about war with Germany.* She had endured fifteen minutes of Lady Busborough triumphantly recounting how she had caught a German spy red-handed, when in actual fact she had merely packed up her personal maid and sent the poor Fräulein back to Berlin because she had caught her reading her private correspondence.

As she cast about for a distraction she heard Mr. Greenberg's voice behind her mentioning Hermione's party for Winston Churchill. *We are not supposed to refer to that,* she thought. And without turning her head, she tuned in.

". . . Still active in her charity . . . supportive of the arts. Her new companion . . ." Clementine detached herself from Colonel Jack Ambrose, who was embarking on another anecdote, which featured a game of polo at Hurlingham where nine ponies had been lamed, and edged into Mr. Greenberg's conversation with Mrs. Crawford-Beamish.

". . . Most accomplished . . . such a remarkable repertoire . . . unassuming and with such musical ability . . ."

She laughed to herself; Aaron Greenberg was positively gushing, another conquest chalked up to the lovely Lady Ryderwood.

"Her father was a violinist *and* composer . . ." Mr. Greenberg prattled on, and Clementine realized he was not talking about Lady Ryderwood. ". . . Miss Gaskell played for us, quite superbly I thought, as she accompanied Lady Ryderwood, whose voice is really quite nice."

Lady Ryderwood's voice is quite nice? Clementine was about to turn and laughingly protest when she realized that Mr. Greenberg's voice was expressing tremendous appreciation; praise was simply flowing—for Miss Gaskell!

"Hermione encourages Miss Gaskell to take lessons from Alfred Engleward and it is she who will accompany Melba at the charity evening, that is how good her playing is," she said in a voice dripping with admiration.

Clementine couldn't believe that he was chattering on about Hermione's upcoming charity event, it was courting disaster especially with someone as thrusting as Mrs. Crawford-Beamish. And sure enough, he was to be punished.

"I would love to hear her play and I have always admired Miss Kingsley's charity . . . the, er . . . Chimney Sweeps. And of course we are complete devotees of Miss Melba. I would be more than happy to make a contribution to the organization." It was obvious that Mrs. Crawford-Beamish had not been invited to the charity evening, but as it was becoming the most fashionable event that December, she was determined to find a way to wriggle in. "Perhaps I might join *your* little party, Mr. Greenberg!" This was said with a fluttery little laugh that wiped the besotted smile right off Aaron Greenberg's face.

"Oh, unfortunately I'm not in a position . . ." he floundered, but Mrs. Crawford-Beamish, a woman of impressive size and with a voice as strident as that of a barker at a fair, would hear nothing of it.

"Oh nonsense, Mr. Greenberg, I know how close you are with Miss Kingsley, I am sure you could find a place for little me!"

Mr. Greenberg had been put thoroughly on the spot; he was not at liberty to invite her and here was this determined woman crying out at the top of her lungs for an invitation. He glanced at Clementine, his expression rather frantic, and she rescued him from further embarrassment by interrupting them, swiftly changing the subject, and then, recognizing an old friend across the room, steered him to safety.

As they made their escape to join Olive Shackleton and Lord Herriot, Mr. Greenberg smiled his thanks and went on to say what a jolly nice young lady Miss Gaskell was, so ready to please and eager to make things right. His relief was palpable, and to cover his humiliating near brush with disaster he continued to natter on about Miss Gaskell.

"Miss Gaskell was not well the other night, you know. But there she was, determined to be useful. I found her running around downstairs after dinner on an errand to find pure spirit, with no one to help her. We found some in the end in the laundry rooms belowstairs."

Clementine was stunned at this new intelligence, uttered quite without thought on his part, no doubt after too much champagne and the relief that he had been rescued from producing an invitation to an event that was not his to extend invitations to. She had to inhale her almost blurted, *But you said you were keeping Mr. Tricklebank company in the outer hall, until you came up to the salon.* To cover her confusion she turned away to talk to Olive, determined not to alert Mr. Greenberg to the fact that he had related a completely different account as to his whereabouts on the night of the dinner party than he had earlier.

It was this that she was still mulling over as she ate her toast and marmalade the next morning, Aaron Greenberg's uncharacteristic lie. Aaron Greenberg, whom she had grown to rather admire and like; courteous, thoughtful, and considerate Aaron Greenberg, who made the Sir Thoms of this world, with their paramours, their affairs with other men's wives, and their double standards, seem shallow and empty.

If Aaron Greenberg had been helping Adelaide Gaskell find pure spirit for Miss Meriwether's spoiled dress, then this gave Adelaide an alibi for the time she had been gone from the salon. But it also blotted Aaron Greenberg's copybook, as he had been careful to establish an exclusive alibi with Trevor Tricklebank. She had taken Mr. Greenberg for a truthful and straightforward man, but perhaps this was rather naïve of her, considering the massive fortune he had made despite the banking sharks of Istanbul and Paris. Perhaps she had completely underestimated him.

She ruminated on this new information as she crunched toast and sipped tea and her mind went back to a chance remark that Hermione had made yesterday afternoon about being betrayed by Sir Reginald.

Hermione had obviously had a falling-out with her old friend, before his death, and since then had decided that her nephew should take his place on the board of governors. Now with Trevor having severely disappointed her, and with an important place to fill on the board, she had resorted to Aaron Greenberg. Being made the chairman of the most influential charity in England would be a plum indeed, especially if it led to a peerage. Perhaps it was Mr. Greenberg who had told the police that Tricky had not gone on with Jennifer Wells-Thornton that evening but had walked off alone into the night. Thereby ensuring Trevor's disgrace with his aunt, and securing his place as chairman of the charity—the only suitable male for the job. She did not like the idea at all, but it did make sense.

She set down her teacup with a clatter on the saucer at her next thought. Mr. Greenberg was certainly fit enough and agile enough to span the gap between portico and windowsill quite easily. And little Miss Gaskell could have ably contributed by making sure that the window was unlatched in the dining room. It was a possibility, and one she did not like.

Trevor Tricklebank as a suspect was home free and clear. The police had not charged him, as his new wife had probably given him an alibi, since this was undoubtedly whom he had been with for those two missing hours. But his lie and his clandestine marriage had put him in a bad position with his aunt.

But on the other hand there was the Clumsy Footman, who had spilled coffee on Marigold's dress to give him the opportunity to leave the salon, and who had spent the crucial time of the murder belowstairs, outside at the bottom of the area steps, possibly to keep watch while his accomplice had gone in through that window into the dining room. Or, if he'd had the time, had run up the area steps, gained entrance to the dining room from the portico, and done the deed himself. Was the footman's accomplice someone inside the house, or had he been planted there to help someone from outside who had climbed in through the window to murder Sir Reginald?

And finally there was this pleasant young woman who hadn't the courage to tell her employer that she was too sick to play for her recital, but who was running around the house at the crucial time of the murder and who had kept a photograph of the dead man under her pillow and then later had torn it in two and thrown it away. Mrs. Jackson had told her that Miss Gaskell worked hard for the charity and that she cared deeply about the work it accomplished, which rang true considering that Adelaide was an orphan. But she didn't have a hope of being appointed to the board of governors, as Hermione Kingsley was hardly a modern-thinking woman who supported other women's right to govern and not just serve.

And she must try to find out why Captain Vetiver had been closeted with Sir Reginald in the dining room; was it significant that these two had spent time alone together with a butler ensuring they were not interrupted? Ordinarily she would not have thought so, but none of the events that evening must be considered as ordinary. There was something too flawless, too plausible about that captain that did not sit well with her.

I have to narrow down the search, thought an overwhelmed Clementine, as she lay back against the pillows, her breakfast tray pushed to one side. I am ignoring one of Conan Doyle's favorite rules for solving a crime. The When and the Where were immediately established. As to the How, we know that access to the dining room could be gained either through the dining-room window or the door when the butler abandoned his post and went downstairs to admonish the Clumsy Footman. So which way did the murderer enter and leave the dining room? The How is the most important because it always leads to the Who.

Chapter Twenty-three

Clementine was still deep in thought when Pettigrew arrived to take away her breakfast tray and inform her that Lord Haversham had sent word he was at the Admiralty and would come over to Montfort House, hopefully in time to join her for luncheon if it would be convenient. Clementine was delighted and hopped out of her bed to be ready in time. Doubtless Harry would have some news about Captain Wildman-Lushington's accident.

As she waited for Pettigrew to hunt down the right shoes for her dress, Clementine made a promise to herself: she would not ask her son critical and uninformed questions about why he was messing about with aeroplanes or joining the RNAS. Her opinions got them nowhere and caused bad feelings. And in this moment of maternal insight she resolved that when she next saw Althea, she would only express interest in daughter's future plans to explore the outer reaches of barbaric lands, even though Althea had mentioned in her last letter, causing more than a ripple of annoyance and concern on her mother's part, that she had heard the Rift Valley was one of the most beautiful, untouched, and least spoiled places left in Africa to explore.

I am not an accomplished woman, she thought, *but hopefully I am an intuitive and sensitive one who can rise above my limited life's experiences, and try to understand what makes my children tick. If we try to force them away from what matters to them, they will only find a way; Tricky is surely an example of that.*

"Right then, Pettigrew, I like what you've done with my hair." She turned from the glass as her maid came back with her choice of shoes. "There is something so graceful about hair arranged low in the neck."

"Thank you, m'lady, you have the perfect shape to your head for this style. Lord Haversham is downstairs in the drawing room. He arrived a few minutes ago and Mr. White says luncheon will be ready whenever you are." Clementine stood up like an obedient child and Pettigrew gave a twitch to her ivory silk skirt and looked her over, head on one side, mouth pursed in consideration. Clementine often felt that Pettigrew's last-minute inspection was one of self-congratulation at having achieved the perfection of her mistress's appearance.

As Clementine went downstairs she hoped Harry had managed to find out something at the airfield concerning the young flying officer's death, but she was too pleased to see him to be bothered with all that for the time being, and once White had served them and left, they settled down to enjoy their luncheon together.

"Do we have a new cook?" Harry finished his game pie with relish.

"Yes, we do; such delicious food. She is quite an interesting young woman, apparently. Jackson told me she cooks French provincial food and sometimes even rustic Italian food for the servants' hall, which impresses Jackson, but not Pettigrew. And she goes by the name of Ginger, which impresses White, but not Jackson or Pettigrew." She took a sip of wine and ate the last bite of pie; the crust was tender, the partridge, in its sauce, rich and succulent. She felt the great sense of well-being that good food and wine can bring to the moment.

"Talking about the *unimpressive*," said Harry as their plates were taken away by the footman, "I saw Tricky Tricklebank at Boodle's yesterday. He was there as a guest of Finch-Hatton; his aunt told him he has to become a member. He was a bit subdued, poor chap—Hermione is laying down the law about him getting married, and is determined he will take over as chairman of the board for her charity."

White returned to offer them Queen of Pudding, and Clementine told him that she would ring if there was anything else they needed. There was something expectant in her son's demeanor, and as soon as the butler had left the dining room he said, "How's everything going on at Chester Square and your investigation, if it is not too outright a question?"

His mother told him she didn't mind his question at all, but that he should not ask it in front of his father, who had left her in London in fear that she might actually discover the identity of Sir Reginald's murderer and cause Lord Montfort untold embarrassment.

"So what will you do if you discover who killed Sir Reginald? Will you make a citizen's arrest?" He was laughing now, no doubt at the thought of his mother and her housekeeper tracking down a desperate killer. Did he think this was some sort of parlor game she had invented to while away the empty hours?

"Our investigation is going quite nicely, thank you, and I'm glad you brought it up because I have some questions for you. But as to Chester Square, I am afraid Trevor is in terrible trouble with Hermione. He has been telling her one thing and then apparently doing another and in the process losing a lot of money. Does he remind you a little bit of Teddy?"

"Not in the slightest, Mama, Teddy was a scoundrel and complete blackguard. Tricky is a bit of a spendthrift, but a decent, well-meaning chap who wouldn't hurt a fly. He's scared stiff of his aunt, and who can blame him?"

"Well, he'll be in even greater trouble if he doesn't toe the line. What is wrong with Jennifer Wells-Thornton? She would be a good wife for him."

"Because he's desperately in love with an actress, that's why—something to keep firmly under your hat, by the way. A well-connected and successful actress, her name is Lena Margaret Ashwell and she appears at Drury Lane all the time. You remember her, she played in *Mrs. Dane's Defence*. She may come from the Liverpool docks, but she has learned to act like a lady . . ."

"That doesn't *make* her a lady, Harry, it just makes her an adept actress and probably one who is looking for a rich husband." Clementine did not reveal that Tricky in marrying his actress had most certainly forfeited his position as heir to the Kingsley millions.

"Margaret is not that kind of an actress. She is capable, with a good brain, and is a capital businesswoman. Beerbohm Tree is going to let her direct the next play at His Majesty's Theatre at the beginning of the season, so she is probably the right sort of wife for Tricky. Jennifer is a nice enough girl but she's such a little priss, and Trevor would make a hopeless bungle of running the charity. As it is, I think he might come out of things quite well if he has the sense to marry Margaret. She's made pots of money and is immensely fond of Tricky."

Clementine said nothing, because here they differed in their thinking. It was all very well to have a friendship with an actress but it was a catastrophe to marry one. It was the sort of thing aging peers did in the late 1890s when they married eighteen-year-old chorus girls from the Gaiety Theatre, embarrassing their children and families and what was worse confusing the line of succession to an estate they were happily squandering away. She swiftly turned the subject away from what she considered Tricky's depressing situation and at the same time firmly crossed him off her list of suspects.

"How was your trip to Eastchurch?"

"It was good, marred only by the aftermath of Captain Wildman-Lushington's accident and his funeral, which also underscored the whole reason why I should be at Eastchurch in the first place. And I think Wildman-Lushington's accident was just that, Mama, a wretched, unnecessary but coincidental accident. According to his copilot's account, Wildman-Lushington lost control of the plane at about fifty feet up, as they were coming in to land. Landing and takeoff are always the dicey part of flying. The problem was entirely due to pilot error in the face of a new machine that has specific idiosyncrasies the poor chap simply wasn't aware of."

"There could not have been any tampering to make the machine fail?"

"Yes, I suppose there might have, but I seriously doubt it from his copilot's description. And anyway the engine was smashed to bits." Clementine looked away, determined not to say a word about her fears for the future of aircraft. So all she said was, "Ah well, it is a tragedy of course, but I am glad someone didn't engineer his death, poor boy. How are things at Kingston—any more on Sopwith, and his factory?"

"Not good. Someone has been snooping all right. Tom keeps all his designs and drawings of planes under lock and key now, but for quite a long time he didn't. Didn't see the need to really, all the chaps at Soppers are old pals, sharing their design ideas, their successes and failures. There was a young draftsman at the factory for a while, bright sort of chap. Stopped working for us with some story that his aunt was ill. Now we find that he was not quite who he said he was and has scarpered." Clementine thought of the Clumsy Footman, who in Harry's parlance had also scarpered. "Tom feels pretty stupid, as this bloke was evidently some sort of spy, and had all the opportunity in the world to copy Tom's designs, which are far in advance of anything out there, even French planes." Harry explained that the only country in Europe that had concentrated time and money on developing aircraft design were the French, and that in the past ten months Tom had been working hard to improve on some of their designs. Now his innovations, especially where safety while flying at greater height and faster speed were concerned, had most likely been stolen.

"Was he German, this young man?" Clementine asked, thinking of *The Adventure of the Bruce-Partington Plans*.

"If there are red-headed Germans I suppose he might have been. He had a Scottish surname, McVitie; probably not his own. We don't know if he was working for another government, or for a competing aircraft manufacturer, or whether we are being unreasonably suspicious. He's simply disappeared. No sign of him at the house he was lodging in, and no one knew much about him. He was a pleasant sort of chap, friendly and hardworking." Harry looked miserable and then added, "I know you won't say anything, Mother. Captain Vetiver is still having the matter investigated and a good deal of what I have told you is conjecture."

"Let's take our coffee in the library." Clementine rang for White and then as they left the dining room made an effort to change the subject away from unfortunate marriages and disinherited nephews. Mindful of her determination not to carp on about her son's dangerous love of flying, she took the time to take an interest in his soon-to-be commission for the RNAS and whether he would be stationed at Eastchurch. "Elmsford and Cynthia Bertholomew are just around the corner from you at Eastchurch, in Kings Sudbury. I know they would be delighted to give you dinner. They would be so glad of your company. I find that part of East Anglia so empty and dull."

"Thank you, Mama, I'll probably take them up on it. It is

pretty primitive at Eastchurch, but they have a decent cook who turns out a pretty good chop. The navy doesn't believe in frills, and I rather like a spare life." His eyes glistened with anticipation of his new spartan airborne life and Clementine realized that Eastchurch and the RNAS were Harry's dream come true.

Chapter Twenty-four

The servants at Chester Square might find Miss Kingsley's draconian house rules intimidating, but Mrs. Jackson was not perturbed when she was informed by Martha that Miss Kingsley wanted to see her in the library. The old lady's feudal hold on the servants' hall might subjugate its inmates effectively, but Mrs. Jackson was exempt. She was in the house under the auspices of her employer, an independent operator bound only by the rules of service and her loyalties to the Talbot family. After her first hours in Miss Kingsley's house she had come to the conclusion that the more repressive and stifling the rules of management, the more anxious were its staff, resulting in mistakes and chaos.

She was wholly aware of Mr. Jenkins's apprehension as he ushered her into the presence of the elderly and wrinkled dragon in the drawing room. A dragon whose fire had probably been extinguished long ago, in Mrs. Jackson's view, but who gave the occasional experimental huff in the belief that it might rekindle. The old lady was sitting in a high-back wing chair with her feet on a tufted footstool, her spine erect and held at the prescribed four inches from the back of her chair. Her thin, twisted old hands, curled around the curved ends of the chair's arms, were covered in stupendous rings and she was dressed in the fashion of the late 1800s, in a dress of her favorite shade of pink, with a tight, high collar edged with lace.

When Mrs. Jackson came to a halt at a respectful distance before Miss Kingsley, the old lady did not speak for some moments but regarded Mrs. Jackson through hooded yellowing eyes, as if trying to decide whether or not to eat her for luncheon.

"Don't stand by the door, I can't see you; come closer."

As Mrs. Jackson approached, Miss Kingsley put her head forward, stretching taut the wrinkled skin under her chin above the high lace collar.

"Did you visit Kingsley House yet, Mrs. Jackson?" she asked without preamble or good morning, and Mrs. Jackson instantly knew that someone had been telling tales: Matron, or perhaps it was Macleod.

"Yes, ma'am, last week, and with Matron's help chose five boys for the charity evening."

"Well, you will have to start all over again, because four of the five have chicken pox. Matron has found some replacements for you. Unfortunately, they are a little older and have no doubt reached that unattractive stage in their physical development of being awkward and gangling, but we shall have to make do. Macleod will drive you over now." And then as Mrs. Jackson turned as if to go, she added, "And this time you will have Matron's full cooperation." *Aha,* thought Mrs. Jackson, *then it was Macleod who blabbed.*

As Mrs. Jackson left the library she found herself answering a question that had been at the back of her mind for the past couple of days. *Why is it,* she thought, *that those who publicly practice the greatest acts of charity, whose entire lives are given over to causes and the energetic raising of the massive funds that support them, who preach reform and know no other way than to take the poor away from their perceived lives of ignorance and deprivation to show them a better and more worthy path, are often so person-*

ally dismissive of their human characteristics? Mrs. Jackson suspected that the individual boys had become no more than numbers in a ledger and her charity an arena for a helpless old woman to wield power and believe she still led a useful and active life.

Mrs. Jackson was met at Kingsley House by a young man who was waiting for her at the main door to the house, and who escorted her up the three flights of stairs to Matron's parlor.

As Matron struggled to her feet, uttering exclamations of welcome, and shepherded Mrs. Jackson to a tiny chair loaded with cushions and antimacassars, she was immediately on the alert. Somewhere in this effusive greeting, Matron was guilty of a cover-up, of striving perhaps to regain a lost alliance. Breaking off from cries of welcome, she yanked on the bell pull, and when the maid appeared she directed her to bring a tray of tea, with minute instructions as to the quantity of butter on the toasted crumpets.

"I am afraid it's slim pickings for the right sort of boy for the charity event, what with all this chicken pox, Mrs. Jackson. But I have six young men who will do a good job for Miss Kingsley and they are waiting for you in one of the dormitories. Now let me see about that tea . . ." She waded across her cramped parlor, miraculously avoiding footstools and other bric-a-brac. Opening the door, she bellowed down the corridor for the maid.

"Drat that girl," she said under her breath, and then, "Drat that little . . . I won't be a moment, Mrs. Jackson." And so ready was she for her heavily iced teatime cake, chocolate fingers, and brandy snaps that she lumbered off to track down the maid.

In the few moments she had before Matron's return, Mrs. Jackson found that she had slid her hand under the bill spike on the desk and pulled forth the little book that Matron had been toiling over so industriously on Mrs. Jackson's last visit. She opened it at the first page and saw a column of dates from three years back followed by a column of figures in pounds: usually five, but sometimes ten and in several cases as much as twenty-five. Next to each amount was a tick *to denote receipt of the sum*? But what was more interesting was that the column with the ticks was headed with the initials RAC. She quickly turned to the last page of entries. Ah yes, here was the last entry, 15th November of this year, for the amount of ten pounds and a heavy-handed tick. Nothing was recorded since then.

A few seconds later Mrs. Jackson slid the notebook into its hiding place, slipped back around the desk, and resumed her interest in the view out the window from her chair. And as she politely drank a cup of tea with Matron and listened to her breathless complaints of the outrageous laziness of young maid-servants these days, she barely acknowledged the speaker, so wrapped up was she in what she had discovered.

According to her ledger, Matron had been accepting money for at least three years from RAC, in payments twice a month that came to an astonishing two hundred and forty pounds a year and in the last two years sometimes as much as three hundred.

RAC? This was undoubtedly Reginald Algernon Cholmonde-ley, whose portrait hung in the hall of Kingsley House next to that of Charles Kingsley, the great Victorian reformer for child labor, author of *The Water-Babies*, and uncle to Miss Kingsley. And Mrs. Jackson remembered that RAC had died on 30th November, the date of his next remittance to Matron for the month.

Sitting there in Matron's room, she felt a thrill of uneasy excitement. *Why had Sir Reginald punctually paid this unpleasant woman such large amounts of money each month, when she was well compensated for her work by the charity?* Blackmail usually being the basis of such monetary gifts, or some sort of service that Matron was performing for Sir Reginald in return for her twenty pounds a month, made Mrs. Jackson's mind reel with endless, illegal possibilities. It was hard for her to concentrate on what Matron was saying as she poured tea and offered sandwiches. The parlor felt stuffy and stale and the voice of the woman before her unbearable. Mrs. Jackson stood up and said that she hadn't much time and would like meet the young men she had come to meet, bringing Matron's catalog of complaints against the hapless housemaids to a halt.

She was taken to one of the boys' dormitories to conduct her interviews, where she stood beside her designated chair and looked at the rows of beds. How old were these children when they came to Kingsley House, she wondered, three years, four? She was not a sentimentalist; she knew what kind of lives these children had led before their rescue by the charity. Any boy coming to this house after living in the Old Nichol at Bethnal Green, or the Rookeries of Shoreditch and Whitechapel, would find Kingsley House overwhelmingly luxurious: three square meals a day, hot milk at bedtime, a warm, clean, comfortable bed, and new clothes to wear and most of all the benefit of an exemplary education to equip them for the future. But what kind of life were they leading now if the woman who looked after them was not only an unpleasant bully but possibly a blackmailer? And if Matron was blackmailing Sir Reginald, then what on earth had the man been up to? She wondered if the boys she had come here to interview were part of the elite corps that formed the Chums.

At Kingsley House, it seemed that once you reached the age of eleven you went away to school, either to the local grammar as a day boy or, if you were of top-drawer material, to board at a minor public or trade school. Well, Mrs. Jackson thought as the first boy came into the room, this young man was clearly not a Chum. He was quite tall for his age, but he was not particularly prepossessing. And sure enough, he said that he was a daily pupil at the

Dulwich grammar school, and that he expected to become an articled clerk to a local solicitor when he was fifteen. Yes, he said, he would continue to live at Kingsley House until he was twenty-one. He was a straightforward boy, pleasant, with nice manners and the usual diffidence that all the boys she had met so far at Kingsley House seemed to possess. "Were you disappointed not to be chosen as one of the Chums?" she asked as lightly as she could.

He shot her a look that was almost derisive and shook his head as he answered, "No, not particularly, they were always swotting for their entrance exams for posh schools. They had to be top in everything. If they weren't cramming they were out on the playing field practicing cricket or field hockey, and some of them were on the rugby team, too. I'm just not that remarkable . . ."

"But you all mix in together, don't you? You all get along well with each other?" Again she kept her voice light and realized she was imitating Lady Montfort, because she would have had this sort of information out of the boy in a trice without his even knowing he was giving it.

"We all share the same schoolrooms and eat our meals together. But in the common room, after school, they keep very much to themselves." And in a rush of confidence that this would not be repeated: "They look down on the rest of us but I think they lead a dog's life; always worrying about making the grade."

"Well, David, would you like to come and spend the evening at Miss Kingsley's house for the charity event, and help us welcome her guests? I have organized some delicious food—would you enjoy it, do you think?"

He paused and looked at her for a moment and then said, "Yes, I think I could do a good job of it for you, and I would like to help out." And Mrs. Jackson decided that she much preferred the ordinary boys to the chummy ones.

When she had finished interviewing all six boys, none of whom had been gifted enough to be part of the exclusive Chums, she asked to speak to Symes again. And after about twenty minutes the young boy arrived and stood uncertainly in the doorway.

"Hullo, Arthur, how are you doing with the not-running walk?"

He brightened up immediately "Very well, miss, I've got it down pat, no more conduct marks since I last saw you."

He was really such a nice little boy, and once he stopped looking so anxious and furtive he was quite a presentable lad.

"Well, it seems as if all your Chums have fallen by the wayside, and so I had to start again. Have you had chicken pox, by the way?"

Arthur looked baffled for a moment, and then he shook his head.

"So all those other boys will be suffering in the sickroom whilst you are having the time of your life at the charity evening." She watched him closely.

"Which boys?" Arthur Symes looked puzzled.

"Why, George, Edwin . . ." She glanced at her list and reeled off the names of the Chums who were spending a wretched time of it feeling feverish, itchy, and daubed with calamine lotion by Matron's uncaring hand.

"Nothing wrong with those boys; who told you they were sick?"

"Why Matron of course."

Just mentioning Matron changed the atmosphere in the room. Arthur looked way.

"Is Matron unkind to you boys?" she asked.

Arthur did not say anything for a moment, but the look he gave her was shrewd and assessing. Orphans of the poor may look like helpless children, but an early life of deprivation made them a lot sharper than the average middle-class child. "Matron doesn't pay much attention to us ordinary boys, unless we mis-behave. But she was different with the Chums, she kept them apart from the rest of us. If they did well in the classroom and on the playing field they were given special favor: treats and the like. If they didn't do well . . . well, I just felt very sorry for them if they didn't do well." And then after a moment's reflection he added, "Will I still be needed?" And Mrs. Jackson assured him he would. "You are my senior boy now that the Chums have all dropped out. Tell me, Arthur, how was Sir Reginald with the Chums?"

"Sir Reginald boasted about them being the smartest boys from the East End and they were always the ones who were shown off to the governors and people who gave money for the charity."

"And Miss Kingsley?" She was almost too scared to ask. "Was she nice to you?"

"We don't see her much. She comes for Speech Day, and for Christmas and for special occasions, and she is strict but nice." He thought a moment and then said, "Is it true that we won't see Sir Reginald again?"

"What were you told?" She was careful to keep her voice neutral.

"That he had been in a terrible accident and had gone to meet his Maker, and we would not see him again."

"Yes, that's quite true, and you won't see him again, ever. But if the Chums are not in the sickroom, where are they?"

"In the classroom, miss. We'll be having our midmorning break in a minute or two and I would not want to miss out on it, it's bread and dripping today."

"Would you bring one of those boys to me, would you bring George?" She fished in her handbag, opened her purse, and pulled out half a crown, careful not to laugh when Arthur's little hand shot out and took it. Whitechapel wasn't quite gone then, she thought with approval; Arthur may have been taught not to drop his aitches but his wits were still sharp and he was alert to a good opportunity—a combination that stood him in good stead for success in the world of commerce.

"Where shall I bring him?"

"To the motorcar I came in, it's around the back of the house by the kitchen courtyard. Will he come?"

Arthur hesitated for a moment and then said, "Yes, he will if you give him one of these . . ." And he flashed his coin for a brief second and repocketed it. She handed over another and he was gone.

Mrs. Jackson dropped in on Matron to say goodbye and to tell her that she hoped her sickroom would empty soon. As she left Kingsley House she decided that she never wanted to set foot in the building again.

She walked around the house to where Macleod was standing by the motorcar in conversation with George, who was looking pale, but chicken pox free. She walked George away from the chauffer's straining ear, and when they were a comfortable distance away she came straight to the point.

"George, I just want to let you know that now Sir Reginald has gone, I doubt Matron will carry on here . . ."

She was quite unprepared for how he seemed to shrink in stature. He had the look of someone who was carefully shutting up shop: locking doors and pulling down blinds.

"I can't go back." The expression of pleading on his young face made her catch her breath. Of course he was frightened that he would be sent back to the orphanage or the street he had been found on, she thought with grim certainty. In that moment she wished quite fervently for a quiet moment with Matron alone.

"Who told you that you would be sent away?" She knew the answer before she heard it.

"Matron did. The Chums represent the charity, if we don't do well, get top marks at school, achieve in sports and get into the best schools, then they will get rid of us."

"Surely not, they don't get rid of the other boys who turn in an average performance. Did Sir Reginald threaten to send you back to the streets?"

"No, he never threatened, but he was awfully disappointed in us when we didn't make the grade; two boys failed and they were sent away." He glanced at her out of the corners of his eyes as if expecting confirmation that he was right.

"But Matron threatened you?" she persisted, and he nodded.

And now the words came tumbling out. The harshness of the woman who looked after them; hours of standing in a drafty corridor, face turned to the wall for the slightest infraction; isolation from one another and from the other boys to toil away over endless hours of homework; nights of swotting for tests and exams; bread and water if they failed to make the grade. Special teas and treats if they achieved, ostracism and scorn if they disappointed; being a Chum meant that you swotted and worried and stayed up late to improve a Latin translation that was already perfect. They were safe from the danger of homelessness, they were fed, clothed, and educated, but their lives were full of anxiety that it was all temporary. No wonder they all yearned to grow up and be shot of the place, Mrs. Jackson thought. So this was why Matron had dreamed up an outbreak of chicken pox. She didn't want a nosy woman like herself talking to these boys and hearing how badly she had treated them—how manipulated and bullied the boys were in her care. With Sir Reginald gone she was vulnerable, she was losing her power, and she didn't want suspicion turned toward her.

Mrs. Jackson put a hand on George's shoulder. "Matron *will* be sent away, George. And things will change here for the better." But deep down inside she worried that it might not. Who was she to make these guarantees? But if not me, then her ladyship will step in, she thought with greater confidence.

When Mrs. Jackson returned to Chester Square she went to the between-stairs office and sat alone with her thoughts. Her mind went back several times to her own childhood in the parish orphanage. It had been a hard life, and their treatment was often callous but no one had been specifically cruel. And no one in the orphanage threatened the children with homelessness if they were disobedient. She waited until she felt quite calm and then she went upstairs to Miss Gaskell's room and knocked on the door.

Miss Gaskell was sitting by her bedroom window with a book open on her lap, but she was not reading.

"How are you today, Miss Gaskell?" Mrs. Jackson crossed the room. "It sounds as if you are coughing a little less." Miss Gaskell gave an obliging little *ahem* into a perfectly ironed, starched handkerchief that had not been used all morning. *No need to keep up with all this malarkey,* thought Mrs. Jackson grimly as she took a chair directly facing the young woman. "Perhaps you would join me in the between-stairs office so we can go over accounts and make sure that everything is ready—after all, the charity evening is the day after tomorrow and I want to be sure you are pleased with what I have done."

"Yes, if you think so, Mrs. Jackson . . . I am anxious not to infect Miss Kingsley . . ." Her voice faltered and she kept her eyes fixed firmly on her hands resting in her lap.

"Oh, I don't think you will do that, Miss Gaskell. But I thought you might be interested in my update from Kingsley House this morning, unless Miss Kingsley has already informed you. The boys I selected for the evening have all come down with chicken pox." Miss Gaskell looked startled. "Yes indeed, Miss Gaskell, just fancy that—every single one of the boys on my list are in the sickroom under quarantine and cannot come to help us out for the charity evening. Hard to believe, isn't it? Of course there are other boys immediately available to help us out, no Chums of course, but nice boys. I think they will do well."

"Chums?" Miss Gaskell turned a look of confusion toward Mrs. Jackson. "I don't know . . ."

"Oh yes you do, Miss Gaskell, you know very well." She strove to keep her voice level, but she sat forward in her chair, eyes firmly fixed on the young companion's face.

"I most certainly do not, Mrs. Jackson. Perhaps you had better explain yourself!" It was a brave attempt at outrage, but Miss Gaskell's tone lacked conviction, making Mrs. Jackson feel like a tyrant.

"I most certainly will, but first of all tell me what you know about this, will you?" And Mrs. Jackson took a sheet of paper with a torn edge to it, where it had been ripped from a notebook, out of her pocket and held it out in front of Miss Gaskell.

"Yes, that's right," she said in response to Miss Gaskell's appalled stare. "You know what this is about, don't you? It's from Matron's private account book. And the initials stand for Reginald Algernon Cholmondeley. 'Cholmondeley' when it is written is rather confusing, isn't it? Not everyone perhaps knows on first reading the name that it is pronounced 'Chumley.' Sir Reginald Algernon Cholmondeley—the Head Chum—and father figure to the special boys." She had to pause here, to make sure that her voice remained calm and matter-of-fact, as she did not want to precipitate a hysterical reaction.

"And these," she continued as she ran her finger down the list of figures on the far right, "are the amounts required by Matron from RAC. And this," she tapped the row of ticks, "represents the amounts RAC paid up to satisfy her bank account and to ensure her silence."

Miss Gaskell, her face white as chalk, sat quite still as she wound her handkerchief around her forefinger.

"What did you find out about Sir Reginald, Miss Gaskell? Why was he paying Matron all this money?" There was a long silence, and Miss Gaskell's eyes slid around the room as if to calculate which exit would be best for her, the window or the door. Finally she spoke.

"About a week before the dinner party for Mr. Churchill, Sir Reginald had a severe chill and he was confined to complete bed rest at home. He was quite ill and Miss Kingsley was terribly worried about him. I was sent over to Kingsley House to pay the bills due at the end of the month. It was then that I found out what he had been doing." She ground to a halt and stared down at her hands. "Miss Kingsley had given me her set of keys to the safe, and I took out the account ledgers so that I could record the payments I had made. They were not large bills, just ones to local tradesmen and suppliers.

"I had been in the office many times to help Sir Reginald, writing letters of thanks for donations. That sort of thing." And now she blushed, her ears went red, and she looked away. "I had always thought that he was interested in me, that he might . . ." She looked out of the window and her eyes filled with tears. Mrs. Jackson decided it was time to help out. "Did Sir Reginald lead you to believe that he was interested in marrying you?"

"It was never specifically said in plain language, but always implied. And then I realized that he was not in the least interested in me after all. Ever since he believed he would receive a peerage for his work. I was perhaps not . . . quite . . ." She looked away from Mrs. Jackson as she relived her shame when she had discovered that she was simply not good enough to marry.

"And then?" A yawning silence stretched on as Miss Gaskell gazed into her lap. "Miss Gaskell, you need to be painstakingly truthful with me now. You are in an exceptionally bad position.

And you can't stay in this room forever. Will you please tell me everything you know? Lady Montfort is a good woman and will do everything she can to help you. You are not alone with this secret. Please share it. Share the burden." She waited, earnest eyes on the face of the young woman in front of her

"I had never been in the office alone before—Sir Reginald practically lived at the charity and never took time away from his duties. I think I was hoping to find something that would help me understand more about him. And why he had lost interest in me." She ended rather feebly as she dabbed her eyes with her handkerchief, now a tight wad of knots, gray and grubby.

"At the back of the safe I found a portfolio and inside it were bank statements in the name of J. Hewitt and Company with Temple Bank. I thought this was rather strange since the charity has always banked with Coutts and I couldn't imagine why another company's bank information would be in the safe. I looked through the charity's income-and-expense ledger, and found there were regular payments made each quarter to J. Hewitt for legal services, and trust management. The sums were consistently large and regular and had been paid for what looked like many years, ten at least. The payments for just one year were in the thousands. There was a small account book in the portfolio and one of the expenses listed was for cash payments to Mavis Biggleswade, many entries amounting to hundreds and hundreds of pounds!

"Sir Reginald had been cheating the charity for years. He had been taking money that was meant for the boys: their education, uniforms, and school fees." She drew breath and stared at Mrs. Jackson with horrified eyes and nodded her head. "I couldn't believe it at first, I simply couldn't take it in. I found the bills for J. Hewitt and Company and decided to do some checking up. I went to their address, but the company no longer exists. The new tenants of the building told me that Jonathon Hewitt was a solicitor who provided legal services many years ago, but he had died and the firm was now defunct. Sir Reginald was paying himself under the false name of J. Hewitt! He was a lying cheat, and that awful woman was in on it with him. He promoted his special boys, to gain larger and larger donations and then he stole them. If he felt his Chums were not trying hard enough he left their punishment to Matron. Have you any idea how much she bullied those little boys when no one was around to see? They were scared to death of her. I came straight home and told Miss Kingsley!" Mrs. Jackson was almost speechless. So, the girl had told someone. *How could I have thought she had carried the burden of this secret alone?*

"Miss Kingsley told me that I it was wrong. She was angry with me, and said that I was a naughty girl, trying to make trouble." Here Miss Gaskell started to cry, harsh, desperate, painful sobs that erupted from the center of her being. "The more I tried to convince her of what I had found, the more upset she became. I asked her to come with me to the office at Kingsley House, that I would show her the books myself. But she became even more distraught and angry and I was worried that she would collapse. I just gave up. Afterwards, I hoped that she did actually believe me; she just wasn't sure what to do about it. When Sir Reginald was found dead, she shut down completely. This is why we are not allowed to talk about the murder."

"You told no one else after this?" Mrs. Jackson asked, knowing that the answer would be no.

She got up and went to Miss Gaskell's chair and took the young woman's cold hand in hers.

"You are good and brave, and it doesn't matter what Miss Kingsley . . ."

The door opened, and standing on the threshold was the patroness of one of England's largest charities for the unwanted, luckless orphans of the poor.

"I am glad to see you are looking a good deal improved, Adelaide," she said, completely ignoring Miss Gaskell's red nose and swollen eyes. In fact she did not even look at the young woman; she was staring directly at Mrs. Jackson.

"We must not be selfish and trespass on Lady Montfort's goodwill. Mrs. Jackson has done a thorough job and I think, since you are so much improved, Adelaide, that you can continue with the final preparations for the musical evening."

"I would be most happy to continue, ma'am; her ladyship was clear in her instructions that I make myself useful until after the event." Mrs. Jackson was determined to show Miss Gaskell that there was no need to fear Miss Kingsley, and at the same time she cursed Macleod, who no doubt had reported on her meeting with George.

"Thank you, Mrs. Jackson, but no. You have done a splendid job; please thank Lady Montfort for me. Now, I see it is almost seven o'clock. Macleod will take you straight back to Montfort House. Adelaide, when you have had a chance to wash your face, please come downstairs to the drawing room immediately."

Miss Gaskell nodded and cast a weary look at Mrs. Jackson. Her face was composed but her eyes as they sought Mrs. Jackson's were quite miserable as she nodded her acceptance to her elderly employer. *You see?* her resigned glance clearly said. *She is trying to pretend none of this ever happened.*

Chapter Twenty-five

"So are you telling me you were chucked out of the house, Jackson?" Clementine asked her housekeeper, who had walked through her bedroom door, looking triumphant.

"Yes, m'lady, it comes down to that I suppose."

"Well come on in and tell me all about it. Something momentous has happened, I can tell!" Clementine had been feeling that she was wasting her time in London, that Mrs. Jackson in acting as her agent at Chester Square didn't need her help, and as a result she was feeling frustrated and bored. Now here was her housekeeper with useful information that would hopefully help them push their inquiry toward a successful conclusion. She put aside the book she was reading and sat forward in her chair by the fire, her face expectant, eyes bright, her demeanor that of a young girl on her birthday when someone has put a particularly hoped-for gift before her.

Mrs. Jackson hesitated for a moment and Clementine asked, "Do you know who murdered Sir Reginald?" And Mrs. Jackson started to nod, and then she shook her head. "I am still trying to work it all out, m'lady," she said.

"I suggest you just blurt it out, Jackson. Then we can see if between us we can't piece it all together."

And then she made herself sit quietly as Mrs. Jackson related what she had found out at Kingsley House, and her interesting conversation with Miss Gaskell. And as she told her tale Clementine's jaw simply dropped and she leaned forward in her chair and for all the world looked as if she might leap right out of it.

"Good heavens above, Jackson. It simply can't be possible. How absolutely unbelievable, how absolutely preposterous . . . and Matron was in on it too? Matron blackmailed him? Oh, my good heavens." Clementine was sitting bolt upright, her wide eyes glued to Mrs. Jackson's face.

"He was a cheat!" she cried in triumph. Appalling as Sir Reginald's criminal activities were, here was information that explained the reason why he had been murdered. "The wretched man cheated his greatest friend, and betrayed the trust of everyone who supported Miss Kingsley's charity. It just amazes me when I think of all his complacent, holier-than-thou prating, and his good works and determination to elevate the lives of the cast-down. He was nothing but a thief . . ."

"He made those boys perform to such high standards, m'lady, so that he could parade them in front of rich donors and increase the size of their monetary gifts! Money he then went and stole." Mrs. Jackson joined her ladyship in outraged disgust.

"And it was little Miss Gaskell who found out about it and went to Miss Kingsley, who told her . . . who told her she was making trouble? Oh dear, oh dear, Jackson, poor Miss Kingsley's world is falling apart around her ears: a nephew who is a dead loss, a partner who steals from her charity and is then murdered in her house. Does she think that Adelaide did it? Of course she does!"

Mrs. Jackson had handed her the torn sheet from Matron's ledger and she read through the numbers. "Did Adelaide say how much he was stealing?"

"Yes, she said it was thousands and thousands—for the past ten years or more. And at that moment, m'lady, Miss Kingsley came into the room and told me that I was no longer needed."

"Then she knew that you had found out."

"Yes, m'lady, she knows, and that's why she wants me out of the house. She is ignoring what Miss Gaskell told her about Sir Reginald, because she simply doesn't want to believe it to be true and of course she doesn't want his fiddling the books to come out. The shame would be too much for her."

"And she is doing exactly the same thing with his murder. If she doesn't talk about it or acknowledge it in any way, then it didn't happen. Miraculously, the police will arrest a culprit, hopefully someone she doesn't know, and all the awfulness and the possibility of scandal will simply evaporate, poor old thing." Clementine felt nothing but sympathy for the elderly lady whose life's work had been reduced to a travesty by a man she trusted. "So, Jackson, do you think Adelaide murdered Sir Reginald?" She watched her housekeeper's face cloud over, a small frown appeared and her mouth came down at the corners.

"If she did, it was on the spur of the moment, a real crime of passion, as they call it. Passionate hatred for what he had done not only to the charity, but to the boys in his care, and of course for leading her to believe that he might marry her. She was sick, and burdened with what she had found out, doubly so because she wasn't believed. So she came down the stairs to the hall on her errand for white spirit. The butler was belowstairs dealing with the Clumsy Footman—and she went into the dining room and confronted Sir Reginald with what she knew, and killed him. She opened up the catches on the window, hoping to divert suspicion to outside the house. Then she left the dining room . . ."

Clementine willingly took up the tale. "Where she met up with Mr. Greenberg, who offered to help her find what she was looking for. But I wonder why Mr. Greenberg went to so much trouble to conceal this from the police. I would have thought . . ." She fell silent for a moment, off on a track of her own.

Mrs. Jackson obligingly finished for her: "Then Mr. Greenberg went upstairs, and a little later she returned to the salon with her bottle of pure spirit. Errand accomplished." Mrs. Jackson sighed, "But somehow it doesn't feel right. Miss Gaskell is too mild, she wasn't angry, she was broken, and not just by what Sir Reginald had done, but because Miss Kingsley didn't appear to believe her."

"Miss Kingsley perhaps thought the same thing as we just did, Jackson. I think she jumped to that conclusion the moment we found the man dead in the dining room. She bustled Adelaide away to her room and told her stay there and keep quiet. Miss Kingsley is one of those people who are extraordinarily loyal. I think it's the greatest quality she offers as an employer and as a friend. For her it's for life, once you gain her trust. If she wasn't such a frail old lady I would almost say she was capable of having killed Sir Reginald herself; after all, it was her trust he betrayed so thoroughly and for goodness knows how many years." Clementine got up from her chair, walked over to the window, and stared out into the street. "I think it's an awful shame that you have been ordered home, Jackson, as there is still a lot you could achieve at Chester Square. I feel we are almost there."

"Perhaps *you* might make some discoveries at the house, m'lady. You said that Miss Kingsley confided to you about Mr. Tricklebank; perhaps she is in need of someone to talk to now."

Clementine nodded. "Yes, but I don't think it is information we want from *Miss Kingsley*. It's information we want about her household. And you are in a far better position to find out about this business with the Chester Square footman than I am."

"Yes, the death of the first footman, Leonard Crutchley, and the disappearance of the Clumsy Footman, Eddy Porter: we still have not accounted for these elements."

"What did Jenkins say about this Eddy Porter again?"

"Oh, that he was a superior sort of person, but not well trained as a footman."

"Of course he must be an accomplice in this affair, but an accomplice to whom? If only we could find out more about the wretched man." Clementine stood quite still and absentmindedly watched the lamplighter at work along the street. In the silence that followed, she guessed they were thinking the same thing.

"There is nothing for it, Jackson, we must tiptoe carefully the rest of the way. I'm going to have to get you back into that house. We must find out more about Eddy Porter. And I have to have a little talk with that nice Inspector Hillary, however bad it makes me look. Because if someone walked into the dining room and confronted Sir Reginald, and then stabbed him, wouldn't their clothes be covered in his blood? Or are we back to looking at someone outside the house again?"

Clementine intended to talk to Miss Kingsley first, then to Hillary, but she was preempted by the arrival of the detective inspector the following morning as she was pondering how she would get Hermione to welcome Mrs. Jackson back to Chester Square.

Hillary appeared at ten o'clock, full of apologies for disturbing her morning but quite happy, it seemed, to do so. Clementine had decided that the best way of tackling this equable young man was to come straight to the point. But first she offered him a cup of Turkish coffee, because she knew he enjoyed such things, and then she sat quietly in her chair, watching him sip appreciatively, and waited for him to begin.

"How long have you known Miss Kingsley, Lady Montfort?"

"Since I returned, with my mother, to England from India for my first Season, many years ago now. Miss Kingsley was a friend of my mother; she gave a ball in my honor at Chester Square."

"Yes, I thought you were old friends, and I think I rather need your help. You see, it is almost impossible for me to talk to Miss Kingsley. Every time I tell the butler I must speak with her on police business, he tells me she is indisposed . . ." He finished his coffee and put down the cup.

"A terrible shock to have your closest friend murdered in your dining room, Inspector, as I am sure you can imagine. Miss Kingsley is an elderly and frail woman." This was not the way she wanted the conversation to go. She wanted him to talk about the murder itself. But she sat still and composed her face to listen sympathetically.

"Yes of course, and I completely understand, but you see, if this goes on much longer I'm going to have to insist, and that would be unpleasant." *Unpleasant,* thought Clementine, *unpleasant? Why on earth is Scotland Yard extending such niceties to its murder suspects?* And the answer came back: since the ex–home secretary and First Lord of the Admiralty had decided that they must tread gently and not allow a scandal to break. That this murder investigation must be conducted with the least fuss lest the newspapers get a whiff of what was, after all, a sensational piece of news involving some of the country's top families and, most important, the First Lord of the Admiralty. She thought of her husband's dismay that the Talbot name would be once more shouted from the headlines and linked with murder.

"I am happy to talk to Miss Kingsley, Inspector, and explain your position to her. I am sure she will come round. In fact I can guarantee it." *So Hillary perceived she had influence with Hermione; what perfect timing and how very convenient.* She poured another cup of coffee for him.

His relief was palpable as he happily sipped his coffee and offered up his heartfelt thanks. And it was now that Clementine decided to press home her advantage and call in the favor.

"I understand that Leonard Crutchley was found—that he

was killed and then his body was thrown in the Thames." She said this without explaining how she knew who Leonard Crutchley was or how she had found out about his death. She left that for Hillary to work out. If he was surprised that she knew who the dead footman was, he did not show it, but she noted with some satisfaction that he looked at her with new respect and became a little more alert.

"Yes. it was Leonard Crutchley, Miss Kingsley's—"

"Footman," she finished, because she really wanted to move this forward a little faster. "Leonard Crutchley was killed to make way for Eddy Porter to be hired in Miss Kingsley's house, so with the disappearance of Eddy Porter we are looking at the possibility of some sort of subterfuge, am I right, Inspector?"

"It might very well look that way, Lady Montfort, but I couldn't possibly comment, as I am sure you will understand."

She beamed at this nice young man with his pleasant manners, and continued.

"But it certainly looks as though there are some outside elements that need to be accounted for, Inspector," she said, to establish an understanding between them.

"I am sure there are, Lady Montfort." He was quick to take her meaning.

"So Eddy Porter, who is not a footman at all, arrived at Miss Kingsley's house with a specific task. Perhaps he was there to provide a distraction on the evening of the murder and to facilitate an entry to the house through the dining-room window, or to help make it look as if someone outside the house gained access to murder Sir Reginald. And I think there were quite a few distractions that evening, from what I can remember."

"So it would seem." The young man smiled at her.

"And it would seem to *me* that this was not a murder of opportunity but a murder that had been carefully planned in advance."

"I'm glad to hear you say that, m'lady, but once again I

couldn't possibly comment." She noticed that Detective Inspector Hillary was no longer sitting back in his chair sipping Turkish coffee but had put his cup to one side and was looking at her with his full attention. Clementine obliged by swapping horses in midstream, a tactic she knew Hillary would recognize in the refined business of discreet interrogation.

"Of course you have my fullest cooperation, Inspector, and I will be happy to talk to Miss Kingsley. I have no doubt that when you call on her, she will be quite ready to talk to you. But of course you do remember, don't you, that tomorrow night is the occasion of her charity event? Yes, I thought you had not forgotten. It would be far more advantageous for you to make your next visit to Chester Square the morning after her event. As a lady of advanced years Miss Kingsley has one goal in mind and that is to make this event a particularly lucrative one for her charity, and it is in such a good cause."

She noticed a flicker of uneasiness in the policeman's face and he hesitated for a moment.

"Yes, I completely understand, Lady Montfort, and if in the meantime I can be of any help whatsoever or you find you might need me for anything, please contact me or my sergeant." *Aha,* thought Clementine, *now it is my turn.*

"There are two things I would like to ask you, Detective Inspector, if I may?" She saw a flash of apprehension. "You see, when I saw Sir Reginald in the dining room, with that knife handle sticking out of his chest, there was blood on his suit and in his lap as he was slumped forward, but there was no blood across the cloth. That was spilled port wine, which I mistook for blood. So if anyone in the house had stabbed him they should have been covered in blood, and surely there would have been more blood . . . well, you know . . . everywhere, and there wasn't; why?"

He had listened to her without expression on his face, but

surely he must have been quite appalled at the vulgarity of her question. She refused to think about that part.

"You are most observant, Lady Montfort. Ordinarily if someone is stabbed in a vital organ, especially the heart, then there is considerable and immediate blood loss, and as you say the perpetrator would be covered in . . . blood. But in this case the knife was stuck into the heart and left there. If it had been pulled out it would have been quite . . ."

"Messy?"

"Yes. In this case, however, the knife blade acted like a plug, and the victim died not from severe blood loss but of a heart attack."

Well for heaven's sake, thought Clementine, *how extraordinarily simple.*

"And no doubt Sir Reginald's murderer stabbed him from behind. So his body also shielded the murderer from getting any blood on his clothing." She thanked God that her husband would never know she had made this observation.

She was rewarded with a brief nod as he assured her that this was no doubt correct.

"It would have to be someone immensely strong then?"

"Not necessarily, but it would have to be someone who knew where to strike and at which angle to hold the knife."

"And nowadays you can look for fingerprints to help identify whoever it was who used that knife on Sir Reginald. Did the knife handle have any fingerprints on it?"

He continued to regard her without expression as he politely answered, "No, Lady Montfort, it did not. Whoever stabbed Sir Reginald was wearing gloves. Gloves that would have blood on them, and which could be discarded. We did not," she noticed that he had relaxed, "find any bloodstained gloves in the house or garden."

"Thank you, Inspector. I have wondered about this of course

ever since I found that poor man." She tried to retrieve a little of her lost dignity but she saw from his face that he was not fooled for one moment, because his face was grave as he said, "Whoever killed Sir Reginald is a dangerous person, Lady Montfort—they certainly possess cunning and audacity; I hope that you will not put yourself in any danger."

"Oh good heavens, Inspector, of course not. It is my morbid curiosity after having discovered the poor man, nothing more." She allowed herself a dismissive little laugh as she rose to her feet.

But the inspector did not look convinced as he said good-bye.

Clementine decided that her next move, that of getting Mrs. Jackson back into Chester Square, might be a little more difficult than her conversation with Inspector Hillary, because it involved a certain amount of bullying. She called for Herne and told him to bring the motorcar around to take her to Chester Square.

Chapter Twenty-six

On the morning of the charity event Mrs. Jackson decided she would join the servants downstairs for breakfast before she returned to her duties at Chester Square accompanied by Mr. White and his first and second footmen. As she came into the kitchen she found the butler seated at the table, reading the morning newspaper and sipping a cup of tea in his shirtsleeves and waistcoat, his tailcoat hanging over the back of the chair. Ginger was busy at the kitchen range making breakfast. Mrs. Jackson, standing quite unnoticed in the kitchen doorway, watched as Ginger turned from the stove and leaned over Mr. White to set his breakfast down in front of him. She placed her free hand on his shoulder and, to Mrs. Jackson's shocked surprise, the butler bent his head and kissed the hand that rested so lightly there.

Mrs. Jackson felt her cheeks flame hot with embarrassment and she quickly left the room to stand outside in the corridor until the flush died from her face and her heart stopped skipping about in agitation. *What have I just seen?* she asked herself in consternation. She flapped her hand in front of her face to cool it. *Calm down for pity's sake,* she instructed herself, *he only kissed her hand.* And then as soon as she was sure her cheeks were not quite so fiery a red, she cleared her throat loudly and made a second entrance.

"Good morning!" she said cheerfully. "I have just time for a quick cup of tea and then we really should be getting under way!"

Mr. White got to his feet in some confusion. "Yes, Mrs. Jackson, the boys and I are almost ready; they have just gone to their rooms to find clean gloves. Perhaps you would brief me as we drive over to Chester Square."

Ginger, Mrs. Jackson noticed, merely smiled and reached for the large brown teapot to pour her a cup. "Take a load off, Mrs. Jackson, and eat a couple of rashers; it will be a long day. Important you make a decent breakfast." She deftly served the housekeeper a plate of eggs, bacon, and fried bread and went about her work. And Mrs. Jackson sat down next to Mr. White and, careful to not look at him, ate her breakfast.

As Mr. White and Mrs. Jackson were putting on their overcoats in the scullery, they were joined by the Montfort footmen, both of them ready and eager to attend a gala event.

"Right handsome you boys look," Ginger said with approval as they all piled into the Chester Square motorcar and she stood at the curb, her shoulders hunched with cold, to wave them off. *For all the world*, thought Mrs. Jackson, *as if we are off on a day-trip to the seaside.*

As they drove through the empty early-morning streets, Mrs. Jackson took a moment to prepare Mr. White before their meeting with Mr. Jenkins.

"When we get to Chester Square, Mr. White, it is important to remember that Mr. Jenkins must not feel usurped in any way. He has worked for the family all his life and no one understands better than he the importance of the charity event. Our job is to provide perfect support to Mr. Jenkins, in his service to the Chester Square guests, and above all to help Mr. Jenkins to not forget *anything.*" She had then explained the extent and erratic nature of Mr. Jenkins's little problem with absentmindedness, which was often exacerbated by stressful occasions.

The collaborative meeting between the members of the Montfort House and the Chester Square servants' halls went well and Mrs. Jackson was reassured as she left the two butlers—never a particularly easy pairing of hierarchical positions, any more than having two ringmasters at a circus—to discuss their schedule of work together. She was pleased to notice that Mr. White was respectfully deferential and she was grateful for his sensitivity toward the older man. Despite his immature years, which counted against him, Mrs. Jackson had decided that she approved of White. His manner was impeccable and he was intelligent, aware, and he managed everything he did with self-contained professional detachment. He had one serious fault though, in her opinion: he was particularly at risk where Ginger's charms were concerned.

Her mind went back to the tender scene in the kitchen. It was almost a domestic moment, she thought. And who said that people who spend their working lives together should not have kindhearted feelings for each other? She remembered Ginger's soft expression as White had kissed her hand. *It's a cold, old world,* Mrs. Jackson said to herself as she remembered the despair in Miss Gaskell's voice when she finally recognized she had trusted someone with her tender feelings who had not been worthy of them. *Is it natural for us to soldier on, on our solitary paths, and then retire at the end of our working lives to be even more alone?* When she had seen that sweet kiss planted on Ginger's hand, her heart had leaped and she had caught her breath. It had been almost painful for her to observe simple human affection between a man and a woman, especially when she had carefully taught herself never to expect more than professional friendship with those she worked with. It was out of the question that someone in her position should ever entertain the idea of an intimate friendship with a fellow servant, let alone marriage.

It's this wretched investigating business, she thought, *it blurs all the lines of expected behavior and propriety and turns everything topsy-turvy.* Thoroughly confused, her hand strayed to Stafford's letter, which was carefully folded inside her skirt pocket. She still had not replied to him. She went into her between-stairs office and drew out the letter from her pocket and read it through again.

There now, she thought, *the man wants to spend the day with you at Kew Gardens, Edith, what is the harm in that? And you would undoubtedly enjoy yourself. So don't be so stiff-necked.* She sighed and put the letter back in its envelope and from there to her skirt pocket and went in search of Miss Gaskell.

"I am only here today to help *you*, Miss Gaskell, I have no intention of interfering in any way at all," she said to the tired young woman. There was something pathetically woebegone about the young companion, as she put out a gentle hand and laid it on Mrs. Jackson's arm. Mrs. Jackson could only imagine how unkindly Miss Kingsley had castigated Miss Gaskell for her indiscretions regarding Sir Reginald and the carefully concealed theft.

"Ever since you came to help us, Mrs. Jackson, you have been nothing but kind and diligent on our behalf. I do not feel you have interfered, and I am grateful that you care so much. I would really enjoy doing the flowers with you, though." For the first time in days the young girl in Miss Gaskell emerged, and Mrs. Jackson remembered third housemaids who had enjoyed the treat of arranging flowers for the house for a special occasion.

They worked contentedly together, trimming and arranging the great golden blooms of the roses and the ivory-white hothouse lilies among dark foliage in large Grecian urns and priceless Chinese vases.

Once the flowers were arranged and left to open in the little sitting room, the remainder of the day became one of organized activity with the three footmen; the two chauffeurs, Macleod and Herne; the gardener and his two lads; struggling upstairs and downstairs, moving chairs and sofas from rooms all over the house and those borrowed from two neighbors. The salon, now opened up into its fullest extent, was lit by early-winter sunshine streaming through its windows, casting a bright light on Mrs. Jackson and Miss Gaskell as they directed the efforts of arranging seating in the salon.

When the men were quite finished and were standing in perspiring, red-faced groups, breathing heavily and probably wondering if anyone was going to offer them a glass of beer with their midday dinner, Mrs. Jackson and Miss Gaskell inspected the setup to make sure that all chairs were turned to their best advantage, giving whoever sat in them at least a partial view of the famous diva as she stood by the piano to regale them with song.

"Oh dear no, this won't do at all." Mrs. Jackson was standing with her back to the window in the small salon, where a grouping of several chairs and a small sofa were so cramped together that it would be hard for people not to sit without their knees being jammed up against one another's. "I'm afraid we will have to move this screen back at least three feet, more if possible. Would you . . ."

"My dear Mrs. Jackson, no one has moved the Chinese screen since it was placed there forty years ago, when the late Mr. Kingsley brought it back from Peking with him, a gift from the dowager empress. It is far too heavy." Mr. Jenkins turned toward her, his spectacles halfway down his nose, a green apron tied around his middle. The butler's memory, Mrs. Jackson noticed, was spot-on when it came to remembering the past.

"Just a tiny foot . . . or two, Mr. Jenkins, couldn't we just slide . . . ?"

"No one here is strong enough to move it, Mrs. Jackson." The butler was at his most indulgent. "I'm afraid we would need at least *five* village blacksmiths." He smiled his gentle smile, no doubt thinking her a headstrong young woman, forever in need of caution.

This was a direct challenge to Herne and Macleod. They were both well-set-up men, proud of their height and strength; Macleod in particular not five years ago had still been driving Miss Kingsley's barouche and taking care of a stable full of horses in the Chester Square mews. He shouldered the footmen aside, namby-pamby lads that they were, and walked over to the corner of the Chinese screen. Herne, not to be outdone, joined him. The gardener and his two lads fell in on either side. And sure enough the heavy screen was eased an inch toward the window.

"Well don't just stand there," grunted Herne, veins standing out on a shining brow, sweat flowing freely. "Git yer back into ut, lads . . ." And the footmen took off their coats and joined in as they slid the heavy screen back a foot, and then another, and, with a concerted communal grunt, one more, as Mr. Jenkins welcomed every move with exhortations not to send the screen crashing through the window.

"Ah yes, so much better! Do you see, Mr. Jenkins? Look at how much light comes into this lovely room now. So, we should move the potted palm into *that* far corner, and we can put this massive Chinese jar over . . . there."

"Oh my dear Mrs. Jackson, please do not *move* the water jar." Mr. Jenkins's voice was faint with horror and shock at the housekeeper's cavalier attitude to what was after all a priceless and irreplaceable treasure. "The jar, as you call it, dear lady, is in fact from the Ming Dynasty, Jiajing to be precise; peerless, without equal."

"I completely agree, Mr. Jenkins, we must keep this lovely

thing quite safe." Mrs. Jackson walked forward to lift the lid off the jar; she didn't want anything broken at this stage of the game. Macleod wheeled the lidless jar into a safe corner, and after thanking him she bent over to fit the lid back onto the jar. And as she looked down she saw something that brought the hairs on the back of her neck up so straight and stiff that she felt quite giddy.

"Well now, everyone, what a splendid job. It's nearly one o'clock, we should take a break for dinner, and then we need to sweep all the floors and carpets through the house again . . ." She ushered everyone out of the room and watched them troop down the back stairs, the housemaids chattering with the enjoyment of working with a group of vigorous men, and the vigorous men ribbing one another over perceived reluctance to pit their weight against the screen. *Give several men a job to do together that involves a trial of strength and it makes immediate companions,* Mrs. Jackson thought as she walked rapidly back to the salon, and locked herself in.

Her heart was pumping away in her chest as if she had run for miles, but her hands were quite steady as she lifted up the lid of the jar and set it down on the floor.

"Well, hullo," she said as she looked into the bottom of the jar. "However did you manage to get in here?"

Clementine did not expect to be called to Chester Square quite so early for an evening of music. She had spent a pleasant afternoon trying on hats and trying to remember what Pettigrew had told her about wide crowns and narrow brims, or perhaps it was the other way around. Every hat she tried on was a delight after the massive half-gardens that people wore on their heads these days, and she had left an order for several beauties with the modiste.

She was looking forward to putting her feet up for an hour with her book, before leaving for Chester Square and the Chimney Sweep Boys charity evening. Most certainly she had not expected to have to jump into her bath and then throw on her clothes to go over to Chester Square an hour early, but she was quite prepared to do so, especially since Mrs. Jackson had never in her life given Clementine what amounted to a direct order.

"Pettigrew, is Lord Montfort at home yet?" she asked as her maid fussed about with handkerchief and evening bag.

Her husband, as promised, had returned to town to do his duty for the charity, fully prepared to part with a substantial sum of money to his wife's friend in the process. When told that he was still at his club, Clementine instructed Pettigrew to leave word with White to tell Lord Montfort that Herne was driving her over early. His lordship would have to take a taxicab to join her at Miss Kingsley's house.

Wearing her most splendid gown of the season and covered in the entire collection of the Talbot diamonds, as this was a most grand occasion with senior royalty in attendance, Clementine was carefully enveloped in her sable fur and sent out into the damp night. There was a mist closing in off the river that would hopefully not thicken into fog later on.

Herne, who had driven over from his day's labors at Chester Square, was already dressed in his footman's attire. Undoubtedly he liked himself in it because he was standing to attention, at least another three inches taller with his chest sticking out, as he held the door of the motorcar open for her.

"Everything going smoothly at Chester Square, Herne?" Clementine asked as he tucked her up carefully in a large plaid traveling rug in the back of the motorcar, making her feel somewhat overheated and claustrophobic as the night had a clammy closeness to it.

"Yes, m'lady, everyone is ready. The French chef came and the food looks jolly good all laid out on the tables with fresh flowers and fruit; very pretty, very festive." Herne's job was to wait outside in the car or downstairs in the porter's lodge when he drove the Talbots to parties and dinners and he was obviously enjoying the novelty of his dual role.

"The young Chimney Sweeps are being put through their paces by Miss Gaskell and Mr. Jenkins; nice lot of boys they are and no mistake. Hard to believe they were all guttersnipes at one time."

Clementine smiled to herself in the dark; Herne had a peculiarly outright and amusing turn of phrase, always appreciated by the Talbot family.

"Mrs. Jackson coping well then?" Clementine asked, searching for possible hints to what awaited her at Chester Square.

"Oh yes indeed, m'lady." Herne was an Iyntwood servant and had enormous respect for the housekeeper and her many talents. "She's got that place looking bloomin' wonderful: flowers everywhere, garlands of 'em all down the stairs, banks of 'em in the hall. The food looks sumptuous and the footmen all very 'andsome. She even got a piano chuner in." He puffed out his chest with pride, as tonight he was one of them. "Our Mrs. Jackson has got them all jumping about all right."

He pulled the motor up to the curb in front of Chester Square. Every light was on in the house; the large sash windows cast a golden aureole of light out into the night and the deepening mist reflected it back so that the house appeared to be quite separate from its neighbors, alone in the night like a great glowing ship putting out into a dark sea.

"You are the first to arrive, m'lady," Herne said as he handed Clementine out of the motor.

"Thank you, Herne. Now where is—?" Clementine looked up and her words hung unfinished in the damp air. "Good heavens, what is Mrs. Jackson thinking?" She and Herne gazed upward to behold Mrs. Jackson, almost hanging out of the second-floor window of the salon, craned forward and bent over from her slender waist. She straightened up and, as she did so, saw Clementine and waved her hand in clear indication that running up the stairs to the salon would not bring Lady Montfort to her soon enough.

As Clementine obediently trotted up steps to the front door, she noticed that another motorcar was coming to a halt at the curb; the first of the early birds were arriving.

"You've found something, haven't you?" Clementine was quite out of breath as she arrived in the salon, having sedately walked the length of a battalion of liveried footmen and pages in the hall and then taken the stairs at a pretty fast clip. Mrs. Jackson said yes m'lady she most certainly had indeed. And as soon as Clementine was safely inside the room she locked its double doors.

"I've found the How of it," she said. And for the first time in their long acquaintance, Clementine saw that her housekeeper was capable of expressing exultant triumph. Her face was flushed, her eyes gleamed with intention, and tiny little springs and coils of hair had escaped from the constraint of her immaculate head and sprung about her forehead and neck, making her look beautifully vibrant and at least twenty years old. She led Clementine over to the Chinese water jar and lifted the lid.

"Look at that, m'lady," she said, and Clementine looked down into the jar and with a jubilant, "Oh my goodness me," reached down and carefully pulled up a lightweight portable ladder made of corded silk. As she coiled the ladder on the floor beside the jar, a rather portentous clang came from inside. It was a heavy lead weight secured to the last rung.

"The sort used by fishermen to keep fishing nets anchored down," her housekeeper explained.

Together the two women stretched the ladder to its fullest extent across the floor.

"It's easily twenty feet long, maybe more," Clementine exclaimed. "I see what you were doing hanging upside down from the window, Jackson. Now, tell me exactly what you have decided."

"Well, first of all I have to set the stage, as it were, m'lady. Before I had them moved, this large Chinese screen stood squarely here in front of the windows, blocking all the light and wasting space." Mrs. Jackson disliked natural light being shut out of a room. "At the edge of the screen was that huge palm." She waved her hand to indicate the potted palm now relegated to a distant corner. "And in front of the palm was this Chinese water jar. Do you see what I'm driving at, m'lady? With the setup the way it was, anyone could go behind the screen and not be seen by people in the room, and then they could step behind the closed curtains, slide up the window, and lower the ladder. It was probably already made fast to the screen." She reached out a hand to shake the screen and it didn't budge. "And look, some of the black lacquer is scuffed here on the screen's foot from a rope burn. The potted palm was right in front so no one would have spotted it. It was quite simple, the person who murdered Sir Reginald was upstairs in the salon with you all evening."

"Good grief, Jackson, here in this room the whole time?"

"Yes, m'lady, except for the time it took for him to climb down that ladder and back again. The Clumsy Footman's job was to cause a distraction by spilling coffee, and as everyone's attention was briefly taken up with that, and the last of the gentlemen arriving from the dining room, the murderer stepped behind the screen, went out the window, down the portable ladder, and landed on the outside sill of the dining-room window. The window had been unlocked by the Clumsy Footman earlier and he had probably secured the portable ladder, too, as no one could possibly have seen it behind the screen. So the murderer only had to slide the window up and climb in right behind the chair in which Sir Reginald was sitting."

"Yes of course, Jackson, how simply brilliant of you. He came into the room behind him and stabbed him with a nice strong backwards thrust right into the heart. He took Sir Reginald completely by surprise."

She then repeated her conversation with Detective Inspector Hillary, saying that blood loss from a wound delivered in such a way and with the knife left in place would be far less messy than if the knife was pulled out.

"And Sir Reginald's body further acted as a shield. Jackson, we are so close!" Clementine finished triumphantly with thrill of delight. *Why was it you pondered a thing for days, waking at night, cudgeling away at an overworked brain trying to make sense of it, and then: voila!*

"Yes, m'lady. I am hoping that you can run over the time upstairs in the salon when the footman spilled the coffee."

Clementine walked over toward the piano. "Pity everything has been moved. Well anyway . . ." She closed her eyes momentarily to conjure up the scene in this room several nights ago. "Marigold Meriwether was sitting on one of two sofas . . . here, with Miss Kingsley. Lady Wentworth and Mrs. Churchill were sitting close, about here. Miss Meriwether was being congratulated on her engagement to Captain Vetiver. I was standing there talking to Lady Ryderwood. Adelaide was by the piano, organizing sheet music . . . Lady Cunard was wandering up and down this wall, looking at the paintings and waiting for the men to join us. Now where was Jennifer Wells-Thornton? Had she gone by then? No, of course not, she was with Miss Meriwether. Oh yes, and here," she walked forward toward the double doors that gave entrance into the room, "were the first of the men arriving to join us from the dining room: Lord Montfort and Sir Henry

Wentworth and that poor young flying officer; followed by Sir Vivian.

"It was as we were talking to Sir Henry about hunting that the coffee was spilled." Clementine turned back to where this had taken place on the sofa. "Hermione sent off the Clumsy Footman, that would be Eddy Porter, and then Adelaide, and then went off herself. Marigold pouted . . . Sir Vivian and Lady Cunard were here looking at paintings. I can't remember who might be missing at this point. Have I accounted for everyone except Mr. Greenberg who came in later, Mr. Churchill, Trevor Tricklebank, and Sir Reginald? We were wholly absorbed in talking about cures for lameness. Wait a moment, where was Captain Vetiver? He came in as the Clumsy Footman was leaving, they passed each other in the doorway. Oh my goodness, Jackson, perhaps it was Captain Vetiver—yes, he came into the room and stood by the door just as the coffee was spilled and reminded Jennifer to go down as Mr. Tricklebank was waiting."

Mrs. Jackson interrupted her and related what happened next: "The Clumsy Footman went downstairs and had a cigarette in the area outside the servants' entrance. So I think he was keeping the servants from going out there, because at that moment the murderer was climbing down the ladder to the dining-room window. Mr. Tricklebank and Miss Wells-Thornton had already left by then. So there was no one in the street to see what was going on. When I looked out of the salon window just now, m'lady, I was checking that it's possible to look up and down the street and see if the coast is clear on the street from both the salon window and the dining-room window, and there is an unobstructed view on all sides. So the murderer came down the ladder immediately after the coffee was spilled, and killed Sir Reginald while Miss Gaskell was looking for pure spirit . . ."

"Helped by Mr. Greenberg," Clementine put in with delight that Mr. Greenberg was completely in the clear.

Mrs. Jackson nodded vigorously, completely caught up in the moment as she took back the account of what had happened.

"It cannot have been Mr. Tricklebank, Miss Gaskell, or Mr. Greenberg . . . or—"

"—Mr. Churchill, who was in the library, shouting down the telephone! Jackson, it simply has to be Captain Vetiver. He cornered Sir Reginald in the dining room, and then was purposefully seen to leave by Mr. Jenkins while Sir Reginald was still alive. Vetiver comes up the stairs to the salon, and when he arrives, this is the signal to his friend Eddy Porter to upset the coffee. Then Vetiver slips behind the Chinese screen, the ladder has already been made ready, and all he has to do is slide open the window, lower the ladder . . . Oh my good grief! Of course it was Vetiver." Clementine was so astonished that she had arrived at this conclusion that she held her breath and stared at her housekeeper, eyes wide with elated surprise.

"What time is it, Jackson?"

"Nearly a twenty minutes to seven; the guests will start to arrive in another fifteen minutes."

"Then we must appear to be normal and everyday. Is Captain Vetiver coming here tonight, can you remember the guest list?"

Mrs. Jackson pulled her lists from her pocket and consulted the first neatly written sheet. "Yes, he is, m'lady." She lifted the lid of the water jar and they carefully lowered the portable ladder back into it and put the lid on.

"All right then, here is what I want you to do. Go downstairs and carry on. When Lord Montfort arrives, and he will be on time if not early, ask him to come up here to me. How is this room secured, Jackson?" In her excitement and agitation Clementine was already making for the corner of the room obscured from sight by the screen.

"Just these double doors for the two rooms remain open,

m'lady. The door from the gallery room at the back connects with the back stairs and is locked."

Mrs. Jackson was on her way out of the room when she turned as if to say something. But Clementine was already taking up her position behind the Chinese screen.

Chapter Twenty-seven

Up until now, Clementine's attention had been focused on what had gone on outside the salon on the night of the murder. Now with the information that someone inside the salon had been able to leave the room unperceived, she wanted to piece together the entire story without interruption. Once more she replayed the scene in the salon just before and after the coffee incident; she knew that she must be thorough and not impatiently jump to the most obvious conclusion.

How long would it take someone to climb down the ladder, murder Sir Reginald, and climb back up the ladder to the salon? She went to the window, slid up the sash, and looked cautiously out. It was quiet in the street below, still a little time before guests started to arrive in earnest. But the mist lying on the river earlier had indeed become a fog and was rolling into the city, thickening with every moment into an impenetrable wall of gray damp. All of Hermione's guests to the charity evening would be cautiously crawling along the streets in their motorcars, anxiously asking their chauffeurs if they would be late. Clementine worried that her husband would not be there when she depended upon his early arrival.

She withdrew her head and closed the window after taking an assessment of the drop below her. It would have been the work of minutes to climb up and down the ladder if someone was agile and strong, she thought. Going down would be easy, coming up more difficult. Again, she tried to conjure up the scene in the salon from the moment the coffee had been spilled and became unsure where Vetiver had been at the time. She remembered talking to Lady Ryderwood about music and the opera, and from that point she carefully went over the arrivals and departures in the room, until she got to Vetiver. Surely he had joined Marigold Meriwether on the sofa, either to commiserate about her dress or to encourage her to buck up and stop sulking. But had he stayed there? She simply couldn't remember.

And why was Sir Reginald still in the dining room after everyone else had come upstairs? He had not joined them because he was waiting in the dining room to meet with his murderer. He was waiting for Captain Vetiver to return. *Yes, of course, that's exactly how it had been done.* Vetiver had kept Sir Reginald in the dining room after dinner. He had left briefly, probably saying he would return, and then come up to the salon to establish his alibi. In the distraction over the spilled coffee he had slipped behind the screen, climbed down the ladder, stabbed the waiting Sir Reginald, and then returned to the salon.

She was quite sure of herself now. And with this surety, all the excitement of working out who had been where and at what time, leading to Vetiver as the villain, evaporated. *Should I be sitting here alone in this room?* she asked herself. *And what exactly am I waiting here for?* She got to her feet to come out from behind her screen when the door into the room opened.

Relief washed over her and she was about to call out to her husband when she heard the rustle of silk. It was not Ralph.

How stupid she would look, she thought to herself, if this was Adelaide or Hermione. What on earth would they think to find her hiding out in a corner of the room behind the Chinese screen? *Oh good heavens, what a fool I am. I hope I am not discovered.* She held her breath and waited, praying that the whoever-she-was would go away soon.

It was at this moment that her mind obediently obliged her earlier summons and revealed an image buried in her subconscious that stopped her preoccupation with social embarrassment dead in its tracks.

Vetiver had been seated next to Marigold from the moment he arrived in the salon until the end of Lady Ryderwood's song. How did she know this? Because Mrs. Churchill had said so: "I'm glad to see that Marigold is being told to rein it in by her fiancé, silly little thing. She should have left the room with Hermione's companion to see to her dress and not sit there like a dowager having us all run in different directions." Clementine had obediently glanced over at the couple and then resumed her hunting conversation with her husband and Sir Henry, immediately after which Hermione had announced that Lady Ryderwood would sing. Vetiver had been there with them all the time! He had not left the salon; he could not possibly be the murderer.

She heard the person who had come into the room moving around. Was it Hermione counting chairs or rearranging flowers, or was it Adelaide coming to check on her sheet music? *Oh dear God,* Clementine realized in a horrible moment, *if this is the murderer then it's the Chinese jar they are after, and it's been moved.* She felt that moment of cold dread when you understand that you have made a terrible mistake. She shivered, the hairs on her arms bristled, and in a flash she knew, as surely as she knew that Lord Montfort had not yet arrived in the house, that she had known all along who the murderer was. "*Che gelida manina!*" Everything came together into a crescendo of understanding, superbly orchestrated. She was alone in the room with the person who had killed Sir Reginald.

Sir Reginald? Here was where inspiration wavered and didn't slide into place quite as smoothly and as neatly as it should. Sir Reginald did not fit as the victim for this murderer at all; there was no perceivable motive, surely? But undoubtedly his murderer was in the room looking for the Chinese jar, the jar that Clementine could see quite clearly in the far corner of the room. And if Clementine could see the jar, then she would also be seen when it was discovered.

There was an exclamation of annoyance and she caught a movement at the edge of the screen, a flash of the shell pink beloved by Hermione. Clementine felt her stomach heave and she thought for one awful moment that she was going to be sick. A wave of heedless panic engulfed her and she wanted to cry out, *Here I am!* to get the awful moment of discovery over with, as if she were a child playing hide-and-seek and now, after a long and exciting wait, could no longer contain the suspense of being discovered.

She swallowed and watched as the owner of the portable ladder walked over to the precious Jiajing jar and lifted the lid.

Clementine felt elation and panic race through her body, practically paralyzing her. For there, bent over in the corner, was an immensely different creature altogether from the one she knew. This woman moved with decisive, brisk movements, there was power in the set of her shoulders and tremendous confidence in her movements; it seemed, somehow, that she was taller. This was not the lovely creature who habituated drawing rooms and theaters; this woman emanated determined purpose. She moved with the elastic confidence of an athlete, the sort of woman who could easily control and train the spirited horse that she said only her husband could ride. *Lady Ryderwood was the true owner of Lochinvar!* Clementine's mind flashed back to the night she and Lord Montfort had left to go to dinner at Hermione's house. Ralph's voice sounded in her head:

"Yes, I remember her husband well . . . he was confined to a wheelchair, poor chap, completely crippled by his war wounds. Awfully bad luck for a man who loved his horses . . ."

The scales, as it says somewhere in the Bible, fell from Clementine's eyes. Everything she had been led to believe about her new friend crumbled to dust. It was Veda Ryderwood who had climbed down the ladder, murdered Sir Reginald, and climbed back in through the window on that bitterly cold night. Her hands had been like ice! She had touched Clementine, seen her shiver, and laughed it off as stage nerves. Stage nerves! This woman had never been frightened in her life.

Veda Ryderwood lifted out the silk ladder and gathered it up into a bundle, and with the weight still swinging she turned and looked straight at Clementine.

Her stare, direct and penetrating, took Clementine in as if she knew she would find her cowering in her chair behind the screen.

Lady Ryderwood said nothing in the second it took her to assess the situation. She dropped her ladder and closed the short distance between them in an agile bound and, reaching out an arm, fastened a grip of iron on Clementine's wrist. She jerked her up out of the chair and turned her around all in one smooth and hideously capable movement. Clementine found herself with her arm twisted up tightly behind her back and pinned between her shoulder blades, with Veda Ryderwood's chin digging into her shoulder.

"Can you feel this, Lady Montfort?" Something hard pressed into Clementine's back and she gasped with pain. "Yes, I see you do; it's a gun. One peep and I'll put a bullet in your liver. Agonizing, and you will die awfully slowly."

Fear froze Clementine from head to foot. She thought her heart was going to burst out of her chest. Lady Ryderwood let go of her arm and she carefully slid it down to her side, hardly aware that the sharp pain in her shoulder had now turned into a dull, aching throb.

"I had you earmarked from the start as one of those women who can never quite mind their own business. How right I was." Veda Ryderwood stepped back, pointing her gun.

"Che gelida manina—your tiny hand is frozen." Clementine said aloud the words that had meant little to her on that night; her Italian was particularly poor, and Lady Ryderwood smiled.

"Yes, that's right. Now you remember. But you remember far too late. I was cold, from climbing up the ladder in my underclothes." She laughed as she saw Clementine's look of disapproval. "My skirt detaches from my dress quite cleverly, it was the work of a moment to unbutton and drop it to the floor so I could climb the ladder. But when I came in through the salon window I brushed against you and you shivered. I thought you more alert than you actually are, and so I passed my cold hands off as stage fright."

"You killed Sir Reginald . . . but why?"

"Yes, I killed him, and now I'm going to have to include you in the last part of my plans and then kill you too. A pity really, as you are the only really decent person I've met since I came back to this godforsaken country with its unbearable, complacent arrogance; so convinced that every one of you is born to rule."

"It's your country too . . ."

"Oh really? I don't think it is. My mother was Dutch, my father German. I married an Englishman certainly, but that most doesn't make me English. He was another stupid fool who thought that the English were God's appointed. Take away your colonies and dominions and what are you after all? A bunch of uneducated, isolated barbarians with nothing to recommend you, and now you will lose your empire to a country that knows how to govern."

"Germany? That's quite ridiculous!" Clementine laughed. *Keep her talking,* she said to herself. *Ralph will surely come through that door in a moment.*

"Yes, that's right, Lady Montfort, Germany. The German culture is more educated, refined, and elevated than that of England any day. I've spent an amusing eight months watching you all. There is nothing this country has of any value, except its industry, its steel mills, and its lucrative colonies. Britain has become a culture wholly obsessed by money, with no real interest or comprehension of music, literature, or philosophy; a culture completely empty of intellect and certainly with no obedience from its social inferiors. Your monarchy is borrowed from Germany, even the cuisine you enjoy is French. It's astonishing that your greatest writer of *this* century is a dolt like Rudyard Kipling and your most notable composer is Elgar!"

"Good heavens, I'm not interested in Kipling and Elgar!" Clementine was calculatedly brusque; she must push Lady Ryderwood into a revelation. "I simply don't understand why you killed Sir Reginald."

"It's quite simple; I was merely doing my job."

Clementine laughed, it was a shaky laugh, but the best she could do. "Your job? Oh, for heaven's sake!"

"I will explain since your imagination only takes you so far. Unlike you, I never had the advantages of birthright. I came from a humble family. My father died when I was fifteen, leaving my mother and me with nothing. I had a natural talent and I worked hard to make it pay; you have no idea how grueling it is to train the voice. Hours of practice require physical stamina and dedicated patience; there is never a day off. I was employed at the Munich Opera House . . ."

"You are Velma Moser," Clementine couldn't help herself as she remembered her conversation with Lady Ripon at the theatre. "You are the Queen of the Night!" The pitiless cruelty of the role was far better suited to this new Lady Ryderwood than the timid and gentle Butterfly. It was an inspired guess, and Clementine was rewarded for it. She had touched on conceit and now Lady

Ryderwood or Velma Moser, or whoever this woman really was, was eager to tell her story.

"Yes, I am *Velma Moser*." And being the diva she was, the woman preened. "My most successful role was the Queen of the Night; no one can sing that aria as well—I was barely twenty years old when I first sang it in Munich. Twenty!"

"But this doesn't explain . . ."

"Then do not interrupt, Lady Montfort." Lady Ryderwood was warming to her story now. "It was in Munich that I met Sir Francis Ryderwood. He fell in love with me, and took me away from the exhausting life of an underpaid performing artist. For the first time I knew what it was like not to worry about money, to eat well and wear beautiful clothes, and with the allowance he gave me I was able to keep my mother in some comfort until she died. Unfortunately, Sir Francis patriotically decided that he would return to his old commission to fight in the second Boer War. No, Lady Montfort, I was not concerned for his safety, but I did manage to persuade him to marry me before he left.

"My concern was for my mother's two younger sisters, my aunts Katryn and Andrea, the kindest, gentlest women I ever knew when I was a little girl. They had gone to live in southern Africa in the late 1890s. Many young Dutch girls emigrated to the Transvaal to marry Boer cattle farmers. The men were happy to have young wives from the old country: strong, willing, working-class farmers' daughters, who wanted the opportunity of a new life with hardworking husbands who would give them big families. When the Witwatersrand Gold Rush fomented even more discord between the Dutch Afrikaners of the Transvaal and the British settlers in the Cape, your government decided it was time to intervene, on behalf of the British immigrants of course. It was a long and bloody struggle and the Boers fought bravely for their freedom to the bitterest of endings.

"When my war-hero husband returned severely crippled

from his war wounds, I did not feel that this was sufficient reparation for the lives of my aunts and my little cousins who had died such terrible deaths in British camps. They just disappeared like that!" Veda Ryderwood snapped her fingers in the air and her face was as cold as stone as she continued. "I was alone and in despair when I heard how my aunts were taken from their farms and corralled, along with thousands of other Dutch Afrikaner women and children. With the Boer women and children incarcerated, the British set about the destruction of their farms: burning homesteads and poisoning wells to deprive the Boer rebels of food and shelter, while their families starved to death in those camps. Yes, I can see that you have perhaps heard of Lord Kitchener's shameful scorched-earth policy. It was successful; it certainly brought the last of the Boer rebels to heel."

"The British army didn't intend for them to die." Clementine felt the story was a little one-sided; at least she hoped it was. "They put them in camps because they were alone on their farms with no one to protect them."

Lady Ryderwood's laugh was bitter as she shook her head, "They starved to death in those camps.

"Even though Francis was in a wheelchair, I knew I could not continue with him. I had to make a plan. Bad investments had reduced his fortune and we had to live inexpensively in Ibiza, so there was nothing to be had from him. I wrote to my old voice teacher, Franz Schmidt, as I knew I would have to earn my living again. He immediately came to visit me in Ibiza and he did something far better than return me to the stage of the Munich Opera House. He persuaded me to work for the German government, to gather useful information and cause chaos within the British government in the event we went to war. Francis was dying anyway, but his title and position in society would be of greater use to me if he were dead."

"You killed your husband? You killed Sir Francis?" It finally came to Clementine just how ruthless this woman was, and she instantly regretted her outburst. *When my time comes,* she thought, *she will show no mercy.*

"I agreed to his death. I have never felt such freedom as I did that day."

Clementine shuddered; the woman was a monster, and she had been stupid enough to fall for her gentle charm and her lies. *But this did not explain why she had killed Sir Reginald.* And then it came to her. Veda Ryderwood had come through a window into a room lit by candlelight, and from behind her victim, seated at the top of the table, she had seen the heavy, balding head sunk down between broad, slouching shoulders. Sir Reginald even smoked the same cigars as Winston Churchill. This woman had intended to assassinate the First Lord of the Admiralty. That was why, when Winston breezed in on her aria, she had beheld his arrival with such an intensity of surprise. It had not been annoyance that he had blundered in on her nearly finished song. Veda Ryderwood had understood in that moment that she had made a tremendous mistake.

"You killed the wrong man, didn't you? You meant to kill Mr. Churchill!"

"Yes, it was unfortunate, I killed the man who was invited to stay on in the dining room after dinner. It was the footman who gave my note to the wrong man. I don't make mistakes."

Clementine was amazed that Lady Ryderwood had the impudence to call the English arrogant, but another revelation dawned: *This is exactly like The Bruce-Partington Plans after all!*

"You are nothing but paid spies, you and your Clumsy Footman!"

"No, Lady Montfort, I am an assassin. My partner, the footman, is the spy." She made it sound as if murder required far superior skill than theft, and if Clementine had not been so thoroughly frightened she would have laughed. "My partner was planted at the Sopwith factory to obtain copies of their designs, and when he had them he came here to help me with my task. It did not work the first time, but it will now. Unfortunately, I couldn't risk his being recognized by your son after I found out about Lord Haversham's involvement at the Sopwith factory, which is why he is not here to help me tonight."

"I knew there was something wrong with the Clumsy Footman," said Clementine. "I could never put my finger on it. His coloring was all wrong for that jet-black hair, pale eyes, and freckled skin. Good heavens, he was a natural redhead. My son even told me he was!"

"Yes, yes, you are so clever, Lady Montfort. So there is a brain in that dull little English head of yours. But you are a bit too late, I'm afraid." Lady Ryderwood jerked on the cord that secured the heavy curtains away from the window. "You will wait here behind the screen with me. And when Churchill comes through that door I will have my chance again—one bullet for him and then one for you, after you have served your purpose as my hostage."

Clementine took a step backward, away from Lady Ryderwood, and now she fervently hoped that Ralph would not come into the room, as if he did he would most certainly be shot. She took another step back and as she did so she tripped over the mounded-up ladder that lay on the floor, bruising her bottom on the lead weight as she went down. Sprawled on her back, she watched in paralyzed fear as Lady Ryderwood, gun in hand, came and stood over her.

"You are so frightfully clumsy, Lady Montfort. Now get up." Veda Ryderwood pointed her gun. And Clementine thought, *That's right, make her shoot you now, the sound will bring everyone upstairs and she will be caught.* A heroic and selfless gesture, to be sure, but then she had a far better idea.

She reached underneath her as Lady Ryderwood motioned

with her gun that she stand up. "Get up, or I'll pull you up by your hair." Things were getting nasty, Clementine thought as her hand closed over the lead weight.

"I may not be able to sing above a top C, Lady Ryderwood," she said in a reasonable and conversational voice. "But"—she lunged forward as Lady Ryderwood stood over her—"I can do this . . ." And she slammed the lead weight down as hard as she could on Lady Ryderwood's foot and heard the most sickening crunch.

"Even if my Italian is pretty patchy . . ." Clementine leaped to her feet, accompanied by Lady Ryderwood's shrieks of pain; she was a little off-pitch, Clementine thought, "and I don't know Verdi from Puccini . . . I am still pretty steady on *my* feet." Lady Ryderwood, staggering off-balance in a circle, shot a hole in the ceiling.

Clementine was off across the room; she slipped the key out of the lock and whirled through the door as Lady Ryderwood fired her gun after her.

"And," she shouted back through the door as she slammed it and turned the key in the lock, "the reason we have a world empire is because we always keep our heads in a crisis."

Chapter Twenty-eight

Standing outside the salon door on the upper landing, Clementine became uncomfortably aware that she had shouted her last remark at the top of her voice and in doing so had secured the fascinated interest of the small crowd gathering below her in the hall. She looked down over the balustrade and saw several startled faces gazing up at her. Her hair was halfway down her back, her gown in ruins. But the upturned faces now frozen in horror were not because of her rough appearance, or her shouted words, but because of the continuing gunfire from the salon.

In a moment her husband had come up the stairs and was at her side. *Better late I suppose than never,* thought Clementine as her legs started to wobble. He was followed by Mrs. Jackson, who, in answer to Clementine's muttered words, turned and called down the staircase to White, who was determined to maintain composure at the bottom of the stairs, surrounded by the Chimney Sweep Boys looking rather sweet in powdered wigs.

"Mr. White, telephone for Detective Inspector Hillary if you please, and tell him to get here as quickly as he can and to bring plenty of police constables." Mrs. Jackson's voice cut across a rising babble of conjecture and exclamations from those below them in the hall.

As her husband walked Clementine down the stairs and into

the library, Hermione stepped forward, regal in her lilac gown, and followed them into the room.

"My guests will be arriving at any moment, Clementine. The dowager queen Alexandra, the Princess Esterhazy, and Lady Ripon will no doubt be among the first. We simply do not have time for any unpleasant behavior and there must be no further interruptions to the evening. Adelaide! Make arrangements to contain that woman, and please tell Inspector Hillary when he arrives that I do not have time to talk to him. I suppose we will have to scrap the duets." And Hermione swept out of the room, leaving Lord and Lady Montfort, Aaron Greenberg, Adelaide Gaskell, Macleod and Herne, and what amounted to the entire staff of servants of Chester Square and all the menservants of Montfort House, to relieve the salon of the veritable tigress that was rampaging up and down it, having shot all the bullets in her gun into its walls and the ceiling.

"Well, Lady Montfort," said Detective Inspector Hillary, having escorted a grimly silent Lady Ryderwood, supported between two policemen, out of the scullery door of Chester Square and up the area steps into a waiting Black Maria parked outside, to the delighted interest of several guests who were walking up the front steps to the house, "if this would be a good time, I would really appreciate it if you would tell me how you made this discovery."

"It was a complete accident, a coincidence," said Lord Montfort, rather too quickly in his wife's opinion as she turned to him and gently laid a hand on his arm. "Darling, might I have a brandy or something? I have asked Mrs. Jackson to join us; we have plenty of time to fill Inspector Hillary in before supper." Hermione's guests were now all settled upstairs in the salon and the first strains of music reached their ears from upstairs and then the exquisite power of Nellie Melba's voice. The door opened and Mrs. Jackson came into the room, looking quite immaculate in her best bombazine silk dress, as if nothing in the world had occurred that evening.

"Have you met Mrs. Jackson, Inspector Hillary? No, I didn't think you had. This redoubtable woman is responsible for your making the arrest of the person who murdered Sir Reginald, and who was planning the assassination of Mr. Churchill." Clementine smiled at her housekeeper as she said, "Jackson, do you realize this one only took us the better part of five days?" She pretended not to hear a long-suffering sigh from her husband and realized that perhaps she was showing off.

A near brush with death and the better part of two glasses of a sixty-year-old Napoleon brandy had left Clementine almost euphoric, and it was in this condition that Winston Churchill found her as he burst into the room, arms open as if he were about to enfold her in his embrace. It appeared that Mr. Churchill always managed to avoid the business of sitting down and listening to other divas.

"Clever and resourceful, Lady Montfort!" he cried, and Clementine turned and positively beamed at her husband. The Earl of Montfort and his Countess did not approve of grandstanding and making too much of a business about things, but at this moment Clementine was feeling positively reckless with elation that she had, after all, avoided being shot.

"It was nothing, Mr. Churchill, just some moments that we noticed," she gestured toward Mrs. Jackson, "and later put together to form a picture of the evening. It was—"

"I am utterly and completely in your debt, always will be. If there's—" Mr. Churchill glowed at her even as she interrupted.

"It was Mrs. Jackson who actually found Lady Ryderwood's portable ladder, the one she used to climb down to the dining-room window. And her accomplice is no doubt waiting for her at her address in Mayfair—if you search the house you will be able to find the plans he stole from Tom Sopwith."

No doubt Churchill had been thoroughly briefed by Vetiver, for he swanned over this scrap of intelligence; even now he would not be lured into any disclosures. His eyes were shining, effortless accolades tripping off his tongue.

"All immediately . . . in hand . . . *dear lady*. England will be . . . forever *in your debt*," Churchill intoned, his pudgy hands flying out to the world that was England.

Mr. Churchill's grandiose regard of his wife saving Britain did nothing to mollify Lord Montfort, who with an exhalation of irritation had turned to the brandy decanter for solace.

Surrounded by the sweet, innocent people who had featured as suspects in their murder inquiry—Mr. Greenberg, Adelaide Gaskell, Trevor Tricklebank, who had also joined them as an alternative to an evening of opera, and Mr. Churchill's punctilious right-hand man, Captain Vetiver—Clementine couldn't help but tease out the last untidy little loop and knit it up neatly to resolve everything that had gone before. Life rarely provided such opportunities.

"Mr. Greenberg, please let me be the first to congratulate you on your engagement to Miss Gaskell," she murmured to him, as he came over to refill her empty glass. "Oh, please don't look so surprised. You gave yourself away the other evening. When we were still . . . were still . . . " She caught Jackson's eye and remembered in time not to go into that unfortunate business at Kingsley House. "If only you had both made your regard for each other known a little earlier, as well as providing each other with an alibi . . ." she turned and reached out her hand to her housekeeper, nay her friend, her clever and fearless friend, Edith Jackson, "you might have saved Mrs. Jackson a considerable amount of work."

"What is to become of the Chimney Sweep Boys, m'lady?" Mrs. Jackson was standing in Clementine's room early the next morning, as Pettigrew directed the footman to take the last of the luggage down to the hall.

"Well, without remotely referring to what Sir Reginald had been up to for years, because that will remain her secret forever, Miss Kingsley of course appointed Mr. Greenberg to become chairman of the board of governors for the charity. And since he is to marry Adelaide, then she will help him run the charity while he waits around for his knighthood or, even better, a peerage. Miss Kingsley, bless her heart, now all this unpleasantness has been resolved, has had a complete about-face. She has put Mr. Tricklebank back into her will—after all, he's all she has—and invited the new Mrs. Tricklebank for luncheon, which should be a very interesting experience for her. Things couldn't have turned out better."

"And the other business?"

"Ah yes, the other business. Well I'm afraid that Lady Ryderwood is for the high jump for espionage, murder, and attempted assassination. Her accomplice, and his name by the way is Gordon, Alexander Gordon, is for the high jump too."

"Awful people; what drives them to such extremes, I wonder," Mrs. Jackson said rather grimly as Pettigrew helped Clementine into her coat, before leaving to make sure the footman put the luggage into the back of the motorcar in the correct order.

"I hope Mr. Greenberg sends that awful matron packing, m'lady."

"Oh, Mr. Greenberg will leave all that to Adelaide. I feel almost sorry for Matron. Mr. Greenberg and Adelaide will do a tremendous job together for the charity. How perfectly it has all fit together. Adelaide and Mr. Greenberg, Mr. Tricklebank and his . . . well, Mrs. Tricklebank."

And they are not the only ones to find companionship—to find love, thought Mrs. Jackson and she set about the business of updating her ladyship on the existing state of affairs in the Montfort servants' hall.

"Mr. White will be giving notice, I'm afraid to say, m'lady. He has been offered a position as head butler at Lady Cunard's London residence. He says it is too good an offer to pass up." Mrs. Jackson radiated disapproval that the butler had done exactly as Miss Pettigrew had predicted.

"Oh no, Jackson, please not that. This is *too* bad. We've solved one problem belowstairs and now another one emerges to take its place. Well, we won't be returning to town until after Easter, so we can jolly well wait until March to hire a new butler. I expect Lady Cunard collared White at Chester Square." Clementine laughed, shaking her head at the perfidious behavior of some of society's more ruthless leading ladies.

"Yes, she did indeed, m'lady. And he's not all she collared either, that Ginger is going with him, they are to be married it would seem. Lady Cunard evidently doesn't worry about what goes on in *her* servants' hall." Because it was expected of her, Mrs. Jackson looked down her nose in utter contempt of servants who did not understand their loyal duty. But ever since she had witnessed that tender scene in the Montfort House servants' hall and seen the rapt worship of the handsome Mr. White as the fascinating Ginger had served him his breakfast, dangerous emotions had stirred in the Mrs. Jackson's bosom. *We give ourselves in devoted and loyal service all our working lives, and then we retire and live alone for those years remaining to us.* She thought of the elderly Mr. Jenkins, who preferred not to retire.

"How silly of them. Lady Cunard will run them both off their feet; she never has a quiet evening from one week to the next. Did you tell them about her entertainment schedule?"

Mrs. Jackson emerged from her thoughts to answer her ladyship.

"No, m'lady, I did not. It's not my place to involve myself in the

Montfort House servants' hall. But it will be nice to get back to Iyntwood and to a staff that keeps to the old ways. And we have a good deal to do to organize for Christmas." She thought of her interrupted afternoon walk in freshly fallen snow to the edge of the village and Mr. Stafford's cottage for a nice cup of tea.

"Yes we do. But Jackson, there is no need for you to hurry home. Why don't you spend another couple of days in town and do some Christmas shopping?"

"Thank you, m'lady, I think I will." Mrs. Jackson glanced at the clock. She had plenty of time to change and catch the half past ten train to Kew, and meet Mr. Stafford at the Lamb and Flag before their visit to the Orchid House.

Author's Note

One of the joys of writing about the early 1900s is the many eccentric true-life characters that populated the time. I found them so intriguing that I wanted to include a few of the more flamboyant ones in *Death Sits Down to Dinner*. Here is a little more information.

Winston Spencer Churchill
NOVEMBER 30, 1874–JANUARY 24, 1965

Success consists of going from failure to failure without loss of enthusiasm.

—WINSTON S. CHURCHILL

Winston Churchill was the son of Lord Randolph Churchill, the third son of John Spencer-Churchill, seventh Duke of Marlborough, and Lady Randolph Churchill (née Jennie Jerome), daughter of an American millionaire. As the third grandson of a duke, Winston would inherit no title and very little money.

Winston loved to live life well. He was never without a Romeo y Julieta cigar clamped firmly between his teeth, and he drank a bottle of his favorite champagne, Pol Roger, as a nightcap in bed every night as he wrote letters or read. One of his favorite ways to relax was soaking in a deep, steamy tub with a good book. He passionately believed in the British Empire, loved the ideal of glorious war, and was horrified that women should be given the vote—a woman's job was to provide heirs, hopefully to adorn her protected world, and to look after the welfare of her husband and family. If she was unfortunate enough to come from the lower orders it was her fate to be burdened with the exhausting life of an Edwardian working mother. Conversely, he was a huge advocate and supporter of welfare reform for the working and poor classes, notably the elderly and those too sick to work. He staunchly supported the prime minister, Herbert Asquith, and the chancellor of the exchequer, David Lloyd George, on welfare reform and the People's Budget, which passed those reforms into law—money for which was garnered from property taxes levied on the landed classes. He was also involved in breaking the power of veto exercised in the House of Lords, which made him hugely unpopular with his fellow aristocrats.

Winston revered his father, a well-known and powerful figure in politics, and it was likely that this need for approval from his disinterested parent drove Winston's early political ambitions. By the time he was thirty-one, he had crossed the floor of the House of Commons, forsaking the Conservative Party for the Liberal Party, a move he was rewarded with six years later with a senior cabinet position as home secretary. His defection from the Conservative Party alienated fellow members of the aristocracy who viewed his actions as treacherous, irresponsible, and self-serving. Eloquent to the point of upstaging the entire House in parliamentary debate, Winston was by turns laughed at, envied, and adored. But many considered him a visionary especially in preparations for what was to be World War I.

In 1911 Winston became First Lord of the Admiralty. Never wavering for a moment in his conviction that war with Germany was inevitable, he spent huge sums in strengthening Britain's navy. He was fascinated by the innovations of aircraft and flight and saw aircraft as potential weapons of war and invaluable in aerial enemy reconnaissance. Future battles would be fought in the air, he decided, and founded the Royal Navy Air Service in 1912.

As Britain was drawn into war with Germany, Winston was not destined to be First Lord of the Admiralty for long. In 1915 he was the leading political and military engineer of the disastrous Gallipoli landings in the Dardanelles. He took much of the blame for the fiasco—450,000 dead and critically wounded—and when Prime Minister Asquith formed a wartime all-party coalition government, the Conservatives demanded his demotion.

There are hundreds of amusing anecdotes told about Churchill throughout his long, ruthless, and sometimes glowing political career, but the one about the Siege of Sidney Street told in *Death Sits Down to Dinner* is quite true, and he certainly did have a precarious moment on a railway station platform with a particularly aggressive member of the militant suffragettes.

Churchill married the beautiful and strong-minded Clementine Hozier after a lengthy and some thought promising friendship with the prime minister's daughter Violet Asquith. Violet was so devastated when Churchill dropped her in favor of marriage to Clementine that the Asquith family feared for her mental health. Winston and Clementine's marriage was a happy one and their relationship remained flirtatious. She called him Pug and he called her Cat.

Gilbert Vernon Wildman-Lushington

JULY 11, 1887–DECEMBER 2, 1913

In deepest regret for a gallant officer of achievement and promise.
—WINSTON S. CHURCHILL, CONDOLENCES ON
CAPTAIN WILDMAN-LUSHINGTON'S DEATH

I don't think if I sat up all night for weeks that I could have come up with such a fabulous name as Gilbert Vernon Wildman-Lushington. Captain Wildman-Lushington, Royal Marines, was originally one of four officers selected for flight training in 1911 out of two hundred naval officers who applied. In late 1913 he was appointed as Churchill's personal flying instructor. He was twenty-six years old when he took Churchill 'up' in his Farman bi-pusher aeroplane. Churchill had enough confidence in his new instructor to take the controls after only a handful of lessons and not only flew the plane but successfully landed it (the most dangerous part of early flight was landing). Churchill was so exhilarated by his experience that he invited the young flying officer to his birthday party that evening. Two days later, on December 2, 1913, Wildman-Lushington was returning from a flight toward Sheerness but as he came down to land at Eastchurch the machine slideslipped into the ground and Wildman-Lushington was killed. He was buried in Christchurch Cemetery on Portsdown Hill with full military honors.

Maud, Lady Cunard
AUGUST 2, 1872—JULY 10, 1948

Let me introduce you to the man who killed Rasputin.
—MAUD CUNARD, ON INTRODUCING THE GRAND DUKE
DMITRI PAVLOVICH, WHO TURNED ON HIS HEEL AND
LEFT HER HOUSE, NEVER TO RETURN

She was the American wife of Bache Cunard, the fabulously rich grandson of shipping magnate Samuel Cunard, who founded the Cunard Line. It was a marriage that she found so unforgivably boring that she abandoned Bache and went to live in London. The couple was to legally separate, but Bache Cunard financially supported his independent wife for the rest of his life.

Lady Cunard was probably the most lavish hostess of her day and entertained fashionable London society at countless scintillating dinners, innumerable extravagant balls, and invitations to ultrasophisticated country-house parties at her husband's country seat at Neville-Holt, where anything might happen. Her celebrated London salon was a center for musicians, painters, sculptors, poets, and writers, as well as politicians (anyone was invited as long as he or she was famous or interesting), but nerves of iron were necessary to withstand Maud's quicksilver repartee and often wounding tongue. Herbert Asquith, the prime minister, considered her a dangerous woman, because although she was not greatly interested in politics, she beguiled senior politicians into revealing state information at her dinner table. Maud was not a particularly endearing character but was renowned for serving up her guests' frailties at dinner after the fish course. However, there was one occasion when Maud Cunard met her equal:

"Do you mind if I smoke?" Lord Birkenhead asked Lady Cunard long before dinner was over.

"Do you mind if we eat?" Lady Cunard responded sweetly.

"Not if you do it quietly," retorted his lordship.

At a time when discreet infidelity was an acceptable pursuit among the aristocracy, Maud was the longtime mistress of Sir Thomas Beecham. The anecdote related by Lady Shackleton in *Death Sits Down to Dinner* about the window-cleaner spotting Lady Cunard in bed with Sir Thomas is actually true, and nearly cost Lady Cunard her powerful place in society.

Sir Thomas Beecham

APRIL 29, 1879–MARCH 8, 1961

There are two golden rules for an orchestra: start together and finish together. The public doesn't give a damn what goes on in between.

—SIR THOMAS BEECHAM

Beecham's grandfather, also Thomas Beecham, was the rich industrialist who owned Beecham's Powders, a laxative and cure-all for headache and stiffness of the joints.

Sir Thomas, who was extraordinarily handsome, deeply talented in music, and possessed of a stupendous ego, bankrolled and conducted his own orchestra and was the impresario of His Majesty's Theatre and the director of the Royal Opera House. Sir Thomas demanded the very highest standards from his players. He once noticed that his leading cellist was not striving for the perfection required of her. He brought the music to a halt and said to her, in front of the entire orchestra, "Now, madam, you have between your legs an instrument capable of bringing pleasure to thousands and all you can do is scratch it!" Sir Thomas, Lady Cunard's lover for many years, was often unfaithful to her as he was so irresistible to women. When his wife died after many years into their marriage, Lady Cunard confidently expected Sir Thomas to marry her, but he abandoned her in favor of a much younger woman.

Constance Gladys, Marchioness of Ripon

APRIL 22, 1859–OCTOBER 28, 1917

Gladys would have appreciated a Beethoven symphony so much more if she had been a personal friend of the composer.

—E. F. BENSON

Lady Ripon was six feet tall and so beautiful that even the most glamorous in her company looked like they needed "a touch of the sponge and the duster," according to the writer E. F. Benson. She was, in her mature years, the most influential patroness of the arts, one of society's greatest leading ladies, and, as it turned out, had a talent for event planning and an excellent head for business.

Lady Ripon was a close friend of Oscar Wilde, who dedicated his play *A Woman of No Importance* to her; her other celebrated friends included the opera singer Nellie Melba, whose success in London was largely due to her support, and Sergei Diaghilev, director of the Russian Ballet.

It took Lady Ripon less than a year to revitalize the half-empty Royal Opera House at Covent Garden, which was verging on bankruptcy, with the help of her friend Sir Thomas Beecham. She made the Royal Opera one of the main events of the London season, second only to Royal Ascot and Cowes Week. She was immensely well connected and invited everyone she knew to the season's operas, carefully making sure that invitations were extended long after tickets were sold out. She also developed the brilliant idea of selling tickets in advance for performances and made it extraordinarily chic to take a box for the entire season at an exorbitant price—paid in advance. But she was singularly feted for the discovery of the flamboyant and fascinating Ballets Russes, which she invited to perform on the night before the coronation of King George V, in 1911. It was a gala event of such magnificence and popularity that the Lady Ripon's Ballets Russes became a sensation for years to come.

Vaslav Nijinsky
MARCH 12, 1889–APRIL 8, 1950

I jump and sort of stop in the air for the moment.

If the Ballets Russes was the crowning glory of Lady Ripon's dazzling reign as society's grandest dame, then Polish-born Nijinsky was its superstar and international crowd-pleaser. A dancer of tremendous athleticism, Nijinsky's theatrical and gravity-defying leaps into the air held audiences spellbound. The dancer was fond of relating how his father threw him into the Vistula River when he was seven, one icy winter night, to teach him how to swim. As he sank to the bottom of the muddy, freezing river he found that he had been invested with superhuman strength and, with one push, shot up through the swirling water and through the ice on its surface to land safely on the bank.

For his solo performance in *Le Spectre de la Rose*, Nijinsky wore a skin-colored silk tricot, which clung so tightly to his athletic body that it revealed every muscle and sinew, onto which were sewn hundreds of red and pink silk rose petals. He gathered a tremendous following among society ladies—who either did not care or failed to notice that Nijinsky was very much in love with his director of the ballet, Diaghilev.

The sets and costumes designed by Léon Bakst were so exotic

that the enthralled devotees of the Ballets Russes paid astronomical sums for their tickets, which were sold out months in advance. The ballet's brilliant savage colors of blue, scarlet, emerald green, and pink and its oriental themes became immediately fashionable among the beau monde. For London's stylish ladies it became chic to lounge in a boudoir made over to look like a Turkish seraglio in a pair of sheer chiffon, baggy scarlet pants, suffocating in an atmosphere of incense. The Ballets Russes had revitalized color!

Nijinsky was the ballet's choreographer and his successful career was assured for many years, until he married and was dismissed from the ballet by Diaghilev. Nijinsky spiraled into debt, alcoholism, and schizophrenia with long bouts in mental asylums until his death of kidney failure when he was sixty.

Nellie Melba
MAY 19, 1861–FEBRUARY 23, 1931

If I'd been a housemaid I'd have been the best in Australia—I couldn't help it. It's got to be perfection for me.

—NELLIE MELBA

At the name of Melba, crowned heads would nod respectful acknowledgment, noble lords and ladies would open their doors, newspaper editors would clear space for headlines, theater managers would turn pale, and the house would be full. The tsar paid tribute; Paris, Monte Carlo, and Brussels were crowns strewn in her path. Nellie Melba was the era's megastar. She was quick-witted, outspoken, and unpredictable as she held her ground at center stage against rival sopranos, male colleagues, and conductors. She alienated Sir Thomas Beecham so thoroughly that she never sang at the Royal Opera House in the years before the

Great War. She did, however, sing for private events, and was singularly generous in her fund-raising efforts.

She came from a well-to-do middle-class family in Australia, was trained in piano and voice, and became something of a minor celebrity in Melbourne. Nellie took the pseudonym "Melba" from Melbourne, her hometown.

Looking for a greater public and a more sophisticated arena to appreciate her unparalleled voice, Melba came to Europe: "... the voice, pure and limpid, with an adorable timbre and perfect accuracy, emerges with the greatest ease," Arthur Pougin said of her in Paris. But she was so unspeakably rude to everyone that it took the intervention of the Marchioness of Ripon to prevent her from being fired from the opera house in Brussels, and it was only with the support of the British nobility and particularly Lady Ripon that Melba made her breakthrough at London's Royal Opera House to become a world superstar. Her technique and coloratura soprano made her an ideal voice for the Italian operas of Puccini and Verdi. It was Melba who made Puccini's *La Bohème* a success (it was not particularly well received on its opening night), but through her role as Mimi, *La Bohème* became one of the world's most favorite operas.

She invariably would finish her concerts with "Home, Sweet Home," leaving everyone misty-eyed and begging for more. And when it was announced (not before her time, some thought) that the diva might soon retire to her native Australia, the editor of *The Musical Times* wrote under the headline THE DIVA TO GO HOME: "And by all means why not? As Miss Melba has melodiously declared, only too often, there's no place like it."

For more information on these and other wonderful Edwardian characters please visit my blog, Redoubtable Edwardians: www.tessaarlen.com/redoubtable-edwardian.